Blaze

HOMECOMING HEARTS
BOOK FIVE

HJ WELCH

CHAPTER

One

REYSE

REYSE HICKSON FELT LIKE AN ALIEN FROM OUTER SPACE. HE sat in the corner of the room, watching the wedding reception unfold joyfully around him, wondering desperately how to join in with the festivities. It was like he had totally forgotten how to be a real person.

Luckily, the room had been darkened for the evening, so he had the shadows to protect him. He could observe in relative safety as flower girls chased one another around the tables and couples slow danced on the floor, colored lights swirling over their heads. Music and conversation filled the air, enveloping him like a cocoon.

Reyse forced himself to take a deep breath and sip his glass of Champagne. All things considered, the day had gone very well. The guests had either been too afraid to approach him or had varying degrees of celebrity status themselves, so they knew how to talk to someone like him or at least try. One little boy had stood for a full five minutes gaping at Reyse until his mother had bustled him away, too embarrassed to even look Reyse in the eye. But Reyse had endured far worse reactions over the years.

The point was, he desperately *didn't* want this day to be about him. It was about one of his dearest, oldest friends. Reyse smiled, feeling some of the pressure release from his chest as he watched TJ rocking gently back and forth on the dance floor with his new husband, Ashby.

They looked so impossibly happy.

Last year, it had been Reyse's sincere advice to TJ that he follow his heart. Reyse hadn't met Ashby at that point, but having finally been introduced today, Reyse knew without a doubt that TJ had done the right thing. Ashby was like a bright beacon, lighting up the room with his easy cheer and delightful smile. Plus, Reyse liked his fashion sense.

It was difficult not to be envious of their happiness, but Reyse tried his hardest. Jealousy was so ugly and it wasn't really what Reyse was experiencing as he glanced around the room, seeking out his other blissfully married friends. It was more like a pang of sadness.

How could he be sad, though? He watched as the music changed to something more upbeat and Blake dragged his husband, Elion, onto the dance floor. Elion was hopelessly outmatched. Blake ran his own dance studio, not to mention starring on the reality show based around it and hosting another competition show to find up-and-coming dancers. But that was what made Blake and Elion perfect. Blake danced with Elion like he hung the moon and stars, never wincing once when Elion stood on his toes.

"Penny for your thoughts?" a perfectly refined English accent asked.

Reyse pulled his gaze away from the dance floor and his friends to smile at his companion as she sat down beside him. "Oh, nothing," he said evasively with a smile.

Bella Dalton was almost as well known as Reyse himself was. She elegantly crossed one long, slim leg over the other and regarded him with her big brown eyes that had helped make her such a Hollywood starlet. "Oh, come now," she scoffed, reaching over and helping herself to one of the mini-quiches Reyse hadn't eaten from his plate. "I know that face."

Reyse sighed and rolled his eyes at her, but there was no malice to the gesture. She was right. She did know that face.

"I am perfectly content," he said, mimicking her accent.

She scoffed and covered her mouth. Once she'd swallowed her quiche, she sipped from her own Champagne flute. "Don't do that, it's disconcerting," she teased.

"Sorry," he said, back to his regular Californian twang. "I was trying to fit in with the locals."

She wagged a long finger at him playfully. "Then you want to try something like 'och aye, ya wee bastard!'" Her Scottish accent was flawless and made Reyse laugh. It felt like the first time he had truly relaxed all day.

She was right. They were currently located in a picturesque castle in the Scottish Highlands. Reyse normally spent his time surrounded by the most modern of luxuries, so he had to say he was basking in the beautiful and awe-inspiring history of the place. The wedding breakfast had been in an honest-to-god stone banquet hall complete with stag heads mounted on the walls and flickering wax-candle candelabras. TJ had arrived on horseback like some kind of knight and Ashby had unearthed a family tartan on his dad's side of the family for the kilt he and his other groomsmen were currently wearing.

The whole idea for having the day in Scotland had come from the kilt. Apparently, Ashby had struggled with the idea of wearing a suit for his big day, but a white wedding dress had equally felt like it wasn't quite right. When his mom had reminded him of his Celtic heritage, the problem had been solved.

The two grooms were currently speaking to a gaggle of guests Reyse thought might have come from the resort

Ashby ran. A plump woman stood arm-in-arm with a man Reyse was almost certain was TJ's dad. Next to them were another younger man and woman. Reyse had definitely seen the guy juggling wine glasses earlier in the evening, amusing several of the children tearing around.

Everyone seemed to know each other. It wasn't just the former members of Reyse's band, Below Zero, but their other halves appeared to have become friends when Reyse wasn't looking. Ashby and Elion in particular looked like the best of friends. Reyse watched as Blake congratulated TJ again. Then they were joined by Raiden Jones, who had most likely just reappeared from sneaking off to an ancient broom closet with his new husband, Levi. The three guys gave cheers, clinking their glasses together.

"Oh, just go over and say congratulations," Bella said, cutting through Reyse's thoughts with a huff. "You've barely said two words to any of them all day. What's the point of flying over here if you're going to ignore them?"

"I'm not ignoring them," Reyse mumbled, crossing his arms. Bella blinked at him. He deflated somewhat. "Okay, so...*maybe* I'm not entirely sure what to say. But that doesn't mean I'm avoiding my friends."

"You say what people usually say at weddings," Bella said in a blasé manner, flicking her slender fingers. "'Congratulations,' 'Don't you look happy,' 'the ceremony was gorgeous,' – that sort of thing."

Reyse rubbed his chin. "Ah, yes," he said lightly, but it was difficult to keep the slight melancholy from his voice. "But then people want to ask difficult questions in return, like 'How are you?'"

"Hmm," Bella said. She patted his hand sympathetically. "That is a tricky one."

"Oh shush," he said good-naturedly.

"I'm serious," she said. "I do understand. It doesn't

matter that you're number one in the charts or the box office." She sighed and looked out over the sea of happy, mostly paired-off people. "They want to know when *you're next.*"

They both looked down at her ringless left hand. Reyse felt the same twinge of guilt he always did at some point when they went out anywhere as a 'couple.'

"That's not what you want, is it?" he asked. Because he would consider it if she did.

"No," Bella told him softly, mustering up a smile. "Forgive me, darling, but I'd like to marry someone who actually loves me."

"*I* love you," Reyse said quickly.

She patted his hand again. "I know, dear. I love you, too. But…not like that."

She turned to watch TJ and Ashby. Even though they were speaking with different people, they were still holding hands. Like it was impossible to be parted, even for a second, on their special day. As Reyse looked on, TJ flicked his gaze toward Ashby. That single look contained so much love and affection it made Reyse's heart ache. Both for his friends' happiness and for what he himself was lacking.

Had lost.

"Do you think a man will ever look at me like that and *not* want to shag me?" Bella asked with a heavy sigh.

Reyse considered his words before he answered. "So you really never feel like…?"

"Nope," Bella replied before he could finish his awkward question. "Sex just doesn't interest me. I suppose I *could,* every now and again. If I wanted children, let's say. But just for fun?" she wrinkled her nose. "Give me a snuggle on a sofa with hot chocolate any day."

Reyse laughed gently, then gave her a one-armed hug. She had always been open about being asexual with him. Not to the public, of course. But it was what made them such a neat and tidy couple.

Neither was remotely interested in bedding the other.

Reyse raised his glass of bubbly toward her. "Here's to you finding someone to *actually* Netflix and chill with," he said with a wink.

She smiled and clinked her own glass with his. A small *ding* rang out over the cheesy nineties music that currently had most of the wedding party on the dance floor. "Cheers to that," she said, taking a sip. "And what shall we wish for you, hmm?"

Reyse shook his head and placed his glass back down. "Let's wish that you 'dump' my ass kindly when you find your Mr. Right, and that my next record goes platinum. Again." He grinned ruefully at her. "Fuck, I'm such an ungrateful brat."

They both laughed, but he could see she wasn't going to let it go.

Bella glanced left and right. There was no one around their table, and anyone nearby was currently being distracted by TJ's manager. The large man was loudly telling a story in his gravelly voice that Reyse was absolutely sure he shouldn't be sharing about a certain well-known TV star. Even though the venue was nonsmoking, he was standing under a cloud of smoke as he entertained the small throng of women with his juicy anecdote. No doubt he was looking for wife number four among them.

Satisfied they weren't being listened to, Bella leaned in close to Reyse. "No Mr. Right for you, sweetie?"

A lump formed in his throat almost immediately at even the mention of such an idea. "Nah," he said, not meeting her eye and forcing a laugh. He should have known the question was coming. After all, Bella was one of the few people on the entire planet who knew the truth. But it still hurt all the same.

Bella huffed and scowled, an almost comical expression for a face that sponsored makeup lines and perfumes across the globe. "You absolutely could, you know?" she insisted. "It's not as if it's *illegal* or anything."

Reyse gave her a patient look. He knew she meant well, but they'd had this conversation both at her premiere for *Fallen Angels Club* and Prince James's birthday party last year.

"Sun City Records is a 'family friendly' company," Reyse recited, using heavily sarcastic air quotes. "And everyone knows the gays are dirty perverts out to get the helpless children with their glitter and sodomy."

Bella snorted so badly into her Champagne a passing waiter almost stopped to help her. But she was able to wave him off. "Seriously, darling," she said, mopping off her chin stealthily, "do you really think they would, what? Drop you?"

"And keep the rights to not just my back catalog, but Below Zero's as well," Reyse said. "In a heartbeat."

He didn't even attempt to keep the bitterness out of his voice. At the moment, the Below Zero records were under a different contract, so when the rest of the guys had come out it hadn't been a breach of anything. Joey had been out when the five of them had still been together, after all.

But Reyse was the goose that laid the golden egg. Sun City had his balls in a vise. If he fucked with the label, his manager, Kevin, would get such a fucking kick out of burning everything to the ground out of spite. He would kick Reyse to the curb and keep every penny he'd earned them, all with a grin on his face.

Reyse smiled at Bella and hugged her around the waist with one arm again. "It's fine," he said firmly. "It's not like there's anyone on the horizon. I can think about love when

I'm old and no one wants me to make music anymore." He wiggled his eyebrows at her. "I'll make a great sugar daddy."

"Eww," she said with a chuckle, pushing him off. "No, you need to be having sex, now. While you're impossibly hot. Just…find someone who can keep a secret."

That sounded awful to Reyse. Not only the idea of sneaking around, but also trusting someone enough that they wouldn't run to the press the second they were done fucking.

No. Staying away from men was safest. But he shrugged at Bella and told her "maybe," in the hopes of making her feel better. He hated being pitied when he was one of the biggest pop stars on the goddamned planet. That was just nuts.

Besides, there were some men he had stayed away from for far too long. Bella had been accurate earlier. They were his friends and he needed to stop hiding in the corner.

"I think I'm going to give my congratulations to the happy couple," he told Bella.

"Good man," she said with a nod, taking another drink and finishing her glass. "I do believe I'm going to go back to the bar and see what I can do about getting shit-faced."

"Splendid," Reyse said with his English accent again.

"Oh, bugger off," she told him with a light smack of her clutch purse to his arm.

Reyse watched her go, sitting at the table alone for a minute while he steeled himself to go mingle. But it wasn't going to get any easier the longer he waited. So he also downed his glass, rose, and began walking through the crowd.

He wished Joey were here.

It had been four entire years since all five of Below Zero had stood together in a room. Normally, that was Reyse's fault. But having only just made Blake and Elion's wedding for a couple of hours and missed Joey and Gabe's entirely, Reyse had created a stink to make TJ and Ashby's.

It was going to be their big 'getting the band back together' moment.

But Reyse honestly couldn't begrudge Joey and his husband's absence, even though he had been dying to see them. Sometimes, the stars aligned a little earlier than you planned, and you had to go where fate took you. Although Joey had been a bit cryptic as to why they had to fly out to China all of a sudden. Something about Joey doing a short job there. Reyse figured if he didn't want to divulge the details, that was his business. It must have been important to miss TJ's big day, so that was that.

All Reyse's fears about stepping out and talking to his old friends were completely unfounded, of course. They were more like brothers than buddies. TJ's face lit up immediately when he saw Reyse make his approach.

"Hicks!" he boomed, clearly on top of the world. "My man, this is for you."

Reyse wasn't even sure where TJ produced the two shots from, but he wasn't surprised. The big guy seemed to always have a never-ending stash of tequila on his person. Reyse laughed and took the proffered glass. Getting too drunk even in a semi-public space like this generally made him nervous. But it seemed Ashby's British friends were all high-level socialites and knew how to behave themselves, and his American friends were decent guys. TJ's guests were either fellow movie stars or Below Zero, so Reyse hoped he could rely on some professional courtesy.

"Cheers," Reyse said, holding up the dubious clear liquid. It burned his throat on the way down and he coughed, but it was still kind of fun to still be slinging back dirty alcohol with TJ Charles like the past four years hadn't happened.

TJ clapped his arm around Reyse's back and hugged him to his side. They stood for a moment by the old stone wall, watching people dance without a care and eat food from the buffet and chat around the tables and raise toasts to the happy couple.

"This is the best day of my life," TJ said.

Reyse looked over at him. "Really?" he asked. He wasn't throwing shade, but TJ had enjoyed a very successful career in music and now movies. He'd been all around the world and seen so much.

Of course, TJ didn't take Reyse's question as an insult. He just squeezed him closer with his muscular arm.

"Yeah, my man," he said, nodding. At that moment he caught Ashby's gaze across the room and the two smiled goofily and waved at each other. "I dunno. They say there's someone out there for everyone. I doubt there's, you know, just *one* person. But I do kind of think there is someone out there for you who, like, makes you the best fucking person you can be. If you're really lucky, you might get to marry that person."

He kissed the top of Reyse's head. TJ was usually affectionate, but this was extra, even for him. Whether it was due to happiness or booze or both, Reyse had to say he enjoyed the intimacy. Even just between friends, he couldn't remember the last time he was kissed by someone he cared for.

"You just can't be afraid to let love in," TJ concluded.

"Ain't that the truth, y'all." Raiden came up on Reyse's other side and nudged him with his elbow. "Even if love starts out as your scary bodyguard who angry fucks you senseless."

"Rai!" Reyse chastised while TJ guffawed.

Raiden just shrugged and grinned, though. Out of all the guys, Reyse had managed to see a fair bit of Raiden recently. They'd worked on a few songs together at Raiden's studio over the past year, so Reyse knew he was joking to break the tension.

But there was no escaping the fact that when the band had broken up, there had only been two queer members. One out, the other very firmly not. Now, one by one, Reyse had been forced to remain in the shadows while his brothers were able to own their sexualities and find the loves of their lives.

He was fucking proud of them. But it didn't make his situation any easier. Now, in interviews, presenters would joke that he was the only straight one left and asked him how that made him feel. And Reyse would have to lie.

The boys knew, though. They'd never talked about it. But they knew. So for a while, Reyse allowed himself to be hugged by Trent. He chatted about crap with Reyse before they were joined by Blake and a few people got excited and took photos of them all together.

His life was good. It was amazing.

He just had to let go of the idea that love was something he could pursue anytime soon. Through a certain amount of luck and an incredible amount of hard work, he was living a dream life with a career so many would kill for.

So he spent the rest of the night counting his blessings, dancing and drinking with dear friends, and not worrying about tomorrow.

Today, he was doing just fine.

CHAPTER

Two

COREY

Corey Sheppard cursed under his breath as he rode down the damn road for a third time, trying to see the numbers on these giant ass houses. Would it kill people in neighborhoods like this to stick a mailbox in their yard or something?

He was looking for one-three-nine-three. At around the start of the fourteen hundreds, he killed the engine on his motorcycle and pulled the stack of several pizzas from the top box on the back as well as the plastic bag of drinks, dips and sides. Then he began determinedly trudging along the sidewalk until he got lucky and spied one-three-nine-seven in the dark.

"Finally," Corey breathed in relief.

He dashed along past two more houses and jogged down the front path. The yard was immaculate. There were marble ornaments on the lawn lit up with discreet spotlights and a Grecian column on either side of the front door. Corey pressed the bell, adjusted his Speedy Pete's Pizza baseball cap and plastered on a smile.

"Hi!" he cried as the door began to open. "You ordered-"

"You're late."

Corey broke off from his usual speech and took in the stoned sloth of a skinny college kid that stood beyond the threshold.

"What was that?" Corey asked, still smiling even though he had a bad feeling about this.

The smell of cheap weed was wafting out from the house and Corey was proud of himself for not flinching. Jesus. Surely kids this rich would be able to afford the good stuff.

The guy ruffled his thick dark hair and blinked slowly, swaying from left to right as two of his equally sluggish buddies came to stand either side of him. The sound of music and more voices floated out into the night.

"You're late," Stoner said with a giggle. "Speedy Pete's gives you the order for free if the driver is late."

"Err," Corey ground out, still smiling. He twisted his arm under the pizza mountain and checked his cracked-but-still-ticking watch. "Nope. I've got three minutes to spare, actually."

"Didn't you hear him, man?" one of the sidekicks demanded, leaning over Stoner to get up in Corey's face. "He said you're late. So hand over the pies."

The three of them laughed and made to grab the boxes. Corey stepped back.

"No, no, no," he said with a big grin despite the steel in his voice. "I logged when I left the store. Now come on, guys. Pay up. With seven pizzas, sides and a two-liter bottle of Coke it's eighty-two, ninety. Plus tip," he added purposefully.

Stoner held up his hands. "Sure, you wanna play it that way?" he asked. He fumbled into his pocket and removed his cell. "I'll just call your boss up right now and tell him what a little bitch you're being. I'm sure he'll have no problem firing your rude, basic ass."

More laughter from his witless buddies.

Corey finally dropped the smile. "I wasn't late," Corey growled. He was bigger than these guys, but there were three of them and who knew how many more inside. Plus, he was on their property. He didn't want to piss them off too much, but at the same time, what the fuck? "If you don't pay, that's theft."

"Ohh," Stoner cooed, pretending to be scared as he hit dial on his phone. "And who do you think your boss is going to believe?" he asked, holding the cell up to his ear. "You? Or me?" He held up his free hand to indicate his mommy and daddy's enormous mansion, snickering as his buddies doubled up in hysterics behind him.

Corey cocked his head. "Fine," he said. He let go of the stack of boxes, letting them slam on the ground. He was impressed the food didn't bounce out, but it was worth it to see those jackasses stop laughing. "Have a nice night."

He saluted to them and walked backward just as he heard Stoner's call connect. "Hey, yeah," he said, his voice all concerned as it drifted over the evening air after Corey. "One of your guys was late, then threw the pizza at us when we asked if it was free."

Corey turned around and gave them the finger over his shoulder.

Shit. He didn't need this. He and his boss didn't exactly have the best relationship to start with. He could only hope that Ross listened to his side of the story.

Corey scoffed as he stalked back up to his bike, jamming his helmet back on and revving the engine back to life. Since when did Ross give a shit what Corey said? The greasy bastard. Corey was just a cog in his machine and Ross would care more about keeping customers like that Stoner asshole than protecting anyone like Corey.

Part of him was tempted not to even go back. He was probably fired anyway. But pride demanded Corey at least *try* and stand his ground. He didn't know, he might be lucky.

Instead of chewing it over, Corey tried to stay positive as he rode back into the heart of the city. LA really was beautiful if you took the time to stop and look. A colorful neon jungle towering over gently swaying palm trees, the Hollywood sign watching over them all from above. It was a city full of possibilities.

It had been Corey's home for as long as he could remember, bouncing around from house to house. He knew these streets like the back of his hand and liked having a job where he got to travel them regularly. He never had been good at staying in one place.

Speedy Pete's unique selling point was that it used motorcycles for its deliveries rather than cars, so their pizzas arrived quicker. And like Stoner had said, they gave you your food for free if they were late.

He kept telling himself he could get another job if tonight fucked him over. But he was going to be tight making the rent for his room as it was and his landlady was nice enough until you were short. Then Corey knew he'd be in for a lot of swearing in Polish and possibly a broom over his head.

His room may be tiny and smell of cigarettes from the previous tenant, but it was his, goddamn it. He wasn't going to lose his job and his place over some dumb college bros if he could help it.

Unfortunately, Ross was about as sympathetic as Corey feared he would be.

"What part of 'the customer is always right' did you forget? Dipshit!" he yelled at Corey in the back of the pizza takeout store.

There wasn't seating or anything there, it was just a place that delivered. 'On time, or your money back!' as Ross reminded Corey. His slicked-back hair looked like dirty oil under the buzzing florescent lights and his thin mustache like old mascara bristles. He poked Corey's shoulder.

"Well?" Ross demanded. "What were you thinking?"

"So you wanted me to just let them rob us?" Corey asked in disbelief. "They were full of shit! I wasn't late!"

He could feel the rest of the team glancing warily at him from where they were making orders or waiting to go out on another delivery. Corey didn't care, he was in the right.

"So you threw the pizzas at them?" Ross spluttered.

Ah. Yeah. He may not have been entirely in the right with that.

"I placed them on the ground," Corey said, attempting a cheeky grin. It didn't look like Ross bought it. "I swear! They didn't lose a single slice. But they were high as kites and they weren't going to pay, so I left before they did something dumb like pull a gun on me."

Scrawny Ross, who was at least five inches shorter than Corey and had probably never done a day's cardio in his life, shook his head in disgust. "Pussy," he muttered under his breath, not bothering to even look at Corey. He was too busy poring over the receipt he'd printed out from the system. "Okay, you don't think eighty dollars is worth showing up on time for or fighting over? It can come out of your paycheck."

"You *cannot* be serious?" Corey exploded. "I can't afford that! Ross, be reasonable! *I was on time!*"

Ross jabbed a finger into Corey's face, the receipt screwed up in his fist. "You're lucky I'm not firing you, you little punk," he spat out. Corey refrained from pointing out Ross was only a couple of years older than him. "This is your last warning. You fuck up again, you're out."

Without another word, Ross spun on his heels, his overly shiny shoes squeaking on the linoleum as he stormed off into his back office, slamming the door behind him.

Corey stood in silence for a moment, absolutely fuming.

Slowly, people began to move around him again, returning to work. Nobody really spoke, but the sound of the radio quietly hummed over the noises from the machinery and the phone was soon ringing again, begging to be answered.

Corey had little choice but to swallow his pride and wait over with the other delivery guys for another order. Hopefully the next one would pay. They might even tip well if there was any justice.

He felt a tug on the sleeve of his leather jacket as he passed one of the workstations. He looked down to see one of the 'moms,' as he thought of them. There were several well-rounded, middle-aged women who chatted to each other in Spanish and often left together once their shifts were done to go grocery shopping together.

This lady's name was Maria and she'd been at Speedy Pete's at least as long as Corey had, probably way longer. She always worked the night shifts on Tuesdays, Fridays and Saturdays. She smiled at him and glanced around to make sure Ross hadn't crept back out. Then she pulled a coin purse out from her pants pocket.

"For Mr. Corey," she said, producing a twenty.

"Oh, no," Corey said immediately, holding up his hands. He knew she had at least two kids at home. *"Gracias,* Maria. Really, that's so sweet of you. But it's my own dumb fault. You don't have to do that."

"No, Mr. Corey," Maria said with a frown, pushing the note into his hands even though he still wouldn't take it. "We all know. Mr. Ross is being the jackass. You take. I tell you." She scowled. "Be a good boy."

"Yes, take." Corey looked around to see another two of the women holding out bills as well. They looked equally formidable.

"Um, okay," Corey said weakly. He couldn't deny that sixty bucks would go a long way to helping him out if Ross was going to screw him over. "I'll pay you back, I swear," he added, meaning it as he folded the bills into his pocket.

Maria blew a raspberry, then hurriedly pulled on a fresh pair of blue latex gloves. She then went back to sprinkling mozzarella on the couple of pizzas that had queued up while she'd been talking to Corey. "Good boy," she said smugly.

Corey didn't feel quite so shitty as he went around to the pickup collection and got the address for his next delivery. He vowed to buy the ladies a box of chocolates on his way back from this drop-off. He was aware he would be using their own money to do it, but he had to show them their kindness meant something.

He'd spend every other penny on bills, he promised himself. And if he could muster up a few good tips, he might not go completely under this month.

After all, he had no one else he could rely on. He was all alone in this world. He argued it was probably okay to accept the kindness of his colleagues occasionally.

It wasn't like a white knight was going to swoop in and rescue him anytime soon. He had to save his own ass.

Just like always.

CHAPTER
Three

REYSE

THERE WERE FEW TIMES DURING THE DAY THAT REYSE COULD generally catch his breath and feel like he was alone with his thoughts. He just never seemed to stop working, which is why it had been such a big deal for him to take a few days off to fly to Scotland for the wedding.

But even though that had only been a week and a half ago, it felt like months. He had stopped off in three different European countries on his journey back, because heaven forbid he miss an opportunity to squeeze in some promo. Since arriving back in LA he had met with a couple of sponsors and done a charity auction.

Now, though, he was in his favorite part of the recording cycle. They were just starting to finalize the tracks for the next album for production next month, a couple of which had been written by Raiden. Reyse was going to push as much as he could for those ones to be recorded and included on the final cut. Not just because Raiden was his friend, but because they were damn good songs. If one of them could get released as a single…

He was getting ahead of himself, but it would be a real

boom for Raiden. His music production business had suffered badly when he'd been hacked last year, and even though he'd done well building up clients again, Reyse knew this would be just the boost he needed.

That and a couple of other thoughts were swirling around his head as he walked down the sidewalk that evening with a protein shake. He normally used the gym in his building, but seeing as he had a couple of quiet days in his schedule he had taken the opportunity to go to one of the uber-fancy places across town. It had a certain level of clientele so he could usually get away without being disturbed too much, although there was often some dickhead who snuck a photo. Like it was super interesting to see Hicks busting his ass on a treadmill looking like a hot mess?

Reyse shook his head. Whatever. He hadn't noticed anything like that tonight and he'd even been able to shower in peace. Now he was enjoying soaking up the sights and sounds of the city as the summer night fell. He felt calm and centered. Maybe he'd order sushi in and watch a movie? He still hadn't seen TJ's latest one.

So of course that was the moment his phone rang.

The noise jarred Reyse, like nails on a chalkboard, even though the ringtone itself wasn't all that offensive. He was just tuned into the particular melody, and hearing it meant he knew he was being disturbed.

For a second, he hoped it was someone fun calling for a chat or about an exciting opportunity. But then he saw Kevin's name and his heart sank.

Kevin was a necessary ball ache in Reyse's life. His manager didn't like Reyse much and he knew that Reyse knew. Reyse thought he probably resented his success in some messed-up way, even though Kevin had been instrumental in so much of that success.

Deep down, Reyse suspected it was more that Kevin

knew about his sexuality and was disgusted by it. After all, it was his idea that Reyse and Bella 'date' for Reyse's public image. Why else would he suggest it? Sure, he'd fed Reyse some line about needing to date because it was good for branding. But what Reyse heard was 'date a woman.'

However, Kevin was damned good at his job, and Reyse adored his own job most of the time. So he took a deep breath, smiled, and answered the call.

"Hey, dude! How you doing? What's up?"

"I'm good, Reyse, thank you," Kevin said. His voice was clipped but pleased. Narcissists like him always preened when you asked about them first. "I was just calling to confirm your schedule for the next couple of weeks."

"It's mostly studio time, right?" Reyse asked. He'd been really banking on that. He just wanted to get locked into the room and make some magic. He was all tingly just thinking about it.

The high he got from creating music was as close as he got to sex these days, he thought ruefully with a chuckle.

"Yes," Kevin confirmed, "but I've squeezed in a couple of telephone interviews with Asia – two in Japan and one in Korea – and I think we might need to change up your nutritionist. So I'm looking into booking a couple of interviews with candidates, just so you know."

Reyse stopped walking on the sidewalk and looked at the protein shake in his hand. "What's wrong with Becky?" he asked, a tiny bit defensively. She was a really nice doctor who never fangirled at Reyse. If anything, she mothered him, and he quite enjoyed that. He wasn't eager to test out a bunch of newbies.

Kevin scoffed. Reyse could practically hear him roll his eyes over the line. "She's gone and got herself *pregnant*, so sometime soon she'll be off, sitting back collecting a paycheck for god knows how long. We might as well replace her now before she goes all baby-brained."

Reyse scowled. "I doubt she got *herself* pregnant," he said. "And I'm sure she'll be okay to keep working until she's in her third trimester." Becky wasn't the kind of woman to sit around idly. He knew she would want to keep busy.

There was a silence from the phone. Kevin hated to be contradicted. "I think it would be wise to consider our options now," he said coolly. "If we sit with our thumbs up our asses we could find ourselves without anyone and then you might get fat again."

An icy wave washed over Reyse. Kevin had managed to be subtly homophobic and also remind Reyse of a time when his body image was at its lowest, all in one sentence. Fucker.

Reyse gritted his teeth, then smiled, even though Kevin wasn't there to appreciate it. "Sure," he said cheerfully. "It doesn't hurt to be prepared. Let's see who's out there and might want to work with-"

It all happened in a split second.

Reyse never even saw the bicycle as it flew past, let alone the hand that reached out and snatched his phone.

His personal phone.

"FUCK!" he bellowed, spinning around to see the guy already several feet away. Reyse dropped his shake and broke into a sprint before he even considered what he was doing. But there was *no way* he could just let someone take off with so much personal information about him when he was on a call and the phone was unlocked. Even if Kevin hung up, the bastard could probably decrypt the passcode easily enough.

If he didn't realize he had Reyse Hickson's phone already, he soon would. Reyse had countless photos saved in his gallery, as well as his Twitter, his Instagram.

His Grindr.

He'd never even been brave enough to meet up with any

guys on there. But he liked to chat from time to time with strangers. Sometimes sext. It helped with the crushing loneliness.

Now it could be the undoing of his entire career.

"STOP!" he yelled. "THAT'S MY PHONE!"

Reyse ran flat out as the asshole weaved between pedestrians, trying to get into the heavy evening traffic. People around him were all jumping away in shock, yelping and squealing as he clipped their arms. At least that made a path for Reyse to sprint through. But he was still losing the guy.

Until the mugger rushed toward a pizza delivery man.

The dude was in bike leathers with a baseball cap, carrying three pizza boxes on top of each other, looking up at the apartment block he was walking past. At Reyse's shout, he looked down to see the thief and Reyse running after him.

Without hesitating, the guy Frisbeed all three boxes at the mugger's chest.

The thief lost his momentum. The bike wobbled too much and he had to put his foot down as the pizza spun out from the boxes. Hot cheese, meat and cardboard scattered all over the sidewalk, making pedestrians jump back from the mess.

The thief was already regaining his balance, but the pizza guy apparently wasn't done. He lunged forward, reaching for the phone in the mugger's hand. The thief shoved him back, but the pizza guy wouldn't let go. They were scrambling over the bike, the pizza guy trying to drag the thief off while the thief pushed and shoved, attempting to pedal away.

Reyse had almost reached them. Just as the pizza guy smacked Reyse's phone from his hand, sending it toppling to the sidewalk, the mugger landed a heavy punch, square on the pizza guy's left cheek.

The pizza guy staggered backward, his ass hitting the

sidewalk, giving the mugger the chance he needed to pedal away.

Leaving Reyse's phone on the ground.

Reyse scooped it up before dropping next to the pizza guy. As thrilled as he was he hadn't lost the phone, he wanted to check on his rescuer more. Reyse crouched to see under the baseball cap and they looked at each other for the first time.

Reyse's heart almost stopped.

The man was fucking *gorgeous.*

Reyse worked in the music industry. He rubbed shoulders with actors and models and dancers all the time. But something about this guy completely stole his breath away. Chestnut eyes and thick, rich brown hair that stuck up from under the hat. Chiseled jaw with just the right amount of dark scruff, neatly trimmed. Even under the leather jacket (which was hot in and of itself, if Reyse was honest) he could see the guy had a good build, bigger than Reyse's owl slim but muscular frame.

He realized he'd been staring. But so had the pizza guy, naturally.

He was face-to-face with Reyse Hickson.

Then, despite the shiner already blossoming around his left eye, the guy broke into a lop-sided smile that melted what was left of Reyse's heart.

"Hey," the guy said happily and pointed to Reyse's hand. "You got your phone back."

The tension between them broke and Reyse laughed. "Yeah," he said sheepishly. "At the expense of your face. And your pizza." He looked around at the mess guiltily. "Sorry about that."

They had a fair crowd of people around them now, several with their own phones out. For once, Reyse didn't care. For once, he was just a guy smiling at another cute guy, sharing a moment.

"Are you okay?" someone cried from the small throng.

"Ahh, I'm fine," said the pizza guy, touching his cheek gingerly. "Nothing broken."

"Not you," the voice said in scorn. "Hicks! Hicks, are you all right?"

"Do you want us to call nine-one-one?"

"I got it all on film!"

"Hicks! Hicks, sign my arm!"

Reyse clamped his jaw and refused to look at anyone. "Back away, please!" he said loudly and firmly. "No photos!" Only about a third of them would listen, but it made him feel better. "You need some ice on that shiner," he said to the pizza guy.

He wanted to reach out and cradle the side of his face, but he was far too sensible to do something like that.

"Nah," the pizza guy said with that half smile again that made Reyse's heart flip. "I'm cool. I better call work and tell them to get another order out." He sighed. "I'm probably fired, though. I was on my last strike." He wiggled his eyebrows at Reyse. "Apparently, I can't stop throwing pizzas at people."

It was obviously meant to be a joke, but Reyse's stomach was too busy sinking. "I'll pay for it," he said in a rush. "I'll tip double. You can't lose your job for me."

People were still jostling and shouting around them, but all the commotion faded away as the guy blinked at Reyse and gave him a smile that tugged both sides of his mouth. It was shy and his expression was somewhere between disbelieving and touched, or so Reyse thought. Maybe he was being too hopeful. But somehow it was hotter than the cheeky grin had been.

"Uh, okay," the guy said. "I'd rather not get fired."

Reyse made a snap decision. "Look, I live nearby," he muttered, not wanting the onlookers to hear. "I can get you a bag of ice, write you a check and give you some peace to call your boss."

The guy blinked again. Reyse knew what he must be thinking. One of the most famous guys on the planet had just invited him up to his place. But Reyse honestly had the noblest of intentions and there was no reason for this guy to think he was flirting.

Who would ever assume Reyse Hickson was gay?

Reyse just wanted to give the guy some first aid and try and help him keep his job. And if he got to enjoy a few minutes of that beautiful smile, well, that was a little indulgence Reyse could keep to himself, right?

The guy smiled and nodded. "Dude, thanks," he said. "Okay, sure."

Reyse's heart leaped and he offered out his hand. The guy clasped it with his own and Reyse helped pull him off the sidewalk. His skin was warm and slightly calloused. It sent shivers down Reyse's spine.

Mercifully the crowd fanned out a little, giving them some room to stand among the pizza. Reyse felt a bit guilty leaving a mess, but a couple of stray dogs had already weaved between the crowd's legs and were having a feast on all the cheese-covered pepperoni and ground beef, so he figured he'd let them enjoy it.

"Thanks, folks," he called out, shielding his face as he began to walk with the pizza guy by his side. "Thank you so much. Enjoy your night."

He expected at least a couple of them to follow, but for once he had a bit of luck. This particular gaggle seemed content to just snap photos and record them as the two walked away. The guy, rather sensibly, pulled his cap down to mostly cover his face.

"I'm Corey, by the way," the pizza guy said, bringing Reyse's attention back to him. He smiled and Reyse smiled back.

"Nice to be rescued by you, Corey," Reyse said. "I'm Reyse." Then he felt like a jerk. Of course he was Reyse.

He fully expected the guy – Corey – to say 'I know.'

"Nice to rescue you, Reyse," Corey said instead with that lopsided grin.

Reyse's heart fluttered. Even if this was just a brief encounter, it was worth it. Well, not Corey's bruised face. But that smile?

Yeah, Reyse was going to remember that long after Corey was gone.

CHAPTER

Four

COREY

ON ONE HAND, COREY HAD ACTUALLY BEEN FIRED THIS TIME. Ross had hit the fucking roof when Corey had called to say he'd been involved in an almost mugging and lost another stack of pizzas. Ross had told him not to come back under any circumstances and to expect what was left of his paycheck in the mail after this order was docked from it too.

On the other, he had just stepped from an elevator directly into Reyse Hickson's penthouse apartment.

Corey was trying so hard not to be a jerk, because, honestly, Reyse – Reyse! He was calling him Reyse like a buddy or some shit! – was being really quite sweet to him. But fucking hell, the dude was always on TV and magazine covers. Corey had *jerked off* to him in the 'Deny Me' video several times.

But he wasn't looking at some famous spank bank material now. He was looking at a cute guy who seemed far more concerned about getting a bag of frozen peas on Cory's face than anything else.

"Come in, come in," Reyse said, leading the way as the elevator doors slid shut behind Corey. They hadn't really

28

spoken on the short walk over while Corey had been calling his work. It seemed like Reyse was kind of nervous. "I haven't had anyone over in ages," he said, proving Corey's point. "Well, except…"

Except reporters, Corey mentally supplied.

"It's fucking sweet," Corey said, glossing over the pause. He meant it, too.

Gleaming wooden floorboards stretched over the open-plan apartment with thick, dark gray rugs spread under white, black and silver furniture. Art deco-style pendant lights hung in intervals from wooden beams that stretched across the ceiling. Opposite the elevator door were floor-to-ceiling windows, showing the view of the sun setting over Los Angeles from the twelfth floor through slightly tinted glass. If Corey had to guess, he would say the glass was mirrored on the other side to stop nosy reporters and bloggers from looking in with long lenses.

Three large paintings hung on one of the walls. Corey wasn't sure what they were of, but they were each in rich jewel tones of teal, jade and sapphire mixed with purples and pinks. They made him think of blazing sunsets over beaches, although they could equally have just been strips of color painted with thick, textured oils.

Corey followed Reyse toward his chrome kitchen, finally taking off his baseball hat and leaning on the breakfast bar that separated the area from the rest of the living room. They passed a TV so large it was practically a movie screen and a couple of floating shelves filled with trophies.

Corey had been back to people's places where they had college sports trophies on display or accolades from work. There was one slightly odd guy who'd had his ninth-grade spelling bee award still up for anyone to see. But these were actual Grammys. MTV moon men. BRIT Awards.

When Corey glanced from the shelves back to Reyse at

the fridge, Corey knew Reyse had seen him staring. "Sorry," Corey said sheepishly. "I didn't mean to snoop."

Reyse shook his head and opened the freezer. "You weren't snooping," he said as he removed a bag of peas and wrapped it in a dishcloth. He smiled as he closed the door and approached Corey with the cold compress. "They're there to be seen. I figured you knew who I was."

Corey swallowed and accepted the veggies to place over his left eye. He couldn't help but sigh. "That feels amazing, thanks," he said. He licked his lips and looked at Reyse in front of him with his good eye.

He was unbelievably beautiful in person. This close, Corey felt like he was going to drown in those big baby-blue eyes. His blond hair looked like it was a dozen subtle different shades, all catching the light at different times. Corey wondered what it would be like to run his fingers through. Soft, from how well conditioned it appeared. His skin glowed like a newborn infant or perhaps a god fresh from Mount Olympus. His perfectly sculpted slim body clad in a tight gray T-shirt and faded blue jeans was certainly divine.

Fucking hell, Corey needed to ease off the metaphors. He'd seen gorgeous guys before. But…well, there was something catching him in the way Reyse was glancing at him.

Was there something there?

Surely not. He was dating that English actress, wasn't he? Or was it that presenter? In any case, it was no concern of Corey's. He was simply here because he had the misfortune to get in the middle of a mugging.

It hit him that he'd saved *Reyse Hickson's* phone. That was pretty cool.

Except he didn't want to think of Reyse like that. He was just a guy standing in his own kitchen, feeling awkward with a stranger.

A mad urge took over Corey. He didn't want to be a stranger to Reyse.

"Yeah," he said, finally addressing Reyse's comment about knowing who he was. "I kind of spotted who you were. It was hard not to. But I don't care about that, man. I care that the shithead didn't steal your phone."

Reyse let out a breath and smiled. His teeth were perfect and so white. "Thank you. I'm serious. Fuck knows what they could have released if they got a hold of my information." He pulled the phone from his pocket and placed it on the counter. "I texted my manager to let him know I'm not dead." He laughed. "But...did I hear you lost your job anyway?"

Corey shrugged and leaned on the breakfast bar. "That job sucked," he said with a chuckle. "Fuck it. I'll find another one."

Truthfully, he knew he was pretty screwed. But he couldn't seem to tap into that same panic he'd had the other night. Probably because he swore he could feel...what going on here? It was as if he could taste something in the air between him and Reyse. Like the crackle of electricity just before a storm.

Reyse was holding the freezer door, running his fingers over the handle and biting his lip. He looked uncomfortable. Before Corey could speak again and try and reassure him it was fine, he suddenly spoke.

"Would it be really weird if I wrote you a check?" Reyse asked. His cheeks went the faintest shade of pink and he rolled his eyes, laughing nervously. "Fuck, that probably sounds so awful and one-percenter. But I don't know if you know how much you saved my ass, and it would make me sleep so much better knowing I'd given you something to tide you over until you got another job, not just for the pizza you lost."

Corey blinked.

Reyse was right. That should have sounded like a total dick move. But Corey's chest tightened. It was thoughtful as fuck, was what it was.

"Would I be a terrible person if I said that sounded awesome?" he asked in a quiet voice.

Reyse's face lit up and he let go of the freezer door. "No, not at all." He laughed and visibly relaxed. "Holy crap, thank you. I'll grab my checkbook. Hey – do you want a beer? Or – oh, do you need to get somewhere?" His face fell a little. It was ridiculous the warm feeling Corey got in his chest from not disappointing him.

"Man, I just got fired," he said, laughing and shaking his head. "I'm free as a bird. A beer sounds fantastic."

Yeah. Bringing that smile back made his heart squeeze just a fraction, but it also affected Corey in his pants. Which was fine, so long as he didn't run away with anything. He was allowed to crush a tiny bit on an international sex symbol.

"I'll be right back," Reyse promised as he placed an opened beer in front of Corey, taking one for himself as he moved toward what looked like a bedroom. "Make yourself comfy, if you want." He grinned and disappeared through his bedroom door.

Corey bit his lip. "Stop it," he growled quietly to himself. Smiling too much was bad for his face, anyway.

The bag of peas was definitely helping, though. He placed it on the counter for a second as he removed his leather jacket and kicked off his boots, leaving him in a white T-shirt and black pants. He checked his socks had no holes in them – they weren't matching but they were intact – and he ruffled his hair. As he sat back down, he found himself grateful that he'd parked his bike somewhere safe for the evening.

He was in no hurry to go anywhere.

Was he insane? If this was just an ordinary guy, Corey

would put his money on getting interested vibes from Reyse right now. Maybe not gay – maybe he was bi like Corey? Reyse had dated girls in the past, after all. Maybe, like Corey, he preferred guys. Maybe he preferred girls and Corey was just lucky?

Corey snorted. He was *not* getting lucky. That was way beyond the realm of possibility. He needed to just chill and enjoy his damn beer and a bit of fun company. If he wanted to think about good fortune, then perhaps he might get to hang out with a superstar in his crazily gorgeous apartment for a while. That would be a cool story to tell for years to come. The night lowly Corey Sheppard saved *the* Reyse Hickson from being mugged and potentially blackmailed. That was kind of nuts.

"Sorry, it wasn't where I left it," Reyse said.

He came back out to the kitchen with his checkbook in hand. He waved it at Corey before placing it on the counter along with his beer. Then he slid a pen out from the holder built into the leather checkbook case. It didn't look like it had come from Walmart like the pens Corey usually used. He wondered how much a pen like that cost.

"So, that's Corey, right?" Reyse prompted him.

Corey nodded and spelled it for him. "Last name's Sheppard." Corey glanced to make sure he spelled that correctly too, then looked away as Reyse filled out the amount. Corey felt okay letting Reyse help him out, but to watch him write by how much felt greedy. He didn't even look once Reyse tore off the check and handed it over. He just folded the slip of paper and put it in his pants pocket.

Unfortunately, Reyse seemed awkward again. He glanced back down at the checkbook, like he'd done something dirty, when all he'd done was help Corey out big-time. But there still felt like a huge imbalance between them.

"I'm allergic to apples," Corey blurted out.

Reyse looked back up at him and blinked. "Huh?" he said.

Corey grinned. "I'm allergic to apples. They make my tongue itch and my lips sore. I was forced into a middle school production of the Wizard of Oz to earn extra credit and I was so nervous the first night I puked on stage. I like anything that goes fast and feel like I spend more on my bike than I do on rent. I don't really like Christmas but I fucking *love* Halloween."

Reyse frowned slightly, but he was also smiling. "Okay," he said. "That's – that's cool," he added, sounding like he meant it. "But…"

Corey tapped his beer bottle against the one Reyse was holding in his hand. "Now we're friends. You know some things about me and I know some things about you. And it's okay for friends to help each other out, especially if they really fucking appreciate it."

Reyse gave a little laugh and looked down where their bottles had connected. "Okay," he said again. But this time he sounded about ten times more relaxed.

He suddenly turned around to one of the cupboards behind him and pulled out a bag of jalapeño-flavored pretzel chunks. Then he fetched a bowl, two more cold beers, and dropped into the seat beside Corey.

"Oh, that's what I'm talking about," Corey said with a grin. He took the pretzel bag without pause and ripped it open, dumping them into the bowl that Reyse pushed between them. "So, you like spicy things?"

Reyse crunched on a pretzel piece and shrugged. "I like most food," he admitted. "Although I have to work out like a motherfucker if I eat whatever I want." He rolled his eyes. "A lot of the time it's just less exhausting to have a salad or plain chicken and vegetables." He nodded at the frozen peas, starting to melt slightly on the bar. "How's your face feeling?"

Corey nodded and took another drink. "Much better, thank you. Shall I put those back?"

Reyse shook his head. "Nah, I have loads, and they've been on your face now."

Corey gasped in shock. "Rude," he said playfully. "I have a beautiful face."

"Yeah, but-"

Reyse seemed to realize what he'd said. He coughed and took another sip of beer.

Interesting. Was he embarrassed because that sounded vaguely gay…or because he actually thought Corey was good looking in an actual gay way?

Corey had led an eventful life. One that had left him with the rock-solid belief that you should live for the moment and not give a fuck about tomorrow, because who knew what would happen then? Life was too short to miss out on the things you really wanted.

God, Corey wanted Reyse Hickson. Not because he was famous. Because he was gorgeous and sweet and kind of a dork.

He touched the tip of his finger to the back of Reyse's hand quickly, not even for a second. Extremely low-level flirting, just to test the waters. "What's your ultimate guilty pleasure?" he asked. "Food wise," he added for clarification with a flick of his eyebrows, although the double entendre was clear. "You must have eaten interesting stuff all over the world," he said, laying on the innuendo.

Reyse laughed softly, rubbing his thumbs along the neck of the beer bottle. It wasn't difficult to imagine what else he could be rubbing, and Corey shifted ever so slightly on his stool. At least Reyse wasn't freaking out. In fact, from the shy smile on his lips, Corey couldn't help but hope he was on the right track here.

"You know, in Japan they have like two hundred flavors of Kit-Kat," Reyse said, still grinning.

He glanced at Corey, who smiled back at him. Fuck, he was having fun. He had that warm, tingly sensation in his chest that came with the possibility of an exciting development just on the horizon.

"Yeah?" he prompted.

Reyse nodded. "Like soya sauce and green tea and banana," he said. "I always go a bit crazy when I'm there and fill my luggage with all the different kinds to last me until I go back."

He picked at the corner of the label on his bottle, then reached for one of the fresh ones. Corey copied him and finished his first beer off, joining Reyse for a second. He was feeling more at home already in this enormous, lavish apartment.

"I booked an unnecessary stop off in London once," Reyse continued, chuckling to himself. "Just because it was Creme Egg season and I had to get the real ones." He waggled his eyebrows at Corey. "American chocolate tastes different than British. Did you know that?"

Corey shook his head. "I've never left the country," he admitted.

"No?" Reyse asked incredulously. There wasn't any malice to the word, though. It must be hard for such a jet-setter to imagine, Corey thought.

"I don't even have a passport," Corey confessed. "I only leave the state if I go for a long ride on my bike."

Reyse shook his head. "You really should, for the candy alone," he joked.

Corey licked the beer and pretzel coating from his lips. "Sweet tooth, huh?" he asked.

Reyse blinked and grinned with a little nervous laugh, the

pink tinge rising in his cheeks again. *Yes,* Corey thought. He was getting under Reyse's skin in the best way.

"Me too," Corey said. "That's why Halloween is my favorite. The candy. That, and getting to pretend to be someone else for a whole night."

"What's wrong with being you?" Reyse asked.

Corey shrugged. "Me is kind of boring," he said with a laugh.

But Reyse didn't laugh. "I don't think you're boring," he said quietly.

"No?" Corey asked. His heart rate sped up, just a fraction.

Reyse shook his head. "Why don't you like Christmas?" he asked instead of elaborating. "Christmas has candy too."

"Ah," Corey said softly. It was his turn to pick at his beer label. "It helps if you have a family at Christmas. Otherwise it's kind of a suck-fest."

When Reyse didn't respond right away, Corey looked back up. Reyse was toying with a particularly large chunk of pretzel. "I spent the last three Christmases on entirely different continents," he said softly.

Before he could stop himself, Corey reached out and laid his hand over Reyse's.

Reyse let the pretzel piece go.

"I always thought being famous might be kind of lonely," Corey said truthfully.

Reyse nodded. Then he laughed ruefully and looked at the ceiling. He hadn't removed his hand from under Corey's yet. Corey rubbed the top of his wrist with his thumb.

"Yeah, poor Hicks in his million-dollar apartment," Reyse scoffed, shaking his head.

Corey looked around. "The place is kind of big with no one to share it with," he told him.

Reyse bit his lip. "You're here now," he said.

"I am," Corey agreed. God, their hands felt fucking

amazing where the skin was pressed together. Corey slid his hand over until their fingers were interlaced. He heard Reyse's breath hitch. "Do you want me to stay?" he asked.

Reyse bit his lip harder.

"I'll go, if you want," Corey continued. His voice was hoarse all of a sudden, barely more than a whisper. "But...I'd really like to stay."

Reyse blinked a couple of times, his eyes glassy with emotion.

Corey was unsure how much to push this. But if Reyse was an ordinary guy Corey had met at a bar, he'd be trying just as hard. He was thrumming with desire. He wanted to taste Reyse so badly it was making his toes curl and his cock throb.

"I..." Reyse said. When he bit his lip this time, he looked close to drawing blood.

Corey reached forward and ran his thumb gently over the lip, cradling the side of Reyse's face.

Reyse looked at him with huge blue eyes. He was scared.

"You're safe with me," Corey said.

Where the hell had that come from? He'd never said *anything* like that to anyone he'd attempted to seduce before. But it felt so right with Reyse in that moment.

How often did Reyse do this? Corey was sure he wasn't out. He felt pretty confident if Hicks was gay, the whole damn world would know. Was he really interested enough in Corey to let go?

"I shouldn't," Reyse said, his words slightly strangled. But he didn't move away from Corey.

"Why not?" Corey asked, leaning in ever so slightly.

Reyse shook his head against Corey's palm. "I can't...I mean, it's not..."

Corey felt a pang of sympathy twang in his chest. "Do you want to, though?" he asked.

Reyse nodded without hesitation. "Fuck, yes," he whispered. His voice caught with emotion on the last word. Like he might cry.

Corey didn't want that. He wanted to make him happy. So desperately. He couldn't believe he might have the power to do that. But sometimes, life took you strange places and you just had to deal with it.

"I really want to kiss you," he said. He slipped from his stool and stood between Reyse's knees, cradling his face with both hands. "Would that be totally out of line?"

There was a beat. Then Reyse Hickson grabbed Corey's T-shirt and yanked his mouth down to crash into his.

CHAPTER

Five

REYSE

THIS WAS ACTUAL INSANITY.

Reyse moaned as Corey's stubble rubbed against his jaw, his tongue strong and wet as it pushed into Reyse's mouth. It had been *years* since he'd kissed anyone like this. For real. Not in some music video or with Bella for show. But because he just couldn't bear it a second longer if he didn't find out what the other person tasted like.

What the hell was he thinking, though? He couldn't kiss a guy! But…holy fucking hell it felt amazing.

Corey had one of his hands around Reyse's back already, pulling him to his feet as their chests collided. Reyse let go of Corey's T-shirt and found the top of his pants, sliding his fingers along the firm, delicious flesh exposed there.

Corey groaned, not pausing in his frantic kissing. Reyse was as hard as a rock in his jeans.

But…this was wrong. He'd only just met this guy. He could screw him over *so* badly. How did Reyse know he wouldn't sell a kiss-and-tell story the second he left the apartment? It was too much of a risk. Even kissing him had been fucking stupid. Reyse couldn't have sex with him, he just couldn't.

"Hey, hey?" Corey's gentle voice cut through Reyse's suddenly frantic thoughts. His freak-out must have come through in some physical reaction. "It's okay," Corey assured him.

"I can't…" Reyse said.

His voice was pained to his own ears. He clung to the bottom of Corey's T-shirt and screwed up his eyes. Corey rubbed his back and rested his forehead against Reyse's. Jesus. It felt incredible to be touched like this. To be held and desired and Reyse was going to break apart, he wanted this so badly.

"We can stop," Corey said, god bless him. He didn't sound like he wanted to stop. His words were rough with lust and Reyse could feel his shaft, hard and thick, pressing against Reyse's leg. "It's okay."

Reyse shook his head. "I want you," he whimpered. "Don't…just don't hurt me."

He sounded fucking pathetic. He cringed away, unable to face Corey.

But Corey cupped his hands around Reyse's jaw again, forcing him to look at him. Corey was a couple of inches taller and gazed down at Reyse with those beautiful chestnut eyes.

"I won't hurt you," Corey said. He didn't blink. "I won't, Reyse. I promise. With everything I have, I promise you can trust me. Whatever you need, I'll give it to you. Just for a night. You're free with me. I won't tell a fucking *soul*."

Reyse could feel himself trembling.

Could he do this? Take the leap of faith and trust a near stranger in the most intimate of ways? Trust him with Reyse's biggest, darkest secret?

In the end, it wasn't so much that he chose to give in. It was that he didn't have the strength to pull away.

He attacked Corey's mouth again with desperation, grabbing his thick, dark hair with one hand and slipping his hand under his T-shirt with the other, sliding it up his back. His skin was so warm it was practically burning to the touch.

"Will you come to bed with me?" Reyse asked between frantic kisses, the words almost swallowed in their mouths.

"Only if I can fuck you senseless," Corey replied.

Reyse shivered so badly he had to stop kissing and take a breath. Corey used the opportunity to kiss Reyse's neck.

"Or you can fuck me," Corey growled. He kissed along Reyse's jaw and licked into the shell of Reyse's ear. "Or I could blow you and eat you out for as long as you want."

"Fuck," Reyse moaned, clinging to Corey to stay upright.

His knees were in danger of giving out. He couldn't think straight. All he could hear was the blood rushing through his ears. All he could feel was his painfully swollen cock rubbing against his jeans, desperate for release.

"You take charge," he uttered.

He buried his face against Corey's neck and dug his fingers into his shoulders, loving the hardness of his muscles. The T-shirt was tight and damp against Corey's body, so Reyse had already guessed he was toned. But to feel it was a whole new level of incredible.

"I'll do whatever you want," he practically sobbed. "Anything. I'll love it. *Corey.*" He knew he sounded desperate, but that was because he was. He didn't care if he was begging. He had been craving the touch of another man for years, and the universe had delivered this angel right into his lap.

Damn the consequences. Reyse was all in. If it came back to bite him in the ass tomorrow or sometime down the line, he didn't care. Right now, it just felt so fucking *right.*

He realized Corey was hugging him. Cradling him. It was

so comforting Reyse felt tears prick in his eyes. "I've got you," Corey mumbled into his hair. "I can look after you. I'll make it memorable."

"It already is," Reyse said. He breathed out and relaxed in Corey's arms. "Jesus, Corey. Where the hell did you come from?"

Corey chuckled. Then he surprised Reyse by picking him up. Reyse wasn't exactly light, but Corey had his legs around his waist and his hands under Reyse's ass in a flash.

"I'm just a figment of your imagination," he said with that lopsided grin that had stolen Reyse's heart in the first place. "I'm just a dream. A fantasy."

Reyse shook his head and held either side of Corey's face. Reyse wasn't smiling. "You're real," he said firmly.

Then he kissed Corey again and again, their lips coming together like waves lapping on a shore. Corey began walking, shouldering his way inside the bedroom with Reyse still wrapped around his body. Reyse had only turned a bedside lamp on when he'd come in here earlier. He was glad of that now.

As they tumbled onto the bed, there was enough light to see each other but it was still dark enough to feel intimate. Through the window, nighttime LA glowed in a thousand tiny spots of light. People getting on with their everyday lives while Reyse's whole world changed around him.

Corey laid him on the bed, then draped his body on top, pinning Reyse down. Fuck, it felt good. His hands grabbed at Corey's back, his ass, his neck, his hair, pulling him closer. The scent of his musk was strong, filling Reyse's lungs with something so undeniably male. The tang of sweat and the taste of beer on his breath and lips.

Without speaking, Corey peeled his own T-shirt off, then stripped Reyse of his.

Reyse thought he might come purely from the sensation

of their bare chests rubbing together. He groaned into Corey's mouth, his nipples hard, tingling pebbles. He knew he was trembling but he wasn't sure how to make himself stop. He wasn't sure he wanted to.

"I'm on PrEP," Corey said. He stopped kissing Reyse and looked directly into his eyes, his hands holding either side of Reyse's ribcage, their noses practically touching. "I'd like to fuck you bareback, but I totally understand if you'd rather use a condom."

Reyse didn't know what to say for a second. PrEP? That was a pill you took to stop you getting HIV, right? You could still get other things, and he wasn't taking it. So he wasn't protected. Fuck, he didn't want to spoil the moment, but...

"I don't have any condoms," he said truthfully. He used to keep some handy. But they went out of date and after a while he just stopped replacing them. It was too depressing to keep throwing them away. Shit. He bitterly regretted that now.

But Corey grinned and lightly ran his fingers through Reyse's hair, playing with the ends. "I do," he said. "I was planning on going out after work, and some guys insist." He winked down at Reyse. "I'm a gentleman like that."

Reyse's heart did a summersault in his chest. "Can we use one?" he asked. "I can't risk anything. I'm sorry."

What he was doing was enough of a gamble. He couldn't chance getting an infection – especially not HIV – and then the press finding out. That could out him as much as a photo with a guy.

He was worried he had just killed the mood, but Corey didn't seem to care. Instead, he kissed Reyse again and grinned. "Whatever you want, gorgeous," he said. He hopped off the bed and headed for the door. "Don't move."

Reyse shook his head and watched him dart back into the main area of the apartment. Reyse tried to slow his breathing down as his stomach flipped with nerves and anticipation.

Not knowing what else to do, he rested his hands above his head and closed his eyes, focusing on taking slow, deep breaths.

"Holy fuck," Corey's voice drifted softly over to him. He opened his eyes to see Corey leaning against the doorframe dressed only in his black pants, flipping a sealed condom over his knuckles like a coin. "Do you have any idea how stunning you look?"

Reyse licked his lips, cautiously drinking in the sight of Corey's half-naked body. "Not as stunning as you," he rasped back. Corey had a gorgeous physique. Not overly pumped, but a washboard six-pack and sculpted arms. His cock was straining against his pants, making a bulge between his legs. Reyse wanted to taste it and touch it and feel it inside of him.

He thought Corey might laugh at Reyse's insistence that he was the better-looking one. Reyse wasn't an idiot. His *job* was to be hot. But he was sincere. To him, Corey was by far the most gorgeous and desirable. Reyse wasn't sure he'd even wanted a man more.

Yes, he was handsome. But there was something about his eyes – there was a kindness there. His patience and understanding made Reyse feel safe.

That was far more attractive than a six-pack. Although he had to admit the muscles didn't exactly *hinder* Reyse's good opinion of him.

Corey walked slowly over, like a lion stalking his prey. His mouth was tugged into that half smile again and he licked his lips as he crawled over Reyse's body. He held the condom in one hand and ran the other over Reyse's chest.

"God, I want to fuck you so many different ways," he murmured, kissing Reyse's neck.

Reyse moaned, letting his eyelids fall closed. "You can fuck me all night," he told him. After waiting so long, he never wanted this to end. He didn't want to waste a single second sleeping. He wanted to try and take as much as Corey could give him.

He needed enough memories to see him through the next god only knew how many years.

He watched as Corey studied his face, then bit his lip. "I kind of want to keep it simple, though. Like this. So I can kiss you and see you."

Reyse was tempted to say to hell with that. He wanted it kinky. He wanted something wild he would never forget.

But he realized that wasn't true. He wanted something *real.* He wanted to memorize every inch of Corey's face and sear it into his brain. Corey would be able to see Reyse any time he wanted. But Reyse might never see Corey again after tonight. The thought he might forget anything about him was already painful, even though he was still right in front of him.

"You're in charge," he murmured, tracing his fingers down the side of Corey's face. Corey captured his hand and kissed his palm.

"We're just two people," Corey said, nuzzling his face against Reyse's hand, "making a connection. I think you have enough people bossing you around. Let's just see what makes us feel good and keep doing it."

Reyse laughed and kissed him again. "I like the sound of that," he said. "I need a lot. I'm making up for lost time."

Corey studied him. Maybe Reyse shouldn't have said that much, but he couldn't say he regretted his honesty. Maybe he wanted Corey to understand how special he was?

"I'll give you everything," Corey murmured, kissing him reverently.

Corey unzipped Reyse's jeans, watching ardently as Corey tugged them off his legs. Reyse lost himself in the here and now. For the first time in he wasn't sure how long, he didn't feel like he had a spotlight on him. He just felt like a normal guy having a normal hookup.

It was incredible.

He moaned and dropped his head back onto the pillow as Corey nuzzled and mouthed at Reyse's cock, straining through his briefs. Reyse briefly thought how lucky he was to have just showered at the gym. Knowing he was as prepared for sex as he could be without having any clue it was going to happen helped ease his nerves.

He didn't want to disappoint Corey in any way. But what if Reyse didn't live up to Corey's expectations? There was every chance Corey could have thought about having sex with Reyse before. It was fucking weird to think of, but Reyse had been in the public eye for almost a decade.

And in that time, he'd only had sex with one man. That had been years ago. What if he was shit?

Corey brought him out of his thoughts by abandoning his cock and coming back to hover over Reyse, looking him square in the eye. "I keep losing you," he said with a slight frown, cupping the side of Reyse's face. "Are you really sure you want this?"

Reyse let out a frustrated growl and balled his fists up, clutching the bed sheets. "I'm sorry," he apologized. "Yes, god, yes, I want this."

Corey licked his lips and nodded, his expression thoughtful. "I could tie you up or blindfold you? A bit of sub/Dom play might get you out of that pretty head of yours."

He smiled but panic flew through Reyse. "No, no," he choked out, jerking a few inches up the bed.

"Whoa," said Corey, his mirth vanishing in a heartbeat. "Sorry. Cool, none of that. Don't even worry about it."

"I'm ruining this," Reyse whispered, closing his eyes. He wanted to crawl out of his skin. How was it he could perform in front of eighty thousand people and love it, and yet this was scaring the crap out of him?

"Reyse," Corey said firm enough to make Reyse open his eyes. Corey lay down next to him and pulled on Reyse's hip, encouraging him to turn and face him. Corey slipped his arm around Reyse's back, hugging their bodies together side by side. "You aren't ruining anything. This is incredible. I'm so fucking happy to be here with you. And not because...you know..."

"I'm really famous?" Reyse suggested weakly.

Corey chuckled and kissed his cheek. "Yeah, nothing to do with that," he said. "I swear. You're fucking hot and sweet as sin and..." He leaned back so they could look at each other in the eye. "We're just two guys, having a great time. Right?"

Reyse nodded. "Yeah," he agreed with as much conviction as he could muster.

Corey nibbled on his own lip. It was slightly plump and red from all the kissing. Reyse had done that. He touched it with the pad of his thumb.

"I..." Reyse said, trying to get the words right. "I haven't done this for years," he settled on. *Years.* So, um, I hope that tells you how unique you are, Corey Sheppard."

For a moment, they simply looked at each other, something unspoken passing between them.

"Get under the covers with me, would you?" Corey asked softly. Reyse nodded. Together they shifted and pulled the comforter back, snuggling under the thick, soft material. Corey made short work of kicking his pants off, leaving them both in their underwear. Corey hugged Reyse side by side again, their limbs tangled together in a seemingly never-ending press of flesh on flesh. Reyse's straining cock soon found Corey's, the two hard shafts rubbing together. It felt so good even with their briefs still on.

"Ohh," Reyse moaned with a laugh. "I might come like this if you're not careful."

Corey grinned. "You promised me all night," he said playfully. "I wonder how many times I could make you blow your load."

Reyse snorted and smacked his arm. "I'm not eighteen anymore," he said, rolling his eyes.

"Thank god," Corey growled. He kissed and sucked at Reyse's neck, grinding his cock deliciously against Reyse's some more. "I like me a man, not some baby boy. Jesus. Can I kidnap you for a few days and we can just *fuck?*"

Reyse closed his eyes, sadness washing through him. "I think we can only have tonight," he said softly.

Corey sighed and hugged Reyse with his whole body. "Then I'd better make it amazing," he said.

He rolled Reyse on his back once again, grinning as he shimmied under the covers, kissing down Reyse's chest.

"Fuck," Reyse breathed, gripping onto the bed sheets and biting his lip. "Fuck. *Fuck.*"

First, Corey slipped his briefs off, freeing Reyse's cock. Then he took Reyse's leaking shaft down in one confident swallow, deepthroating him with his hot, wet, *wicked* mouth. Reyse whimpered and writhed, but Corey held him tightly by the hips as he swallowed again and again, rubbing his tongue against Reyse's sensitive dick.

"Corey," Reyse cried out. *"Corey."* It felt important to say his name out loud. It was like it anchored him here with Reyse.

Corey slid his mouth from Reyse's cock for a moment, giving him a second to catch his breath. Reyse half wished he could see him, but he had to admit the heavy feel of the comforter enveloping him made him feel safe. Secure.

Corey must have sucked or spat on his fingers, because

when his lips wrapped around Reyse's shaft once more, two fingers began rubbing at Reyse's hole.

Reyse liked to fuck himself with his fingers and dildos. It seemed the only thing he could do when dating or hookups were totally out of the question, so his body was used to feeling the intrusion there. He focused on his breathing and relaxed, eager to allow Corey into him as fast as possible. But it seemed like Corey was content to play for a while.

It felt like he spent ages under the covers, fingering Reyse and playing with his cock and balls. He sucked and kissed and swallowed and licked, making Reyse a babbling, tearful mess. After his fingers had stretched him a bit, Corey switched to using his tongue, rimming Reyse just like he'd promised he would. By the time he resurfaced, red-faced, glossy-lipped and grinning, Reyse felt like a wreck.

"Oh my god," Reyse hissed. He seized Corey's face and kissed him sloppily, loving the tang of his own intimate flavor on his lips. "Holy fuck, Corey, I can't…that was…"

"You liked that, huh?" Corey asked playfully. "Well, sir, I'm happy to inform you the big finale is still yet to come."

"Yeah?" Reyse asked weakly. "You don't want me to suck you or anything first?"

Corey shook his head and grabbed the condom. "No offense, but I'm so fucking turned on I'm going to come any second now." He rolled the condom on and threw the packet away. "And I *really* want to do that in your gorgeous ass. Got any lube?"

Reyse nodded and jerked his thumb at the nightstand. "Second drawer down," he stammered. Corey was mesmerizing in his confidence. When Reyse had begged him to take charge, he'd meant it.

Corey found his pump of lube in no time, slipping his hand back under the covers to slick up his cock and Reyse's entrance. Then he wiped his hand on the side of the mattress, pulled the comforter back around his shoulders, then snuggled close on top of Reyse as he angled his cock against Reyse's tight ring of muscle.

"Ready?" Corey asked playfully.

Reyse kissed him hard, biting at his lip and thrusting his tongue into his mouth. "You have no fucking idea how ready I am," he rasped.

Corey pushed, forcing his way in. It burned, but Reyse took it all. He knew it would ease soon enough and he quivered at the pleasure of the intrusion. Corey felt like he was pressing against the entire inside of Reyse's body, from his toes to his chest to his throat. Then he was pressing against Reyse's prostate and Reyse was gone.

"Fuck me," he gasped. "Oh, Christ. Fuck me, Corey. *Hard.*"

Corey grunted and nodded, sweat running down his face. His dark hair was sticking up in odd tufts and Reyse loved how wild he looked.

"So good, Reyse," he cried as he began pounding into his ass. "Fuck, amazing, *fuck.*"

They didn't talk after that. There were only kisses and desperate breaths and the *slap slap slap* of skin against skin.

"Gonna come," Reyse panted, digging his fingers into Corey's back. He wouldn't be surprised if he'd scratched the poor man.

Corey didn't seem to care if he had. In fact, he looked like he was having the time of his life as he grinned and screwed his face up, his own orgasm probably building too.

"Come for me, Reyse," he gasped. "Come. *Come.*"

The bed was rocking against the wall. Reyse wailed and threw his head back, his balls tightening before his climax exploded. He shot everything he had between him and Corey while Corey slammed mercilessly into his ass. Reyse lost track for a few seconds, his vision blacking out as the orgasm stole his breath. Then Corey arched his back, shouting out as he came to completion.

Reyse felt glued to the bed, like he couldn't move a muscle as he began to come down. Corey laughed and bent down to kiss Reyse on the lips.

"Good?" he asked, his voice hoarse.

Reyse blinked and focused on Corey's beautiful face. For a very brief second, pain lanced through Reyse's chest. He didn't want this to be over. But he made the decision not to ruin this perfect moment. Because it *wasn't* over yet.

"Spectacular," he said weakly. He smiled and touched his fingers to Corey's face. "Oh, Corey."

"Reyse," Corey replied. His name sounded so good on his lips.

Reyse got lost in his chestnut eyes for a while. Then Corey winced and pulled his softening cock out of Reyse's ass.

Reyse had recovered enough of his wits that he was able to fish his briefs out from under the covers and use them to wipe off most of the mess from his chest and between his legs. He was sweaty and satisfied, but his anxiety was starting to creep in. What was Corey thinking?

Corey plucked the underwear from Reyse's fingers with a grin and used it to wipe himself, too. Then he dropped it and the tied-off condom over the side of the bed and flopped down beside Reyse.

"Come here, you," he growled, yanking Reyse to his side and cuddling him close. He inhaled deeply and placed a kiss on his temple. "How do you feel?"

The tension eased in Reyse's chest. "Are you going to stay?" he asked.

"Yes," Corey replied without even looking up at Reyse. He just nuzzled his face into Reyse's damp hair and kissed it. "It stinks of man sex in here. I love it."

Reyse laughed. It really did. Cum and sweat and musk hung in the air. "Thank you," he whispered.

Corey hugged him tighter, then lifted his head and rested it on the pillow. Reyse looked into his eyes.

"You didn't answer my question," Corey prompted gently. "How do you feel?"

Reyse had just had sex for the first time in years with a gorgeous man who was going to fall asleep in his arms.

"I feel free," Reyse replied truthfully.

CHAPTER
Six

COREY

COREY TRIED HIS BEST TO STAY AWAKE, BUT IT WAS IMPOSSIBLE. After the adrenaline and physical exertion of the sex, he passed out within minutes of snuggling up with Reyse in his arms.

When he woke several hours later, he was still tangled up with his lover. While Reyse was still sleeping he looked like any other guy. Of course he was still breathtakingly gorgeous. But his hair was flattened in patches and sticking up in others. His mouth was slightly slack and his fingers twitched as he dreamed.

Corey didn't think of himself as a particularly sentimental person. But in the faint light of dawn, he carefully ran his fingertips lightly over Reyse's hair and cheek.

Reyse hadn't needed to spell it out last night. Corey wasn't super smart, but he'd worked out that Reyse didn't do this often, if at all. He said he hadn't had sex for *years*. Corey couldn't imagine that.

How strange to think someone had it all, only to find out they were missing something Corey thought of as so essential. Not just the sex. But that kind of closeness with another person.

It had to be some sort of music biz bullshit that was keeping Reyse in the closet. He didn't struggle with what he'd wanted last night. At least Corey didn't think so. The battle had been whether or not he should give in.

Fuck, Corey was glad he had.

Corey had a lot of sex. He didn't see anything wrong with that. Boyfriends, girlfriends, relationships…not so much. Corey didn't like to rely on people. People were fickle and selfish and just let you down. But connecting between the sheets with another person? Corey was always down for that.

So, yeah, he'd had some buck-wild nights in his time. At twenty-eight, he felt pretty experienced and really enjoyed a good fucking.

But there was something different about last night.

He'd never been with someone when it had meant so damn much to them, and he'd even taken a few people's virginity. But it wasn't just what it had meant to Reyse. It had been special for Corey as well, as much as he didn't want to admit it.

Because this wasn't a normal hookup. He couldn't take Reyse's number and see if he wanted to go out for drinks and do it all again next week. Fuck. The thought flitted across Corey's mind that he wanted to take Reyse to dinner or some shit. What the hell? Corey didn't normally feel the need to do any of that romance crap. How typical. His heart was tugging for the one guy who was totally off limits.

It was just the fact that Reyse was vulnerable and he had trusted himself with Corey. That was all. Corey couldn't read too much into it. He just wasn't used to people treating him like he was anything noticeable. Exceptional.

So…he was just the right guy at the right time for Reyse, and he was just feeling honored at having being chosen for something. It wasn't that he was experiencing anything more than that for Reyse. He might have known his name for years, but he'd only just met him in real life.

It didn't matter that Corey liked the fact he was cute and kind of insecure. Or the fact he knew he had a sweet tooth that he indulged with candy from around the world. Or knew the exquisitely beautiful face he pulled when he came.

Right?

There wasn't anything actually here between them. It was just circumstance.

Corey swallowed. He needed to leave.

For the briefest moment, he considered if it would be better to sneak out. Some people, especially guys who were closeted or in denial, preferred not to be reminded of the previous night when they woke up. But it didn't even take Corey a second to work out that if he did that to Reyse it would be a dick move of monumental proportions.

It had taken a lot of courage for Reyse to open himself up to Corey last night. Not just to get naked and let himself be fucked, but to trust Corey with his secret.

Corey was almost certain Reyse was fully gay. Otherwise he'd just date women, right? Corey loved sex with women every now and then, but he was pickier when it came to the ladies. He liked confident women who'd give him a run for his money. But he'd fuck almost any cock going. He loved rugged, raw sex with men as much as he loved it slow and sensual. He liked a bit of BDSM and quickies in public. He loved taking care of other guys, like he had with Reyse last night.

But Reyse...Corey sighed and stroked the side of his face again. He was pretty sure Reyse wanted a boyfriend. Someone he could trust. The poor guy would probably settle for vanilla sex in bed once a month if he could just have someone to hold him at night.

Jesus. Corey needed to quit with this bleeding-heart crap. He wasn't here to be Reyse Hickson's shrink. They had shared something awesome together and that was the end of their story. Corey needed to move on with his life and so did Reyse. It wasn't like they had anything in common, anyway.

Apart from the explosive sexual chemistry.

Corey rolled his eyes. Reyse had said it himself. It was a one-time deal.

Dawn was climbing over LA as the city woke. Pink and orange streaks warmed the dark sky. It was early enough that people would be around, but it was unlikely anyone would spot a strange man coming out of Reyse Hickson's apartment.

He kissed Reyse's shoulder and rubbed his back. "Hey, gorgeous," he murmured. "Reyse?"

Reyse frowned a little and began stretching his body, unfurling like a cat as he slowly came into consciousness. "Hmm?" he mumbled.

"It's Corey," Corey said, feeling a bit stupid. But Reyse wouldn't be used to waking up naked with anyone. Corey didn't want to freak him out. "It's morning."

Reyse blinked. Christ, his eyes were so blue it was almost startling. "Corey?" Then he opened his eyes properly, raised his brows, then focused on Corey's face.

Uh oh.

So much for Reyse not freaking out. Corey could already see the panic forming and he'd been awake all of two seconds.

"It's okay," he said warmly, rubbing Reyse's arm. Because it really was as okay as it could be. "You're all right."

Reyse cleared his throat, scrubbed his face, then pulled the covers around him. There was a small amount of space between them, but now the comforter was acting like a sort of barrier. "Hi," he said, his voice unsure.

Fuck. Corey desperately didn't want to leave. But it was too risky to stay. Someone could see him leave or...

Well, he had a suspicion the longer he stayed, the harder it was going to be to leave.

But for Reyse he smiled, easy and bright. "Hey," he said. He still had his hand on Reyse's arm and he rubbed his warm skin with his thumb. "It's early. You can go back to sleep. But I wanted to let you know I have to go."

"Oh," Reyse said. He looked around the room, perhaps thinking about what they'd done the night before. "Uh, do you want a shower or breakfast?"

Corey's heart contracted. He needed to get a hold on this. He'd find someone else who he wanted to stay with when they offered him breakfast in the morning. Because he couldn't stay with Reyse, despite the bit of his heart that was desperate to.

"Thanks," he said sincerely, "but I'd better head out. I had an amazing night."

Reyse swallowed and nodded. He was looking out the window. Corey suspected he was avoiding looking at him, for whatever reason. Whether because he was regretting last night or because he wanted it to continue now, Corey couldn't tell.

"Me too," Reyse said gruffly after a few moments. "I, uh... thank you." A weak smile tugged at his lips. "That doesn't seem enough."

Corey smiled back at him, trying not to let his sadness show. "Can I kiss you goodbye?" he asked.

Reyse sighed and laughed. "I'd love that, but I have morning breath."

Corey snorted and waggled his eyebrows at him. "I've got someone's cock and ass all over my tongue," he said devilishly.

Reyse barked out a laugh, then hid his face under the covers. "Oh my god," he said with a chuckle.

Corey tugged the comforter down and shifted his body alongside Reyse's. He pulled the blankets so they were no longer bunched up between them, but still covering them both, keeping them warm. Then he slid his hand over Reyse's hip, cuddling their chests together as Corey dipped his head down for a kiss.

Reyse's lips and tongue were hot against Corey's. His skin tasted of salty sweat, and where their thighs pressed together it wasn't difficult to miss their cocks lolling about, getting harder.

If Corey didn't leave now, he was going to spend all day in this bed, tenderly fucking this stunning man.

But if he did that, he would want to come back and do it again. And again. All it took was one asshole reporter or some crazed superfan to notice a pattern and Reyse's secret might leak out. What that would do for his career, Corey couldn't say exactly. But there was a reason Hicks was not out to the great wide world. So Corey had to respect that.

Feeling like he was wrenching his heart from his chest, he pulled himself away from Reyse's perfect body. He touched his thumb to Reyse's cheek and looked him in the eye. "I should go," he said firmly.

Reyse bit his lip and slowly nodded. "Yeah," he said, looking away to the ceiling. "You know I want to ask for your number?"

Corey nodded. "I know," he said.

But he didn't give it to him.

Instead, he extracted himself from the bed, not looking at his lover as he found his briefs, socks and pants, dressing himself again as quickly as he could. Only when he had his T-shirt on again did he look back down at Reyse.

Reyse had been watching him. He met Corey's gaze with

a smile, even if his eyes looked a little glassy. "I'm so glad I met you, Corey Sheppard," he said, his voice only slightly shaking.

Corey sighed and nodded. "You too, Reyse Hickson," he said. "Take care of yourself. I-"

What did he want to say? That he was never going to forget this? Did he want to ask Reyse to remember him?

That was too sad. He didn't want to make Reyse sad. The whole point of last night was to make him happy.

"You're incredible," Corey said, giving him his cutest, cheekiest grin instead. The one he knew made his eyes sparkle. He usually used it to charm people into bed. Not to ease himself out of one. "Don't forget that."

Reyse managed a small smile and tilted his head. "So are you."

Unable to drag the moment out any longer, Corey turned on his heels, walking swiftly out of the bedroom and back toward the kitchen. He jammed his feet into his boots and slung his leather jacket back on.

The elevator felt like it took forever to arrive, but once it did, it was like Corey blinked and he was back out on the sidewalk, breathing in the warm California morning air.

That was it. It was over. He marched purposefully back to where he'd parked his bike overnight. Someone had stolen his helmet, but the bike was otherwise intact. Corey revved the engine and rode back to his crappy apartment on autopilot.

Back to real life and away from Reyse Hickson.

CHAPTER
Seven

REYSE

REYSE ALLOWED THE MAKEUP GIRL TO TOUCH UP HIS FACE while half a dozen women in latex hot pants stood around him holding oversized lollypops, looking bored.

On days like this, he wondered what the hell he was doing with his life.

He was sprawled out on a leopard print futon while the crew fussed with the lighting and wind machines. His costar, Mega Daddy, was shouting angrily into his phone while choosing which diamond-studded ring to wear from a selection being presented to him in a velvet-lined box.

"My ass is chafing like a bitch," one of the dancers whispered behind Reyse with a giggle. But then she moaned like she might actually be in pain.

"Did you put talcum powder down there first?" one of the other girls asked sympathetically. Reyse didn't want to look around in case it seemed like he was ogling them. But he guessed the first girl shook her head. The second one sighed. "You might have time to get some if we break. But Hemal likes to get all the shots in one go once a scene is set up."

Hemal was their director for the music video. Reyse

hadn't worked with Hemal much in the past, but Reyse had done a last-minute vocal guest star on Mega's record, much to Reyse's annoyance. Kevin had insisted it was great for getting his name back in the charts between his own releases, but it had also meant pushing back the start date for recording his own album by a couple of weeks.

His agent, Martha, had agreed with Reyse that work like this wasn't exactly on brand for him and went against her own personal taste. But Kevin had more pull than Martha, despite her representing Reyse since before his days in Below Zero. But they had both learned when to back down when Kevin and Sun City dug their heels in.

So here they were, throwing a trashy video together to get the single released in less than five days.

The premise for the video wasn't exactly all that original. Girls shaking their asses in skimpy outfits. Lasers and smoke machines. Brightly colored walls and tilted camera angles. It was a by-the-numbers kind of job. Which was good, because Reyse was definitely phoning this one in.

He would much rather be back in his own studio, working on some songs that had more to the lyrics than fucking and how awesome he and Mega were. It was a bit tiresome. But these kinds of songs charted really well and would help keep the money rolling in until he released his own next record. Because heaven forbid he stopped bringing those dollar bills in for Sun City.

He scoffed. Like this was 'family friendly'? Sun City was quite happy for him to objectify women like this, but Kevin and the other suits would drop dead if Reyse announced he was in love with another man.

He wasn't in *love,* he reminded himself scornfully.

But he was having a hell of a time getting Corey Sheppard out of his head.

He chewed on his thumbnail and tuned out the hustle and

bustle around him. Three weeks and Reyse could still feel an ache in his chest when he thought of Corey. It was beyond ridiculous. But Reyse kept finding himself playing with his phone, typing out dumb messages about his day with no number to send them to.

It was typical that Corey hardly had any social media presence at all. He didn't have a Twitter, his Instagram only had a few images of pretty scenery from around LA, and his FB profile was simply his profile picture (his face all but covered by a baseball cap) and cover photo (a sunset). He was also one of those people you couldn't add or message unless you already had mutual friends. Not that Reyse was dumb enough to try and add him.

He just wished he had *something* to look at to remind him of their night together – other than Speedy Pete's pizza, which Reyse might have shamelessly ordered a couple of times since. He knew Corey wasn't working there anymore, but it was the last little tether Reyse could think of between them.

He sighed and wondered what Corey was doing today. Had he gotten a new job? Had he thought about Reyse at all?

Reyse had given up telling himself it was just about sex. He'd been driven nuts with lust with guys he'd worked with over the years. This wasn't that. He kept thinking about Corey's devilish smile. The way he'd paid attention to what Reyse had said. His jokes and outrageous flirting. His tenderness.

Corey had been one in a million. And now he was gone.

"Okay, girls and boys!"

Hemal clapped his hands as he arrived back on set. He was a skinny white guy with a Guy Ritchie-type cockney London accent. During the entire shoot, he'd not stopped puffing on a strawberry-scented vape, exhaling smoke with no regard to who was around him. He sucked air through his teeth and surveyed the scene. Mega Daddy was still ripping a new hole for whoever he was on the phone with. Hemal narrowed his eyes at him, then turned back to Reyse and the girls.

"Those plants need to be moved to the green screen area along with the rain machine," he yelled to the crew as he advanced on the leopard print futon. Several stagehands burst into action to carry out his orders. Hemal stopped in front of Reyse and steepled his fingers in front of his chin. "Now," he said. "What to do with you lot?"

In a professional capacity, Reyse had encountered many kinds of people in his career. Directors, producers, interviewers and the like usually treated him with reverence or deep respect. But every now and again, a cockroach would surface who thought they were oh so much better than a dumb pop star.

This dude had roach written all over him.

"Wardrobe, get me those baseball caps for the ladies!" The way he said 'ladies' had little to do with his valuing them and more him trying to get in their tight, latex pants, Reyse was sure. "She needs more hair. She needs more lips. Oh, for Christ's sake, someone get this one some tits, will they? I'm supposed to *fancy* these birds. Wardrobe! Get them fishnets while you're at it. The neon ones we discussed. You, Blondie, and you, Pocahontas. Congratulations! It's your lucky day. You're getting solo spots. Wardrobe! Strip them down, paint them blue and dump glitter all over them."

He said most of this monologue all while looking Reyse directly in the eye with a smirk on his face. Reyse held his gaze, not flinching away for a second. He had his ankle perched on a knee and his arms resting on the back of the futon. He wasn't going to be bossed around by some dickhead who thought he had big balls.

"You all right there, mate?" Hemal asked, smacking Reyse's elevated foot.

Reyse didn't budge.

"Fine, thank you," he said with a smile he knew didn't reach his eyes.

Hemal nodded and puffed on his vape, looking around the studio. "Yeah, sure. Anything you need, just let me know."

"Talcum powder," Reyse said without missing a beat.

Hemal frowned and looked back down at him. "Beg your pardon?"

"Talc," Reyse repeated with a bigger smile. "As soon as you can, *mate.*"

Hemal slowly blinked, then unclipped his walkie-talkie from his belt and clicked it on. "Yeah, some talcum powder to the set for Mr. Hickson, asap."

He didn't look at Reyse. He just stalked off, screaming at the next unfortunate crew member about moving a set of mirrors on wheels around to the next filming location.

Reyse glanced back. The dancers that were left had taken themselves a few feet away and were practicing the choreography while they had a few minutes before wardrobe came back with their new items. They were crazy talented. Reyse spent a few moments simply admiring them run the moves. He would have loved to have jumped up and joined in with them, but the choreography was incredibly sexual. Feminine.

He sighed. God, he missed dancing with the guys, especially Blake. Blake had always been the star when it came to the choreography, but he also made those around him better just with his energy to bounce off. Reyse often still got to dance in his videos and on tour. But it wasn't quite the same as with his brothers.

He turned around and fished his phone out of his pants pocket to distract himself. Seeing as they weren't filming yet and weren't likely to be for at least another half an hour, he figured it was safe to turn it back on. He'd shut it off after taking a selfie for Instagram, looking as happy as he could manage on the set with Mega.

It was stupid, but every time he restarted it after turning it off for a recording session or flight or whatever, he hoped he might see something from Corey. Reyse's team handled the private messages on his social media, so even if Corey contacted him on there, chances were the guys would just dismiss him as some overeager fan. But Reyse could still daydream about seeing Corey's name popping up on his phone.

As it was, several unexpected messages *did* show up on Reyse's screen once the phone came back to life. They just weren't from Corey.

Three text messages and a voicemail from his mom.

Reyse sat up in his seat, his heart racing in cautious excitement. He never got to talk to his mom. He never knew the right time to call and never knew what to say. And heaven forbid his dad should pick up.

The texts were vague.

Hi sweetheart can you call me? LOL

He assumed she meant 'lots of love,' rather than 'laugh out loud.' He read on.

Its urgent

Everythings fine its just your father has had a bit of a scare. If you could call id really appreciate it

A scare? A cold sweat ran over Reyse's body and he punched in his voicemail code, holding the phone anxiously to his ear.

"Oh, hi, hon. I'm not sure if I'm supposed to call you on this number but it's the only number I have. You're probably busy. I rang a bunch of times but it went to voicemail each time. So...sorry if this is disturbing you."

"Come *on*, Mom," Reyse growled, feeling like he was going to be sick. "What's up with Dad?"

"So, um, anyway. I just thought you should know that Dad had a stroke." She laughed nervously. "He's fine. I mean, he's stable. He, um, hasn't woken up yet. But he's still in the ICU, so he's getting the best care. The doctors can't really tell me when he's going to wake up...or what state he'll be in when he does. But, uh, well. I just thought you should know. You don't have to call me back. Love you, sweetheart."

"What the *fuck?*" Reyse cried, leaping to his feet and startling a couple of the dancers. He was punching redial as one of the PAs came up to him with a bottle of talcum powder. "Oh, give it to the dancers. Thanks," he added with the best smile he could muster as he walked past them. It wasn't a great smile. His head was swimming with too many thoughts and his stomach churning like a cement mixer. "Mom! Hi!"

"Oh, sweetheart," her voice came down the line. He hadn't heard it in weeks, maybe months. His heart contracted. "I said you didn't have to call back," she said, almost accusingly.

Reyse shook his head and pushed his way out of the studio space, jogging down the hall until he found a door out into the lot. "Mom, you said Dad had a *stroke,*" he said. He stepped outside and shielded his eyes from the bright LA sunshine.

There was a brief pause. "Um, yes. Sorry."

"Mom, why are you sorry?" Reyse cried in exasperation. "I'm glad you called, I wanted to know! When did it happen? Is he really going to be okay?"

"Yes," his mom said immediately. But then it was like she struggled with what to say next. "I mean, the doctors don't know. They keep warning me that...that there might be, uh..."

Brain damage. Reyse got that. He tried to swallow, but he felt so nauseous.

"Dad's strong, Mom," he said, trying to convince the both of them. "Tough as a ram, right?"

That got a very small, weak chuckle from her. But his dad had spent all his life in the Army. He *was* tough. Reyse couldn't imagine him sick, lying in a hospital bed. That was just unfathomable.

"Yes, yes," his mom agreed. "You're quite right. He's going to be fine. Oh, hon, you didn't have to call, really. I saw on the Instagram you're shooting a music video today."

Reyse sighed. He knew his mom loved getting her news from Insta. Not just from him. She followed all kinds of people on there, preferring that to other actual news outlets. It made Reyse a little sad that was how she got *his* news, though, rather than simply texting or calling him. But he knew he didn't contact her enough either. Communication was a two-way street.

"I am, but it's fine," Reyse said truthfully. Quite frankly, they could be screaming at him to come back in that moment and he wouldn't care. "This is more important. What happened?"

"It was all so fast," his mom said, her voice trembling. "Your dad was just tinkering in the garage and he came over all funny. The ambulance was here in no time and our insurance covered most of the costs. So that's good, at least."

"I can cover it, Mom," Reyse said, not even hesitating a second. That was the least he could do.

Guilt was making him dizzy. He leaned against the studio wall for support. How long had it been since he'd seen his parents, let alone talked to his dad? His mom kept him updated as to what they were up to, but that wasn't the same. Home just seemed like a foreign land to him. He had nothing there now, and his dad had always been distant, even before Reyse got famous. When he wasn't deployed it always felt to

Reyse like he wanted to be anywhere but around his one and only son. So Reyse had stayed away.

And now he was unconscious with no clear prognosis as to when he might fully wake up…and what his mind might be like if he did.

When he did. He had to. Reyse wasn't sure of a lot of things about his dad, but he was a tough old bastard and he wasn't going down without a fight. He would recover.

And Reyse would be there when he did.

"I'm coming home," Reyse blurted before he could really think about what he was saying.

"W-what?" his mom stammered.

Reyse experienced a brief moment of panic. But this was his *dad.* If there was ever a time to drop everything and go home, it was now. Kevin would just have to deal with it. Off the top of his head, Reyse knew he had an appearance booked on the Kimmy Kovac show, but she would totally understand his need to reschedule. He was only going to play a game and get himself covered in gunk rather than promote something specific. Reyse would ask her wife which of the new Lego boxsets she was missing and get her a couple to apologize for the inconvenience.

It was typical Kevin and Sun City were okay with him going on a lesbian talk show, just because it was popular, but heaven forbid Reyse himself be gay.

Aside from a few phone interviews, he mainly had studio time on his calendar for the next few weeks. As much as it pained him to postpone that again, he wouldn't hesitate. The record could wait.

His family could not.

"I'm coming to see you," Reyse said. He rubbed his eyes, probably messing up his makeup. "I should have come home ages ago, so…yeah. I'll be there as soon as I can."

"Sweetheart," his mom said, not sounding sure. "You can't just drop everything like that. You're so busy. We're *fine.*"

"But you're not!" Reyse countered, trying not to snap. But he was feeling horribly guilty. "What if it had been worse and Dad…what if I couldn't talk to Dad again?" There was still a chance he might not. Anguish squirmed in his gut.

"Reyse," she said, her voice cracking. He knew she was fully aware that was a possibility, too. She was a smart woman, despite all her unsureness.

"I'll get through today," Reyse told her. "I'll tell them to cut my shots in half, or just do a couple of takes." It would give him immense pleasure to tell Hemal he wanted off his shitty video as soon as possible. "My people can book a flight for the next day or so, once I've got everything else in order. I'll let you know when I know."

There was a pause. Reyse could tell she was still wrestling with inconveniencing him. But he'd make her see this was his priority, without a shadow of doubt.

Thankfully, she let out a big sigh, and said, "Okay. That would be just wonderful, sweetheart. I'd love to have you here. And it would mean a lot to your dad."

Reyse honestly wasn't sure about that. But maybe a scare like this would be enough for them to try and talk a bit more. Reyse didn't know, but he'd try.

"I'll be home as soon as possible," Reyse promised. "I'll get the first flight I can."

"Will Bella be able to come with you?" his mom asked, a touch of hope in her voice.

Damn. Bella. His 'girlfriend.' His mom had never met her, but she was a huge fan, and not just of her movies. She followed her social media accounts as much as Reyse's, always saying how lovely and sweet she seemed.

Reyse wasn't sure if it was lucky or not, but he knew for a fact Bella wasn't available. "Ah, I'm sorry, Mom," he said.

"She's filming in England for the next six weeks. There's no way she could fly out."

"That's okay," his mom said quickly. "I just…well, it would have been nice for you to bring her, I guess. But I'm overjoyed you're going to come, in any case. You hurry back to work now and let me know when you've booked a flight."

Reyse promised he would and hung up the phone. But he didn't head back into the studio right away. His guts washed with worry, like acid, but now his heart was aching, too. God, it would be so amazing to bring a partner along with him in a situation like this. Someone to hold his hand and hug him and tell him his dad was going to be okay. Bella would have been nice, but Reyse had a moment of rage that he couldn't have a *boyfriend* to stand by him. He did every goddamned thing by himself. Was it too much to wish for once he could have someone take care of him?

What was worse was he had a face flash up in his mind when he thought about who that boyfriend could be.

Reyse allowed himself a moment of self-pity. Then he steeled himself for a fight. They already had several shots of him. They could just rush his other segments through, then work with Mega Daddy and the girls tomorrow.

Tomorrow, Reyse was flying home.

Alone.

CHAPTER

Eight

COREY

COREY SIGHED AND CLOSED HIS LAPTOP DOWN. YET ANOTHER rejection email had him feeling like maybe now was a good time to get on his motorcycle and see where the evening took him. He wanted to forget everything and just feel the road beneath his tires.

Maybe 'forget' wasn't the right word. He just wanted to escape his thoughts for a little while. But he didn't want them gone.

He leaned back against his pillows and tossed his laptop on the end of the bed, rubbing his face. If he picked it up again now, he was likely to check on a certain singer's Instagram, and that wouldn't do anybody any good.

He sighed and stretched his arms up before sliding further down the bed, raising his knees and drumming his hands on them. Yeah, a long ride on his bike would be a good way to get through the evening. He needed to do something to occupy his time.

He wasn't *desperate* for work just yet. Reyse's overly generous check had seen to that. Corey was still kind of stunned when he thought about how much he had given

Corey without a second thought. A couple of times he'd worried he should feel more guilty about that. Dirty. But damn it, Reyse hadn't paid him for sex. He'd helped him out because stopping that mugging had cost Corey his job.

The mind-blowing sex had just been an unexpected and thoroughly enjoyable bonus.

Corey had half a thought about jerking off, but his heart wasn't in it. As hot as the memory was, it was tinged with sadness.

Was Reyse Hickson okay?

It seemed crazy, but Corey felt like he was the only person on the planet who might be having that worry. Sure, there would probably be a couple of other people who knew what the man was going through. But from the vulnerable state he was in during their night together, Corey couldn't help but feel there weren't many others who truly knew his plight. And if they did, they were unlikely to have experienced his distress firsthand. They didn't know how he'd shaken when he'd come. Or how he'd been so heartfelt in his gratitude when Corey stayed the whole night, holding him tightly and tenderly.

It had been three weeks and Corey was apparently not getting over Reyse Hickson anytime soon. He pulled his phone out from his pocket and defied himself by logging into Insta anyway.

This was creepy. Corey needed to stop pining over a man he couldn't have. Fuck, he'd been gifted five grand, no strings attached. So long as he got a decent enough job over the next few weeks, he'd be more set up than he had ever been in his life. He could afford to *breathe* and take a moment to relax just a little.

It was only natural that he'd think about Reyse. It wasn't every day you got to fuck an international pop sensation. It had occurred to Corey a couple of days later that he'd never be able to tell anyone about this. Not that he really had any friends right now to confide in. But he honestly couldn't trust anyone with this information. He'd just have to sit on it.

It paled in comparison to the secret Reyse had to keep, so Corey would just have to deal with it. But, damn, it would have been nice to talk it through with someone. Maybe he could see a shrink? They had to keep stuff like that private, right? But that might mean having to talk about other shit, too, and Corey wasn't down with that. He much preferred the 'shove your feelings down' kind of approach.

He huffed and looked at the crack in his ceiling as he paused scrolling through Instagram. This was the trouble with not having a job to take your mind off shit on a regular basis. Delivering pizza might not have been his dream ambition in life, but he'd enjoyed seeing Maria and her crew regularly, and sometimes the customers could be really fun and friendly. Not to mention the excuse to ride his bike everywhere. He'd gone back once since he'd been fired to get the ladies another box of chocolates and pay them back their very kind loan. But Ross had made it clear he wasn't to drop in again.

No, Corey needed to get up and do something, he told himself firmly. A ride would do the trick nicely. He even had a full tank of gas, so he just needed to get changed and ride out of town. The sun would be setting in about an hour, so it would be the perfect time to go.

He decided if he was going to be productive, he was allowed to take a quick peek at Reyse's Instagram feed. Rather than scrolling through all of the people Corey followed, he went straight to Reyse's account to take a glance at his posts in chronological order.

The first photo was from today of him on the set of a slightly trashy-looking music video. 'Excited for an opportunity to work with Mega Daddy!' the caption read. Corey rolled his eyes. He questioned that, knowing a little bit about Reyse now. But did one night make Corey an expert? Maybe having half-naked girls jiggle around him really was Reyse's thing. Somehow, Corey doubted it.

He was about to swipe down to see a few more posts, when a comment on the first photo made him stop dead in his tracks. 'Sending you thought and prayers, babe' one user had written.

'No one says 'thoughts and prayers' anymore,' another had replied underneath. 'But we are thinking of you and your family, hon. BIG HUGS!'

Corey's heart was fluttering in his chest. It really wasn't his business, but he was panicking all the same. What had happened to Reyse?

A quick assessment of several other comments and a Google search gave him some answers. Thankfully, Reyse himself appeared to be okay. But he had left the video shoot early because his dad had been rushed to the hospital, possibly with a stroke. Corey couldn't say he knew exactly what that would feel like, not having any family of his own, but he wasn't a coldhearted bastard. Reyse would obviously be upset and worried, so that made Corey distressed.

He didn't even bother trying to argue with himself that he shouldn't feel so keenly for a guy he'd spent literally one night with. He was up and pacing his room, his phone clutched to his chest as his thoughts tumbled over one another.

Reyse was bound to be in a state. Who did he have looking after him? His shitty homophobic label? In fact, some of the comments had suggested his label – they were called Sun City Records, Corey had learned – were fucking pissed that he'd dropped everything to run home.

What if Reyse was on his own?

"Don't be stupid," Corey said out loud.

But it was too late. He'd had an idea.

After all, he had been about to take a bike ride, anyway.

Corey growled, giving in and snatching up his bike helmet from the corner of the small, messy room. He shoved his feet into his boots and found his jacket and keys. Fine. He'd drive out to Reyse and just...see what was what. Chances are the door staff wouldn't even let him in the building.

Oh...that was bad. But...it just might work. Maria would help him, and...yes.

He also picked up the Speedy Pete's baseball cap he hadn't bothered to return when he'd been fired. Corey wasn't above a little subterfuge to get what he wanted. If Reyse was fine, or had already left, so be it. No harm done. But if he needed someone to just vent to, even for a few minutes...

Corey paused at the door. Was he insane?

Yes, quite possibly. But Corey had to try. The abhorrence he felt at the idea Reyse might be hurting on his own was all consuming. He couldn't let it lie. Corey had looked after Reyse once before, and if he let him, he might be able to look after him again this evening.

Just as friends, of course. For once, Corey wasn't thinking with his cock.

Life was too short – that was Corey's mantra. So he wasn't about to start second-guessing himself now. This wasn't a booty call. It was a sympathy call. Nothing more.

He repeated that to himself throughout the whole drive over.

———

He'd called the order in as a pickup and texted Maria to ask her to come out with the pizza once he was close. "You're up to something, Mr. Corey," she said with a grin, handing over the large box. Then she wagged a finger at him. "I think it's for love, no?"

Corey blinked at her. "No," he spluttered, rather unconvincingly. "I mean, something like that, I guess," he admitted under her knowing stare and raised eyebrow.

She chuckled to herself as she went back inside, not bothering to count the generous tip Corey had given her. It was strange, but he did miss her. He didn't speak Spanish, shamefully, but he wondered if she might want to meet for a coffee one day, just to catch up.

He shook his head. That was silly. She wasn't his mom. She had her own kids.

Corey got back to the matter at hand, driving over to Reyse's place, weaving through the evening LA traffic. This time, he parked his bike a little closer to the apartment. Once he'd chained it up, he took his new helmet with him. He may have a spare bit of cash these days, but he still didn't want to lose a second helmet in a month.

He approached the apartment building with his heart in his mouth. There were a dozen ways this could go, most of them horribly, embarrassingly wrong. But he was here now, so he had to give it a go.

He smiled as he pressed the buzzer, adjusting the cap he'd hastily shoved onto his head. He had his helmet under one arm and the pizza balanced on the other, making him feel pretty awkward. "Hi!" he said into the intercom once it clicked, waving to the guys behind the desk. "I've got a delivery for the penthouse."

He almost said 'Mr. Hickson,' but he realized there was no way Reyse would give his name on the order. However, he was still out of luck.

"I'm afraid there's been no delivery organized for that address," the guy said. He wasn't mad, but he didn't sound like he was going to make any exceptions either. Damn it. Of course that would make sense for security. When Reyse ordered anything, he probably let the front desk know so they could take it in for him. "Are you sure you have the right building?" the security guard asked.

"Oh," Corey said with a small laugh to cover his disappointment. "Sure, man, I'll check. Sorry to bother you."

"No trouble at all," the guy said. At least he didn't chew Corey out.

So he turned to walk away from the building to reassess his options. Could he just wait here and see if Reyse came in or out? That was super fucking creepy. Maybe he could leave a message for Reyse? Would his security even pass anything on to him, though?

Corey bit his lip and looked up from the hot pizza box into his hands.

Just as Reyse stepped out from a sleek black car by the side of the curb.

They both froze, looking at each other with disbelief. "Corey?" Reyse said, his voice catching.

Corey's heart almost stopped. But then Reyse's eyes went wide and a smile played on his gorgeous mouth. He looked hopeful.

"Hey," Corey said.

He looked from the pizza to Reyse again as Reyse closed the door and the car drove off. Fuck, if possible, Reyse looked even better than when they had met before. Corey supposed he'd been in his workout gear then. But now...well, technically, he was just in jeans like Corey was. But Reyse's jeans probably cost a grand and fit him like a glove, making his ass look incredible. His sneakers were so white they practically glowed. He'd paired the pants with a cream shirt, a black buttoned vest and a skinny burgundy tie. The top button of his shirt was undone, revealing the dip of his throat.

On someone else, the outfit might have been kind of nerdy. But on Reyse, it was mouthwatering.

Corey couldn't get distracted, though. He and Reyse had made a kind of unspoken agreement not to see each other again. Yet here he was, acting like a goddamned stalker.

"So, uh, you're probably wondering why I'm here?" he said sheepishly.

Reyse shrugged and moved toward his building's front door. People were already starting to notice him as they walked past. "Kind of," he said. But then he smiled a little more. "It's nice to see you, though. I'm having a pretty awful day. Do you want to step inside for a second?"

"Sure," Corey said, his heart in his mouth. "Oh, I kind of told the guys at the desk you ordered a pizza."

Reyse looked down at the box, his smile becoming wry. "That's sort of brilliant," he said.

Really? He wasn't mad? Corey exhaled as Reyse let himself through with a fob and a PIN code. Then Corey followed behind him.

"Sorry," Reyse called out to the desk. "I forgot to phone ahead. Thanks for being diligent."

The big security guy nodded to him. "Sorry about that, sir," he called over to Corey. That was decent of him, at least.

It made him feel just a fraction less nervous as he and Reyse stopped in a small lobby with purple sofas, the glass wall looking out over the sidewalk behind them. "Is everything okay?" Reyse asked.

That pulled at Corey's heart. Here he was having a terrible day, yet he still asked about Corey first. It gave Corey a bit of courage.

"I'm totally fine," Corey said. "But I got this crazy idea and…I hope you don't think I'm a maniac."

"I don't think that," Reyse said. "I…I know we had an agreement. But it's nice to see you again."

Corey licked his lips. *Focus,* he told himself. He was here as a friend. Not as a fuck buddy.

"I saw the news about your dad," he blurted out. "And I was worried about you. So I thought I'd come back on the off chance you were here and see…I don't know." Christ, it sounded nuts now he was explaining his thought process out loud. "Honestly, I just wanted to make sure you had people looking after you. If you needed someone to talk to, just as a friend, or…it's not my place. You have friends. Sorry, I shouldn't have tried to trick my way into your building, but I knew your security was tight and-"

He made to turn away, but Reyse caught his wrist.

"I can't believe you did that," he said, shaking his head.

Corey winced. "I'm sorry. It was creepy, I-"

"It was incredibly thoughtful," Reyse said. Corey was alarmed to realize that tears were pooling in Reyse's eyes. "Fuck, do you have any idea how much I didn't want to be alone right now?"

They stared at each other. Corey's heart rate began to slow, just a fraction. "I wondered, yeah," he said quietly. "Do you want some comfort food?" he added with a shaky laugh, offering him the box in his hands.

Reyse laughed too, taking the pizza from him. "That sounds amazing," he said with a sigh. "What toppings?"

"I wasn't sure what you liked," Corey admitted. "So I got ham and pineapple on one half, then jalapeño pepperoni on the other."

Reyse frowned and looked up at him with a strange expression. "I love both of those," he said.

Pride flushed through Corey as well as something else – happiness? He loved those toppings too, and knowing he and Reyse had that in common made his heart flutter. "Well, you know," he said, rubbing the back of his neck. "You have that sweet tooth, then, uh, the jalapeño pretzels we had…"

Reyse was sort of gaping at him. Then he shook his head and held the box with both hands. He went to speak, closed his mouth, then tried again. "I have also just had a crazy idea," he said. Corey raised his eyebrows and nodded, encouraging him to go on. "I could really use a friend right now."

Corey smiled. "Sure, that's why I came over. We could hang, watch a movie or something." He glanced to make sure the security guards couldn't hear, but they were engrossed in some kind of sports on their TV. "Just as buds, I know you have to be careful of…you know, anything else."

Reyse nibbled his lip. "Actually…oh god, it's insane. Forget I said anything."

Corey touched his arm, just for a second. Nothing too scandalous if anyone was watching them. "Try me, man," he said. "I'm here. And…like I said. I can just be a friend if that's what you need. Nothing more."

He meant that, as much as it pained him. Reyse smelled so good and Corey just wanted to wrap his arms around him and take his pain away.

"I'm heading home tomorrow," Reyse said in a rush. "Upstate. I…would you come with me? Just for a few days? I haven't spoken to my dad in forever and it's super weird but I'm so worried about him and my mom's a mess and-"

His voice was getting higher in pitch and tears were pooling in his eyes again.

Corey would have done anything to make that stop. If he couldn't comfort Reyse with his body, he could try the next best thing. "Yes," he blurted, interrupting him. "Yes, I can come. I haven't gotten a new job yet. I'll be your buddy, no problem." He smiled as Reyse's relief was evident on his face.

This was madness. What was Corey doing? He'd just thought maybe he'd give Reyse a hug if he got to see him. Maybe talk for an hour or two. Not fly out to see his estranged folks for a few days.

But the fact Reyse even suggested it meant he must have been pretty desperate for some company. He was asking Corey of all people. He could either be disbelieving, or take it as the honor it was.

"I'd really appreciate the company," Reyse said softly.

"Then let's go," Corey said.

He'd have plenty of time to second-guess himself later. For now, he was just going to go with the hand the universe had dealt him. Reyse needed a friend, and it just so happened Corey was on hand to be that person.

Nothing more. That would be too complicated. But he could keep his hands to himself, especially while Reyse's family was going through a crisis.

Of that he was sure.

CHAPTER
Nine

REYSE

For the hundredth time since they boarded the private jet, Reyse wondered if he was genuinely insane. Could he really trust Corey? He knew he *wanted* to. But he hardly knew the guy.

He'd wondered if he'd been remembering him with rose-tinted glasses, right up until the moment he'd unexpectedly opened the car door to him. But the second Reyse saw that relieved smile, he knew he hadn't been imagining things. Corey was just as easygoing as Reyse had remembered from a few weeks ago, not to mention gorgeous in that damn leather jacket and worn jeans.

Reyse couldn't believe he'd come and found him, just when he needed him the most. And as much as he would have loved Corey to have thrown himself at Reyse, he truly respected that he hadn't. Reyse didn't need sex complicating his life right now. He wanted a friend to tell him things were going to be okay, to stand in his corner when his family inevitably turned against him.

Well…what he *really* wanted was a boyfriend. But seeing as Corey couldn't be that, this was the next best thing.

Undoubtedly, this was a complicated situation Reyse had gotten himself involved in. But as the plane touched down at Sacramento International, he found his worries over Corey giving way to his concerns about what was about to come.

"This is it," Reyse murmured.

Corey took his hand. Although there were a handful of other free seats, it was just the two of them on the tiny aircraft aside from the small crew. The one flight attendant that had looked after them for the past hour and a half wasn't currently hovering over them. Reyse appreciated the brief moment of contact.

"Are you sure you're ready for this?" he asked Corey.

Corey snorted. "No, probably not," he said with a grin. "But let's give it a try anyway. Your folks know I'm gonna be there with you?"

Reyse nodded. He probably should have talked this through with Corey earlier. "I told Mom you're a friend," he said while the airplane completed its short taxi, slowly coming to a halt on the tarmac. "I told a bit of a white lie," he admitted. "I said you did catering on my last tour and we just really clicked. That you treated me like a normal guy. I hope that's all right?"

Corey nodded. "Clever," he said. "You wouldn't want to make me a school friend or anything. I'd be expected to know too much about you."

Reyse glanced at the flight attendant at the back of the small plane. He didn't appear to be listening in. "It doesn't bother you?" Reyse muttered. "All these complications?"

Corey shrugged and smiled. "It is what it is, right? No sense getting my panties in a twist if I can't do anything about it."

Reyse sighed, resting his head on the seat, tilting it to take Corey in. "You do make me feel like a regular guy, you know," he said appreciatively. "That part is true."

Corey regarded him. They were sitting across the small aisle from one another. Corey had worn a forest-green T-shirt with a logo Reyse thought might be from a video game and a new-looking pair of jeans. His thick, dark hair defied gravity as usual, standing up to attention like a hurricane couldn't flatten it down. He was gorgeous.

Even more so when he licked his lips and leaned forward in a conspiratorial manner to whisper to Reyse. "I hate to break it to you, bro," he said quietly, "but nothing about you is regular."

Reyse blushed and gave Corey a shy smile. He could have meant any number of things, but Reyse's mind immediately provided the memory of Corey on top of him, his cock buried deep inside his ass as they both shuddered in the wake of their orgasms. Judging by the smug look on Corey's face, that was exactly the moment he had been thinking of, too.

The flight attendant bustled through the plane, which Reyse realized had come to a full and complete stop. He gathered up his belongings as the steward opened the door out onto the wheeled stairs that had been positioned by the plane. "There we are, gentlemen," he said with a professional smile. "Thank you for flying with us today, Mr. Hickson."

And Mr. Sheppard, Reyse wanted to say, but he didn't want to embarrass Corey any further. People often liked to pretend those around Reyse were invisible. Whether due to spite or jealousy, Reyse couldn't always tell. This guy was giving him petty vibes, though. Maybe he was envious of Corey for monopolizing Reyse's time?

Reyse put it from his mind. He soon forgot about the flight attendant as he and Corey walked down the stairs to meet the ground crew who had removed their luggage from the hold for them. He said a little prayer in thanksgiving for airport security. He didn't have to brave the main belly of the building, so for once there weren't any fans waiting for him with cell phones and things for him to autograph. There was a private car on the asphalt, however.

"Wow," Corey said as the driver ran to take their suitcases from them and load them into the trunk. "A guy could get used to this."

Reyse hummed. It was true, he didn't feel shocked at this treatment anymore. It was no longer out of the ordinary. But he couldn't say he loved it. He'd rather jump in a car and drive upstate or fly coach like normal folks. But, like Corey had wisely said, it was what it was. Reyse couldn't make himself be un-famous, so he just had to get on with it. He hoped Corey got a kick out of it, at least.

It was about a twenty-minute drive to his parents' new house. Reyse had only made this particular journey a few times, so he didn't know the route all that well. But he could tell when they were getting closer to Fort Ladrillo. His guts were in knots. It was only when Corey took hold of his hand that Reyse realized he hadn't spoken a word for the past ten minutes.

"Sorry," he said, shaking his head. "I guess I'm kind of nervous."

"Why?" Corey enquired. "I hope you don't mind me asking."

Reyse scoffed and shook his head, running his thumb against Corey's hand. God, it felt good to hold him. They had tinted windows in the car, so they were relatively safe, even from the driver's backwards glances.

"Of course not," Reyse said, looking out the window again. "You're in the middle of this now. You deserve to know what's going on."

Fort Ladrillo had a real mix-match of architecture. There were plenty of one- and two-story houses that looked like a lot of towns across the west coast, nicer-than-average trailer parks and high-rises uptown that might even be called skyscrapers. But his folks' neighborhood was downtown. The center there was full of Victorian buildings with triangular roofs all bunched together on three- or four-story buildings that looked like haunted mansions right out of Disneyland. Reyse noted that since his last visit the clock on the tower in the cobblestone main square had stopped working at eight sixteen.

"This thing with my dad is so stupid," Reyse admitted, feeling a bit like a fool. "It's not...my folks don't know about...you know." He squeezed Corey's hand. Of course he hadn't come out as gay to his mom and dad. That would be insane.

"So..." Corey said, stretching out the word. "It's the phenomenally successful career and stacks of cash that's really bummed them out?"

Reyse sighed, feeling sick. "Kind of, yeah," he admitted. "My dad was in the Army. I'm an only child. He was never really home, but when he was, he talked a lot about me enlisting and defending my country, too. It took a long time for him to understand that I was never that kind of guy." Reyse grimaced. "Even then, he didn't *understand.* I think he felt betrayed that I didn't want to follow in his footsteps, you know? And I felt less of a man..." He swallowed, trying not to let his emotions get the better of him now. But the shame was still there. "When I left home it just got worse, even when he was honorably discharged a few years ago and retired. We just...never have a single thing to say to each other."

"You think your success made him feel like he'd gotten it wrong or something?" Corey asked. Reyse gave him an inquisitive look. "Like, you were right not to follow in his footsteps, and being a big star just reminds him of that?"

Reyse blinked. He wasn't sure he'd ever thought of it like that before. "You know," he said with a cautious smile. "Don't take this the wrong way, but you're a lot smarter than you make yourself out to be."

Corey grinned at him, though, rubbing his thumb over Reyse's palm where their fingers were linked, making him shiver. "I don't know what you mean," Corey murmured, probably knowing exactly what Reyse meant.

"So, what's your deal?" Reyse asked, figuring he should make an effort to know *something* about the guy he was shortly going to be introducing to his parents. "Do you see your family much? Are you close?"

"Ah," Corey said ruefully. Reyse could tell immediately he'd asked a tricky question, but Corey didn't look too upset about answering. Just maybe about the answer itself. "I'd have to *have* a family to be close to them in the first place."

"I'm sorry," Reyse said automatically. Shit, he felt like a jerk, moaning about not being best friends with his dad when Corey had, what? Nothing?

Corey shrugged. "I was adopted when I was a baby," he explained, "so it started out well. But then my new mom and dad got killed in a car crash when I was three." He sucked on his teeth and smiled, but it was more of a grimace. "Went into the system until I was eighteen. Bounced around several homes that never stuck. Apparently, I was a difficult child." He winked at Reyse, like he was letting him in on some joke, but Reyse didn't find the situation very funny.

"You really didn't have anyone looking out for you?" he asked.

Again, Corey shrugged. Reyse sensed he was trying to make light of his situation. "I had some buddies at school, but they were straight, didn't get the home situation, and went off to college. I don't know. It always seemed easier to look after myself."

"How old are you?" Reyse asked.

It was pure coincidence they were driving past his own

former high school. He didn't have much love for the place, but he'd opened up a new theater for them a couple of years ago that he'd paid for. So he always thought fondly about the arts kids that had somewhere to go now.

"Twenty-eight," Corey said, surprising Reyse. He'd assumed he was closer to his own age, if not older from the way he'd looked after Reyse and taken charge. "You?"

"Thirty-two," Reyse said. "Weren't there other gay kids you could hang out with?"

Cory shrugged. "I'm bi, so it was hard to feel 'gay enough' at that age."

That hit Reyse a bit like a sucker punch. "You're bi?" he said. For some completely irrational reason, he felt fractionally betrayed by that. Like he'd lost a comrade. But that was dumb as all hell. Corey was still here with him, wasn't he? But still, Reyse had to ask. "Why not just date women?"

Corey smiled like he'd heard that question a hundred times before. "Because I like men, too," he said, rubbing the back of Reyse's hand. "Why deny myself half the people I could be seeing?"

"Sorry," Reyse mumbled.

"Don't be," Corey replied. "I'm sure you'd appreciate the opportunity to be attracted to women as well, right?"

Reyse's managed a small smile. Corey was very insightful. *But then I might not have met you,* he thought with a pang.

Even if they were just going to stay as friends for this trip, Reyse was glad he'd gotten the opportunity to meet Corey, even just for a short while.

It felt so soothing just sitting holding hands, with no pressure of anything else. Fuck, Reyse wished they could do this all the time. But the fact they were drawing nearer to his parents' place reminded him that they couldn't.

Corey still knew how to ease his tension a little bit,

though. "See," he said sagely. "Now we know all kinds of things about each other. We're practically BFFs."

Reyse laughed. "Definitely," he said.

He even sort of meant it. He wasn't sure he'd ever been this open with the guys when they'd been in the band together. All those years on the road and Reyse had been too ashamed to admit why he never wanted to call home. That it would have been better if he'd been phoning from some base in Iraq rather than a European tour.

If he was going to know enough about Corey to be his best friend, now was the time. Their driver swung up to the entrance gate of Reyse's parents' neighborhood, buzzing his way inside.

Corey squeezed Reyse's hand as they passed through the gate. "Are you okay?" he asked.

Reyse thought of how he'd asked if he was okay after sex. If anything, the question was harder to answer now. But Reyse nodded. "I'm all right," he said, mostly telling the truth. "Thanks for, you know…"

Being here. For some reason, the words were too difficult to say.

Corey nodded and gave Reyse's hand one last squeeze before the car swung into his mom and dad's driveway. Then Corey let him go.

"Anytime," he said, smoothing down his jeans as the driver killed the ignition. "Okay, what do you say we go and face the music?" he asked.

Reyse nodded. It was now or never.

"Let's do it."

Ten

COREY

Corey was trying to put on a brave face for Reyse. But damn, what the hell had he been thinking? A guy like him did not belong in a place like this. Reyse's mom was going to take one look at him and *sense* the fact he used to deliver pizzas to this kind of neighborhood.

What did he care what she thought, though, really? He wasn't there as Reyse's boyfriend. Just a friend. Still, he didn't want to shame the man. As the car swung into the circular driveway, Corey attempted to flatten his unruly hair.

But Reyse glanced over at him with a kind smile. "You look great," he murmured.

Corey felt a flare of rage at the situation they were in. If Reyse was a regular guy off the street, they wouldn't have to pull their hands apart like they had now. They could entertain the idea of maybe dating, of seeing if they made a good couple after the novelty of amazing sex wore off. If it even did.

As it was, they stepped out either side of the car, acting as if they were just buddies. Nothing more. One bro looking after the other while his dad was in the hospital, hanging on by a thread.

Jesus. Corey was selfish for even thinking about this relationship stuff while Reyse had so much going on. He may not be close with his dad – or at all from the sounds of it – but he obviously cared that he might die without them being able to sort their shit out. Corey got that. He needed to stop thinking with his dick and think with his heart. Reyse just needed a friend right now to make sure he didn't fall apart.

Corey had to say, he was pretty honored to be that friend. This time yesterday, he'd thought he wasn't going to see Reyse again. Now here he was, rolling up to his parents' home.

He looked up as they made their approach. The house was set a few dozen feet back from the street, the lawn circular and meticulously maintained. Leafy green trees swayed in the afternoon sunshine, surrounding the property in a way Corey suspected was intended to keep anyone from trying to look too closely inside. He felt a pang for Reyse's folks. They probably had to deal with all kind of security issues thanks to Reyse's fame.

The house loomed over him and Reyse as they closed the car doors, their driver materializing with their luggage, then slipping back behind the wheel like a silent ghost. Corey was too busy gaping to pay much attention to someone who was being purposefully discreet. Before he knew it, the car was driving around the other side of the circular driveway, leaving them alone.

Reyse's parents' place had three stories visible from the front, but from the way the ground sloped on either side, Corey would bet there was another basement level that opened up to the backyard. The first-floor walls were rough-cast and the rest of the walls painted a coffee-cream color. The tiles on the roof and awnings between floors were a rich brown, as was the wood on the massive front door and window frames.

"So, this is where you grew up, huh?" Corey asked to deflect away from his nerves. How much did a pile of bricks like this cost, anyway?

"Oh, no," Reyse said. He slowed his walk as they climbed the couple of steps that led to the front porch. "I grew up in town, about fifteen-minutes' drive from here. I bought this place for my folks a couple of years ago."

The idea that someone his age could afford somewhere like this for someone else, not even themselves, was mind-boggling to Corey. But Reyse wasn't just well-off. He was *mega* rich. Corey needed to not freak out, otherwise he was going to make Reyse feel like a jerk.

"Wow," Corey said with a grin and an appreciative tilt of the head. "Must have been an awesome Christmas present for them," he said sincerely.

Reyse gave him a tight smile, resting his suitcase on the slate stone porch and looking at the doorbell. "Mom likes it at least, I think," he said.

Corey frowned. Before he could dwell too much on who *wouldn't* like being given a house like this, Reyse reached up and pressed the bell. Rather than continue their conversation, Corey clutched at the strap of his old backpack over his shoulder. It was hard not to compare it to Reyse's top-of-the-line suitcase and carry-on set that had probably come from Europe and cost several hundred dollars.

Corey remembered the days when he moved from house to house with a black trash bag full of all his worldly possessions. At least the backpack was a step up from that.

"I-" Reyse said, catching his attention. But then the door clicked and swung inwards, making them both look at who was on the other side.

"Uncle Dave?" Reyse spluttered.

He was clearly thrown by the gray-haired man who had come to meet them. Dave was even taller than Corey, so well over six foot, with a solid build that suggested he was still fit even if he was in his late fifties or early sixties. He wore cream pants and a navy polo shirt, and had a no-nonsense air about him. Corey looked to Reyse for a reaction. Because this was the kind of guy Corey was sure he didn't blend well with.

"I – what are you doing here?" Reyse asked. "Not that it isn't good to see you, sir."

Sir? Corey got even more of a bad feeling about this.

Dave nodded. "The family wanted to be there for your mom, son," he said sagely. "I have to say it's a pleasant surprise to see you." Reyse's eyes dropped to the ground in shame. Corey felt that him implying Reyse wouldn't come when his dad was on death's door was a dick move. "Come on in, why don't you," Dave said.

"Uh, sure," Reyse said, looking back up. If he felt anything like Corey, he was probably kind of pissed at his uncle 'allowing' him into the damn house *he* bought. "This is my friend, Corey Sheppard. He's been a real rock."

Corey swelled a little inside with the praise, but he tried not to let it show. Instead, he stuck out his hand and attempted to be his most manly as he squared off with Reyse's uncle. "Pleasure to meet you, sir," he said, adding on the epitaph for Reyse's sake. In Corey's opinion, people weren't owed respect. They earned it.

Dave's bushy salt-and-pepper eyebrows knitted together as he clasped Corey's hand with his own plate-sized one. "You his secretary or something?" He snorted and rolled his eyes at Reyse. "Too good to carry your own bags home, hey, boy?"

What the actual fuck? This old bastard was mocking one

of the most internationally recognized pop stars of the last decade. Fury rose in Corey.

But Reyse smiled, that hundred-killer-watt one that had made him so famous in the first place. "Corey's the one with his shit together," Reyse said, nodding. "I wouldn't have made it here otherwise."

Well, that was bullshit. Reyse toured the *world* on a regular basis just fine without Corey holding his damn hand. But for some reason it seemed to work on Dave. He nodded, his expression serious as he looked back at Corey. "Glad to hear it, son. A man should have a fella who'll watch his back. Your daddy never let a man down in his life."

Corey wasn't sure what exactly had just happened, but he got the feeling he'd somehow gone up in Uncle Dave's opinion. Corey didn't know why that might be, nor did he care. He didn't crave approval from a jackass like this.

"No, sir," Reyse agreed, his expression pained. "Is there any news?"

Dave shook his head. "He's pretty much the same. Why don't you come in? Your mom can tell you all about it."

This time, Reyse accepted the invitation to step inside the front door. He made a point of picking up his own two bags with ease. He may have been on the small side, but he was damn strong. Corey allowed him to go ahead. Then he walked with his backpack behind him into the house, nodding at Uncle Dave as he did. If the smile he wore was more like a defiant smirk, Corey really couldn't say.

The door swung shut, enveloping them in the air conditioning that was a pleasant relief from the hot Californian afternoon. They were led through a cream marble entrance hall past a dark wooden staircase that rose upward to the second and third floors. As Corey had suspected, there was another flight of stairs that descended into a basement level that they headed toward. Along the way, they passed what Corey thought might have been a living room, if that was where rich people kept their grand pianos and collections of top shelf-liquor.

It also appeared to be where the Hicksons stored extended family members. Or so Corey guessed from all the people of various ages that peered out through the open door as Reyse and he walked past with Uncle Dave. They weren't dressed in black exactly, but their clothes felt pretty somber in tone. Corey was glad he'd bothered to wear something he felt to be respectable. But he still felt pretty scruffy compared to these guys in their dark suits. Women young and old were in the kind of dresses that would be acceptable for working in the office, or even at a funeral.

As he and Reyse walked by the door, Corey spied at least a dozen people in his line of sight. He suspected there were more in the room beyond. They all looked to be drinking alcohol and several people were smoking pensively, their lips pinched as they inhaled the tabacco.

Trays of puff pastries and glazed mini-sausages, complete with leafy garnish, were placed on various tables. The TV was on showing an old rerun of The Kimmy Kovac Show – the sitcom she had before she came out as a lesbian and the network canceled the whole thing. Joke was on them. She now had the number one daytime chat show in the US by the same name. Not that anyone was paying attention to the screen right now.

Most were talking quietly among themselves. An older dude with a prosthetic leg and the air of a military man nodded at Reyse. The guy sitting beside him had a supportive hand on his shoulder, and he also nodded at Reyse. One woman turned her back on him.

Corey's mouth worked before his brain did. He leaned into Reyse with what he was sure was an alarmed look on his face. "Your dad isn't *dead*, right?"

Reyse had gone very pale. He didn't appear shocked at Corey's black humor, but the sort of joke pulled him out of stunned silence.

"Uncle Dave, why does it feel like there's a wake going on?" he asked, somewhat hysterically. "Who *are* all these people? What are they doing in my parents' house?" Oh, so not all family then, Corey thought. It would make sense if the two guys who had actually appeared pleased to see Reyse were his dad's old army buddies.

Dave snorted as they approached the stairs down to the basement level. "You know your mother," he said, shaking his head. "She doesn't know what to do if she's not feeding people. We just wanted to support her, be there for Donny when he wakes up. But she can't help turn the whole thing into a cocktail party."

Corey felt his eyebrows crawl up his head. The woman was worried about her husband and had been thoughtful enough to feed her guests. And this jackass thought that was a good excuse to insult Reyse's mom *to his face?*

"Not sure what kind of parties you're used to, man," Corey said, trailing after Dave and Reyse down the stairs. "But I'm sure a little food and booze are going a long way right now."

Dave paused on the stairs, forcing Reyse and Corey to stop, too. He gave Corey a searching look, as if trying to discern if he was being serious or not, then turned and continued on his way.

Reyse glanced at Corey. "Sorry," Corey mouthed. He didn't want to get Reyse in any shit with his relatives, after all.

But Reyse shook his head. "Don't worry about it," he said. However, he looked extremely worried at all the people in the house. The two of them followed Dave down the remainder of the stairs.

The last few steps curved around to the right, depositing them in an open-plan floor that led out onto a patio with a pool in an enormous garden, much like Corey had expected. There was a kitchen to the left with a large marble breakfast bar, a huge flat-screen mounted on the left-hand wall with a corner sofa in front, partitioning a sort of den area from a dining table big enough for twelve people. A couple of ceiling fans spun overhead and on top of all the cupboards and sideboards, leafy plants with delicate pink flowers tumbled out, filling the space between the units and the ceiling but not hindering the use of the cupboards.

Another dozen people were loitering here too, either sitting on the couch or at the table, sipping drinks and nibbling on hors d'oeuvres. They all stopped whatever they were doing to turn and gape at Reyse. The only sound left in the room was the quiet noise of the rerun of the old NFL game on the television.

"Jesus fucking Christ," Reyse hissed under his breath, so low probably only Corey heard him. But he was clearly freaking out at having close to fifty guests sprung on him when he'd been nervous enough about just seeing his mom and dad. Corey almost grabbed his hand in solidarity. He caught himself at the last second. Instead, he just stepped closer to Reyse to show his support.

Everyone was either looking starstruck or overly eager to say hello to the mega celebrity.

All except one.

"Oh, *sweetheart!*"

The voice that cut through the near silence pulled both Corey and Reyse's attention to the kitchen on the left. It was easy to identify the woman who had spoken. She was the one suddenly moving in a blur to get to Reyse.

"*Mom,*" Reyse cried back. He let go of his carry-on handle with such force it almost slammed to the ground. But Corey shot his hand out and grabbed the suitcase before it could fall, setting it right again. As he did so, Reyse and his mom crashed into each other's arms.

Corey was kind of stunned at the lump that rose in his throat, but it was pretty emotional to see a mother-son reunion that had been years in the making.

Reyse clearly took after his mom. They were both slim, her almost painfully so, while he was muscular despite his petite stature. They both had golden blond hair and high cheekbones. Before she closed them for the hug, Corey saw that her eyes weren't the same piercing blue as her son's, but a light brown. She rocked him back and forth, and slowly the room returned to the state it was in before, conversations slowly crawling back to life.

"Ahh, it's good he's here for her," Dave said gruffly. Corey turned to see him nod, his arms folded across his chest. "A house needs a man in it. She's been falling apart."

Corey hummed but said nothing. He felt pretty strongly that people were allowed to be worried about their loved ones when they were sick. It had nothing to do with having a man around or any bullshit delicate feminine sensibilities. But he wasn't sure Dave was down for that kind of conversation, so Corey left it.

"Mom, this is my friend, Corey," Reyse said, interrupting Corey's thoughts. Reyse had stepped to the side of his mom, but was still hugging her with one arm. "I was a wreck when I got the news about Dad. Corey got me here and helped me pull myself together. Corey, this is my mom, Clementine."

Corey hadn't met many people's moms, but he knew they were generally supposed to be treated with the utmost respect. Besides, he got a good vibe from Clementine Hickson.

"Pleasure to meet you, ma'am," he said, stepping forward to touch her arm and carefully kiss her cheek once. "I'm so sorry to hear about your husband. Hopefully you'll hear something soon."

Clementine nodded as he broke contact with her, blinking tears from her eyes. "No news is good news," she said determinedly.

She pulled at the silk scarf around her neck over the cream blouse tucked into perfectly fitted jeans. Even though they were indoors, she still wore heeled leather boots. A simple outfit, but Corey could tell from the cuts of the garments they were expensive. He'd been around enough rich people to see the difference between what they had and he didn't.

Her style didn't scream of pride in being upper-middle class, however, unlike some of the people Corey had spied here who were dripping with bling and labels. People like that were so desperate to let others know how well they'd done in life, they didn't care if they literally had to write it on themselves to make it clear.

For all his wealth, Corey realized Reyse wasn't like that, either. He was just quietly understated. Corey liked that about him.

"I'm worried we're going to run out of olives," Clementine said anxiously, looking around the room. As Corey followed her gaze he realized Dave had wandered off to watch the football game, standing behind the sofa with a fresh beer bottle in hand.

Reyse huffed. "Mom, no one gives a damn about olives," he said firmly. "How are you? What actually *happened* with Dad?"

"Hey, why don't I give you guys some space," Corey said. He felt like these were two people in dire need of a catch-up and he didn't want to intrude.

Reyse's face fell. "No, you don't have to go," he said. But Corey could tell it was because Reyse didn't want him to be at a loose end. He was gripping onto his mom like a small child who'd gotten momentarily lost in the mall.

Corey shook his head. "Hey man, it's cool," he assured him. He nodded at Clementine, who gave him a weak smile. "I'll grab a beer and hang. You guys need some time."

Reyse swallowed. "Thank you," he said with a look of gratitude.

"No problem," Corey told him convivially.

He just had to hang out with a bunch of wealthy strangers who were already looking at him like he didn't belong, without giving away to a single one of them that he'd had the most spectacular sex with their golden boy.

Nothing to worry about. Right?

CHAPTER
Eleven

REYSE

REYSE WATCHED COREY CONFIDENTLY SNAG A BEER FROM THE silver bucket of suds on the dining table and saunter out onto the patio. He flicked his sunglasses from where they were perched in his thick hair down onto the bridge of his nose, smiling at one of his parents' friends as he passed them like he knew them. Reyse wished he could be more self-assured like that.

But that was the trouble when pretty much everyone in America knew his name. He was always at a disadvantage.

He could worry about whether or not he was supposed to introduce himself around to people later. Right now, he had his mom clinging desperately to his side. He was so thrilled to see her in person after all these years. Yet he couldn't think of a single thing to say.

He knew she had wanted to come out and visit him many times over the past several years. But his dad always made airports and the TSA and even something so simple as hailing a cab seem like a military operation. Clementine Hickson probably didn't know if she could do anything like that on her own, because since she had met Donny Hickson at twenty-one years of age, she'd never been given the chance.

Reyse was convinced his dad did things like that out of love and care. But it had essentially held his mom hostage if his dad didn't want to go to a certain place.

And he'd never felt the need to come see Reyse perform. Not even once.

So he and his mom had talked a lot over the phone as well as FaceTime and via text. But recently, even that had dwindled away. Reyse had been dying to chat to his mom for months, to spill out a hundred – a thousand – little stories and problems and triumphs. But now, he found he couldn't say a single word. The irony that he used his voice for a living was not lost on him.

"You must be hungry," his mom said suddenly, stepping away from their half hug. She didn't look at Reyse as she began fussing over a plate, dishing up several side salads and marinated chicken skewers from the spread on the kitchen counter. "Do you want a beer or some wine? Maybe a soda?"

Reyse didn't want her fussing over him when she had so much else on her mind. But he couldn't deny it felt amazing to have his mom look after him again, even if it was just fixing him a late lunch.

"Uh," he said sheepishly. "Do you have any grape soda?"

Her face broke into a beautiful smile, and for a brief second, he saw the girl he knew from old photos. The girl who had won both homecoming and prom queen in her senior year. The head cheerleader. The young woman who had gotten herself on a bus in 1986 down to Los Angeles to protest for nuclear disarmament. That had been only a couple of months before she'd met her would-be husband. Six months before she'd fallen pregnant with Reyse. It was nice to see that person resurface in real life occasionally.

"I always have grape soda," his mom said. She spun around to the fridge to grab him a can.

Reyse tried not to drink this kind of stuff regularly as it was full of sugar and all kinds of additives. But damn, he loved it. Partly for the taste itself, but also because it reminded him of his childhood.

He also knew he was the only one out of his family who liked it at all. They couldn't stand it. He'd hoped maybe she might have gotten some, but was she serious? Did she really always keep some in the fridge?

"Thanks, Mom," he said quietly as he cracked the tab and took a sip.

She held the plate of food she'd made him in two hands, clutched to her front, and rocked on her heels. Glancing at the room full of guests, she bit her lip. "Why don't we find somewhere a little quieter?" she suggested, looking back at Reyse. Her eyes were glassy.

"I'd love that," he said sincerely.

Before he could offer to carry his own plate, she scuttled out of the kitchen, heading for the stairs. Reyse had his soda can in one hand, so he just grabbed his carry-on with the free one. That was the case that had his most-valued possessions that he'd brought with him. They were both locked, but it comforted him to know he had his laptop and tablet in his sight, not to mention his favorite sneakers and lucky T-shirt.

His phone was in his pocket. He was usually careful with it, but since the almost mugging, he was obsessively aware of where it was now.

He was able to follow his mom with ease as she jogged up the stairs. She was obviously still keeping fit, despite being in her early fifties now. He was glad to see that hadn't slowed her down.

"Tina!" someone called from the front room. Reyse thought of it as the music room, as that was where the piano was. Not the old one he'd learned on. This was a Steinway, bought to match the fancy new house he'd gifted his parents. He wondered sadly if anyone had ever played it. He'd put his old one in storage. It was worth pennies, really. But for sentimental reasons, he felt he couldn't give it away.

Some guy stepped out of the room and touched Reyse's mom's arm in an overly familiar way. Reyse caught her very slight flinch and the contact. The guy didn't appear to. He had a long face, brown hair and a sleazy sort of half smile tugging at his lips. He readjusted the sweater tied over his polo shirt and nodded at his mom.

"Still playing hostess, Tina?" he asked. Then he tutted and shook his head. "You should have people looking after *you* in this difficult time." He didn't even so much glance Reyse's way.

Reyse's mom swallowed and gave the guy a sweet smile. Reyse knew how much she hated people shortening Clementine to Tina, but since that was what his dad's family called her, it kind of stuck.

"Jeremy," she said politely. "This is my son, Reyse. We haven't seen each other in quite some time."

Jeremy took a second to swirl the whiskey in the tumbler he was holding, then slid his eyes over to Reyse. He chuckled. "Oh, the prodigal son has finally returned, has he?" he asked with mild incredulity. He didn't bother to offer to shake Reyse's hand. "The pop star, right? Donny said you were in that *'Oh Oh Oohh'* band my girls used to be so crazy about." Reyse didn't miss the inflection on 'used to.' "Things calmed down these days?"

Reyse gave the guy a small smile. "Not really," he said. "Nice to meet you, sir."

His mom didn't need telling twice to pick up on his cue. She just smiled and nodded, already walking around to the next staircase to lead them up to the next floor. "Who was that creep?" Reyse murmured when they were halfway up.

"Oh, just a neighbor," his mom said cheerily. But her smile didn't meet her eyes.

Once they reached the landing, she automatically walked down one of the hallways and went to the room on the left by the bathroom, using her butt to bump the door open. Reyse followed after her with his carry-on, looking around the room that was technically his.

He'd guessed this was where she would take him. It made him a little anxious to be two floors away from Corey. He didn't want him feeling like he'd been abandoned. But he got his mom's need for a little space. The whole house was filled with people who were treating his dad's stroke like a goddamned party.

He might not recognize the room with its dark wood furniture and chintzy lampshades over the lights. But he recognized his old Thriller poster hanging on the wall, now in a frame. He also knew the stuffed Dalmatian dog on the bed, Spot. His dad had never allowed any pets in the house. He said they just made a mess. So Spot was the closest Reyse had ever had to a puppy. He let go of his suitcase and picked up the soft toy with a fond smile, feeling where the fur had rubbed away on his ears after so many years of cuddling.

He knew his dad meant well. He was a practical man, and he was aware that dogs took a lot of looking after. But Reyse had always wanted one so desperately. He moved around so much these days there wasn't much chance of keeping one responsibly. But he still dreamed someday of having a little pack of his own. Friendly faces and wagging tails who would always be happy to see him when he got home.

"You look good, baby," his mom said fondly as he sat on the bed. He placed Spot back down and rested the soda on a coaster on the dresser, then took the plate she offered him.

As she sat beside him, she reached out and carefully brushed back a strand of his hair. "I'm so glad you're here."

A lump rose in Reyse's throat. Suddenly, he wasn't so hungry anymore.

"I should have visited more often," he said, shaking his head. He didn't feel able to look at her, so he stared at the homemade potato salad instead. But she rubbed his knee, drawing his attention anyway.

"Honey," she said patiently. "It's okay. I know you have this fabulous life-"

"But that doesn't mean it's okay I left things the way they were all these years," Reyse interrupted. All the guilt he'd been bottling up was coming out. He set the plate on the nightstand and bunched up his fists. "What if Dad dies? He's not even sixty. This shouldn't be happening. He's going to die and I never got the chance – I never said-"

"Hey, shh," his mom said firmly. She scooted over and wrapped her arm around his side, resting her temple on his shoulder. "He's not going anywhere. He's fine."

"Mom," Reyse protested. He felt horrible. He'd come up here to look after her and yet here she was, taking care of him.

"Nope," she said stubbornly. Her voice wobbled slightly. "He's as tough as a ram, remember?"

Reyse had to give her a weak chuckle. His dad had been as hurt at Reyse's lack of interest in football as he had in his refusal to join the Army. It hadn't escaped Reyse's notice that although there was a lot of chintz fabric in this house, it was all blue, white and gold. The colors of the LA Rams. It was kind of cute his dad had compromised with his mom like that.

"Go Rams," Reyse said weakly, punching the air with about the same enthusiasm. But it made his mom laugh. He waited while she wiped her eyes, expertly dabbing underneath her lashes so as not to smear her mascara.

"He'll be okay," she whispered.

Reyse rubbed her arm and sighed. "He will," he told her, even if he didn't necessarily believe it.

He may not get along with his dad. But that was because they were just different people. Reyse could look at Donny Hickson and see a good man, even if he had different values than him. He just wished his dad could look at him and see the same.

"I assumed we'd go see him tonight," Reyse said. He wasn't particularly in a rush to get over to the hospital, but at the same time he *was* here to visit his dad.

"Oh, um," his mom said. "I don't really want to go back there just yet. Not until he wakes up. I don't like sitting there, just waiting, thinking..." Her eyes glassed over and she sniffed. "You could go, though. With your friend?"

Reyse could tell it freaked her out, so he shook his head. There was no way he was going without her beside him. "I'll wait," he said.

"Your friend seemed nice," his mom said casually. "Corey, yes?" He couldn't tell anything from her words, but anxiety immediately spiked in Reyse's chest. Did she suspect something? She couldn't, could she?"

"He is," Reyse said genuinely. "Obviously, it would have been better if Bella could have come. But Corey is a real pal. I – I don't know where my head would be at right now without him."

That was also true. Yes, Corey represented a complication. A massive one. He muddled Reyse's mind, offering him such a great temptation that Reyse simply couldn't give into again. But Corey was also rock solid. Considering Corey's own life sounded like it had been nothing but upheaval most of the time, he had a simple, steady outlook on life. He made

Reyse feel grounded. It was like Reyse was a boat bobbing on choppy waters and Corey was the anchor tethering him in place.

"He has kind eyes," his mom remarked.

That surprised him. He would have thought she'd have lamented on Bella's absence over complimenting Corey. She always raved about 'Beautiful Bella' when they spoke on the phone. Reyse knew his mom was a huge fan of her movies and always said she was 'so classy.' Yet...she seemed more interested in Corey right now.

"I guess," Reyse said, scrambling around for what a straight dude would say about his bro when his mom said he had kind eyes. *Yes*, Reyse wanted to say. *He's kind and sweet and funny and awesome and I can't get him out of my head.*

His mom patted his knee. "I'm glad you have a friend like that to rely on," she said.

Reyse nodded against the side of her head, not trusting himself to reply. His voice might crack. But he thought, *me too.*

"How about you?" he managed to ask after a minute. "Have you got a friend that's been helping you the past few days with..."

How did he finish that sentence? With Dad almost dying? With this invasion of people into her home?

"Oh," she said, sounding vague. "The Pilates girls have rallied around. They're so sweet," she told him. "The neighbors have all stopped by. And then family flew in. I don't know if I need another delivery from the store if I'm going to keep this up. Luckily they all seem to want to stay in hotels..." She trailed off. "Oh, Aunt Evangeline is here, too."

"Oh," said Reyse carefully. As much as he adored her, he honestly couldn't say if having his mom's sister in the mix was a good thing or bad. But it was certainly something.

His mom smiled at him. "But Corey will stay here, won't

he?" she asked, handing him his plate in an indication she wanted him to start eating. "He hasn't booked a hotel or anything, has he?"

Reyse did his best not to frown as he picked up his fork, toying with some rice and beans. "Oh, no," Reyse admitted. "We didn't know there would be so many people around. I figured he could have one of the spare rooms."

"Of course," his mom said, jumping to her feet, startling him. "You sit and eat, and I'll make up the room next to this one, okay?"

"Mom, wait," he said, but she was already rushing off toward the door. He could practically feel her anxiety levels rising. To be fair, he knew once she had an idea in her head, she wouldn't relax until it was done.

"I'll just be a second," she insisted, disappearing through the door.

He kind of wanted her to just sit for two minutes with him. But at the same time, he got a funny warm feeling that she would rush off to look after Corey. Obviously, she couldn't know what he meant to Reyse – he was scared to admit that to himself when he was supposed to be keeping him at arms' length. But still, it was nice to think she was welcoming him when Reyse very much wanted him around.

Now, he just had to get through the night with the only lover he'd had in the past five years, sleeping ten feet away. One who had cared for Reyse, not just fucked him.

Simple. He just had to stop himself knocking on his door at any point once everyone had gone to bed.

How hard could that be?

CHAPTER
Twelve

COREY

COREY SQUINTED AS HE STEPPED OUT INTO THE SUNSHINE. He dropped his sunglasses from the top of his head so they landed on his nose and took a swig of beer. It was good stuff, cold too. "Hi," he said to a middle-aged guy who passed him on the way back into the house.

The guy flat out ignored him.

"Oh-kay," Corey said to himself and shook his head.

He stood on the patio, taking a moment to assess the scene. The yard was split into a couple of different sections. A small brick wall ran along where the large patio met the lawn. In the middle, a fountain rose with a fat cherub pointing a cupid's bow into the air. There was a short set of steps on the right of the yard where the lawn dropped down a couple of feet, so Corey headed that way.

Several people were sitting on wicker lawn furniture on the patio under umbrellas, sipping on an assortment of drinks. Presumably, they came from the small bar to the left that was actually manned by a guy in a white shirt who Corey got an immediate 'staff' vibe from. The people – family or friends of Reyse's folks, Corey couldn't tell –

watched Corey as he walked on by. He swore the conversations dipped as he did.

Wow. Was he really that interesting?

He'd learned from experience he could either shy away or put his 'Corey' mask on. He chose the latter. "Hi," he said cheerfully to anyone that caught his gaze, also giving them a nod or a wink for the ladies. "How are you?"

Nobody replied, but Corey felt less of a leper as he jogged down the steps.

A winding path took him around some rose bushes in full bloom. It reminded him of Alice in Wonderland. "Off with their heads!" he muttered to himself with a laugh. "Oh, not you," he said awkwardly to the older lady he hadn't noticed hobbling past with a cane. She shook her head in scorn and muttered something about 'no respect' as she continued up the path.

Corey swallowed and kept walking. The path was leading him to a kidney-shaped pool with a few people loitering around. No one was in swimwear. They were just standing by the water.

Or so he thought.

The pool was surrounded by trees and trailing plants on trellises. He didn't realize some of these trellises formed little alcoves until he walked past them, let alone that any of them were occupied.

"Hello, you there?" a woman's voice floated over the late afternoon air. Corey paused. The accent was so refined it was practically British, although he definitely still caught an east-coast twang to it. He stopped and looked around.

He was by one of the alcoves. This one contained a large wicker lounger shaped like a clamshell. Sitting among the many scatter pillows like a pearl in an oyster was a slim middle-aged woman in a one-piece black-and-white-striped bathing suit. She also wore an open silk kimono and a sun hat so large the brim practically touched her shoulders. She peered over horn-rimmed, diamanté-studded sunglasses and pointed a closed, hand-held lace fan in Corey's direction.

"Yes, you," she said imperiously. "Who are you?"

Corey blinked and looked around, but there was no one else around. So he took a couple of steps into the shade of the alcove and removed his own sunglasses. "I'm Corey, ma'am," he said from the foot of her clamshell lounger.

The woman shifted on the circular pillow that covered the base of the seat, causing a couple of the two dozen throw cushions to move around. She had laughter lines around perfectly smoky eyes, bright red lips and nails, and a red rose clip holding up a mess of dark brown curly hair. The hand not holding the fan swirled a cut crystal flute filled with Champagne. Corey had done several waiter gigs in his time, and bet anything that was the hundred-dollars-a-bottle-type stuff.

"Oh, *don't* be boring," she said, flouncing on the pillows. "Corey *who?* Who are you with? You don't look like everyone else." She batted dark eyelashes at him. "Be exciting."

Corey laughed and rubbed the back of his neck. "Well, I don't know if *I'm* exciting, ma'am, but I'm a friend of Reyse's. He's plenty exciting enough for the both of us, I'm sure."

To his relief, the woman's face lit up. Not in the way those others had in the house, like Reyse was a walking gossip column piece, but with genuine delight. "Oh, *Ricky!*" she said gleefully. "How is my darling nephew? Come, sit, Corey, Friend of Ricky's." She patted a spot on the lounger not currently covered in a pile of cushions. Then she rummaged around in the pile beside her. "Ah ha!" she cried in triumph. She produced another crystal flute as well as a half-finished bottle of Champagne. Corey couldn't read the label of because it was all in French, but that just meant it was probably *very* good. "Put that beer down, share the good stuff with me."

Cautiously, Corey placed the beer bottle in his hand on the patio and sat himself down. He was aware of the fact this woman was in her bathing suit, even if she was wearing a kimono, and didn't want to be too informal.

But she wasn't having any of that.

"Oh, don't be silly," she scoffed, waving the second flute around. "Come closer. I'm not interested in propositioning you. You're far too young." She turned her hand around and showed Corey an enormous diamond engagement ring on top of a wedding band. "I'm on husband lucky number four," she said with a grin. *"This* one's the keeper."

Now she'd mentioned the familial connection, Corey could see the same high, sharp cheekbones on this woman as Reyse and his mom had. She shoved the glass into Corey's hand as he inched a little nearer, not really sure what he was getting himself into. "Thanks," he said, holding the flute up.

"No. Cheers," she said. She held her glass up as well, but held off clinking it just yet.

"Cheers to what?" Corey asked.

The woman shrugged. "Oh, I don't know. There's usually something to celebrate, isn't there? Pick something."

"To Mr. Hickson's recovery?" Corey suggested.

The woman blew a raspberry. "That old codger will outlive the cockroaches, you'll see. Pick something *funner.*" She looked at him devilishly through eyelashes thick with black mascara.

"To...Reyse?" Corey ventured. He couldn't think of anything else and immediately worried he'd said too much. But the woman's glossy red lips broke into a wide smile of perfect white teeth.

"Excellent choice," she said with a nod, finally tapping their glasses together. The *ding* rang out over the still water of the swimming pool to the indifference of the people milling around. "I'm Evangeline," she announced after taking a sip. "Clementine's sister. I assume you've met Ricky's mother already?"

Corey nodded. He had to say, the Champagne was seriously good. Not like that cheap stuff you got at the store for under twenty bucks.

"Lovely lady," he told Evangeline.

"Quite," said Evangeline sincerely. She frowned slightly as she looked out over the sunny yard. "My baby sister. Both lovely and a lady."

"So…" Corey said, searching for a suitable discussion topic. "You guys must have a really big family."

It was more of a probing question than a statement. Evangeline peered over her sunglasses again. She seemed happy to have them sitting on the tip of her button nose rather than taking them off as Corey had done in the shade.

"Oh, nonsense," she scoffed, swigging more Champagne and then refilling her glass. She refilled Corey's, too, even though he'd only had a couple of sips. "Vultures, the lot of them," she said, not bothering to lower her tone. "They all have these little in-jokes and titters about how Ricky is a bit of a family embarrassment. Yet they're perfectly happy to come enjoy the fruits of his labors." She scowled as a young couple walked past their alcove, laughing arm in arm. "Most of these people are from this ghastly, superficial neighborhood. They just like to tell people that 'Reyse Hickson isn't all that, don't you know I'm friends with his mommy and daddy? Kissy kissy, *urgh*. Take me back to New York."

Corey's eyebrows shot up. He couldn't help but warm to Aunt Evangeline. "You're from New York?"

"Naturally," Evangeline said with a frown. "Where else would one live? Oh, London of course. But they don't quite have the Big Apple's *grittiness*, you know?"

"I can't say I've ever been to either, ma'am," Corey admitted.

Evangeline slapped his thigh with the closed fan, making him jump. "Enough of this 'ma'am' nonsense," she said and rolled her eyes. "Oh, Foofy!"

Corey's gaze was drawn to a sudden shifting of several pillows. From underneath emerged a small dog with long hair, big with static from the cushions. The pooch had a pink, diamanté-studded bow on top of their head in a ponytail and their tongue stuck out, making them look kind of dopey. Especially when the pup wobbled on their legs then shook themselves, making their fur even bigger and more disheveled.

Evangeline dropped the fan and scooped the dog up into her arm. The dog didn't even seem to notice. "Corey," Evangeline announced in delight. "I'd like you to meet Lady Bonniford Honeydew the Third, or Foofy for short. Foofy, this charming young man is Ricky's friend, so we like him very much." She deftly repositioned the dog in her grip, then held her out in her hand in front of Corey.

"Oh, okay," he said, quickly taking Foofy into his lap. The dog looked up at him and blinked, the tip of her tongue still poking out. "Hey there, little lady. Aren't you beautiful?" Foofy's tail wagged weakly, like she couldn't be bothered. Then very suddenly, she went completely stiff in Corey's arms, her small head snapping to look out into the sunshine. She barked several times and growled, startling Corey.

"Whoa, there, Evie," an unfortunately familiar voice came from by the pool. Then Uncle Dave stepped into the shade so Corey and Evangeline could see him. He held his hands up and smiled at them, but it came across as more of a grimace. "That dog is a menace."

Evangeline regarded her brother-in-law coolly. "Shih Tzus were bred to protect Chinese emperors from would-be assassins," she said with a bat of her long lashes. "She's simply protecting her mommy."

Corey preened. "She didn't bark at me," he told Dave with a grin and nod.

Without a trace of humor, Dave slid his eyes toward Corey, then back to Evangeline. "I just wanted to welcome you to the house," he said with a thinly veiled attempt at civility.

"Oh, Clementine and Donald's house, you mean?" Evangeline said with an equally fake air of innocence. "Yes, I saw my sister several hours ago. Thank you."

Dave didn't react in any particular way in terms of his expression. He simply turned and walked away. Foofy immediately relaxed in Corey's arms, flopping into his lap and staring back into space with her tongue lolling out between her lips.

Evangeline shook herself and blinked a couple of times, then she returned her attention to Corey with what felt like a genuine smile. "Sincere apologies." She picked the fan back up and sipped her Champagne. "You weren't in that band of Ricky's, were you? You're someone new."

She tilted her head and continued to stare at Corey. His natural reaction was to feel like he didn't measure up when people scrutinized him. But in this instance, he felt like Evangeline was merely trying to work him out. Like a puzzle piece.

"Uh, yes, I am new," he told her, resisting the urge to add 'ma'am' at the end. "Reyse and I met on his last tour. I worked for the catering company. We just hung out."

A big smile crept over Evangeline's crimson lips. "Oh, wonderful," she said. "You're a *real* person. You must be very special for Ricky to have trusted you." She signaled to a passing man, looking away from Corey. It turned out it was the guy from behind the bar. "Hello there, darling. We would very much appreciate another bottle of the Bolly. *Merci beaucoup.*" She saluted him with her glass.

The bartender smiled and nodded at Evangeline, then went on his way again.

Corey's brain was a little stuck on Evangeline stating that he must be 'very special' for Reyse to have picked him as a friend. He didn't know how to expand on that, however, without straying too close to their actual relationship. He also didn't want to be grilled on any details about the supposed tour that he'd been on. So he shifted the subject slightly.

"Why do you call Reyse 'Ricky'?" he asked.

Evangeline's smile became genuinely fond. "I always used to call him 'Ricky Reese's Pieces' when he was little. A silly little nickname that stuck. But when everyone in the world felt like they knew him simply because they knew his name…" She shrugged. "Ordinarily I find pet names tacky. Foofy aside, naturally. There have already been two Lady Bonniford Honeydews before her." She reached forward and scratched the small dog's head. "But in the case of my nephew…well, I stuck with 'Ricky' even harder once that 'Oh Oh Oohh' song topped the charts."

Corey got the feeling Evangeline knew exactly who every member of Below Zero was and that the song in question was actually called Hearts Bound. He could feel the protective vibes radiating from the stiffness of her shoulders.

Corey fiddled with the corner tassel of one of the nearby pillows. "The internet and tabloids call him 'Hicks' a lot," he said. "It's nice to get to know Reyse behind the scenes. But I bet he appreciates being called Ricky still."

"Oh, he hates it," Evangeline said flippantly. Corey wasn't sure he believed that, but he still shared a smile with her.

Abruptly, Evangeline snapped open her fan and began to

waft herself with it. "You're staying at the house, yes?" she asked.

Corey raised his eyebrows. "Uhh," he said. "I have no idea. We had no clue the place would be full with so many friends and family."

Evangeline snorted, obviously disagreeing that some of these people could truly be considered friends. "I'm the only one actually staying," she said, then rolled her eyes. "Well, David is staying too, but that can't be helped. Clementine promised me she wouldn't give in and house any of these vultures." She rested the fan on her collarbones. "We'll make sure you're in the room next to Ricky's. I have a feeling you'll keep an eye out for him, won't you?"

Corey gulped. She wanted him to sleep next to Reyse? Well, claim the room beside him. If there was just going to be a wall separating them tonight, there was no way Corey would be getting a wink of sleep.

"Yes, ma'am," Corey said sincerely with no trace of humor. He would damn well look after Reyse, he was sure of that. However he could.

Evangeline gave him a smile. "I'll let that 'ma'am' slide because I believe you. I also believe that if you do get up to any mischief, you'll make sure it stays between the two of you." She began fanning herself again. "That boy deserves a little fun."

At that moment, their fresh bottle of cold Champagne arrived with a flourish. The bartender made a show of opening it for Evangeline and topping up her glass. It gave the anxious butterflies a moment to settle in Corey's stomach.

Was she suggesting what he thought she was?

No, surely not.

After that, the conversation moved on to theater. Apparently, Evangeline was a big off-Broadway fan, seeing anything and everything going. He got the feeling she might have a hand in investing in productions as well, maybe as a sort of patron. But she downplayed any involvement if there was any. Corey was starting to see where Reyse got his creative flair from.

As she regaled him with scandalous opening night gossip from one of the major musicals, Corey's mind kept drifting back to her earlier words.

Was she seriously suggesting he pay Reyse a midnight visit?

Part of him worried if she *had* worked out their little secret, could other people? Another part worried if he gave into temptation, would that be fair on Reyse? They had to protect his career.

There was another part of him that ached, though. If she was giving them her blessing, that was pretty big. Corey had never had a partner long enough to be introduced to their family before. But if he was going to get approval for anyone, goddamn it, he wanted that person to be Reyse.

This was dangerous. He was so desperate to get permission to try again with Reyse to see if they had enough between them to make a go of a relationship, he was willing to jump on the first hint of approval that came his way. But Evangeline obviously cared deeply for Reyse. If she meant as much to him, her endorsement would carry more weight than most.

As evening turned into night, Corey drank a little more Champagne, but not enough to lose his wits.

He had an important decision to make.

Thirteen

REYSE

"Son, pass the salt, would you?"

Reyse was a trained performer with years of acting on screen and stage under his belt. Yet he almost failed to conceal his flinch at Uncle Dave calling him 'son.'

He knew he didn't have a model relationship with his dad, but Dave was certainly not his father.

"I've got it," his mom said, stretching just beyond her reach to get the silver shaker to pass to Dave. She smiled and handed it over.

"I can't believe you cooked us dinner, Mrs. Hickson," Corey said. He shook his head and grinned. "After all that party food? I didn't think I was hungry, but these noodles are incredible."

Reyse felt a warm glow in his chest. This may have been a strange meal, but with Corey here, things weren't so bad.

"I know I told you to order in, darling," Reyse's Aunt Evangeline said, swigging from a Champagne flute, "but this is delightful. I do love Thai."

"I know," Reyse's mom said fondly.

Evangeline's Shih Tzu, Foofy, barked from her lap, as if in

agreement. Evangeline dropped a small shred of chicken into her mouth.

Dave huffed and scowled. Unfortunately, now all the other dozens of guests had left for the night there wasn't much to disguise his disgruntled attitude with Reyse's aunt. "I've said it once, I'll say it again," he said between gritted teeth, waving his knife and fork around. Everyone else was using chopsticks. "It's unhygienic." He didn't look at Evangeline when he spoke, but Foofy gave a little growl all the same.

"Yes, dear," Evangeline said cheerfully, looking directly at him. "But if you wear a napkin in your collar – like a bib – it will catch all that food you drop." She grinned her cherry-red, glossy lips and watched him while she slowly took another slow sip of Champagne.

Corey snorted. It seemed he'd met Evangeline that afternoon and was acquainted with not only her humor but her relationship with Dave.

Reyse had to say he was glad. He'd always been fond of Aunt Evangeline as a child. She'd always been so free and wild, but had visited less and less as he grew older. However, she had been the one to gift him that old piano back when such a purchase has seemed wholly extravagant for Reyse's mom and dad on just his Army salary.

Evangeline and Dave had always butted heads. Apparently, he had flirted with her at Reyse's parents' wedding and she'd dumped a whole tray of shrimp in his lap. It seemed neither of them had ever forgotten about it.

Dave glowered at Evangeline and Foofy, but chose not to respond, instead turning his attention back to Reyse's mom. "Tina, you're doing too much. You should just be sitting with Donny, not running around playing waitress."

He said it like he cared, but Reyse's hackles immediately went up. He saw Corey frown, too, and Evangeline rolled her eyes. Even Foofy tilted her head in apparent disbelief.

"Well, who invited all those insipid people?" Evangeline demanded. "What was Clementine supposed to do? Have them sit on their hands and starve?"

"It's okay," Reyse mom said brightly, looking between the two of them as if debating which one was going to explode first. "It's okay. They just wanted to show their support. I appreciated them coming. It was sweet that they all just sort of…showed up," she said with a tinkling laugh. "The least I could do was provide refreshments. Besides, cooking soothes me." She looked down as she rearranged the napkin on her lap. "Sitting next to bleeping hospital machines in a place that smells of chemicals, not knowing what kind of brain injury my husband is going to have, does *not* soothe me."

Reyse reached over and squeezed her arm. She was at the head of the dining table next to him. Dave was at the other end, with Evangeline opposite Reyse and Corey. They had minimized the dining table so it now only sat eight, but it still felt like Dave was trying to lord over them.

"Mom, no one thinks any less of you for not sitting vigil over Dad," Reyse said firmly. "The nurses told you they'd call when he woke up properly, right?"

His mom nodded earnestly. "He's still sleeping and out of it," she said, looking around the table.

"Of course he is," Evangeline scoffed. "His neural pathways are rebuilding themselves. He's going to be confused and disorientated for a good few days." She looked from Reyse's mom to Corey, who was staring at her, presumably not expecting her to have such knowledge. She smiled at him. "Husband Number Two had a stroke," she explained. "Don't worry. He made a *full* recovery to go on and cheat on me with his twenty-three-year-old physical therapist." She grinned. "I did *very* nicely in that divorce."

"The point is, Mom," Reyse said firmly, still holding her

arm, "Dad is going to be fine. But he needs time. You hanging around all hours isn't going to change anything."

"Besides," Corey said, shaking his head. "Hospitals are creepy as f-" He stopped and cleared his throat, smiling at Reyse's mom. "They're really creepy."

Dave put his knife and fork together with unnecessary clatter, causing the rest of the table to look at him again. "All I'm saying," he said as he stood from the table and plucked up his beer, "is I'm sure Donny would appreciate his wife being there when he comes around. That's all."

"That's why you're there now, by his side?" Corey said, raising his eyebrows. "Doing the big brother thing?" He grinned. A little flutter of fear flitted through Reyse, but Corey didn't seem to give a shit.

Dave frowned down at him. "Son, you're a guest in this house," he began coldly.

"Yes," Evangeline chimed in cheerfully. "Ricky's guest. And you don't have any children, do you, Dave?" She sighed and pouted. "Probably because no one ever wanted to marry you."

"Enough!"

Everyone turned to Reyse's mom. Her small fists were bunched on the tablecloth and tears teetered on the brim of her eyes, one falling as Reyse watched in horror.

"Oh, Mom!" he cried. He jumped to his feet and wrapped his arms around her. It didn't help that he felt guilty himself for not seeing his dad yet. But Dave really wasn't helping the situation. They just had to wait for Dad to recover.

"I'm going to bed," Dave muttered, stalking from the table with his beer.

"Oh, shucks," Corey said to Reyse's mom. He sounded genuinely sheepish. "I'm so sorry, Mrs. Hickson. That was a dumb move on my part. I'll go apologize."

"You'll do no such thing," Evangeline said firmly. "If you

really want to help, you'll help me clear the dishes." They all had about half of the food still left, but if the others felt like Reyse, they were no longer hungry.

Corey looked at Reyse, pained. Reyse smiled at him as his mom sniffed in his arms. "Don't worry," he said. "Uncle Dave likes to see things one way and, well, that's it."

"Come on," Evangeline said, rising gracefully to her feet.

She'd seen fit to wear a floor-length, black, gauzy negligee-type dress to dinner over her bathing suit. She swept from the room on a pair of red heels with several plates like the mistress of a gothic castle. Foofy trotted obediently after her with her little pink tongue still peeping out.

"Let's refrigerate the leftovers still in the pot," she called to Corey over her shoulder. "It'll be something to feed the ravaging hordes tomorrow."

Corey gave Reyse a small smile, then hurried after Evangeline.

It was a kind of torture, having him this close and not being able to touch him at all. Especially when Reyse's nerves were frayed from dinner. The afternoon hadn't been much better either, with everyone wanting to talk to him and treat him like a piece of meat rather than the son of a seriously ill father.

But now was not about Reyse or Corey or really anyone else. It was about his mom.

"Hey," he said softly to her after she'd gently dabbed her eyes for the umpteenth time that day. "Do you want a cup of tea? Bella drinks the stuff by the gallon when she's had a bad day." That much Reyse knew to be true. Bella was extremely British in her dedication to tea consumption and had taught him how to make a good restorative brew.

His mom smiled and patted his hand. "Actually, I'd really just like to go to bed. Will you walk me up?"

Reyse nodded. "Sure," he said.

Her room was on the top floor. They walked arm in arm until they reached her en suite and he sat on the end of the bed while she took her eye makeup off. He felt like a small child again.

He hated when he got stuck in the middle of conflict like that, as if he *was* a kid again. He knew a lot of performers were supremely confident while on stage or in front of a camera. But in real life, they were full-blown introverts. It didn't make it any easier on him to feel like he hadn't defended his mom enough purely because he'd gotten tongue-tied.

"I'm sorry about Uncle Dave," he said to his mom. She'd partially closed the door to change. When she came out in flannel pajamas covered with daisies, she was shaking her head.

"Honey, don't be silly," she said fondly. "Dave is just worried. He didn't mean any harm."

Reyse watched as she took her jewelry off and placed it into a music box on her dresser. Reyse realized it was the same box she'd always had. She even took the various pieces in the same order Reyse always remembered her doing. Earrings, necklace, bracelets, then rings last. A warm feeling of nostalgia crept over his heart. Even under these dire circumstances, it was so nice to be with his mom again.

"He could have been a bit politer about it," Reyse grumbled.

His mom laughed, squirting some moisturizer in her hand and rubbing it between her palms then up and down her arms. It smelled different than the one he remembered. Not that he could recall that scent. Just that this wasn't it.

"It'll all be better in the morning," she assured him. Reyse hoped she was right.

He stood up and walked over to her dresser where she was sitting. "Night, Mom," he said, kissing her cheek.

He made his way to the door. "Reyse?" He turned back to look at her at the threshold. She smiled at him. "It's good to have you home."

Reyse smiled back at her. "It's good to be home," he said.

The house was quiet as he jogged down the stairs to his own bedroom. Either everyone had gone to bed in the time he had walked his mom up, or they were being very stealthy.

Reyse looked at the door next to his own, pausing before going into his room. Was Corey in there? Was he all right?

Was he thinking about Reyse?

That was stupid. Reyse couldn't let his mind go in that direction. With a sigh, he pushed the door in, only mildly disappointed not to find Corey already waiting on the other side.

He was, however, grateful to have his own en suite. He took his time brushing his teeth and stripping down to his boxer briefs. His body was weary, but his thoughts were whirling like a tornado. It didn't help that his phone was full of emails, texts and voicemails from Kevin just 'keeping him up to date.' Bombarding Reyse was Kevin's way of reminding him of all the trouble he'd caused by dropping everything to come home. Not that he'd ever say such a thing out loud to Reyse. He'd simply keep guilt-tripping him so he knew what a fuckup he was.

Reyse's mind warred over what to worry about more. Family, work obligations, or the man sleeping ten feet away from him.

A soft knock at the door made Reyse freeze. Had he imagined that? He blinked and sat up, turning on the lamp sitting on his nightstand. "Hello?"

The door opened a crack. The corridor was dark outside, but there was no mistaking Corey's beautifully sculpted physique. He was just in boxers and a tight white T-shirt, his expression apprehensive. "Uh," he said, like he was already regretting this decision. But he swallowed and gave Reyse a half smile. "May I come in?"

Reyse didn't trust himself to talk, so he just nodded. Corey came inside and quietly closed the door behind him. Reyse tried very hard not to look at the outline of Corey's cock in his loose boxers as he dashed across the room and sat on the end of Reyse's bed.

Reyse felt like his heart was going to beat out of his chest. He wanted to lift the covers up to hide his naked torso. Instead, he bunched the comforter up in his fists, licking his dry lips.

"Hi," he said, finding his voice again. "What are you...are you okay?"

Corey crossed his arms over his chest, then immediately uncrossed them, placing his palms down on top of the bed sheets. "Me?" he asked, his voice kind of a squeak. He cleared his throat and his lips twitched in a nervous smile. Why was he here? Why was he nervous? God, Reyse had to work hard not to let his hopes climb. "I'm fine, dude. I wanted to check on you. You got ambushed by like fifty people and your uncle's a douche and you gotta be worried about your dad and looking after your mom..." He frowned and appeared to mentally backtrack a step. "I mean, your uncle seems..."

"Like a douche," Reyse agreed with a grin. He felt himself relax just a fraction. "Yeah. He makes my dad look like a hippy in comparison. Sorry he was weird with you."

Corey shrugged. "He was weird with everyone," he said. His gaze was on his fingers, tracing patterns in the bedding, like a child playing in the sand. "Your aunt is cool, though, in a slightly scary sort of way." He laughed and Reyse laughed with him. "She loves you like crazy. So does your mom."

Reyse swallowed. "Thanks," he said. "I, uh, well, I guess it's been easy to let those feelings fade when I haven't felt like I could come home. But it's nice now."

Corey nodded. "Yeah," he said.

Reyse's heart ached. Corey didn't know what it was like to have a mom or an aunt or *anything*. "Hey," Reyse said. Before he could overthink it, he reached out and took Corey's nearest hand in his own. "I'm glad you're here."

Corey looked down at their linked fingers. "Here at the house, or…"

Here in Reyse's room.

If he was honest, he was scared shitless. But that was only because he was terrified what could happen. He didn't trust himself to do the right thing. Or, rather, his opinion on what the right thing was had become fuzzier. Right thing for who?

Fuck, it felt so good to hold Corey's hand after all afternoon and evening apart. Was that insane? They'd only had one night together, after all. But even just this small skin-to-skin contact was exhilarating.

"I'll take what I can get from you," Reyse admitted quietly to Corey.

Corey shifted closer, making Reyse look up. Corey's chestnut eyes were a warm brown in the soft light of the bedside lamp. His eyelashes cast shadows on his cheeks. Reyse's heart skipped a beat.

"Do you mean that?" Corey asked.

Reyse did his best to swallow but there was a lump in his throat. "Before…" he said, sidestepping the question. "When we…Well, I asked you not to hurt me."

Corey nodded. "I remember."

"And you didn't," Reyse said. "But…my heart hurts anyway. Seeing you. I…" He trailed off, biting his lip.

Corey rubbed his thumb against the back of Reyse's hand. "I'll be honest, man," he said, shaking his head. "I can't stop thinking about you. And you're right here." He sighed and licked his lips. "I tried to sleep, I really did, I swear. But then I thought I'd just come and *ask* you how you felt."

"About what?" Reyse asked.

Corey lifted his gaze so they were looking at one another. "About one more night together," he said evenly. "I know we can't…it's not possible. In the long run. But for the next few hours?" He exhaled and gave Reyse a shaky laugh. "It's killing me thinking about the time we'd be wasting when no one would ever find out. But if that's cruel, if you don't want that, I'll leave right now. I'm not going to put you in a position where-"

Reyse didn't know what Corey meant to say after that, because he rocked forward on his heels, grabbed Corey's face, and kissed him hard on the lips.

In a flash, Corey's hands were on his bare torso, holding either side of his ribs as he kissed him back. "I'd give anything for one more night," Reyse whispered into Corey's mouth.

Corey held Reyse's face, too, their noses almost brushing. "You don't have to give anything," he said. "We can share this together."

Reyse swallowed. There was still a raw sort of panic in his chest. But a happiness was also blossoming. Sheer relief that he could have this precious gift, even if it was only one more time.

"I want that," he confessed. He'd been wanting this since Corey had come back to him with that damn box of pizza in his hands.

"Me, too," Corey said.

This was it. The point of no return. Reyse was pretty sure his heart might not recover from this.

But right then, it was totally worth it.

CHAPTER

Fourteen

COREY

As much as Corey had hoped Reyse would say yes, he'd not really let himself believe it was possible until they were toppling gently back down onto Reyse's pillows, their kisses hot and a little desperate. Side by side, their bodies lined up, their legs entwined and their rapidly hardening cocks rubbing together through their underwear.

Every worry had been worth it to finally knock on Reyse's door. To be here, now, getting this chance to be with him again, made Corey's heart sing. Reyse just made him so damn happy. He was sweet and earnest and seeing him at home like this it was like he'd totally forgotten he was a fucking pop *sensation*. Here, he really was just Reyse Hickson, a guy who was nice to his mom and shy about asking a guy to bed.

Corey loved it.

He couldn't afford to think of this as anything more than just another hookup, but he found himself grinning at Reyse and tickling his side. Reyse yelped, then immediately slapped his hands over his mouth. "My *family*," he whispered scandalously.

Corey tried to taper his grin, but he couldn't. "Are all on different floors," he assured Reyse, but he stroked along Reyse's flank where he'd tickled anyway. "Sorry, I won't tease you."

Reyse shook his head and looked up at Corey through his golden lashes. "I…I like it when you tease me a bit," he said. "I mean, I like sex to be fun."

Corey sighed and nuzzled his face against Reyse's neck, inhaling his scent deeply. "You're fun," he said. "My little fire-cracker."

Reyse stiffened in his arms, his hands clinging on tighter to Corey. Ahh, shit. Maybe he shouldn't have said 'my'? Reyse couldn't be his. Thinking that would just hurt them both. But in that moment, he couldn't take it back. Instead, he just began to kiss Reyse's neck.

A thought crossed his mind, though, that stopped him in his tracks. "Oh, fuck," he said, pulling back to look at Reyse. "I don't have anything. Do you?"

Reyse shook his head, but he didn't seem that upset. "I'm not sure I feel like anal," he said, but then he raised his eyebrows. "Unless, you…"

Corey quickly shook his head. "I kind of like this," he said, cuddling Reyse closer. "But fewer clothes, maybe?"

Reyse chuckled and rested his head against Corey's, rubbing his back. "You just make everything easy, don't you?" he murmured.

Corey was pretty sure he made Reyse's life ten times more complicated than it needed to be. But he took the compliment for what it was.

"Come on, then, Romeo," Corey said playfully as he tugged at Reyse's briefs. "Let's get rid of these, shall we?" Reyse chuckled and shimmied free of his underwear, allowing his cock to spring free. It was hard and eager for attention already.

But Reyse immediately reached out for Corey's T-shirt, wrestling it off him before tackling his boxers. In no time at all, they were lying under Reyse's sheets, naked again.

Reyse ran his fingers over Corey's abs with a reverent look in his face. "You're *so* gorgeous," he whispered. "Perfect. Seriously."

Corey smiled and kissed Reyse's lips once to bring his attention back up to Corey's face. "You know that's kind of funny, coming from you?" he said, gently teasing. "Haven't you been given literal *awards* for how hot you are?"

Reyse rolled his eyes. "Shut up," he mumbled. But Corey just grinned harder, skimming his fingers over Reyse's own abs and lower.

"I think I want to see these cum gutters live up to their name," Corey rasped, tracing down the defined groves that led from Reyse's hips to his crotch in a V-shape. He was thrilled when Reyse blushed and bit his lip.

"You're so bad," he admonished.

But Corey shook his head. "I'm going to show you just how good I am, Reyse Hickson," he said. "Now how about you lie back and let me take care of you?"

He reached over, intending to turn off the lamp and plunge them into darkness. But Reyse suddenly propped himself up on his elbows. "No," he said urgently. Corey looked back to meet his gaze. "I…is okay if we leave it on? I want to see you."

Something either terrible or wonderful lanced through Corey's heart. Of course he could see Reyse whenever the hell he liked. A quick internet search would bring up thousands of photos of him from over the past decade. But Reyse wanted to see Corey now. It didn't take a genius to work out that their time was limited. Typing 'Corey Sheppard' into a search engine brought up dozens of guys from all over the world, almost none of which were Corey. He had made sure not to have his face plastered everywhere.

It didn't take a genius to figure out that Reyse wanted to see as much of Corey as he could while he had time. To commit him to memory, perhaps.

Jesus fucking Christ. This was so unfair. Corey had never felt this strongly about anyone. If Reyse was the guy next door, Corey would just take that leap and ask if he wanted to date. But he wasn't. So Corey could get pissy about it or he could continue looking after Reyse like he said he would. They were supposed to be having fun.

He gave Reyse his most sultry grin and slipped back into the bed, leaving the light on. "Sure thing, gorgeous," he said as their bodies slid against each other once again, like two jigsaw puzzle pieces, slotting together perfectly.

Reyse looked at Corey with wide eyes. "Can I suck you?" he asked, his voice almost giddy.

Corey beamed at him. "Oh, hell yeah," he said, kissing Reyse on the lips in excitement. "I'd love that. Do you want to make me come like that?"

Reyse shook his head. "I liked the cuddling plan," he said with a nervous laugh. "I just thought I could start you off with a blowjob. If that's okay?"

"Babe, that's more than okay," Corey assured him.

He allowed Reyse to move them around so Corey was lying on his back. Then he scooted down Corey's body, running his hands along his sides as he did. Corey pushed back the comforter. If they were going to keep the light on, he wanted to witness every second of this delicious show.

Reyse rested his hands on Corey's thighs, rubbing down the coarse hair there as he trailed openmouthed kisses along Corey's left hip. Then he lifted up his right hand and began stroking Corey's hard cock with his fingertips. There was a reverence to the movement, especially as he nuzzled his nose against Corey's thatch of dark pubic hair.

Corey bit his lip and did his best not to move, despite wanting to thrash around. It felt like his heart was fluttering in his mouth as he watched Reyse's ministrations.

"You smell good," Reyse murmured, running his cheek along the side of Corey's dick.

"You look good," Corey rasped. Fuck. He was going to have to work hard not to come down Reyse's throat after all.

Reyse smiled bashfully and licked the tip of Corey's cock. Then he wrapped his lips around the shaft, pressing his tongue on the side as he bobbed his head up and down. He didn't attempt to take Corey down too deep, instead sucking and licking the top half of his length. He curled his fingers around the bottom half and pumped, making Corey moan. Corey respected Reyse's wish not to be too loud, even though he was sure they were pretty safe on this floor. But if keeping quiet meant Reyse was more relaxed, it was worth it.

"Reyse, oh my god," Corey hissed.

He had to admit, it wasn't the most confident blow job he'd ever had. But Reyse's attentiveness and consideration were so sweet and his mouth so hot and wet it more than made up for it. Besides, the *emotional* connection was really what was setting Corey's heart racing. He'd take this intimacy over spectacular head from a stranger any day.

He ran his fingers through Reyse's soft hair, loving the feeling of his head bobbing up and down under his palm. Reyse looked up at him, his eyes still sky blue and bright in the dim illumination from the lamp. They were like sapphires sparkling just for Corey.

"Come here," Corey suggested. If he didn't stop this now, he was definitely going to come and that wasn't what Reyse said he wanted. "Kiss me, gorgeous."

Reyse slid his lips off Corey's cock and wiped his mouth before crawling back up his body. "Was that okay?"

Corey grinned and cupped Reyse's face to kiss him tenderly. "Really good," he said honestly. He almost said next time he could teach Reyse exactly how he liked it. But there wasn't going to be a next time.

Although…that was what Corey thought before. Yet here they were.

"I don't know about you," Corey said playfully, "but I'm pretty keen for an orgasm." He wrapped his hand around Reyse's hot cock and kissed his lips. "Unless you want to play around a bit more?"

Corey didn't mind waiting for a climax sometimes. It was fun to edge with other guys or make himself hold out if he was with a girl, making her come several times before he even penetrated her. There was something amazing about knowing you were causing your partner so much pleasure. But he could tell he and Reyse were both close, so he didn't mind at all when Reyse shook his head.

"I'm ready," Reyse said. "Can I go under you?"

This was why Corey liked sleeping with people more than once, even if he'd been bad at dating. It was cool to learn what your partner enjoyed. Reyse might not have had any inclination for bondage, but he certainly liked Corey to physically take charge and be on top. Corey was more than happy to use his size to make Reyse feel safe and secure.

They rolled around so Reyse was on his back. Corey leaned behind him and pulled the comforter over them again, snuggling them up. He straddled Reyse around his thighs and lined up their cocks, wrapping his hand around them both. They were both leaking and Corey was wet from Reyse's mouth. It was enough to make them a little slippery as they began to frot, rubbing their chests and hot, hard dicks against one another while they kissed.

It was bliss.

Reyse clung to Corey's back, moaning into his mouth. "Yes, Corey, yes," he whimpered.

Corey had a sudden pang, realizing that both tonight and their night before were tinged with a slight sadness. A knowledge that they could never fully let go because doing so would make walking away all that harder. But Corey banished that thought. If he was going to get mopey, there was no point in doing this at all. They needed to have fun while they had the chance.

"Fuck, you're so beautiful," he gasped while he grinned down at Reyse between kisses. "Does that feel good? Do you like it?"

Reyse nodded frantically and grabbed the back of Corey's head. "Close," he uttered.

"Can you hang on for me, beautiful?" Cory asked, breathless. He was peaking but wasn't quite there yet. Besides, it gave him a kick to ask Reyse to follow an instruction, especially when he nodded again, his eyes alight with passion. "We can come together."

"Yes, Corey," Reyse said. "I'll wait. Just tell me. I can hold on."

"Good boy, so good," Corey murmured.

He didn't talk after that. He simply focused on letting his body relax, allowing his climax to build quickly. He kissed Reyse and sucked on his lower lip, looking into his eyes as their breaths mingled. They were both damp with perspiration, and where Corey touched Reyse's skin, he was as hot as Corey felt. Like they were burning up and melting at the same time.

"Oh, god," Reyse stuttered. "Corey – I – please!"

But Corey was just about there too, thrusting in his hand against Reyse's hard cock. "It's okay, baby," Corey uttered, not bothering to stop himself using the pet name. "Come for me. Come, Reyse, I'm ready."

Reyse made a strangled noise and gritted his teeth, digging his fingers into Corey's flesh as he started pumping hot cum between them. The erotic sight tipped Corey over, pushing him into his orgasm, like plunging into water. Waves of pleasure wracked his body, making him shiver as he came. He let go of both their cocks, hugging Reyse to him as they both quivered, coming down from their highs.

When Corey could summon the energy, he nuzzled their temples together. Then he gently kissed from Reyse's neck over his cheek until he captured his mouth for a sweet, unhurried kiss.

"That was perfect," Corey said.

Reyse bit his swollen lip and smiled. "Amazing," he agreed with a nod. "I – thank you."

"I didn't do much," Corey joked, not wanting to dig too deep. But Reyse wasn't letting him get away with that.

"Thank you for being brave," he said. Although his voice was quiet it was also firm. "I was too scared to let you in again. Thank you for coming in here tonight. Thank you for coming back to my apartment."

Corey stroked along the side of his face with the back of his knuckles. "I'm here to look after you," he said. Damn it. Here went nothing. "Day and night. If you want, we can do this again. Just while we're here."

Reyse sighed and pressed his face against Corey's neck, placing a kiss on his skin. "I want to look after you, too," he said.

"You do," Corey assured him, not really sure what he meant. But he felt it was true. He might be the one obviously administering the sexual healing, but Reyse gave him as much back, he was sure. Maybe it was simply how much Reyse wanted Corey. It made him feel validated. Part of something.

"If it's not too much to ask," Reyse said cautiously, "then, yes. I...I would love to spend more time with you. So long as we're careful."

He looked pained to add that last part, but Corey understood completely. He made the decision to take what he could get from this relationship.

"Discretion is no problem at all," he assured Reyse. "Speaking of which, do you want to do something about this?" He laughed as he leaned back and pointed at the sticky mess sandwiched between their chests. "Then I should probably head back to my own room."

Reyse laughed too and covered his eyes briefly. "I forgot how bad it can get when you're not jerking off into a tissue," he said. For some reason, Corey found the admission adorable.

"Come on," he said, peeling himself off Reyse. "Is that a bathroom behind us?"

Reyse nodded, so Corey took him by the hand and led him across the room. They were comfortable around one another as they used washcloths to rinse the cum from their naked bodies. Corey couldn't stop himself sneaking a little kiss on Reyse's cheek, making him giggle. He was so cute.

"Do you have to go right away?" Reyse asked as he walked back to his bed, pausing to slip his briefs back on.

Corey did likewise, leaving the T-shirt off for now. It just felt better not having his junk swinging around during what felt like quite a tender moment. He shook his head. "I could stay a minute," he said. Reyse got into bed then held the covers back, inviting Corey to join him.

It couldn't hurt to cuddle for a bit, could it? Reyse smelled so good after sex, and Corey didn't want him to think Corey was only interested in getting off. This visit had been about far more than just orgasms.

So he slid in easily beside Reyse, wrapping him in his

arms and kissing the top of his damp hair. "Goodnight, Reyse," he said fondly.

"Goodnight, Corey," Reyse replied, holding on to Corey's arms and snuggling against his body.

Just a few minutes, Corey promised himself as his shut his eyes and inhaled Reyse's scent deeply. Then he would sneak back to his room. No one would find out he'd been here and their secret would remain safe.

CHAPTER

Fifteen

REYSE

THE KNOCKING AT THE DOOR WAS PERSISTENT ENOUGH TO wake Reyse from his deep sleep. He was completely confused as to where he was, not to mention why there was an arm wrapped possessively around him.

It all came rushing back to him as his eyes flew open, blinking in the morning light. He was at his parents' house. Corey had fallen asleep in his bed. And someone was about to walk in on them.

"Corey!" he hissed, batting his arm frantically. "Corey, wake up! You need to get into the en suite!"

"Reyse? Are you awake?" Damn. That was Aunt Evangeline's voice. She was not going to wait much longer before barging in.

"Nuh fuh?" Corey mumbled. Panic was rising in Reyse's chest. Shit, they were going to get caught!

"Corey!" he hissed, hating how hard he jolted Corey's shoulder, but it did the trick. Corey's eyes snapped open. "You have to hide!"

Corey frowned and blinked as he came back into consciousness. "Huh?"

"Young man," Evangeline called out cheerfully. "I've given you more than enough time to stop masturbating. Either reply, or I'm coming in regardless on the count of three. One!"

"Fuck," Corey gasped.

"Two!"

In one fluid motion, Corey rolled off the bed and underneath it.

"Three!"

Reyse had just enough time to gather his sheets around him to hide his morning wood before his aunt came sweeping in, looking far too glamorous for this early in the morning. The floral maxi dress could have been casual enough, but combined with the large diamond necklace, three-inch heels and full face of makeup, it was quite the sight to behold.

"Cat got your tongue?" she asked with a grin as she swept across the room and perched on the end of the bed. As usual, she had Foofy in her arms, a little green diamanté bow in her static-ridden hair and small tongue peeping out.

Reyse swallowed and shook his head. "Sorry," he said, his voice hoarse. "I was dead asleep. Is everything okay?" A sudden fear gripped him. "Is Dad okay?"

But Evangeline nodded and let Foofy down on the bed so Evangeline could touch his knee. "He's fine. No change. Stable but groggy. Your mom is still reluctant to visit again until he's awake. But if you want, Dave is going over to the hospital this morning."

Reyse felt torn. He'd expected to have seen his dad by now, but he wasn't thrilled at the idea of going anywhere with Dave. "Maybe Mom and I can see how he's doing this afternoon?" he suggested. A few more hours wouldn't make a difference, not when his dad was essentially just sleeping the whole time.

Evangeline patted his knee again and nodded. "Quite sensible," she agreed.

Foofy hopped off the bed, then turned and looked around. Underneath the bed frame. Reyse froze. "Uh, so, what can I do for you?" he asked Evangeline, trying not to sound or look alarmed as Foofy trotted under the bed and out of sight.

Evangeline smiled genuinely with no trace of humor or silliness. "I just wanted to see if you'd like some breakfast," she said. "It's been far too long since we caught up. I thought we could eat on the patio before it gets too hot."

"Oh, yes," Reyse stammered. "Th-that sounds lovely." Out of the corner of his eye he saw a pair of hands place Foofy out from under the bed again. Foofy looked around confused, then pawed at Corey's T-shirt, discarded on the floor from the night before, growling as she scratched it.

"Darling, what's the matter?" Evangeline asked, bending down to her dog.

"Oh!" Reyse blurted too loudly. "That…T-shirt is really gross. I worked out in it. I should, uh, put it in the wash."

He leaned down before she could and scooped it up, throwing it in the direction of his suitcase.

"Yes," Evangeline said in approving tone. Mercifully, she sat back up. Unfortunately, deprived of her distraction, Foofy trotted back under the bed. "You should never let your standards slip, Ricky," she said, wagging her finger at him. "No one wants to pick up your mucky underwear."

Despite stressing that Corey was underneath them right now wrestling with a very determined Shih Tzu, Reyse had to admit this was nice. "I have missed hanging out, you know?" he told his aunt. "Give me five minutes to brush my teeth and I'll meet you down for breakfast?" he suggested.

Evangeline nodded. "Marvelous," she said. "Oh, where did Foofy get to?"

The pair of hands only just dropped the little dog back on the carpet before Evangeline looked down. Reyse scooped Foofy up before she could try and visit Corey again. "She's so sweet," Reyse said, trying to calm his heart rate down. "I hope she's living up to her namesake?"

Evangeline took Foofy back and rolled her eyes. "Well, each Lady Bonniford Honeydew is different in her own right," she said sagely, rising to her feet. "But I have to say this little one will surprise you from time to time." She winked at Reyse. "No rush, now. Meet me downstairs in half an hour?"

Relief washed over Reyse. "Sure," he said.

Evangeline paused at the door's threshold and looked back at Reyse, something sparkling in her eyes. "Let's make the most of Dave's absence, hmm? I'll get Clementine to cook for us, and you rouse Corey. He's probably still fast asleep at this hour, isn't he?"

"Oh, uh, yeah," Reyse said. Fucking hell, he was normally a much better actor than this. But then, he wasn't normally woken at the crack of dawn with the threat of his biggest secret being discovered. "I'll go knock on his door."

Foofy barked angrily and wriggled in Evangeline's arms, trying to get back down again. Evangeline just smiled and snagged the door handle, pulling it behind her. "See you shortly," she said.

Reyse held his breath until the door clicked shut, then flopped down on his bed, flinging his arms out. "Fuck me, that was close," he whispered in case Evangeline was still close enough to hear.

Corey's chuckles came from under the bed. His thick, disheveled hair and grinning face soon followed. "Well, that was fun," he said, cocking an eyebrow.

Reyse knew he should be more freaked out, but his heart

felt lighter just seeing Corey again. "Sorry," he said, meaning it. He hated that Corey had to dive out of sight.

Luckily, Corey seemed over it. He bounced up from the floor and snuggled back in the bed beside Reyse without having to be asked. "Did they never catch you with a guy when you were at school or anything?" Corey asked. He brushed Reyse's hair back and rubbed his back. The easy familiarity he was displaying with Reyse's body was so nice it almost hurt.

Reyse managed a smile. "Nah," he said ruefully. "I was always too terrified to make out with anyone I knew growing up. I guess I somehow knew deep down it could come back to bite me in the ass. Besides, I spent every minute I could hauling my ass to auditions and choir classes and all the other things my dad didn't approve of." He rolled his eyes. "I managed to sneak into some bars and clubs though, so until I landed Below Zero, any hookups were anonymous." He felt a pang of sadness. "I never told those guys my real name and we always went back to theirs, so…"

Corey studied him for a moment or two. "And when you joined the band?" he asked, surprising Reyse by not probing any further into his childhood.

Reyse bit his lip. Did he want to talk about this?

He'd never really talked about it with *anyone*, though. Suddenly, he couldn't bear it another second.

"His name was Jon," Reyse began. Immediately, a lump rose in his throat and his eyes got itchy. But he wanted to own this part of his past for one damn time in his life. "He was a backing dancer on our second world tour, for the second album five years ago. He was…wonderful. A phenomenal dancer with a Pokémon obsession and a smile for everyone. He always set up a Buddhist shrine no matter how crappy his hotel room was, and burned this beautiful sandalwood incense." He paused and sighed, recalling the scent all these years later. "We were very careful, but we spent most of that tour together, stealing every second we could. Then… then the tour ended and the record label dropped the band and suddenly I was the golden boy working twenty-four seven. It just wasn't possible, and I couldn't put him through all that. Especially after my first album went platinum."

"You didn't want to make him a dirty little secret?" Corey asked.

Reyse felt guilty confessing this to Corey. Like he was cheating on him or comparing the two of them. But it wasn't like that. Jon was a lifetime ago. Corey was here and now.

"No," Reyse agreed. "I had to let him go. I didn't keep in touch, but I heard on the grapevine a while ago he's married, even adopted a kid." Reyse blinked back tears, not wanting to cry anymore over this. "I'm happy for him," he said sincerely. "He was…such a beautiful light. He deserved everything. I didn't want to take that away from him."

For a while, Corey just hugged him. "That must have been so hard," he said. There wasn't a trace of envy in his words. Was that because he was secure enough in his own self? Or because he didn't feel a need to be jealous as he knew there was no future between him and Reyse either? That their time was limited, so why get upset about a former lover?

It was stupid, but Reyse hoped it was the former. He liked to think of Corey as this resilient survivor, not threatened by Reyse's past. Because if he was honest, it would hurt too much to think he didn't care about what little time they had together.

"It was hard," Reyse admitted. Then he decided to be fully honest, hoping his instinct that he could trust Cory was on the mark. "It still is, some days. Fuck, I hope you don't think I'm this ungrateful brat. I've got everything I could ever want, right? A dream career I fucking love, incredible fans who I honestly adore – you should see some of the sympathy stuff coming through right now because of my dad. Videos and artwork and fanfiction and essay-length messages. I've managed to create a body of work that affects people all around the globe, that makes them want to care for me when I'm down. Yet…" He sighed heavily. "God, I'm so selfish."

"Hey, no," Corey said with a frown. "It's not too much to ask to be yourself. Living a lie has got to be exhausting. I know it's none of my business, but the guys at your label are fucking jerks for keeping you in this bind. It's got to be shitty on your mental health."

Reyse breathed slowly in and out for a minute, resting his head on Corey's chest and stroking his fingers gently up and down the warm skin of his arm. "I don't want this to sound like I'm anything less than completely thrilled for my best friends to have all found love and marriage and happiness. The boys from the band are my brothers, it doesn't matter about blood."

"But you're the one that's been left behind," Corey guessed correctly.

Reyse bit his lip. "I know it was hard for them when they got dropped in favor of Sun City focusing on just me," he said. "It was hard for us all not to see the divide. Especially Joey. God, it killed him."

"But they've all landed on their feet," Corey interjected. Reyse appreciated it. He knew the guys were all good, but he still felt a twinge of guilt at being the one selected to carry on with the solo career.

"Yeah, of course," Reyse agreed. But, having been the one to get ahead to begin with, now I'm the one on my own and…" He gritted his teeth. This was the real kicker. The one he hated himself for, but he had to say it out loud, just once. "Blake, Raiden, TJ…they were never out as queer before. They didn't know it about themselves. Joey was allowed to be out and I wasn't and they did have the easier career paths. Yet they all met these amazing men and…oh fuck, I can't believe how petty I am."

"Reyse," Corey said firmly. He took Reyse's face between his hands. "It's okay to be mad. In this day and age, your job shouldn't hold your love life hostage. That's nuts. But I'm telling you right now, it *will* change. Someday, soon. It has to. They can't keep this up! It's fucking homophobic and you've given them more than enough to prove your worth. They either see your value and accept you for who you are, or you part ways."

And they keep the rights to my entire back catalog, Reyse thought to himself. But he didn't want to pour cold water over Corey's enthusiasm. So he smiled at him instead.

"That was quite the speech," he said.

Corey huffed. "Yeah, well, the situation is fucked up. You need to realize the light is at the end of the tunnel. Maybe not today or tomorrow or even next year. But…I believe it. One day, you'll be able to sing *and* be with someone you love. Out, not in the closet."

Just for a moment, Reyse studied Corey. *But that person won't be you,* he thought with certainty. Corey was a fleeting moment. There was no way Reyse could ask him to hang around in the shadows until Reyse was free to come out. No matter how much he wanted to ask him to. It wasn't fair.

He didn't want to think about that, though, let alone talk about it. So he just snuggled back into Corey's arms. They only had a few minutes before they needed to hustle and get ready for breakfast.

"Thank you," he simply said in response to Corey's optimism.

He needed to let Corey go back to his own room to shower. But, just for now, he could pretend that this was normal. That he wouldn't lose Corey like he did Jon. At least

Corey had been the one to come back, to suggest a short-term thing while they were in this little bubble of home. It made Reyse feel less needy. So long as nothing took a serious turn with his dad, Reyse could afford to take a little break from his crazy reality.

And the practical, logical side of his brain argued they would have to leave it when they went back to LA. But the other, wistful side of him argued that if they were in the same city, maybe they *might* run into each other again.

It didn't do much harm to indulge in a private little fantasy. Reyse could have that for a moment before he checked the coast was clear, kissed Corey goodbye, and let him run back to the safety of his own room.

CHAPTER
Sixteen

COREY

Corey could tell Reyse was on edge. Corey sympathized with his situation. He was clearly anxious to see his dad, but his mom didn't want to hang around until Donny was awake properly. So Reyse still hadn't visited the hospital, the whole purpose of this trip.

But the kicker was, Corey could tell Reyse was *terrified* of seeing his old man. The way a child is scared they've screwed up and they're just waiting for the blowback. Or, at least, that was Corey's own experience. He'd had a couple of foster dads with short tempers. And while he didn't think Mr. Hickson was physically abusive – far from it – Reyse was scared of him for entirely different reasons.

He was scared of not being enough. Despite his crazy success, Reyse Hickson somehow didn't live up to his own father's expectations. That was pretty messed up, in Corey's opinion.

Reyse was good around his mom and aunt. They had a fancy damn breakfast out on the patio, just like Evangeline had suggested. Clementine really did seem to love cooking. Corey felt that was her easiest way to show affection when words failed. She made her son pancakes and eggs and bacon and doused it all in maple syrup. Corey felt honored to be a part of it.

Evangeline kept the conversation going, mostly by talking about people and places in New York. Even though Corey had no idea about most of what she said, she was a gifted storyteller and managed to keep him, Reyse and Clementine laughing over these people they had never met.

Yet again, Corey was roped into doing the dishes, which he didn't mind, but Foofy kept running around his feet, barking. Why did he get the impression she was trying to snitch him up for hiding under Reyse's bed earlier?

Seeing as Evangeline *couldn't* read minds, Corey didn't worry about a bit of extra attention from her dog. She was a cute little thing, even if she did walk into table legs more often than was probably good for her small head.

But once the dishwasher was loaded and the coffee pot rinsed out, Corey wasn't sure what to do. At least breakfast had lasted so long it was pretty much midday. Corey killed some time making his bed and straightening up his suitcase. He was always in the habit of being ready to leave somewhere at the drop of a hat thanks to his unstable childhood. Then he checked his emails to see if he'd heard back from any of the crappy jobs he'd contacted. He hadn't, and he couldn't say he was disappointed.

But then it was early afternoon and he couldn't stop his thoughts drifting back to Reyse. He'd given him enough space now. Corey didn't want Reyse thinking he was ignoring him. But he was aware of how close they'd been this morning.

On one hand, he wasn't sure if he should seek Reyse out. He didn't want to smother him or give the game away. On the other, he was here *for* Reyse, as his buddy. Surely his mom and aunt wouldn't think it was weird they were hanging out?

It didn't take long for Corey to locate Reyse. He was sitting in the deserted front room on the piano stool. The room looked much bigger without a couple dozen people loitering in it, tiring themselves out with showing just how concerned they were for Donny Hickson's recovery. Corey sighed internally. Why did some rich people have to be so fake?

Reyse didn't even seem to notice Corey slip through the half open door. He was staring at the piano keys, his hands in his lap.

"Do you play?" Corey asked as he approached. It was nice to genuinely not know something about Reyse Hickson from pop culture.

Reyse blinked out of his reverie and looked over at Corey, then his face broke into a delighted smile. It made Corey's heart trip up. There was nothing fake about that smile. Reyse was happy to see Corey simply because he liked him.

Damn it. Corey liked Reyse, too. This was getting less simple by the day. When the time came to part ways, it was going to be hell.

But for now, Corey sat himself beside Reyse on the long stool and raised his eyebrows, seeking an answer to his question.

"Oh, yes," Reyse said. "I love playing the piano. I started when I was really young. I think I was five or six when an old lady down the road started teaching me for five bucks an hour." Reyse chuckled. "Gosh, I can't even remember her name now. Isn't that sad? I had so many music teachers and dance instructors through school, and then I started singing, too." He shook his head. "There's something incredible about playing and singing all by yourself. It's...pure."

Corey loved the faraway happy glint in his eye when he talked about making music.

"Play something for me," Corey murmured.

Reyse bit his lip. "I didn't want to disturb the house," he said sheepishly.

Corey frowned. "Surely your mom and Evangeline won't mind?" he asked.

Reyse ran his fingers lightly over the white keys, not pressing any of them down. "It feels…raw. To just impose my music on them without asking. Does that make sense?"

Not really, Corey couldn't help but think. They could turn on any number of radio stations or music video channels and accidentally hear Reyse's voice. Hell, they could search on the internet and see him anytime. But for some reason, Reyse making the music here and now was too much for him. Didn't he feel proud of his accomplishments? Probably not, considering his dad seemed to think being a pop star was dumb. Like his son hadn't changed the lives of millions of people for the better?

"Sort of," Corey said in response to Reyse's question. "But…how about you just play for me? Forget anyone else is here. Even if they are, though, I bet they'll love it."

Reyse thought about that for a second. "What would you like to hear?" he asked after a few moments.

He stroked down the length of a couple of the raised black keys. The sight was mildly erotic and in the relative privacy of the living room, Corey felt a surge of daring. He slipped his arm around Reyse's waist and beamed at him.

"Whatever would make you happy to play," he said.

For a few breaths, Reyse just stared at Corey. Corey wondered if he was debating asking Corey to take his arm down. But then he gave him a shy smile and nodded. "Okay," he said.

All across the globe, people paid hundreds of dollars to

hear Reyse Hickson sing live. But in the quiet of this living room in little Fort Ladrillo, Corey suddenly found himself privileged enough to get a live show, all to himself.

Reyse started with a song Corey didn't recognize, something about catching a chill in his heart. It was mournful. Corey wondered if it was an album track or something rarer. But Reyse came alive as the pitch-perfect notes soared from his mouth, filling the room with something impossibly beautiful.

He segued flawlessly into a fun, upbeat Below Zero song that Corey had forgotten about but recognized as soon as the chorus hit. Then Reyse played a couple of his solo songs, his enthusiasm and confidence growing with each number. Then he mucked around, playing a couple of tracks by Britney Spears and Michael Jackson, encouraging Corey to join in, even though his voice ruined the performance. Reyse didn't seem to mind about that, though, and Corey was having too much fun to care.

Reyse's fingers found their way back to the ice song, the one about his heart freezing over.

"Without your love, you left me out in the cold," he sang. His voice was stronger now it had warmed up. *"I broke your heart, you broke my soul. Can we ever make this right?"*

He wandered his fingers up and down the keys for a few more notes, expertly petering off. "Beautiful," Corey murmured.

Reyse looked at him. Their faces were so close.

"Oh, honey!"

Corey and Reyse both jumped and Corey tried to slip his arm down from Reyse's waist as subtly as he could. But Clementine didn't seem to have noticed that.

She had obviously slipped in at some point during Reyse's impromptu performance and was perched on an arm of the sofa closest to the door, as if she were ready to bolt at any moment. But she hadn't. She clasped her hands to her chest, tears clear in her eyes.

"Sweetheart, that was just – oh – I don't have the words!" She chuckled and wiped her eyes, careful not to smudge her makeup. "It's so nice to hear you sing again."

Corey nudged a bashful-looking Reyse. "Told you," he muttered with a wink.

The moment was quite ruined as the door banged open and Reyse's Uncle Dave strode inside the room. Corey hadn't heard him come back from the hospital. He glanced down to note Dave hadn't bothered to take his boots off as he traipsed all the way through Clementine's house.

"What the devil are you doing in here?" Dave demanded. "I was calling, but obviously you didn't hear me over your little sing-along."

Anger flared through Corey. "Man, what crawled up your ass? Reyse was just playing the piano." He was sure if Dave had really bellowed, they would have heard him. He was just being obtuse on purpose.

"Yeah," Dave said with a raised eyebrow. "Making me come all the way through the house to tell you Donny woke up. Or don't you care?"

Clementine and Reyse both shot to their feet as shock jolted through Corey's chest. "What?" Clementine cried. "The nurses said they would call me!"

Dave shrugged. "Those ladies are busy. I said I'd come get you. I know you don't like to drive," he added in concern. Or at least, it *sounded* concerned. To Corey, it felt patronizing. Dave shook his head. "This is why I said you should have been there, Tina. But we can get going right now, if you want?"

"Yes, yes," Clementine said. She wrung her hands and looked between Dave and Reyse, who had gone as white as a sheet. Corey stood up next to him. "Was he okay?" Clementine asked. "Is everything all right?"

Dave smiled and placed a hand on her shoulder. "Yeah, honey. He's pretty damn strong, that man. Nurses were pleased with his responses, said he was looking good. Why don't you go get your purse and we'll head over?"

"Yes, of course," Clementine said, then turned to Reyse. "Reyse, you're coming too, right?"

It looked like Reyse took a second to shake himself back to his senses. "Yeah, absolutely. Corey, will you come too?"

Panic flared inside Corey's chest. Reyse wasn't thinking straight. Corey couldn't go with him. All it would take was one moment of upset and he might look at Corey in a vulnerable moment or, worse, reach for his hand, and they'd be caught. But he didn't want Reyse to feel like Corey wasn't supporting him.

Corey grasped Reyse's shoulder and smiled. "It's cool, buddy," he said firmly. "This is a family moment. I'll be here when you get back."

"Well said, son," Dave said. Perversely, Corey felt like he'd earned a sliver of respect from Dave for admitting he wasn't part of the family. It made Corey grind his teeth in frustration. If Corey were Reyse's girlfriend, he'd bet any money Dave wouldn't talk to him like that. "Come on you two. Get your things. I'll wait here," Dave said fondly, as if they were a naughty couple of school kids.

Reyse gave Corey a lingering look before following his mom out of the room. Dave stood by the door, waiting for them, but also kind of blocking the doorframe. Corey didn't feel like pushing his way past him, so instead he sat back down at the piano and ran his fingers over the keys where Reyse had been playing.

"You haven't served, have you, son?" Corey looked up to confirm Dave was indeed talking to him.

Corey cleared his throat. "In the military? No, sir. I thought about enlisting," he told him truthfully. "Right out of high school."

"What stopped you?" Dave asked, folding his arms.

Corey shrugged. He refused to feel any less of a man for this. "I've got too much respect for what you guys do," he said, again, speaking the truth. "I can't follow orders for shit. I couldn't serve my country, not like that."

"No," Dave agreed, nodding. "You couldn't, could you?"

Corey felt the sting of those words but refused to look up. Instead, he focused on the piano keys.

"I don't know how you wormed your way into my nephew's life," Dave continued regardless, "but that boy has been enough of a disappointment to Donny. He doesn't need someone like you making him softer."

"Excuse me?" Corey asked, looking up with a scowl. "Reyse isn't soft." He didn't give a shit what this jackass thought of him, but Corey didn't like hearing someone that was supposed to be Reyse's own blood, his *family*, talking smack about him like that.

Dave scoffed, his arms folded. "All Donny wanted was a boy to carry on his legacy, to follow in his footsteps. Instead he got a namby-pamby."

"You do realize Reyse is an honest-to-god musical legend?" Corey asked in disbelief. "Like, I seriously have to check at this point in case you really didn't know."

"And how does that help his country?" Dave asked. "How does that honor his dad?"

Corey rose to his feet. "Maybe Reyse's dad shouldn't have such a fragile ego he only sees one way for his kid to honor him," he snarled, clenching his fists, his heart racing.

Dave laughed, which unfortunately only fueled Corey's anger. "Oh, and what would you know about honoring your dad, huh? I bet your old man's real proud of you, serving soup at some mobile kitchen – is that right?"

Corey didn't care about the dig at his job, because that was fake anyway. He'd never defined himself by his work. But, despite it being none of Dave's damn business, Corey was going to set him straight on one thing.

"I don't have a dad," he said, smirking and digging deep for the twisted pride he got from whenever he had to tell anyone this. "Or a mom. I cut my own *damn* way through the foster system and I stand on my own *damn* two feet. I don't need to answer to *anyone.* Not some dad who only cares if I do the same job as him to validate him, and certainly not some stranger like you."

Dave shook his head. "I should have known," he said with a scoff. "Someone like you ain't worth keeping around. Seems Mommy and Daddy knew that right from the moment you came squalling into this world." He curled his lip. "Still squalling now. Pathetic."

"Dave! We're ready!" Clementine's voice came floating from the other side of the door, accompanied by the sound of two pairs of hurried footsteps racing down the stairs.

Dave chuckled cruelly. "See you around, kid," he said, turning his back on Corey.

Corey was too stunned to respond in any way. He just simply listened as Dave, Clementine and Reyse exited through the front door, slamming it behind them.

Then Corey was left in the silence of the empty house. He wasn't sure where Evangeline was, but she apparently hadn't gone with the others, and Corey couldn't hear her or Foofy now.

He just stood by the piano that Reyse had used to bring him such joy only a few minutes ago. Now Corey felt hollow. Emptied out.

Every day he told himself that he was his own man. That

he may have been alone, but he was still standing and he was making something of his life.

But all his words were just a house of cards, waiting for someone like Dave to come and speak stronger, bigger words out loud.

Corey wasn't worth anything. He was forgettable. His parents, whoever they were, hadn't wanted him, and he'd been too difficult to ever adopt.

Now Reyse was going to forget him too.

He had to get out of here, just for a little while.

Seventeen

REYSE

It was a short but tense drive to the hospital. Reyse sat in the back of Dave's big, shiny four-by-four, letting his mom ride up front while Dave made quick work of navigating the streets of Fort Ladrillo.

Reyse felt strangely small. His dad was okay, he was out of the woods. Yet Reyse was still scared stiff at the prospect of seeing him. What the hell was he going to say?

Without anyone around to stop him, Reyse chewed on his perfectly manicured thumbnail. He wished so badly he could turn back time. Why the hell hadn't he just swallowed his pride and visited before? The longer he'd left it, the worse he had made it.

Deep down, he kind of knew a childish part of him had been hoping his dad would relent and come visit Reyse, to see the life he had made for himself. When it really came down to it, Reyse just wanted his dad to be proud of him.

He knew his mom was. It had been such a joyous moment to realize she'd been listening to him play just now. But as usual, it had been cut short.

Dave's disapproval was rolling off him in waves as he

drove. It was confusing, because he kept saying soothing things in soothing tones, about how great Reyse's dad was doing and how thrilled he would be to see them. But then he'd tack a 'finally' onto that in the same concerned tone, not to mention his shoulders were so tense Reyse could practically see his frustration and irritation in the air.

Reyse's mom was visibly consumed with guilt for not being there the second his dad had woken up all the way. But what was she supposed to do? Sleep in a place that wreaked havoc on her nerves and mental health when Reyse's dad wouldn't even know she was there? That wasn't fair.

But then…Reyse hadn't been there for either of them for *years*. So who was he to talk, really?

None of that mattered. It didn't matter that things could be awkward or that Dave was being a bully or that a special moment between him and his mom had been interrupted. It didn't even matter that he and Corey had been caught almost before they kissed.

What mattered was that his dad was all right. That he'd come around and the nurses said he was doing well and if luck was on their side he would make a full recovery. Everything else paled into significance when Reyse reminded himself of that.

All too soon they were pulling into the hospital parking lot. Reyse's mom looked wrecked with nerves, but Dave rested one of his big hands on her back and smiled at her as he led her over the asphalt and into the main lobby. Reyse trailed behind them, keeping his head down.

Shit. He really should have thought to wear a baseball cap or sunglasses. Or both. He'd been so eager to rush out of the house he hadn't thought of any of his usual security measures.

Instead, he pulled out his phone and wrote a quick text to his manager Kevin while following Dave through the maze of corridors. He obviously knew where he was going. Reyse studiously ignored all of Kevin's emails and texts and voicemails, simply telling him his dad was awake and he was just about to see him. Then he put the cell on airplane mode and slipped it back into his pocket.

The hospital itself was all very clean and airy, designed with lots of natural light pouring through large windows. Each department was marked with a large mural painted on the wall depicting multiple cultures in swirling effigies. Reyse had to say for a hospital, they had made the place as calming as possible.

That was, until he rounded a corner and, despite being behind both his mom and uncle, almost ran into a young nurse in pale blue scrubs.

At the sight of Reyse, she gave a short, sharp scream and dropped her armful of notes in a flurry of paper, clasping her hands over her mouth.

"I – I'm sorry," she stammered, clutching her trembling fingers in front of her chest. "Oh, I, you're Reyse Hickson, aren't you? Of course you are. Oh my god, how embarrassing. Don't – uh – is there anything I can do for you, Mr. Hickson?"

As fan encounters went, it was a very sweet, innocent one. The nurse was wide-eyed, clearly embarrassed and now attempting to put on a professional air amid the paper still slowly floating to the floor. The trouble was, now everyone in the corridor was looking their way, pointing and whispering as they realized who exactly they were looking at.

Reyse glanced at his family. His mom just looked stunned, but Dave rolled his eyes. "No, thank you, miss," Dave said in a tired voice. "We know the way. I've been coming here all week. Thank you kindly."

Awkwardly, Reyse maneuvered out of the paper explosion, careful not to tread on any of the poor woman's notes.

She was obviously rushed off her feet. "Can I help you put those back together?" Reyse asked.

"Son, we're on a schedule here," Dave said firmly.

"Oh, no," said the nurse, blushing. "I'm fine, honestly. I'm just a butterfingers." She laughed and crouched down to start reassembling her pile. "You have a good day now."

"You too," Reyse said.

Although people openly stared as he followed his mom and uncle down the last couple of hallways, thankfully nobody else approached him. He wouldn't have been surprised if someone had stopped him for an autograph – it had happened in the strangest of places before – but the universe took pity on him and he was able to reach his dad's room without incident. Good thing. Dave was obviously pissed enough as it was that Reyse's fame had slowed them down.

Dave knocked on the door but didn't wait before marching inside. Reyse let his mom go on ahead of him, then he followed last. He closed the door behind him, then took a deep breath as he turned around.

There was no hospital staff in with them, so it was just him, his parents and Dave.

The first thing that Reyse couldn't help but notice was the assault of the Rams' white, gold and navy blue on his eyes. There were scarves and foam fingers and team jerseys propped up and draped over everything in the sparse, private room. Even the vase of gladioli – his mom's all-time favorite flowers – that were perched on the nightstand were a mixture of white, yellow and sky blue. Not quite the right color blend, but close enough Reyse could tell she had tried.

Dangling from the lampshade next to the vase were his dad's dog tags. It was a jolt to Reyse's heart to see them not around his dad's neck. Reyse couldn't think of a time he had ever witnessed his dad without them.

All around the bed were beeping monitors. His dad had an IV in each arm, a blood pressure cuff on one bicep and a finger clip on the index finger of the opposite arm for his oxygen levels. He was pale and looked so much smaller than Reyse remembered. He watched his dad reach his diminished arms out for his mom as she approached. It didn't feel like he'd even noticed Reyse enter the room.

"Clementine," his dad said, his voice hoarse. Reyse's mom was tearful as she gently leaned over the side of the bed and hugged him.

"Oh, Donny," she said, sobs making her chest shudder as she tried to keep her composure. "You *scared* me!"

"I know, honey. I'm sorry," Reyse's dad said, petting her hair and hugging her close. "It's okay, I promise. Shh, there now."

A lump rose in Reyse's throat. His mom had clearly been keeping a lot inside. He wondered if he should have insisted they come to the hospital earlier. Maybe she would have been less anxious with Reyse sitting next to her. Had Reyse let his fears over seeing his dad get in the way of his mom's being here when his dad came around?

Reyse clenched his fists briefly then let them go. No. He hadn't got so far in life by second-guessing every little thing. He'd gotten on the first plane he could and looked after his mom as best he knew how. They were here now. That was all that mattered.

"You son of a bitch," Dave said loudly, breaking the moment by clapping Reyse's dad loudly on the arm. By the way his dad winced, Reyse wondered if he was up for getting slapped like that just yet. Dave didn't seem to notice, though, as he stood between Reyse and his dad with his arms folded. Now Reyse couldn't see either of his parents as they presumably looked over at Dave. "I knew you were just messing us around, you old dog. I *told* you you needed to start taking it easy." He shook his head. "Will you listen to your big brother now, huh?"

"Sure, Dave," Reyse's dad said. He sounded tired.

Reyse cleared his throat. He couldn't put this off any longer, so he stepped out from behind his uncle's bulk. "Hi, Dad," he said in a small voice, his hands in his pockets. He looked up through his lashes and felt his lips tweak in half a smile. His heart was racing like he was about to step on stage at Madison Square Garden. But at least there he knew what he was doing. This was all uncharted territory. "It – it's good to see you. I'm glad you're okay."

Dave scoffed. "He's had a stroke, son. He's hardly 'okay.'"

Reyse ignored him as he and his dad locked gazes. His dad's eyes had more lines around them than Reyse remembered, but they were sharp as ever.

"Reyse," he said, like he couldn't quite believe it. He then looked at Reyse's mom. "You called him?" There was a touch of accusation to the question that made Reyse's blood run cold.

"I didn't know what to do," his mom said, looking conflicted as she wrung her hands.

"I wanted to come, Dad," Reyse said firmly. He took a step forward. "I should have come home sooner. I'm sorry."

He swallowed, the words leaving his throat dry and his skin hot and prickly. He held his breath.

His dad looked away, taking his mom's hands and gazing at their entwined fingers. "I-" he said, then pursed his lips together. "Okay."

Okay? Was that it? Reyse stood for a moment, not sure what to do. But his dad just kept looking at his mom's hands in his. Reyse could feel Dave's weighted gaze on him. His mom looked between him and his dad, her eyes wide as she bit her lip.

"Uh…" Reyse scrambled around for something to say. "Do you, uh, need anything? Water or, um, a nurse?"

A smile twitched at his dad's mouth, but it didn't meet his eyes. From what Reyse could see of his profile, he looked sad.

"I'm fine," he said. Then he looked up and smiled for real at Reyse's mom. "I'm so glad you're here, petal. I feel like hell," he added with a chuckle.

"I should have been here, waiting," Reyse's mom fretted.

But, to his credit, Reyse's dad shook his head. "Naw, none of that. I've just been sleeping." Reyse felt Dave bristle. Reyse was sure Dave felt strongly that his mom should *definitely* have been here. "But you're a sight for sore eyes now, I can tell you."

Without warning, Dave's heavy hand dropped onto Reyse's shoulder. "Come on, son. Let's give them some space, huh?"

Reyse frowned. No. He wanted to stay here and try and talk with his dad. But…he did look incredibly weak and tired with purple shadows under his eyes and his usually tan skin so pale. Maybe Reyse shouldn't be putting any extra pressure on him right now.

The childish side of him wanted to cry or stamp his foot. This was his *dad.* He knew they'd never played catch in the yard with a pigskin or talked about girls or any of the other things he knew his dad really wanted in a son. But they were still blood. Reyse didn't want to be dismissed.

His dad nodded, though. He didn't look at Reyse, just glanced at somewhere around Reyse's feet for a second before looking back at his and his mom's linked hands. "I'll see you later, Reyse," he said in a croaky voice, then cleared his throat. He opened his mouth, as if he wanted to speak again. But then he closed it once more, his shoulders slumped.

"Sure," Reyse stammered. "I'm here for a few days. I'll

come back and see you whenever you want. I…it's nice to see you."

He watched as his dad gave a single nod, but that was all the response that followed.

"Reyse," his mom began.

"It's okay," he told her with a tiny smile he didn't feel.

Feeling defeated, Reyse turned and walked toward the door before Dave could rest a hand on his shoulders. Out in the corridor, he stopped only long enough for Dave to shut the door behind him.

"I'll get a cab," Reyse said. He'd already vetted a private company that passed his team's security criteria. He could have a car within ten minutes from anywhere in town. "I don't want to intrude."

Dave sighed. "That's probably for the best, son," he said.

Reyse gritted his teeth. For the umpteenth time, he wanted to apologize to his dad. He had obviously been given the wrong child in this life. But the door was closed now and Dave was standing in front of it, like a bodyguard.

"I'll see you and Mom back at the house," Reyse bit out. Then he turned on his heels and walked out of the hospital, not looking up to see if anyone was paying attention to him.

The need to get back and see Corey was all that consumed him. He just wanted to feel someone's arms around him.

To feel loved, even though he knew Corey didn't… couldn't love him.

For now, Reyse just needed to pretend.

CHAPTER
Eighteen

COREY

AFTER HIS ALTERCATION WITH DAVE, COREY'S FIRST INSTINCT was to march out the front door, start walking, and just keep on walking. But when he opened it, he came face-to-face with a brown-haired man with a sweater tied around his shoulders. His hand was raised as if he was about to press the doorbell.

"Hello?" he said in an accusatory tone. Corey translated that into 'who the hell are you?'

Corey mustered up his best bullshit smile and did his utmost not to tarnish the Hickson family name. "Hey, there," he said cheerfully. "How can I help you?" Hopefully this guy was just selling something and Corey could send him on his way.

But Sweater Dude clasped his hands behind his back and rocked on his feet, smiling tightly back at Corey. "I was just calling on Tina. Checking if there was anything she needed?" He shook his head as if he was deeply concerned, but Corey got a weird vibe from him.

"Tina?" he asked, confused.

The guy raised his eyebrows. "Yes, Tina. You're standing in her house."

"Oh, *Clementine*," Corey said, choosing to ignore the barb about being in Reyse's mom's house. Like this guy had caught Corey robbing the damn place or something. "She's not here, I'm afraid."

Sweater Dude frowned. "Well, where is she?"

Corey amped up his smile. "I'm sorry, I didn't catch your name. I can tell her you've called, if you like?"

"Jeremy," the guy said, narrowing his eyes. "One of her neighbors. I said I was going to swing by. I expected her to be in."

Wow. Creepy much?

Corey shrugged. "Reyse's dad woke up, so he took his mom to the hospital to see him." Corey flicked his eyebrows up and grinned. "You did know Clementine's married, right?"

Jeremy the Creep bristled. "Of course I did. *I'm* married, so I'm not quite sure what you're implying."

Yeah, right. Corey could detect his interest a mile off. Sleazeball.

"Nothing, man. I don't know anyone here, so just keeping the facts straight."

Jeremy sniffed. "So, you work for Tina?" he asked in an entitled tone.

Corey was tempted to tell him it was none of his damn business, but he *burned* to tell the truth. He wanted to be validated for once in his life. "Actually, I'm a friend of Reyse's," he said with a smile. "Just helping out while things are a bit tricky with Donny's recovery."

"Oh, yes," Jeremy said slowly. "Reyse. Her son from the band."

"I think he's won a few Grammys by himself since then," Corey told Jeremy cheerfully.

No disrespect against Below Zero, but Reyse had achieved so much over the last four years on his own. This guy Jeremy evidently thought about as much of Reyse as his old man did. Jesus, what was it with people around here not thinking Reyse was anything to shout about? He was one of the biggest pop stars around for fuck's sake! Was it jealousy, or did they really not think what he'd achieved was all that impressive?

Corey was aware he was biased on the matter. Before he probably would have admitted that Reyse had done well for himself. But now…now that he knew all the fears and doubts that lay behind those beautiful blue eyes? It made him want to defend Reyse Hickson until he ran out of breath.

Perhaps he was so possessive because he knew he couldn't keep him. But whenever this thing between them was over, Corey knew he would never stop fighting Reyse's corner, wherever he was in the world.

Jeremy stepped back and looked Corey up and down with a critical eye. "A friend from high school?" he asked.

Corey's cheer vanished. He didn't like the suspicious hint to his words. "Just…a friend," he said flippantly. "Like you and Clementine." Let him make of that what he will. He smiled and pushed the door shut. "I'll be sure and tell her you called. Catch you later!"

Jeremy opened his mouth, but Corey had already closed the door.

He took a deep breath. Damn. There went his escape route. He just wanted to get out of the house for a while and away from Dave's shitty words. Now Jeremy had come along and *also* made him feel like crap. Corey didn't like the assumption he was a member of the staff, but he liked the last look Jeremy had given him even less.

It would take a wild leap for anyone to connect the dots and guess that he and Reyse were intimately involved. That Reyse wasn't straight. But some people were damned shrewd. Corey chewed his lip. Great, that was another thing to worry about. The shittiest thing he could possibly imagine doing would be to accidentally out Reyse as being gay.

Corey balled up his fists and let out a frustrated snarl. Fuck Reyse's family *and* his label. It was unbelievable that an international superstar could be treated with such contempt by so many people that should have had his back. Why did Corey feel like he was the only goddamned person on his side?

There was the rest of Below Zero, too, he reminded himself as he began stalking through the house. When Reyse talked about them it warmed Corey's heart. It was as if they were his biological brothers. Corey let a little of his tension go as he assured himself that whenever he and Reyse had to part ways, his brothers would be there for him.

If Reyse let them.

God. It broke Corey's heart to think about, but before he went, he was going to have to try and convince Reyse to let them in more. He *needed* people to love him and be close to him. If he couldn't even officially come out to the guys he considered family – all gay or bi themselves – then he was doomed for a very lonely life.

Corey tried not to even entertain the notion that he wanted to be the one to look after Reyse. To hold him at night and remind him that not only he was a living fucking legend, but also a good, sweet, beautiful person. Why couldn't Corey be the one to make him laugh? To chase away his demons? To kiss him until all his troubles melted away?

He knew why.

Life had never been particularly fair on Corey. He'd trained himself not to rage at the universe. Shaking his fist at the sky wasn't going to bring back his parents or get him adopted, so it wasn't going to deliver him Reyse Hickson either. He needed to honor the agreement from last night and take what he could get, here and now.

That was, if Reyse even wanted him around anymore. Now his dad was awake, maybe he wouldn't need Corey. They might have already made up. Or, if there was still no hope of a reconciliation, Reyse might want to pack his bags and head back to LA

The thought made Corey's stomach twist. He wasn't ready to let Reyse go yet. Just a few more days – would that be too much to ask?

He hardly realized he had stomped downstairs and out onto the patio until he reached for his sunglasses that were dangling around his collar. He took a deep breath of warm air and tried to figure out what he wanted to do. This house was suffocating him.

"Darling?" a voice rang out over the yard. Corey squinted through the dark lenses and saw Evangeline stretched out on a deckchair, sunning herself by the pool. "Whatever is the matter?" she called out.

Corey sighed and jogged down the steps to her level, walking over to where she was resting. The swimsuit and kimono combo was back, complete with enormous sunhat. She sipped what looked like a long island iced tea from a tall glass and a candy-striped paper straw, arching her eyebrow as Corey approached. Foofy was settled under the deckchair in the shade, asleep on her back with her four paws in the air and the end of her long-haired tail dipped into her water bowl.

"Hi, Evangeline," Corey said heavily. He offered her a rueful smile as he came to a halt, careful not to cast his shadow over her.

"What is this?" she asked with a frown. "Why are you all gloomy? I thought everyone would be all singing and dancing now that Donny is awake again."

Corey couldn't help but sigh once more. "I don't belong here," he said matter-of-factly.

Evangeline tutted. "Well of *course,* darling," she said. *"No one* belongs here. It's all lovely make-believe." She twirled her hand and smiled like a beauty queen. "This is the kind of place where people settle down to convince themselves they have wonderful, shiny lives with nothing dark lurking in the closets. Some people genuinely like a simple, polished life. That's fine. But a community like this…?" She shook her head. "It's not *really* a community. It has no history. People don't stick their necks out for one another. So you don't belong? Good. I'd be disappointed in you if you did."

She plucked up her fan to open with a snap and observed Corey as she sipped on her drink once more. Corey chewed on his lip, then sat on the edge of her deckchair without stopping to consider what he was doing.

"You don't think I'm a bad influence on Reyse?" he said. He felt like a small child, asking for the acceptance he had never gotten. But he didn't have the strength to police himself like he usually did.

Evangeline rested her fan on her chest and quirked a small but genuine-looking smile for him. "I think you're a *marvelous* influence on him," she said warmly. "You're a bit rough and ragged, darling. You're the kind of real person he needs to keep him grounded. So"- In one fluid motion she snapped the fan shut and smacked his knee with it. Corey wasn't even surprised this time. He just grinned. -"stop this moping and cheer up. He's going to be in a stinker of a mood when he gets home, so you need to think about how you're going to cheer him up. Hmm?"

Corey frowned. "But…his dad woke up?" he said, confused. "Don't you think he'll be in a good mood when he gets back?"

Evangeline sighed sympathetically and tapped him more

gently on the knee with the fan. "I'd love to think so, but somehow I doubt it. But you can make him happy, can't you, sweetie?"

Corey looked at her for a moment. But her face gave nothing away. "I guess," he said slowly.

"I have no doubt," Evangeline said confidently. "So, you're all cheery again, yes?"

Corey chewed his lip and pushed his sunglasses back up his nose where they'd slipped a little. "I was actually hoping to go for a walk and clear my head," he said. "You know a direction I could point myself?" He'd planned on checking Google Maps, but he'd prefer a personal recommendation.

Evangeline beamed at him. "That sounds splendid. If I were you, I'd trot down to the very end of the yard. You see where those big oak trees are?" Corey nodded. "Well, through there, there's a gate out to a pathway. You follow that down for about ten minutes, you'll reach the security gate and it'll spit you right out onto the beach."

"The beach?" Corey repeated without thinking.

He probably sounded far too excitable for a grown man, but he didn't care. Ever since he could remember he had always adored the sight and sound of the ocean lapping against the shores of a warm beach. Even just thinking about it made his body relax.

"Ah," Evangeline said, knowingly. "You're that sort, are you? I thought so. Wonderful." Before Corey could ask what sort she meant, she jutted her chin at him. "Off you go, then. Take a blanket if you want. There's plenty of picnic things in the kitchen. I'll send Reyse your way whenever he returns." She snuggled down on the deckchair and closed her eyes with a sigh. "I'm going back to sleep. And if anyone else asks, I have *no* idea where you two could possibly be."

A lump rose in Corey's throat. "Thank you," he said, grateful for so many things. Mostly for this veritable stranger making him feel more at home than anywhere he'd lived in his life. For her endorsing Corey and Reyse without them having to come out and confirm anything. For simply being kind when the world felt like a pretty cruel place at times.

Evangeline huffed. "Oh, do go away now. I shan't have you being sappy all over the place."

Corey chuckled and sniffed and he stood. "See you later," he said with a nod.

She peeked up at him through a half-opened eyelid. "Enjoy the day," she said simply back to him.

Corey vowed to do his best.

CHAPTER
Nineteen

REYSE

REYSE HAD NO IDEA THIS PATHWAY EXISTED. IT WASN'T surprising, considering he hadn't spent much time at all in his parents' house. But still, the thrill of finding a hidden gem in the backyard lessened his anger and anxiety somewhat. He felt like a little kid again, taking himself off on an adventure.

He'd churned over his meeting with his dad the whole drive home from the hospital. What had he expected? A big hug and for everything to magically resolve just because he'd had a health scare? The real world didn't work like that. And honestly, his dad had been cool with him, but he hadn't shouted at him or been as rude as Dave had been. The indifference cut Reyse to the bone, but he had to allow his dad some slack for being so sick. He'd been in and out of consciousness for days, after all.

So, it wasn't the worst outcome. They'd exchanged a few terse words and Reyse was still glad he'd made the effort to come home and see him in person. Perhaps he could try again tomorrow, on his own? His dad might be open to more of a conversation without Dave looming over them both.

For now, he just needed Corey desperately. It was selfish,

he knew, to expect so much from Corey when he couldn't give him much in return. But he hoped Corey would at least be eager to see him too. He'd been the one to suggest they keep up their private arrangement, after all.

Evangeline had been rather blasé about telling Reyse where Corey was. He wasn't sure what to make of it. But he knew that Corey was down on the beach and he was expecting Reyse.

He bit his lip as he pushed through the slightly overgrown tree branches and tried to suppress the bubble of happiness in his heart. After feeling so low, his brain was trying to lie to him and tell him this felt like a date. He couldn't go on a date with Corey. They shouldn't even be having sex. But as he opened the security door and exited the neighborhood compound, the fresh sea breeze took his breath away.

The vista was awfully romantic.

He crossed a quiet road and headed for a wooden, railed pathway that led down a windswept, dried grassy ridge and onto the sandy dunes. It was a quiet beach with only a couple walking a dog far off in the distance. The shoreline was winding in both directions, with small cliffs rising up right beside the beach to the right.

It was a cloudy day for California, so there wasn't a desperate need for shade from the late afternoon sun. It was easy to spy Corey's familiar form, sitting on a blanket a few dozen feet away, his shoes off and his toes buried in the sand.

Why did seeing him feel like home? Reyse stood for a moment and cursed his heart. This was insane. He couldn't fall as hard as he was. But there wasn't anyone Reyse wanted to see more after getting torn down by his family than Corey Sheppard.

Well, for now, he could. For this precious moment, he could take all his frustrations and anger and hurt and find solace in the person who had come to mean so much to him.

He could either taint it by feeling guilty, or embrace the relief that filled his heart.

It was an easy choice to make as he sank down onto the blanket and smelled Corey's spicy cologne mingled with the sea breeze. He looked over at him and smiled.

"Hey," he said softly.

"Hey," Corey replied.

He was close enough their shoulders could just brush. It was probably a bit too intimate for guys who were just buddies. But if Reyse couldn't throw his arms around his lover and bury his face against his neck like he wanted, he'd take what he could.

"How's your dad?" Corey asked.

He was playing with a long, dried blade of grass between his fingers, but he glanced up at Reyse. His sunglasses were hanging from his collar, despite squinting against the sun. It meant Reyse could see his eyes and gauge his reactions better. He wondered if Corey knew that it meant a lot to see him properly. He wanted total honesty between them in that moment. They were hiding enough already.

Reyse sighed. "He's awake and his vitals are good," he said. "So that's good, but…"

Corey moved his hand and linked his pinky finger around Reyse's. It made Reyse's heart flip. "Wasn't he pleased to see you?"

Reyse pulled his lower lip between his teeth and clicked his jaw. "I don't think he knew *what* to think," he finally blurted out. "He just…didn't really react at all," he cried in frustration. "It was like he was paralyzed and I didn't know what to say either so I just left." He grabbed a fistful of sand with his free hand and shook it out between his fingers. "Dave was pretty embarrassed to have me there. He couldn't wait for me to go and leave them all to it."

"Dave's a prick," Corey said dryly. "Sorry."

"No, you're not," Reyse said with a sad chuckle. "Thank you, though."

Corey shook his head and scowled, looking out over the rolling waves. "I just don't fucking *get it*," he practically snarled. "I know you said things were kind of weird, but it's like they're ashamed of you for being phenomenally successful. Like you're this big embarrassment."

Reyse scoffed and ground his teeth. "But I am, right? Some sissy pop star who just jumps as high as he's told and says all the right things to keep everyone happy. Who the fuck even am I? I'm just…so fake and I'm tired of it."

"Hey, no," said Corey firmly.

He surprised Reyse by grabbing his face with both his hands and kissing him firmly on the lips. It was only for a second and he released him immediately, but Reyse's heart went into overdrive. He couldn't believe Corey had risked that. There was no one around, but it felt incredibly thrilling to kiss in public. Dumb, but also kind of awesome.

"Sorry," Corey said sheepishly, crossing his arms. "I shouldn't have done that. But…you make me so mad. The whole situation is infuriating. You shouldn't let your family or your label make you feel like you're less than you are. You're *insanely* talented. It's their fucking fault they've put you in this bind. If you could just come out, you'd be so much happier."

"And lose millions of fans and sales and probably half my sponsors," Reyse said heavily. For a moment, they just looked at one another, the weight of their situation settling heavily on their shoulders. Then Reyse shook his head. "Fuck it. I don't want to talk about this anymore."

"What *do* you want?" Corey asked.

"You," Reyse said automatically.

Corey gave him a small smile and linked their pinkies

again. "You have me, dummy," he said fondly. "For as long as you want."

"No," Reyse said. "Only as long as I can." He squeezed their fingers together. "Fuck this moping. I'm so over it."

Corey laughed. "Evangeline told me I wasn't allowed to mope anymore, either," he said with a sparkle in his eye.

"I bet," Reyse said.

He stood suddenly, peeling off his T-shirt. Corey laughed. "What the hell are you doing?" he cried.

Reyse grinned. "Having some goddamned fun for once. Get in the water with me."

Corey laughed again and sprung to his feet. "Yes, sir," he growled. Reyse's cock twitched with interest, but he tried to control himself.

It was difficult as Corey also stripped down to his briefs, revealing his delicious abs and muscular thighs. Both now only in their underwear, they raced across the sand, leaving their clothes with the blanket as they kicked their way into the cold surf, yelping as the waves hit their bodies. Reyse's sensitive balls didn't know what to do as they were confronted with both the cold shock of the sea as well as the tantalizing sight of Corey dripping with water, splashing him playfully.

For a while, they swam around, adjusting to the temperature and simply enjoying the feeling of being in the water. A few people walked past them, but on the whole, this seemed to be a private beach for the neighborhood and not one many people were really using just then. Reyse was glad. He'd taken a risk, leaving his phone in his jeans. But he was just so tired of fretting over every damn thing. For once, he was going to be reckless.

The sun began to dip, streaking pale lavender and peachy tones across the sky. He and Corey were a fair way out, though not enough they were in danger of getting swept away. Reyse could just about make out their clothes in a little pile on the beach.

He locked eyes with Corey. "Come here," he said clearly. He was confident his words wouldn't carry over the waves, even if there was anyone around to hear them.

He had the same thrill buzzing through his veins that he got before he stepped on stage or before he did a live TV interview. That tantalizing sense that *anything* could happen, but Reyse was in command. He was in charge of his destiny when he was performing. Out here, away from the world, he surprised himself by finding some of that confidence again. He knew it had been lacking until now when he'd been with Corey.

But Reyse was tired of being everyone else's property, of being their business, their product. This was his damn life and he only got to live it once. So when Corey swam close enough, Reyse grabbed his hip, hard, and they treaded water together, their faces inches apart.

"Take a deep breath," he commanded. Corey did as he was told.

Then Reyse dragged them both under the waves.

It was tricky, but he was able to yank Corey's solid chest to his. Pressing his tongue to the roof of his mouth to keep the water out and the air in his lungs, he kissed Corey fiercely. Corey's hands held him tightly, their bodies entwining, and they made out under the waves. With the water pressing all around them, filling their ears and keeping their eyes shut, Reyse's world was reduced down to just Corey's lips and hands and hard cock bumping against Reyse's.

It couldn't last, obviously. Too soon, they broke apart, breaching the water's surface and gasping for air a few feet apart. But they were grinning and flushed as they kicked their legs to stay upright and afloat, wiping the salt water from their faces. The sunset had turned into a blaze of reds and oranges, hanging over them like a protective blanket.

"You're so fucking gorgeous," Corey said, his expression one of pure devilment. He was only using one hand to keep afloat. He waggled his eyebrows at Reyse. "I'm going to take you back to your room and fuck you like an animal."

Reyse swam as close as he dared. To the outside observer, they were just two guys bobbing about in the sea, shooting the shit. But Reyse reached into his underwear, taking his rock-hard cock in hand, not breaking eye contact with Corey for a second.

"What are you going to do to me?" Reyse asked, his voice hoarse. His heart was racing as he began jerking himself off, just like Corey was doing.

Corey grinned sinfully and bit his lip, dropping his head back a little in pleasure and he touched himself and stared at Reyse. "I'm going to drag you in the shower with me and scrub you clean, because you're a filthy little minx," he said. Reyse moaned. "Then I'm going to suck you off, but I'm not going to let you come."

"But I want to come," Reyse gasped, breathless. "So badly, Corey."

Corey shook his head. "You're a very bad boy, and you get to come when I say. If you're a *good* boy, you'll lie on your bed with your ass in the air and face in the pillow. That way, when you scream, no one will hear you."

Reyse squeezed his cock and stroked his balls and taint for a moment, trying to pace himself. "Why am I going to scream?" he whispered. "I'll be such a good boy, I swear."

Corey groaned and sucked in air through his teeth. "I'm going to eat you out slowly, Reyse Hickson. I'm going to use my tongue to stretch you out for as long as I want. And when you're ready to take my big cock, I'm going to fuck you on your knees, hard."

Reyse shuddered. He was getting close. "I want your hands on my cock," he begged. "Now, please, come here."

They scrambled through the water to close the couple of feet between them, frantically grabbing for each other's dicks. Reyse wailed as Corey took him in hand. It was sloppy and difficult to get a proper grip while bobbing in the water, but Corey was just as turned on as Reyse was and all it took was a few tugs between them for Reyse to come. Reyse arched his back and gripped Corey's cock and hip tightly, seeing him through his own orgasm. Then they clung together, panting as they drifted like flotsam on the waves.

"That was so hot," Reyse breathed when he remembered how words worked again.

Corey grinned. *You're* so hot." He pulled Reyse in for a hug. It was risky if anyone was paying close attention to them, but it was still just about acceptable to the unsuspecting observer. "I…Reyse," Corey murmured into his neck. "I…care about you."

Reyse bit his lip, feeling Corey's cool skin against his own and how fast his heart was beating. "I care about you, too," he said.

Another word floated around Reyse's mind instead of 'care.' But that was ridiculous. He couldn't say that. It was stupid to even think it. Even if he and Corey weren't destined to part at some point in the near future, it was too soon to feel like that. He still didn't really know Corey.

But how much did you need to know someone to realize you loved them? Was this just the sex endorphins talking, or was the way Reyse felt so damned *complete* when he was with Corey the real deal?

He couldn't risk exploring the thought any further. He just took Corey's words and held them close to his heart.

They let each other go and swam back to shore, the sea washing away any evidence of their tryst. "Were you serious?" Reyse asked playfully as they dragged their clothes back over their damp bodies. Thankfully, his phone was exactly where he'd left it. The sunset was transitioning from orange to a more somber purple and dark blue behind them. "What you said back there – what you're going to do to me."

Corey balled up his T-shirt and stepped closer to Reyse, risking a quick touch to his arm. "I can," he said. "Or I could snuggle with you while we watch the rest of the sunset on your bed. Then I'll kiss you gently and sweetly, and touch every inch of you with reverent hands. If you want, I can slide inside you, or we can just lie together. Either way, we can come at the same time, quietly, and hold each other until we fall asleep."

Reyse just stared at him, his chest tight and his mouth dry. "T-that one," he stammered. "I'd like…that…very much."

Corey looked down at him through his dark lashes, his chestnut eyes full of sincerity. "So would I, gorgeous," he rasped.

Reyse swallowed as he watched Corey put his shirt back on. Then they were crossing the road and walking through the security gate. The pathway was narrow and deserted, and night was falling, giving them darkness as protection. So Reyse took a chance and reached out for Corey's hand, entwining their fingers so they could walk side by side like real lovers did.

He could fight it all he wanted, but his heart knew the truth.

He was falling in love with Corey Sheppard. And there was nothing he could do about it.

CHAPTER

Twenty

COREY

COREY SHOULD HAVE KNOWN THEIR LITTLE BUBBLE OF BLISS would pop. He just didn't think it would happen so soon.

Or so spectacularly.

They'd managed to avoid the rest of Reyse's family for most of the evening, just joining them for a quick dinner of Mexican takeout after they'd come back from the hospital. Corey could tell Reyse was happy to hear from his mom and uncle that his dad was doing well, but he was also a bit sad he was missing out on the visits. Corey touched their feet together under the table. He hoped that showed Reyse that Corey had very much appreciated having him *here* instead.

The rest of the evening they'd retreated to Reyse's room and locked the door, feeling brazen and not caring if anyone came knocking. The thing was, most of the night had been pretty innocent. They missed the sunset, but they'd stood at the window and looked up at the stars for quite some time. Reyse had stood in front of Corey as Corey wrapped his arms around him, resting his chin on his shoulder. It felt so peaceful.

They'd made love, just as Corey had promised, and after he hadn't even tried to go and sleep in his own room. The temptation to wrap Reyse in his arms again was just too strong.

When morning came, he was incredibly glad he'd taken the chance to stay the night while he could.

Because their little fantasy was over.

"Oh *shit*," Reyse hissed, dragging Corey into consciousness. He blinked his eyes open to see Reyse sat up in bed, staring at his phone in absolute horror. "Oh fuck, no, *no!*"

"Baby, what is it?" Corey said, not thinking twice about using the overly familiar epithet. He couldn't help it. Every protective instinct was going off in his head like an alarm.

Reyse was horrified.

Tears were already pooling in his wide blue eyes as he turned his phone around with a trembling hand to show Corey the screen.

He was expecting bad news about Reyse's dad, which already had him on edge.

He was not expecting to see a photograph of himself.

Several, in fact. They were kind of blurry, liked someone had zoomed as far in as they could with the camera on their phone. But there was no mistaking Corey and Reyse's forms as they sat together on the blanket yesterday, or stripped on the beach, or ran into the water almost completely naked. Their tight underwear didn't leave much to the imagination. But most damning of all was a candid shot of them hugging in the water. Even though they were small in the photograph, it was clear the way they were clinging to one another.

And above all the photos blared the title: *"Hicks in the mix with gay lover tryst???"*

"Jesus fucking Christ!" Corey yelled, sitting up and grabbing his hair. Nausea washed through him as the blood rushed from his head, making him so dizzy he was amazed he didn't pass out. No, no, this couldn't be happening! "Who? How?"

The photos themselves weren't completely incriminating. But the words were. A quick scan of the article showed the reporter (if people who wrote for trashy blogs like this could even be called that) didn't have any details on Corey himself. But they didn't need to.

'Yesterday evening,' someone called Dez Starr wrote, 'Reyse Hickson was caught frolicking in the sea with a mysterious boy toy. According to the eyewitness that snapped these shots, the pair got pretty cozy, kissing, hugging and holding hands as they watched the sunset on the private beach in Fort Ladrillo, California.

'Hickson was supposed to be taking a break while his dear old dad recovered from a stroke, but it looks like Hicks might have had something more sordid on the brain.'

The text was broken up with a couple of photos of Reyse performing on stage, then one of him and Bella at a recent movie premiere.

'Hickson's management has always fiercely denied the superstar is anything less than straight and he's reportedly been dating British actress Bella Dalton for the last year and a half. But with the rest of Below Zero all throwing themselves out of the closet, it only seemed a matter of time before Hicks joined the club.

'Speaking to numerous fans, this news comes as a devastating blow. "I can't believe he would lie to us like this!" one tearful tween proclaimed on her Twitter feed after these damming photos were released late last night. "It's just disgusting," an older Hickson enthusiast denounced. "I've been a fan for years, but I'm burning my CDs. I don't want my kids seeing this perverted behavior!" "Poor Bella!" another young woman decried on her Instagram with a photo of the stunning Brit. "She deserves better!"

'So far, Hickson's label has refused to comment. But surely

they'll have to fess up soon. Has Reyse been lying to us this whole time? Has this shifty stranger bamboozled our beloved star and corrupted him with his wicked ways? Come on Hicks, tell the truth!'

Corey looked up at Reyse to see him white as a sheet and trembling. "It's everywhere," Reyse whispered, fear cracking his voice. "I've got twenty missed calls from Kevin. I don't know…it's…"

"I'm so sorry," Corey said, tears burning behind his own eyes. He grabbed Reyse and pulled him in for a hug. "This is all my fault. Oh my god, I should have stayed away, I should have-"

"*No,*" Reyse said fiercely. "No, Corey, *no.*" He leaned back and held Corey's face either side. His eyes were blotchy and his cheeks wet, but his expression was furious. "Don't you dare apologize. *I'm* sorry you have to go through this. I'm sorry I couldn't be normal. But I'm *not* sorry we had these few days together."

Corey swallowed, the lump in his throat so big it was painful. "But it's over, isn't it?"

Reyse's lip wobbled and he let Corey go, reaching for his phone. "I have to speak to Kevin," he said in a tiny voice.

There was nothing for Corey to do but sit and watch his lover put the phone to his ear and wait for the call to connect. "Kevin, I-"

Corey couldn't make out what was said exactly, but he could hear the screaming from where he sat. The only clear word he made out was *'fucking'* used many times over. "*Are you fucking kidding me?*" he ended with after a minute of beyond furious berating.

"He's *just a friend,*" Reyse shouted back. He managed to keep his voice steady, but his hand groped until it found Corey's, squeezing it painfully tight. He screwed his eyes shut, forcing the tears to tumble down his cheeks, but he kept his words strong. "I don't know who took those pictures, but there was no kissing. Just two buddies getting drunk and blowing off steam, okay?"

Of course Corey didn't like hearing that, but it needed to be said. He lifted Reyse's hand and kissed the back of it, showing his support. His heart ached. He would do anything to try and make this better.

Kevin seemed to calm down at that. Corey could hear he was still speaking on the other end of the line, but he wasn't spitting feathers anymore. Corey guessed he was still pissed as all hell, but at least he seemed to be listening to what Reyse was saying. Even if it was a lie.

"Uh, no," Reyse said, glancing at Corey. He looked guilty. "I guess. Couldn't we just- Okay. But- But he *is* a friend. I don't get why-"

The screaming started again. Corey shifted over and hugged Reyse's side. "It's okay," Corey whispered into his ear. "Just do what he says. I can take care of myself."

Reyse screwed his eyes up again, more tears leaking between the lids. "I'm sorry," he mouthed to Corey. Corey kissed his shoulder and rubbed his arm. "Okay. Okay, yes, *fine,*" Reyse said loudly. "We'll do it your way. I give up."

He jabbed the red telephone icon to end the call and threw his phone across the room. Luckily it just hit the carpet, so it didn't crack or break. Then he turned and buried his face in Corey's chest.

"Shh, shh," Corey said. As much as he wanted to scream and punch things himself, he had to hold it together for Reyse's sake. "It's okay."

"It's fucking not," Reyse growled. He rubbed his face and looked up at Corey, his eyes blazing in fury. "I have to claim you're an obsessed fan. That after you saved me from that mugging you wouldn't leave me alone and Kevin wants a restraining order placed against you."

Corey had a pretty good poker face. But he had to admit that hit him like a sucker punch to the gut.

"What the fuck?" he whispered. "I – you don't need that. I'll just stay away, I promise."

"A restraining order looks good for any press digging around," Reyse snarled. The tears were free flowing from his eyes now. He hardly seemed to notice as they ran down his face.

"Better than two friends just hanging out?" Corey asked in disbelief.

"He *knows* we're not just friends!" Reyse cried, slapping the mattress. "He's fucking *punishing* me!" He balled his fists up and pressed them into his eyes. "I'm sorry. I'm *so* sorry, Corey. But I have to fly back to LA immediately, do a press release, then fly out to see Bella in England and work on damage control."

Corey couldn't speak for a moment. "It's okay," he bit out eventually. His mind was spinning, like he was on a bad high, struggling to focus. "We knew this couldn't last. It had to end sometime."

"Not like this," Reyse said pitifully. He dropped his hands and looked at Corey. "I hoped…I thought maybe…"

Maybe there was some way they could keep this up. Yeah, Corey had fooled himself with that daydream too. But it was a fantasy. This was reality. To give Reyse false hope now would be cruel.

Corey leaned forward, gently cradling Reyse's face as he gave him a sweet, chaste kiss on the lips. "I will never, ever forget you, Reyse Hickson," he said, keeping his voice as even as he could. "I'm so glad I met you."

"I won't forget you, either," Reyse said. He gripped

Corey's wrists so hard it hurt. "This isn't the end. I'll find a way."

Corey took a deep breath. "Come here," he said gently, pulling Reyse in for a hug. Corey held him until the sobs stopped wracking his chest and his breathing became steady once again. Then Corey brushed any lingering tears from his face and ran his fingers through his soft, blond hair. "It's okay."

He encouraged Reyse to embrace him again, resting his head on Corey's bare chest. Then Corey reached down to the floor for Reyse's phone and opened the camera app with a single swipe. Corey had always thought people that took these sorts of photos were kind of stupid. But as he captured the image of Reyse hugging him tightly, Corey looking longingly down at him, he thought maybe he finally got it. They didn't have anyone else to take a photo like that for them, so they had to try and immortalize the moment for themselves, even if it was a little staged.

"There you go," Corey said, holding the photo up for Reyse to see when he opened his eyes.

"Oh," Reyse said softly. "That's beautiful."

Corey could kid himself that maybe Reyse Hickson, international superstar, might not forget his face now. But everyone forgot about Corey. That was just the way of it.

Unfortunately, they had no time to linger. Kevin already had a car on the way to collect Reyse and take him back to the private plane he'd be riding back to LA Corey needed to book his own ticket and find his own way home. That seemed right, in a twisted sort of way.

"I'll pay for it all," Reyse promised as he hastily packed his bags and threw on some clothes.

Corey shook his head. "You already did," he assured him. Corey had barely touched that five grand sitting in his bank account. "I'll be okay. What about your dad?"

Reyse looked pained. "He didn't want to see me anyway," he mumbled, aggressively aiming socks at his messy case. "I'll talk to Mom, she can explain…" He trailed off, going pale again. "Oh…god. They'll see the photos. They'll know."

"Tell them what you told Kevin," Corey said firmly. "Not that obsessive fan crap, but that we're friends who got a bit wasted and the article is bullshit. It'll be fine."

Corey wasn't wholly convinced of that, but he had to make Reyse believe it. "Okay," Reyse said, letting out a breath. "Okay." He zipped up his carry-on and stood it with his suitcase.

He was ready to go.

"I don't want-" he began.

"Shh," Corey said, standing up and hugging him. He was grateful he'd slept in his underwear for modesty. He hugged Reyse to him, inhaling his particular musk for the last time. "It's all right, I promise. It'll be okay." Reyse nodded against his neck. "Can I ask you to do me a favor, though?"

"Anything," Reyse said, looking up at him.

Corey brushed his knuckles against Reyse's cheek. "Talk to your band friends. Tell them the truth. Open up. They love you. They'll look after you."

Reyse bit his lip. "Okay," he said, his voice barely audible.

Then his phone started flashing. It was still on silent, but that was the driver calling to say he'd arrived. There was nothing for Corey to do but kiss his sweet, beautiful, incredible lover goodbye and close the door behind him.

He picked up his clothes and dressed like his body belonged to someone else, then set Reyse's room straight. Once he was certain Reyse would have gone, he carefully opened his door, then ran to his own room, closing the door and lying on the bed he'd never slept in.

Only then did he allow the tears to silently fall. He didn't wipe at them, he just blinked, encouraging them to slide down past his ears and onto the pillow. After a few minutes, he steeled himself and pulled out his phone.

Then he began the miserable task of deleting and blocking Reyse from every possible means of communication he could think of before booking his flight home.

Twenty-One

REYSE

THE FIRST REYSE TRULY BELIEVED IT WAS OVER WAS WHEN HE realized he no longer had Corey's contact details. They had never swapped numbers, but now Reyse couldn't find him on Facebook, Instagram, anything. He was gone.

He did his best not to cry on the jet, but he stared numbly out the window for most of the short flight, trying to rub his aching heart through his chest.

For all he'd known this was coming, he was still bowled over by shock. Somehow, this was ten times worse than Jon. With Jon, they had been able to have a sweet goodbye, to slip gracefully from each other's lives. It felt like Corey had been ripped from Reyse's grasp with no chance at all to really process what was happening.

It was done.

Reyse stared at the one and only photo he had of the two of them until he completely zoned out, losing track of time as the plane began its descent into LAX. Somehow, Corey had managed to make it look like someone had taken a candid photo without them noticing. Not like those vulgar snapshots yesterday by whoever had invaded their privacy.

More like a photographer at a wedding. Although Reyse's cheeks were a little blotchy, he looked peaceful with his eyes closed against Corey's bare chest. The expression on Corey's face as he looked down at Reyse could only be read one way as far as Reyse was concerned.

It was full of love.

And now it was gone. Without any way to contact him, Reyse would have to try and hold on to the particular timbre of Corey's voice. The way his shoulders moved. The exact shade of chestnut of his eyes. The ways his hands felt on Reyse's skin.

He hardly heard the flight attendant as they disembarked, taking his luggage back on the tarmac like he was a puppet on a string, moving on the whim of someone else. Kevin was waiting for him by a privately rented black car, his arms folded across his chest as he glared at Reyse through the black sunglasses he hardly ever removed. He was skinny with slicked-back brown hair and a downturned mouth.

"Get in the car," he snapped in his incongruous gravelly voice as soon as Reyse was close enough. Like a parent picking their kid up after getting in trouble at school. Reyse was sure Kevin would love nothing more than to ground Reyse for breaking the rules as he saw it. But that wasn't a possibility.

"Kevin-" he began as he sat down.

Kevin slammed the door on him and stormed around the car to get in the other side. Reyse shot the driver an apologetic look as he buckled up. The driver locked eyes with him in the rearview mirror, offered Reyse a single nod, then turned his gaze forward.

"Our PR people have worked on a statement," Kevin said as he threw his ass in the car. As soon as he closed the door after him, he banged on the window to instruct the driver to move. "It's already been released, but you need to memorize it word for fucking word or so help me god I'll book you on nothing but kids' TV shows for the next month and shut you out of the writing process entirely for the next record."

He thrust his tablet in front of Reyse's nose then smoothed down his tie, calming himself. His words made Reyse's blood run cold. Not so much the threat about the TV shows. He didn't feel like working with kids was the hardship Kevin imagined he did. But he'd worked *so* hard to get his feet under the table for the production of the new album. It was incredibly important to him to have at least *some* control over the direction of his music.

So he took the tablet and read the paragraph Sun City had written for him, swallowing the lies without saying a thing.

It was exactly what Kevin had told him they were going to do. The statement basically said that Reyse had indulged an overenthusiastic fan too far. It painted Reyse as someone with a heart of gold, not wanting to upset the guy who had saved him earlier in the month from the mugging. But it very much depicted Corey as a loser who had latched on to Reyse and tracked him down while Reyse was trying to spend time with his family.

It also stated that the restraining order was already being put in place.

Reyse's eyes burned. Anyone who looked at those photos would surely see the ease and affection between two people who were at least friends, if not lovers. He wanted to challenge Kevin and tell him that no one was going to let them get away with this. But Kevin's mulish expression made the words die in his throat.

What did it matter now, really? There was no chance he and Corey could be together. Their parting was already bitter enough and Corey had made his feelings clear by blocking Reyse from every possible means of getting in touch. Whatever they'd had was now gone.

So Reyse handed back the statement with a single, resigned nod. So be it.

Kevin didn't give him a chance to breathe. He escorted him back to his apartment and sat on the sofa, angrily jabbing at his phone while Reyse took a shower and repacked his suitcase.

Then it was a brief stop to be seen having lunch at the exclusive sushi place, Urasawa, with a big-name producer. He was more interested in telling Reyse about his new line of underwear than he was discussing music. He didn't even seem to be aware of the controversy that was chasing Reyse since that morning. But he was a tough, manly-looking guy who brought along a couple of women as arm accessories for them, so it was good for Reyse's image, apparently. Reyse numbed himself to the whole stupid thing.

After that, he was whisked off to the airport again with a first-class ticket to London Heathrow and the understanding that Bella knew he was on his way to 'make a big show of affection for his scorned lover.'

What a load of horseshit.

Reyse hadn't even spoken to Bella yet, but he hoped she would be sympathetic. In the meantime, he allowed himself to be bustled into the front of the plane, cold Champagne pressed into his hand as the jet took off.

Every step taking him further and further away from Corey.

Dealing with his parents hadn't been much better. Or his mom, Reyse really meant. Of course he hadn't spoken to his dad.

She had been upset and concerned to find both him and Corey gone by the time she'd woken up that morning. He'd sent her a text, but she hadn't been happy until he'd given her a call while waiting for the plane to start its taxiing. Even then she'd been obviously distressed.

"But…you didn't say goodbye?" she said several times.

"I know, Mom," Reyse replied with a sigh. Fuck, he was a shitty son. "It's an emergency."

"I don't get why anyone would say these things," she replied. "Corey was so nice."

Reyse couldn't fault her there.

He'd passed on his sincerest apologies several times and she'd promised to talk to his dad. Evangeline sent him a curt text chiding him for not speaking to her before he left. He knew she was trying to be funny and lighten the mood, but her words just made Reyse feel even more hollow.

Dave had been most likely relieved to see the back of him.

Reyse slept for the majority of the flight, unable to even listen to music he was so preoccupied. But it meant the eleven hours passed quicker than he wanted it to.

To his complete lack of surprise, there was a throng of British reporters waiting at the gate when he walked through. A wall of flashing lights greeted him with a chorus of shouts and bellows as he dragged his suitcase out of customs, looking for his driver.

"Reyse! Are you a poofter?" one guy yelled with a thick East London accent.

"What does Bella have to say about all this?"

"Who's the guy, Hicks?"

Reyse pulled the peak of his baseball cap down further and kept walking toward the man holding his name. There was also a hefty crowd of fans all clamoring to get photos on their phones. But Reyse's driver was big enough to play defense for the Rams – or on a rugby team, considering this was the UK – and did his best to put himself between Reyse and all the lenses. He deftly took the handle of Reyse's case and marched them through to the parking lot.

"Come on, mate," he said in a gravelly voice. "Ignore all those wankers. Let's get you to your missus."

Reyse didn't know if a guy like this would be so nice if he knew the rumors about him being gay were true. But he liked to think he would. He got Reyse into his pristine car with minimal fuss and whistled as he switched the radio to an easy listening station playing George Michael.

They were meeting Bella at Pinewood Studios, one of London's biggest film lots. Apparently, Reyse's people had bullied her people into allowing her the afternoon off to be seen out with Reyse, all happy like they were a real couple with no problems whatsoever. Because heaven forbid her job came before Reyse's PR.

He'd managed to grab a couple of hours sleep in the car, but he was still groggy from jetlag and snippy from the whole infuriating situation when he arrived at Pinewood. He thanked his driver, though, who had made him feel at ease with chitchat about the weather and Arsenal football club, as well as being generally respectful without ingratiating himself.

"You take care of yourself now, all right?" he told Reyse with a clap on the shoulder. He'd dropped him off on the side of the lot near Bella's trailer. Reyse had to make sure he was seen being escorted there by security so it would get back to the media that he was here to visit Bella. What a joke.

The security guards waited outside while Reyse knocked on the trailer door. He felt like a teenager being escorted on a date rather than a thirty-two-year-old man. But at least when the door flew open, Bella's beaming face made some of his troubles fade away, even if just for a few minutes.

"Darling!" she cried, flinging her arms around him. She was dressed in a simple pair of black leggings, fluffy slippers and a large T-shirt covered with bumblebees. Her hair was set in rollers and her makeup was half done, but she was still stunningly beautiful. Maybe it was just her open, happy smile that made her look so pretty to Reyse. His heart lifted as he hugged her back.

"I'm sorry about all this," he mumbled into her neck.

"Oh, nonsense," she said briskly. She let him go and ushered him and his suitcase inside. "I mean, yes, I must admit I'm quite perplexed, but I'm always happy to see you. How's your father?"

Great. So Reyse's people hadn't told her what was actually going on. Unless she was just being polite.

"My dad's awake and on the mend," Reyse said, putting the most positive spin on it that he could. "I was happy to see him. But, uh. Did you see the story about me this morning?"

Bella blinked at him as she opened her fridge. Her trailer was delightful, covered with flower-fairy lights and sparkly throw cushions and her collection of Funko-Pop characters, some of which were her own characters. The scent of her fresh but spicy perfume lingered in the air. "I was on set at five this morning, sweetie," she said gently, passing him a bottle of sparkling water. "Why, has something happened?"

Reyse sighed and sat on her couch. He retrieved his phone from his pocket, found the most damning article by that Dez guy, and handed it over for her to read.

He watched her eyes scanning the screen for a few seconds. "Oh, the *bastards*," she shrieked, her face contorting in horror. "The little *shit weasels!* Who took these photos? The dirty fuckers, I'll have their guts for garters."

Reyse had to admit her outrage made him feel the smallest bit better as he took his phone back.

He sighed. "No idea," he admitted. "But...they're not wrong."

Bella sat back at her dressing table and fiddled with her mascara wand. "Oh," she said softly. "Who is he?"

"He's gone," Reyse said abrasively. But he did manage to

offer her a tight smile. "Kevin made sure of that. And anyway, it's not fair to put him through this fucking circus. So, here we are, ready to be a madly in love couple. If you don't mind?"

It was Bella's turn to sigh. "Of course, sweetheart," she said. But Reyse detected some hesitation.

"What's wrong?" he asked.

Bella turned around in her seat, biting her lip. "Uh," she said, clearly uncomfortable. *"IthinkIvemetsomeone,"* she said in a rush, her pale cheeks blushing furiously.

"You've met someone?" Reyse repeated. "Oh, hon, that's wonderful!"

Bella smiled bashfully at him. "Maybe. I don't know," she said. "He knows about…our situation. But, well, he's my new tennis coach and he's very lovely. He's funny and clever and a bit of a dork." She smiled into her lap, unable to conceal her happiness. "And he likes holding my hand and is a simply wonderful kisser and he doesn't want to have sex with me at *all.*" She looked back up at Reyse. "Isn't that *marvelous?*"

Reyse chuckled. "That's amazing," he agreed. "I'm so happy for you."

A beat passed between them.

"I know, I know," Bella said, waving her hand and turning back to her mirror. "It can't really be a thing. I'll keep it completely quiet."

Reyse balled up his fists. "No," he said firmly. "That's what I thought with…that's what I tried to do. The least we can do is turn this shitty situation into a positive for one of us." He stood up and leaned against her dresser and looked down at her. "We can use this as an excuse for you to break up with me. No one would blame you. Then you can be free to date…"

"Tony," she supplied. But her expression was one of

concern. "No, darling, I couldn't leave you in the lurch like that."

Reyse shook his head. "Screw it," he said vehemently. "One of us should be happy, don't you think?"

Bella frowned. "So…does that mean you'll go back to…"

Reyse's heart lanced with pain. "No," he said softly. "I can't be with anyone like that. Nothing's changed. Except… well, I think it might be a little harder now, knowing what I've lost."

Bella huffed and crossed her arms. "This is so silly," she said heatedly. "They can't force you to be something you're not."

"With the number of sales at stake, they can," Reyse said sadly. "I'd be seen as perverted, a bad influence on teenage fans across the globe."

"Oh, and I suppose writhing around with that half-naked temptress in your last video was the peak of family-friendly entertainment?" Bella snapped, genuinely furious. "No, I'm sorry Reyse, but it's outright homophobia and there should be no place for it in this day and age."

Reyse shrugged. "It's just the way it is," he said, his voice hollow.

Bella snarled and threw her mascara across her dresser. "So, what?" she demanded. "You're just going to let this boy go, the same as Jon? For heaven's sake, Reyse! Life's too short! If your father's stroke taught you anything, it should be that."

"I don't want to fight," Reyse said. He couldn't stop the catch in his throat, or the tears that sprung in his eyes. He tried to regain his composure, but Bella had already seen it all.

Immediately, she mellowed and stood up, wrapping her arms around him. He hugged her back, sniffing.

"Oh, sweetie, I'm sorry," she said. "I just find the whole

thing so grossly unfair. It makes me livid. I didn't mean to push."

"It's fine," Reyse assured her.

"It's bloody not," she said. But as she leaned away, she smiled, brushing back some of his hair. "But as long as you aren't cross with me, I'll leave it alone. For now."

Reyse chuckled. "Hell, no. How about we hit the town and get really drunk?"

Bella gasped and clapped her hands together. "That sounds like a *glorious* plan," she declared.

So, for a few hours, Reyse allowed himself to be entertained in London. He and Bella had dinner and drank cocktails in an exclusive bar and managed to avoid most of the British press, but were seen just enough to get a few pictures in the press the next day. He laughed and let himself be hugged and hugged her in return, all the while trying to keep thoughts of Corey at bay.

But when he finally crawled into his hotel room, flinging his suitcase open to rummage around for his toothbrush, he found something he realized didn't belong to him.

It was just a plain white T-shirt. Reyse might not even have noticed it wasn't his if he hadn't spotted the label and not recognized the make. Frowning, he pulled it from the tangle of other clothes he had thrown into the case when he'd first packed it at Fort Ladrillo. Then he realized.

It was Corey's.

The shirt he'd been wearing when he'd first sneaked into Reyse's room. Foofy had shown too much interest in it, so Reyse had picked it up and chucked it into his suitcase to try and stop the little dog from investigating it further.

It smelled like Corey.

The tears sprung from Reyse's eyes before he had a chance to stop them. Feeling empty and dejected, he peeled off his own clothes, then pulled Corey's T-shirt on with his own boxers to wear to bed.

All he could hope was that, in time, the pain in his chest might fade. But for now, he embraced it, hugging a pillow and thinking of Corey until he finally fell into an exhausted sleep.

Twenty~Two

COREY

COREY KNEW ABSOLUTELY NOTHING GOOD WOULD COME OF looking at photos of Reyse and Bella Dalton together. But it was like he was addicted.

They made a beautiful couple. Even though Corey knew it was all fake, it was hard not to be swept away by their charade as he flicked through picture after picture of them smiling and hugging and walking down the street together.

Eventually, Corey angrily returned to his phone's home screen and locked the damn thing. He dropped it beside him on his crappy bed and pressed his fingers into his eyes, as if that might blot the images out from his mind and stop the tears from stinging. It certainly didn't stop the sob that rattled in his chest. He couldn't be with Reyse, so he needed to stop tormenting himself. He needed to be grateful for the time they had been able to have together.

But this was the *twenty-first century*. Why should he be grateful for some borrowed time like some dude from the Victorian or Georgian era? It wasn't *illegal* to be gay! He and Reyse weren't going to be hung or thrown in jail. It was just because some fucking asshats had decided they didn't like it, they got to pull Reyse's strings like a puppet.

Corey looked at the ceiling of his tiny, funky-smelling room and balled up his fists. He couldn't change anything by being angry. Not when it came to Reyse, anyway. He had his own path to walk, as did Corey. He needed to think what he was going to do with himself.

It had always been pretty simple for Corey. He just drifted from one job to the next, one hookup to the next, never truly committing to anything or opening himself up. It was easier to protect himself that way. But what kind of life was he living, really?

This was no way to live at all. He was almost thirty and he had nothing to show for himself. No career, no friends and no boyfriend or girlfriend.

But what he did have was close to five grand sitting in his bank account.

For a fleeting moment, he resisted the idea of spending it at all. Like he would lose his connection to Reyse if he did. But that was crazy. Because whatever he spent that money on would always be *from* Reyse. So…what did Corey want?

Other than Reyse. He laughed ruefully to himself and rubbed the tears from his eyes. Normally, he'd go for his favorite comfort food when he felt like this (not that he'd *ever* really felt like this before.) But every time he even looked at a pizza, his stomach turned into knots. It reminded him of Reyse too much. In fact, he'd not been able to eat much for days.

Just like he'd never really believed in love before, he'd not believed in heartbreak either. But now it was like all those sad songs made sense. He left like he'd been ripped in half and a part of him was missing.

He took a long, slow breath in and massaged above his eyes. He was in danger of getting a headache. This is why he needed to stop dwelling obsessively about Reyse. He couldn't do anything to fix it. He was just going to make himself sick.

No, what he needed was *purpose.* He wanted to mean something, the way he had to Reyse. For that, he needed a job he cared about with like-minded people to hang out with. Thanks to Reyse's money, he had a while to catch his breath and maybe find those things.

He swung his legs off his bed and grabbed his laptop from where it had been charging on the floor. He opened a job-hunting site and began to look. If nothing else, it might take his thoughts off his broken heart for a while.

The trouble was, all these places filtered by what kind of work he wanted to do. But Corey didn't know. He just wanted to do something worthwhile, fulfilling. He wasn't exactly sure what form that would take. He wasn't trained in anything and he didn't have a college education, so he felt like that limited what he could consider. But he felt like there were plenty of things he could learn, if he just put his mind to it.

If someone was willing to teach him.

Yeah, right. No one would want to take a chance on some smart-ass nobody like him. The best he could probably manage would be to work his way up from another delivery job. Maybe work his way up to manager at some fast-food joint. No disrespect to anyone that did that kind of job, but it didn't feel like that was where he was going to find his calling, or other people like him.

Who were his people, though? Who did he want to make friends with? Guys his own age, sure. But then he thought of Maria and the other awesome women he'd met at Speedy Pete's. He didn't necessarily want to isolate himself from meeting people outside of his own narrow demographic.

But what then? An office? He could type pretty well and was tech-savvy. He bet there were plenty of places in LA that would be willing to take on a grunt to do data entry or fill up the copy machine with paper or whatever people did in offices at the bottom of the ladder. As long as it was a good company, maybe he could start there and see where it took him? It might take a while to get anywhere, but it would look better on his resume than a bunch of delivery places.

Half an hour scrawling through admin positions on offer, however, had him feeling disheartened again. They all wanted two years' experience, except for the ones who were offering unpaid internships. Corey chewed his lip. With Reyse's money, he could consider that to get him experience. But he couldn't live off five grand for two years. That would last him a few months, if he was careful. He needed to be making a living of his own.

Maybe he could try bar work? There were plenty of gay bars around LA, some of them were bound to be hiring.

Unless…

Corey sat up on his bed, staring at nothing for several moments.

Here he was raging about the inequalities for LGBT people…what if there was a job he could do to help that? What if there was an LGBT organization in the area that he could do admin work for? Or web design, or marketing promo, or fuck, he'd make coffee for a place that was working for the betterment of queer people.

He opened a new tab on his internet browser, excitement tingling in his chest. He started by searching for LGBT charities and organizations in the city or a drivable distance away. Then he went page by page, seeing if any of them were hiring.

When he got through the first ten and realized none of them were advertising positions available, he went back through them and began dropping them emails on the off chance. He explained he was looking to give back to his community and would be willing to consider anything.

Then he found it. The Rainbow Roofs Trust, based right here in good old Los Angeles.

'*RRT is a voluntary organization dedicated to aiding lesbian, gay, bi and trans young people in the California region who find themselves in a housing crisis situation. Homeless, sleeping rough or unsafe living environment, RRT can help young people in their time of need. We can offer many forms of assistance, including finding emergency accommodation, mentor plans, helping youths developing key life skills and much, much more.*'

Corey blinked, trawling through every inch of their website. They didn't have anything to indicate they were hiring, but his heart was pounding in his chest.

This was the one.

If he could find a way to help kids like him, the way he'd never been helped when he'd been left to flounder in the foster care system, he considered that to be a pretty worthwhile goal. Hell, if he couldn't find a job here, he wanted to volunteer for them, or something. They were accepting runners for the LA marathon in March and asking people to donate time to their food centers. Somehow, Corey was determined he was going to get involved with this organization.

Reyse was stuck under the thumb of people who believed he was less than them because he was gay. As much as it pained him, Corey couldn't do anything to help him more than he had already. But he *could* help to build a better tomorrow for LGBT people. The more queer kids who grew up with support, the more parents and teachers that could be educated, the better tomorrow would look for the LGBT community.

Corey quickly typed out an email...then spent the next hour fretting over every word, tweaking it until he couldn't see straight. He took a deep breath, clicked send, then immediately closed his laptop. As much as he would welcome an email back from any of the other places he had contacted, he had only sent them a vague couple of lines expressing his interest. He'd practically begged RRT for a chance.

He stared at the closed laptop for several seconds before lurching to his feet, grabbing his wallet and keys, thrusting his feet into his boots, and heading out the door. If he stayed in his room, he was going to go nuts.

By the time he reached the bar down the street, he felt vaguely able to breathe again. He ordered a beer and resisted the urge to check his emails or to Google Reyse Hickson. Neither subject was completely off his mind, but as Corey ordered a burger and fries and another beer he was able to slowly relax.

His life had *possibility*. That wasn't something he had really considered before. He was still only able to pick at his fries, because there was no escaping the emptiness losing Reyse had left him. Not just yet. But the gaping hole in his chest was slightly smaller thanks to the hope contacting Rainbow Roofs had given him.

And when he finally cracked and checked his email, he was rewarded with a message from Rainbow Roofs, excitedly asking if he'd like to come in for an interview next week for an admin role.

Corey wasn't generally an emotional person, but he did get a lump in his throat as he wrote back a reply saying he'd love to.

If he had to choose, he'd pick to be with Reyse. But if he couldn't have that – which Corey honestly *did* know he couldn't – he decided to take this heartbreak as the kick up the ass he needed to sort his life out.

If he opened himself up to other opportunities, if he became more involved with the queer community, who knew where his life would take him? He could honor his and Reyse's time together by making life better for others. If Corey helped just *one* kid out there to be able to stay with the person they loved, then maybe their sacrifice would be worth it.

It wasn't until Corey was back at his apartment, several beers inside him as he lay in bed, that he realized he's admitted he was in love with Reyse.

His smile from the email faded.

Reyse was the only one he wanted to tell about his job interview, but he couldn't. He wanted to cuddle up with Reyse and celebrate, just the two of them. He wanted Reyse to tell him he was proud of him.

Corey closed his eyes and felt the room spin around him as he brushed the tears from his cheeks. He didn't appreciate it was possible to miss someone so much it made you physically ache. He'd never known his biological parents nor his adopted parents, so he'd not been able to grieve for them.

But he grieved for him and Reyse.

In the morning, he'd remember that he was happy and excited about his new job opportunity. He was going to get on with his life, just like he hoped Reyse would. But for now, in the privacy of his own room, Corey cried, hard, like he hadn't since he was a teenager.

Eventually, he calmed, running out of tears. It felt better to let it all out. He fell asleep, wishing Reyse sweet dreams, wherever he was.

Maybe, if the universe was kind, Reyse might just know Corey was thinking about him still. That he'd be thinking about him always, in one way or another. But for now, he let the darkness claim him, washing away his sadness.

THE T-SHIRT NO LONGER SMELLED OF COREY.

It was bound to happen. It had been weeks since they'd seen each other. But still, the realization made Reyse's heart hurt.

Corey's social media profiles were well hidden, if they existed at all. So even on a general browser, Reyse could find nothing of him. All he had left was one photograph and a generic white shirt that smelled more of Reyse than it did of Corey now. Still, Reyse wore it to bed every night, even after he'd washed it. It made him feel slightly less alone.

He'd also saved the photo as many places as he could while making sure it was still secure. If he got hacked like Raiden had a couple of years ago, it could be bad. But at this point, Reyse didn't care. His security was top notch, but also as far as he was concerned, the damage had been done. It mattered more to him now to make sure he never lost that picture.

Sure, Kevin's little stunt had put a Band-Aid on the issue for now. But blogs were still running daily speculation pieces about Reyse's sexuality. Apparently, his fake-dating Bella wasn't quite enough anymore, not once they'd realized that Reyse hadn't dated anyone else at all in the past decade.

More than that, though, Reyse didn't *care.* He and Bella were in the process of their fake-breakup whether Kevin liked it or not. Because there was no way he was putting Bella and her new boyfriend through the same hell as he and Corey had endured. Even if they'd postponed their 'parting' for the time being, just while the dust settled around all these articles. Reyse felt bad for delaying her and Tony's relationship in the meantime. But the press was also dragging her for not being supportive enough and making up stories about more of his sordid encounters with men. Anything to get clickbait.

So Kevin's new great idea was to have Reyse reschedule his interview with Kimmy Kovac, the nation's favorite daytime talk show. Not ignore it all and work on the new record like Reyse wanted to do. No, Kevin wanted to make sure any *hint* of Corey was dead and buried. That sadistic asshole.

Apparently, the label's PR people were convinced that because Kimmy was a beloved lesbian, she could talk about Reyse's gay 'rumors' in a safe environment without it becoming too tricky. She would be a sympathetic ear, allowing Reyse to tell his side of the story. He could explain that he had absolutely nothing against the LGBT community, just that wasn't who he was. Then he'd present a big, fat check for some charity Kevin was going to choose for him, and continue to try and sweep Corey firmly under the rug.

As he drove out to Kimmy's studio, Reyse cursed to the high heavens whoever had taken those fucking photos. Being a celebrity meant giving up a certain amount of anonymity, he had always understood that. There were a lot of things he was prepared to go without. But whoever had made a fast buck out of snooping on him and Corey had robbed Reyse of one of the best people he had ever met in his life.

In moments like this, he tried to convince himself he was crazy. That he couldn't be sure he was in love after such a short amount of time. But his heart wasn't lying, not after all these weeks apart.

He missed Corey like he was missing a part of himself. Like he'd lost a limb and now had no idea what to do with himself.

It wasn't a long drive, so he closed his eyes and tried to meditate, or at least take deep breaths and clear his mind. This was an important interview. The kind that could decide the course of his career. He trusted Kimmy. He'd worked with her several times before and she genuinely seemed to have a good heart. All he had to do was follow her instinct, and allow her to help him lie through his ass.

Somehow, this felt like even more of a betrayal of Corey than leaving him and agreeing to that damn restraining order. But it had to be done.

———

Kimmy's studio was all light blue and shiny chrome, her smiling face and the show's logo plastered on every surface. PAs ran all over the place, ushering the guests around who would appear before Reyse, including a guy with a live hawk on his arm and a six-year-old girl who'd uploaded a version of herself singing Lolita Charisma on YouTube and gone viral.

Luckily, the audience was kept well away, so Reyse didn't have to deal with anyone gawking as he was escorted to makeup. Kevin met him there, although he spent the entire time out in the corridor on the phone, angrily debating something with someone, looking like a jackass with his shades on indoors. Reyse was sure it wasn't to do with him for once, so he tuned it out.

The makeup artist was a super sweet twinky guy who had better highlighter and brows than most people Reyse had ever seen. Reyse tried not to stare as a PA got him into a chair, then dashed off to deal with the hawk and their feeding time.

The makeup artist smiled warmly. "My name's Billi with an I, and I'll be looking after you today. Okay, sweetie?" He winked at Reyse.

Reyse wondered what it would be like to be that out and proud. He wasn't inherently that camp – the only way his career had survived thus far – but he felt a mixture of envy and pride as he smiled at Billi with an I.

"If you can make me look half as good as you, I'll be impressed," Reyse said with a nod and a wink toward Billi's flawless foundation.

"Oh, *stap*," Billi said with a limp wrist, owning the gesture that Reyse had seen used in such a derogatory way for gay men so many times. Billi spun on the spot as he fetched facial cleanser and cotton pads. "She's good, but she's not a miracle worker, honey."

Reyse laughed. He knew he was in safe hands with someone who wasn't afraid to tease him.

He watched Billi quietly as he worked his magic while bantering easily with the rest of the makeup, hair and wardrobe team. Billi was absolutely nothing less than one hundred percent himself the entire time Reyse was there.

Completely camp. Completely gay.

"Howdy, howdy!" a voice rang out from near the door. Reyse looked up from his chair while Billi smoothed over his cream bronzer. Reyse couldn't help but smile at the gangly ball of energy that bounded into the room like Tigger from Winnie-the-Pooh.

It was difficult to feel down around Kimmy Kovac. A small woman with a pixie cut in her midforties, she was already wearing her signature jeans, sneaker and button-down combo, ready for filming. Reyse was surprised she wasn't wearing something crazy, but then he figured this was her version of somber in honor of the serious situation he was in.

Last time he'd been a guest, she had scared him with a gorilla costume he'd thought was a lifeless prop until she'd jumped out at him. The cameras hadn't even been rolling. It was just her sense of humor to hide in cupboards and scare her friends and coworkers.

"Hey, buddy, how you doing?" she asked, lightly smacking his arm and pushing her black-framed glasses up her nose. She had a squeaky voice that added to her youthful, energetic persona. "Billi taking care of you?"

"He is," Reyse said, smiling at his makeup artist. Billi squeezed his knee, then carried on working.

Kimmy perched on the edge of the counter where Billi had his supplies laid out. "I just wanted to say howdy, you know," Kimmy said, nodding to herself. "Check you were a-okay. Nothing to worry about. I got all the questions from your, uh, manager-friend-person out there." She waved her fingers out toward where Kevin was still ranting on the phone. "It's tough when the boss gets mad, huh?"

Reyse licked his lips, unsure what to say. He felt strongly Kimmy was in his corner, but he was conscious of making things any worse with Sun City than they already were. However, he would be a fool to forget that she was speaking from firsthand experience. Back in the nineties, when Kimmy had been one of the first celebrities to come out of the closet, she'd lost everything. Her network had dropped her sitcom just like Sun City was threatening to do with Reyse's record contract.

But she'd built herself up again, stronger than ever before. Her show was such a huge success now she gave checks away weekly to send underprivileged kids to college. She once gave her whole audience a damn car each. She launched entire careers just by featuring people like the six-year-old Lolita Charisma girl on her show. Her opinions shaped the way America thought.

"I'm just sorry this whole mess happened," Reyse said evasively. "Thank you for understanding. I'd *never* want to offend the LGBT community."

Kimmy blinked and grabbed his hand between her small ones. "Oh, hon, no. You didn't offend – we're not offended, are we, Billi?"

"No, ma'am," Billi said, shaking his head.

"It's just so funny how people get these ideas into their head, isn't it?" Kimmy said, shaking her head. "But we'll fix it, you'll see. You just go out there and give 'em hell. 'Kay?"

Give 'em hell? Reyse didn't really feel like that. He felt more like a puppy with his tail between his legs.

But Kimmy was grinning at him, scrunching up her button nose. So he squeezed her hand. "Sure," he said.

"There you go, honey, all done," Billi said, spinning Reyse in his chair to look in the mirror.

Kimmy let go of him and hopped to her feet. "Okay, hon, I'll see you out there!"

"Bye," Reyse said as she jogged from the room. Then he looked at Billi in the mirror's reflection. "I look great," he said genuinely. "Thank you."

Billi nodded. "You do," he agreed, somewhat seriously, considering how flamboyant he'd been acting.

Reyse pulled the tissues from around his neck and stood up, offering his hand out to shake. "It was a pleasure meeting you today, Billi. Really," he said.

He expected Billi to scoff and brush him off. But Billi

took his hand, then placed his other one over the back of Reyse's as well. "You too, baby," he said sincerely.

Reyse walked out into the hall, aware he was frowning and chewing on his lip. Kimmy and Billi had been so supportive, thinking he was straight yet wanting to still support the LGBT community. But it was a lie, *it was a fucking lie.* He was as gay as either of them, just too afraid to admit it out loud.

Kevin scowled at him while still talking on the phone. The two of them followed yet another PA who escorted them backstage, taking Reyse behind the entrance screen for his entrance.

He was so scared of losing everything…but that was what Kimmy had done almost two whole decades ago. She had been given the ultimatum of living as her authentic self or keeping her career safe. She had chosen to jump without a parachute, giving the middle finger to those who'd tried to hold her down.

Give 'em hell.

Reyse couldn't even tell the truth. How could he stand up for himself?

For Corey?

The lights changed and the music cued, giving him only a second to compose himself as the doors slid open, revealing him to a hysterically screaming live audience and half a dozen cameras, broadcasting live all across America. Later, it would go all over the world.

Reyse smiled and waved. Apparently, the audience had been given no clue they'd be seeing him today, judging by the way some of the women were crying and pulling at their hair.

The usual adrenaline kicked in, forcing him to react on instinct as he jogged to the center stage and hugged Kimmy before taking his seat on the couch. It was incredibly humbling to see people react to his presence like that.

He couldn't let them down.

Yet, it was like he was behind a glass wall, not really able to fully process what was in front of his eyes, or what was coming out of his mouth. He told Kimmy it was a pleasure to be back, and he meant it, and they swapped a little chitchat about how Reyse would soon be recording his new album. At least he hoped he would, but he didn't say that out loud.

"So, you've had a tough couple of weeks, am I right, buddy?" Kimmy asked.

She tapped Reyse's knee and smiled. She always reminded him of one of his favorite school teachers from when he was in second grade. Fun, but fair, with a glint in her eye that said it would be a good idea not to mess with her or anyone she cared about.

Did she really care about Reyse?

He hoped so.

"Uh, yeah," Reyse said, nodding, going for his most sincere expression. "There's been a lot about me in the press lately, and not much of it about my music, sadly."

There was a slight reaction from the audience, like a soft *"ahh."* Reyse gave them a small smile and looked back at Kimmy. The studio lights were pretty bright in his eyes and he felt hotter than usual. He reached out for his Kimmy Kovac Show mug and swallowed a mouthful of the honey and lemon tea he'd asked for.

"Some people do like to gossip," Kimmy said with sympathy, before grinning impishly at the audience. "Don't they, folks?" That got a little bit of laughter. "But seriously, it's put you in kind of a tight spot, hasn't it, Reyse? People out there are saying you've been cheating on the lovely Bella Dalton, and that's not true, is it?"

"Absolutely not," Reyse said with complete honesty. He'd

never cheated on Bella because they'd never for one moment really been together. "Bella is my girl, my rock. I'd be lost without her."

A louder chorus of *"aww"* went around the studio.

Kimmy laced her fingers together and pressed them to her chin for just a second, before dropping her hands to the sides of her armchair again. "But that's not all, is it? Because these folks are saying you cheated on Bella with a *man.* Now, I don't want to make you uncomfortable, but you wanted to come and talk with me about this today, didn't you?"

She'd taken her glasses off for filming and Reyse looked into her blue eyes. She was smiling, but he got the feeling there was a lot more going on behind those eyes.

"Yes," Reyse said carefully. "I wanted to make sure people understand how I felt in my own words. Because in no way do I think being gay or bi is a bad thing."

Kimmy offered her palm to him and raised her eyebrows. "All your bandmates, the guys from Below Zero. They're *all* very happily married to other guys, aren't they?"

"Well," Reyse said with a twitch of his lips before he could stop himself. "Ashby is nonbinary. But yes. All the guys from the band are gay and bi, and I love them deeply."

He wasn't going to get into the definition of being pan versus being bi live on air. He just hoped Raiden and TJ wouldn't mind.

"Exactly, exactly," Kimmy said, bobbing her head. "But that's just not you, right? The person taking these photos got it wrong."

Give 'em hell.

Reyse's smile became fixed. "Yeah, yeah," he croaked out, still smiling as he reached for more tea. *Damn it. He needed to do better!* His career depended on telling this lie. "I went home to spend some time with my family. My dad's recovering from a stroke. I don't really get many days off, so while my mom was at the hospital, I went goofing off on the beach with a buddy of mine." Reyse determinedly swallowed the lump before it even rose in his throat. "He's a great guy. We just got a little drunk and the bloggers made up their story from there."

There was a motion from behind the camera. Reyse tried not to let his eyes dart too obviously, but he glanced enough to realize Kevin had thrown his hands up in the air and was all but snarling at him. He'd ripped his sunglasses from his face, so Reyse could see he was furious.

What the hell?

Kimmy nodded and tilted her head. "This is the same guy that saved your cell phone from getting snatched a while back, right?" she said. To Reyse's horror, pictures from that day were suddenly on the screens above them for the audience – for America – for the *world* – to see.

In all his pining for Corey, Reyse had never once thought to look up those images. How stupid was he? Now there they were. The research team had probably managed to pick the best one they could, but Corey's face was mostly hidden by his baseball cap. Reyse could still see he was looking up at Reyse with a smile. Reyse was reaching down, offering to help him up.

Reyse didn't get long to enjoy the surprise glimpse of Corey. Kevin was going out of his mind, not verbally, but physically. He was drawing stares from members of the audience now as he hopped about, balling up his fists and mouthing *"NO!"* at Reyse. It looked like he was going to snap his sunglasses, he was clenching his fists so hard.

"Uh, yeah," Reyse said. Had they turned the lights up? Why was his tea all gone? "I was lucky he was there that day."

Kimmy bit her lip. Her eyes were just fractionally too wide as she tilted her head and pressed her hands together. "But you're not friends anymore, right? Because this guy got all whack-a-do on you. That's why you tried to let him down gently, but then…"

"The restraining order…" Reyse said faintly.

No wonder Kevin was losing his shit.

Reyse had just completely undone all his PR work by telling the *wrong* lie.

Cold panic washed over Reyse. "I…" he stammered. He blinked sweat away from his eyes and tried to keep his focus. "It's complicated," he said. His voice sounded strangled to his own ears.

"Is it?" Kimmy asked. She leaned forward in her seat, like she genuinely wanted him to make it all okay.

Give 'em hell.

Reyse had never once in his entire life suffered from stage fright. He'd been nervous before performing and he'd fucked up lyrics and dance moves and said dumb things in interviews. But he'd never frozen in front of an audience before.

Until now.

He looked between Kimmy's concerned face and Kevin, who was standing with his palms pressed to his cheeks like the Scream painting, and the audience who were staring at Reyse, holding their collective breaths. Even the crew seemed to be waiting for a pin to drop.

There were so many cameras aimed at his face. The lights were dazzling and the AC buzzing even though Reyse was hot as hell. His whole body prickled with goose bumps under his clothes as he turned his gaze to the photo still being shown, larger than life, above their heads.

It was Corey. *His Corey.*

His face grimaced before he even knew what he was doing, hot tears pooling in his eyes. Blood rushed through his ears. Dizziness overwhelmed him so much he felt like he was going to pass out.

"I'm gay," he whispered.

The whole studio went nuts. People shrieked and gasped, jumping to their feet. Cameras zoomed from left to right, one rolling right up close to him and Kimmy. Kevin bellowed a string of profanities that had security grabbing him around the waist and hauling him out within seconds. Kimmy herself didn't move much, but her eyes went like saucers.

"Sweetie, what was that?" she asked, leaning forward.

"I – I'm gay," Reyse said tearfully, unable to look away from the photo. "I was never dating Bella. She's my friend. But I was – I – he…"

"This guy here?" Kimmy asked. "Are you dating him?"

Reyse covered his mouth with his hands. It was like he'd dropped under the ocean and his heart was going at a million miles an hour. He could hear Kevin still yelling, trying to halt the interview, trying to make Reyse stop talking.

"I can't," Reyse cried, his voice gaining pitch. "I can't do it anymore. I *can't!* I can't lie or hide! I'm sorry. I'm *so sorry* to let you all down, but I've been forced in the closet for my whole life and now I've lost him and I just – I can't!"

He stumbled up from the couch, trying to pull at his body mic. He needed to get out, get away.

"Wait, Reyse!" Kimmy said.

She held her hands out and stood with him, shouting over the din of the audience. Reyse could tell people were moving everywhere, but he didn't know where he should go. He had to get *out.*

"Reyse, who kept you in the closet? Your label, Sun City?" For just a second, America's most-beloved lesbian looked absolutely livid. "Did they tell you you weren't allowed to be out?"

Reyse gave up on the mic, his hands falling numbly to his sides. He turned and looked at Kimmy. "What have I done?"

Kimmy blinked in surprise. "What have you done? What have *they* done?" she asked, leaning back and throwing out her hands. "Reyse, this isn't okay. What happened to this guy? Is he okay?"

"I don't know," Reyse said thickly, looking up at Corey's slightly blurred image where they'd zoomed in on as much of his face as they could see. It wasn't enough to identify him behind the cap, but Reyse recognized every millimeter of that beautiful smile. "I hope I'm not too late, though."

"Right, that is IT!" Kevin screamed. He stormed in front of the cameras with a couple of big guys standing up to Kimmy's security. Reyse had no idea where they had materialized from. He didn't care.

It was over.

His career, his life, everything he had worked for. It was about to go down the drain. Kimmy looked stunned as her people stood protectively by her and Kevin's goons put their hands on Reyse to escort him from the set.

Reyse twisted in their grip, his eyes never leaving the image of Corey until he'd been dragged from the studio, Kevin's voice screaming in his ear.

He wasn't sure what he'd just done.

Had it been worth it?

He guessed he would find out.

CHAPTER
Twenty-Four

COREY

COREY DIDN'T REALLY WANT A COFFEE. HE WAS JUST NERVOUS and for some reason he had come to the conclusion that a coffee would help him. He'd knocked into a woman on his way into the shop, babbling an apology to her that she didn't even hear thanks to her headphones over her ears. He forgot how to spell his name when the server asked him so she could write it on the cup. Then when the guy handed him the finished drink, Corey almost wished him happy birthday.

All in all, he was kind of a wreck.

He wasn't really sure why. He'd had his interview at Rainbow Roofs last week and it had been fine. Great, even. It had just been an informal chat between Corey and a couple of the management people, then they'd offered him the job on the spot. He'd looked over the offer and was more than happy with the pay and all the surprisingly generous health benefits. As he'd been there the week before he knew where the office was and he wasn't late.

Still, he was all over the place for his first day, his heart banging like a drum in his chest. He tried telling himself it was going to be awesome. He'd gotten a great vibe from the place, after all. But there was a nasty voice in the back of his head that kept suggesting it was all a big mistake. That they didn't mean it. He was going to show up and they were all going to laugh at him because it was all just a big joke.

Corey poured another sugar in his coffee and tried to convince himself that was complete nonsense. But he couldn't seem to quite make himself believe it.

It was hard when he wasn't even sure how offices *worked*. Corey only had TV and movies as references. Did they actually have a water cooler? How friendly was he supposed to be? What did he do if he needed the bathroom?

Corey wasn't the kind of person people wanted around. He had no special skills. And yet these guys had said they'd liked his attitude and saw potential in him. So here he was, about to start his first nine-to-five job.

Shit – should he have bought a box of donuts? What was the protocol here? Was that a new guy thing to do? At Speedy Pete's you just showed up and got a pizza shoved into your hands to deliver. There was no team building or getting to know anyone. How did Corey know if he should have brought donuts or candy or goddamned flowers with him?

They should have hired someone who knew all this stuff already. But they hadn't. They'd hired Corey, and he was out of time.

At nine o'clock on the dot, he and the rest of his coffee jogged up the couple of steps to the multistoried glass-fronted building, finding the button marked 'RRT' and buzzed it, his heart in his mouth. What if they realized he was a dud and kicked him out? What if being bi wasn't gay enough and they kicked him out? What if-

"Come in!" the cheerful southern voice called over the intercom. The door clicked and opened when Corey pressed his hand to it. All right. There was no going back now.

He jogged up a couple of stories and headed toward the

door to the left that had the Rainbow Roofs logo emblazoned on it. Before he could worry about knocking or awkwardly making his way inside, it jerked inward, revealing a young blonde woman with green tips in her braided pigtails, black glasses, overalls and an enormous smile.

"Corey!" she cried. "I'm Ellie Mae. We didn't meet last week but we're meeting now!" She laughed and stuck out her hand. Once Corey shook it, she bounced back and ushered him into the open-plan office. "Well, come on in. I'm so glad we were able to find a new guy so fast. Orchid said she didn't even get a chance to advertise for anyone yet you popped up like a prayer on Sunday. It's like the universe brought you to us!"

She scrunched up her button nose and placed her hand on the small of Corey's back to lead him toward the kitchenette. She was almost a foot shorter than him, but her enthusiasm made her seem much bigger.

"Did you find the place okay? Can I get you a coffee? Oh, no, you already have one. How about a slice of pizza?"

"Pizza?" Corey blurted.

Ellie Mae giggled. "I know right? For breakfast? Hamish always gets a couple for us on a Wednesday morning, on account of us generally doing karaoke on a Tuesday night and being a little fragile after. He wants to make us all fat." She waved to the director Corey had met last week. "Lurve you, Hamish!" she cried in a singsong voice across the office.

Corey's gut twisted at seeing the pizza boxes. It was so dumb, but it just made him think of Reyse now. His coffee churned in his stomach and he dropped the rest of the cup into the trash. He wished he had brought that box of doughnuts now.

Hamish waved back to Ellie Mae, then spotted Corey. "Oh, hey," he said and began making his way over. Several other people looked Corey's way as well. Some of them he recognized, others he didn't, but they all smiled and looked generally welcoming. The knot in Corey's chest eased a little. Maybe he was going to be okay.

There were probably about fifteen people sitting at various desks with room for half a dozen more. Everyone was partitioned into cubicles short enough that everyone could still see over the top when they were sitting down. The foot-high borders gave people places to stick knick-knacks with colorful pushpins. It immediately made the room feel more homely.

At the end of the room was a large meeting space with a long table, sectioned off from the rest of the office with a wall half made of brick, the top half glass. Next to that were three bathrooms. One was marked 'differently abled' and all three were gender neutral.

A small detail, but it immediately put Corey at ease. This was an inclusive place, through and through.

Hamish was a slim, petite guy, although he was a wiry kind of small with defined biceps peeking out from his baggy T-shirt. He also wore glasses, frameless ones unlike Ellie Mae, and had a nose ring and bright smile. He was probably late thirties, but he had a youthful energy about him that could have easily made him in his twenties if it weren't for the slight laughter lines and confidence with which he carried himself.

He approached Corey with his arm outstretched and pumped Corey's hand twice. "So nice to see you again, dude," he said. He was one of those true Californians who called everything and everyone 'dude' – from his friends to his houseplant to his stapler. "I see you survived an Ellie Mae attack."

"Oh, hush, you," she said. She slipped her hands into her enormous overalls pouch and rocked back and forth. "I'm a darlin'."

Hamish snorted. "We keep trying to ship her back to Georgia, but it isn't working."

"Try harder," Ellie Mae sang, skipping off into the belly of the office.

Corey noticed several people were half watching them with amusement, as if they were used to little shows being put on by certain members of staff. It made feel Corey feel even more at ease.

"Now, don't worry," Hamish said. He poured a coffee for himself from the percolator. "We'll break you in gently."

"Speak for yourself," a voice piped up. A redheaded guy waggled his eyebrows at Corey.

Hamish rolled his eyes and steered Corey into the bullpen. "You can *definitely* ignore Lucas. He's from Canada."

"Oi!" Lucas cried, throwing a balled-up piece of paper Hamish's way. Hamish deftly dodged it.

"Pick that up, Lucas," he said cheerfully without looking over his shoulder. Several people chuckled while Lucas huffed and trudged his way over to fetch up the paper ball.

"So, you guys are, like, from all over the place?" Corey said, looking around.

Then he froze.

Now he could see more people's cubicles, he realized over half of them had almost identical pictures and articles printed out and pinned to their walls.

They all featured Reyse Hickson.

A cold sweat sprung over Corey's body. Was this some sort of sick fucking joke? Did they *know?*

"You guys, uh, like Below Zero a whole lot, huh?" he said, trying to sound casual. But his alarm was probably showing on his face judging from the way Hamish looked at him in concern.

Hamish raised his eyebrows, then looked around himself. "Oh," he said as he realized, smiling broadly. "No, we're just fucking stoked, dude. I mean, what a legend, right?"

"Sure," Corey said reluctantly. It seemed odd they would all have very similar pictures up of him, not a variety. Reyse looked to be sitting with Kimmy Kovac on her show. It hurt to see Reyse like it always did, but to have him plastered everywhere on Corey's first day at work seemed a bit cruel of the universe.

"Y'all have seen the interview, right?" Ellie Mae asked him, popping up over her partition like a meerkat.

Corey felt like he was missing out on some office in-joke. Hopefully they would be kind and let him in on it without too much ribbing.

"What interview?" he asked, genuinely not having a clue. Had something happened on the Kimmy Show?

Several people gasped. "How have you missed it?" the woman Corey recognized from his interview as Orchid said. "It's been everywhere!"

"What, the beach photos?" Corey asked. He was trying not to get defensive. His new coworkers could have *no* idea how close to home they were hitting.

"That was ages ago," someone else piped up.

"Hicks came out as *gay!*" Ellie Mae cried. "Right there on the TV! Bless his heart, he cried and everythang."

"You *have* to see it," said Lucas, typing rapidly on his keyboard, presumably to bring up the video.

"No!" Corey blurted out before he could think. But the idea of seeing Reyse breaking down was too much for him to bear. "Sorry, um," he said sheepishly as people looked at him. "I'd rather not."

"Sorry, man, my bad," Lucas said, holding his hands up.

Corey shook his head. "No worries," he assured him.

He felt like his whole world had tilted on its axis. This couldn't be happening, not after everything they'd been through. Everything they'd lost. It wasn't fair. Fuck – had Reyse really *come out?*

"Wow," Corey said with a nervous chuckle, trying to play it cool when his whole world was falling apart. "Um, so he's gay?" he asked, like it was news to him. "What happened? Is he okay?"

"Kimmy tricked him," a guy piped up from across the room.

"No, she didn't," replied another dude with a slight speech impediment. Corey spotted he had hearing aids and he half signed as he spoke. "He got confused."

"Jack's right," said Ellie Mae, also signing her words as she looked at him. Corey guessed he could hear them okay and read their lips, but the signing was an added bonus. "Reyse was talking about those photos and said the guy was a friend, not a stalker like the official statement said. Then the poor dear just *lost* it when Kimmy asked which was the truth."

"I mean, the dude didn't shave his head or anything," Hamish agreed, nodding his head. "But it was a pretty significant meltdown."

"Oh," Corey said. "Damn."

It felt like little fissures cracked down his heart. He hated to think of Reyse in that situation. He'd obviously got confused, like Jack had said. If he'd been telling his family and maybe other friends that Corey was a friend, he probably forgot the stalker lie he was supposed to spin to match Kevin's.

But neither of those were true. Corey was neither a crazed fan nor a casual buddy.

He was Reyse's, body and soul.

What had Reyse gone through, live on air? After almost a decade in hiding, he'd slipped up.

Because of Corey?

No, not really. Indirectly. Because of the situation Corey

had put him in by sleeping with him. He'd accidentally outed himself and possibly ruined his career. He'd finally told the truth, but at what cost? Corey tried to be happy that Reyse was potentially free after all this time, but worry ate at his guts.

"Hang on," Corey said suddenly. "What about Sun City Records? His label?"

"They sound like real jerks," Orchid said, crossing her arms and shaking her head.

"I heard Hicks is already suing them for the rights to his music," Lucas said, his green eyes wide.

"It got real nasty, *real* fast," Ellie Mae agreed.

"What about the guy?" Corey asked, his heart in his mouth. "Who is he?"

"Nobody knows, sugar," Ellie Mae said.

"He's a mystery," Jack added with a *'woooh'* sound, like a ghost.

"It looks like he's out of the picture now, from what Reyse said," Lucas added with a shrug.

Corey's heart dropped. Any hope he'd had that this had been inspired by him faded away. No. This was the way it should be. He'd done it. He'd actually done it. Reyse had come out. For himself.

Corey wished it had been with him at his side, but he was happy for him nonetheless.

Hamish gave a rueful smile and shook his head. "Still, it's incredible for someone like that to publicly state that they're gay. Hopefully, when things die down, he'll be an incredible role model."

"Oh, honey, he already is," Lucas said, pretending to faint and he touched his fingers to the picture of Reyse he had pinned up by his desk.

The chorus of laughs made a good segue for Hamish to finally lead Corey through the rest of the bullpen and show him to his cube. He began by sitting with him to log on to the relatively new PC that was going to be his and start looking around the system. They were going to start him on some light admin work for the office before they got him doing anything with the promo, but Corey was fine to go slow with some mindless photocopying tasks.

His head and heart were completely full of Reyse.

He wasn't sure he could bring himself to watch Reyse go through that pain. It was probably best if he didn't go find the interview online. Corey ached to reach out to Reyse, to comfort him in what had to be one of his greatest hours of need.

But Reyse's life was complicated enough. He'd accidentally tripped himself up and been caught out in the lie his manager had spun for him. He now had to pick up the pieces and fight those assholes for the rights to his life's work. Who knew if he'd recover from this?

He didn't need Corey confusing things further. The press was probably camped outside his apartment. Corey couldn't exactly drive over there again and make a grand gesture in case they caught him and uncovered his identity. What if Reyse didn't want that?

They'd agreed it would just be a dalliance while Reyse had been home, after all. Now he was out as gay, he could date some other famous person. The blogs were probably already pairing him off with movie and sports stars. It would do nothing for Reyse's image to date a nobody like Corey.

No. It was best to leave things as they were. For what his new colleagues had just said, Reyse had a nasty court case on his hands to get the rights back to his entire back catalog, just like he'd feared he would. His whole life was up in the air.

He didn't need Corey making any more trouble than he already had.

Corey swallowed and tried to focus on his computer. His

and Reyse's lives had already been drifting further and further apart. This was like an exit on the interstate. Reyse was gone beyond where Corey could reach him now.

It was for the best, he told himself firmly. This was what Reyse deserved, to finally be free. True, it hadn't come without consequences, but it was still the right thing. Corey was happy for him, he was.

He just wished he could be happy for himself, too.

CHAPTER

Twenty~Five

REYSE

Joey: OMFG DUDE R U OK??????????????

TJ: Who? What?

Blake: Joey, calm down, don't scare people like that x But Reyse ARE you okay?

Raiden: What's happened to Reyse?

Joey: How have you not seen the internet??

Raiden: OMG

TJ: Dude

TJ: Congratulations

Joey: Yeah, it's totally awesome, FUCK Sun City, it's about damn time. But that was pretty extra. What's happening????

TJ: We're here for you buddy

Blake: Absolutely. Anything you need.

Raiden: I see Sun City are being fuckers as usual. We've got your back bro. How are you feeling?

Raiden: Also GRATS! WELCOME TO THE QUEER CLUB!

Raiden: Although I guess you were here first xx

Joey: Please tell us you're okay Reyse

TJ: Wow. Twitter has gone nuts

Blake: Yeah but a lot of it's good!

Joey: Reyse

Joey: Reyse

Joey: REYSE REYSE REYSE REYSE REYSE

Joey: I can see you've seen the chat. ARE YOU OKAY???

Reyse: I'm okay guys. Thank you xxx My head's a mess. I'll talk to you soon. Love you x

Joey: LOVE YOU TOO

Blake: Stay strong buddy

TJ: Hugs, my man x

Raiden: Don't let the bastards grind you down

Reyse looked over the conversation again in the band group chat, feeling numb. That had been three days ago and he still hadn't talked to the guys.

Luckily, hardly anyone had his private number, otherwise he was sure his cell would have been ringing off the hook. But the silence was almost worse, even with the blowout from Sun City still sounding in Reyse's ears.

Kevin hadn't stopped screaming at Reyse the entire drive back to the label's headquarters where he proceeded to haul him in front of the managing board. Namely, three dusty old suits who still thought of Elvis as 'too much.' The rest of Below Zero had always referred to them as 'see no evil, hear no evil, speak no evil.'

Reyse really couldn't remember much of what they'd said, he'd been so shell-shocked. He did recall the spark of joy he'd felt at finally defying them and the rush of adrenaline at laying his heart on the line for Corey. But that faded as reality came crashing down on him.

They had been deadly serious in their threats all these years. They were dropping him like a stone and they would contest any claim he made over the music he'd produced with them. Which, aside from a couple of collaborations and any songs recorded for soundtracks, was his entire back catalog.

It had seemed worth it for a few hours, their livid shouts and condescending sneers washing over him like water off a duck's back.

But then he'd been cut off and kicked out, left with nothing much to do but go home to his empty apartment... and wait.

His agent was the busiest she'd been in years. Sun City had done all the work for a long time in representing him and Kevin had kept a cast-iron grip on all his publicity. But now Martha had her work cut out for her as she'd suddenly become the one and only option for getting in touch with Reyse Hickson.

Apparently, unlike Reyse, her phone had been going nonstop the past three days with people clamoring to book him for interviews on TV, radio and online. However, so far Reyse had refused everything. Martha was probably cursing his name. But he had no idea what the hell to even tell himself, let alone the world.

Why had he done it? For himself, to finally be true to who he was?

Or for Corey?

In retrospect, it seemed like a pretty dumb thing if it was for someone else. Who the hell wanted to deal with this media frenzy? Who wanted to ruin their life when he and Reyse hadn't even worked out if they were compatible to date, let alone for a public gay relationship with people dogging them at every step?

Reyse rubbed his face and looked over to the paintings on his apartment wall from where he was lying on his couch. They had always made him think of a blazing sunset on a beach. Now all he saw was his and Corey's last night together, making love in the sea.

He was pathetic. He hadn't left his home in three days because he was terrified Corey might come to find him like he had last time and he'd miss him. With no other way to contact him, Reyse was being held hostage by the *slimmest* possibility that Corey might still want him.

Tragically, the last thing Reyse had asked for – demanded – from Kevin was Corey's address where he'd sent the restraining order to. Kevin had snarled in triumph that they had never actually *filed* the order, just threatened it.

So, there was a distinct possibility Reyse had gambled everything over a ruse that Kevin had used to manipulate him one last time. Now Reyse was hanging around like a lovestruck teenager in an old nineties high school movie, waiting for his crush to throw pebbles at his window.

He rubbed his face and inhaled slowly. He needed a plan. Life went on without Corey, as much as it pained him, and he needed to work out what the hell he was going to do now. Money wasn't an issue, but that was beside the point. Reyse may have had a good number in the bank, but he needed something to *do.* He hadn't been idle once in his entire life. He wasn't about to start now. But if he couldn't perform his songs, what did that leave?

He might have got some comfort from the fact that Sun City had lost the goose that laid the golden egg. But while they still had control over Reyse's music, they were still earning all the royalties. And naturally, since the scandal broke, radio plays and Spotify listens had shot through the roof.

He sighed and wondered if he should eat something. What time was it, anyway? When was the last time he had something to eat? But he wasn't hungry and he could still see the sun shining brightly in the sky, so the drive to move faded away.

He checked his phone again. He *wanted* to message the guys, but he had no idea what to say. *Congratulations! You were right all along! I'm gay but was too chicken shit to tell you face-to-face!*

Reyse wondered what his life would have been like if he'd been like Joey and been out from the start. He wouldn't have had a solo career with Sun City, that was for sure. But what if he'd been able to sign with another label? An LGBT-friendly one. Were there even any labels out there that were openly queer?

The ping of his private elevator scared the ever-loving crap out of him. People couldn't get in without his permission, so who the hell was this? Within half a second, he'd jumped to his feet and was looking for something to fend off any deranged reporters or fans that had slipped through security.

Or what if it was Corey?

He barely had time to finish the thought when a loud bark snapped his attention back to the opening doors.

"Aunt Evangeline?" Reyse spluttered.

Evangeline swept from the elevator and into Reyse's apartment, her long dress billowing behind her as she whipped her sunglasses from her face. Smoky-painted eyes assessed the main living area from under a large sunhat as her glossy, cherry-red lips pursed.

"Yes," she said with an air of surprise. "This is actually very lovely."

Foofy squirmed from the crook of her arm, launching herself onto the floor and scrabbling over the wooden boards to sniff at everything that came in her path. Reyse looked between dog and owner, completely lost for words. Then he remembered his manners.

"I wasn't expecting you," he spluttered, rushing to the fridge. He had no idea what he had. He was just grateful at this moment that he had pants on. "Would you like some water or coffee?" Evangeline gave him a long-suffering sigh, rolled her eyes, then locked on him with a piercing glare. "Vodka?" he tried again.

"Good boy," she said with half a smile. Then she lowered herself down on the sofa and continued to look around Reyse's home. "I trust they're not fleecing you for this?" she asked as Reyse fixed her a cosmopolitan. "As nice as it is."

Reyse managed a smile. "No, it's fine," he promised. For what it was, it was actually a pretty reasonable price. Besides, his definition of 'reasonable' was vastly different from other people's. "Uh, so…"

None of his family had called once the news had broken. For a while, Reyse convinced himself that they were just busy looking after his dad and hadn't seen the story yet. But as one day turned into another, he knew that *someone* in that busybody neighborhood *must* have seen something and run over to tell his mom.

The fact she hadn't contacted him broke Reyse's heart all over again.

"Oh, like this was a conversation that could be had over the phone," Evangeline scoffed, snapping her fingers for her cocktail. "Um, I'm not drinking alone," she said, shaking her head as Reyse handed it to her. "Go on, back you go and don't return until you have something far stronger than a beer in your hand."

Reyse's felt his lips twitch in a reluctant smile. First, he set a dish of water down for Foofy (who sounded like she was exploring the underside of Reyse's bed). Then he set about making a large jug of cosmos, because Evangeline had already almost finished her first glass and he had a feeling he might need some liquid courage for this conversation.

"Dear lord, stop moping and come over here to toast with me already," she demanded as Reyse picked up the pitcher and his own martini glass. She broke into a big smile and beckoned him over to where she had taken over his sofa, lounging like a star of the silver screen. "Come on, come on!"

She was practically bouncing in excitement, which made Reyse a little confused but also relieved. That was better than a face like thunder. He sat himself down and poured his own glass, offering it up to Evangeline to tap with her own refilled drink.

"Thank *fuck* for that!" she cried in utter glee. "Cheers, you big queen. It's about *time*."

Reyse was too stunned to move. He just froze while she clanged their glasses against one another, almost sloshing the drink over the sides onto his couch. Then she took a long sip, her lip gloss imprinting on the side of the glass.

"You *knew?*" he finally spluttered.

At that, Evangeline did actually spare him a look of sympathy. "Oh, darling," she said with a sigh. "Of course. I've been dying to tell you to fuck the whole miserable lot of them. But it wasn't my place and you simply had to go at your own speed. But now!" She shimmied her shoulders and batted excitedly at his leg. "Now it's all out and wonderful and-" She stopped as if something had just occurred to her. "Where's Corey? Why were you all crestfallen when I came in?" Her expression turned scandalous. "If you tell me he's not here-"

"He's not," Reyse interrupted before the pain in his chest could get any worse.

"Well, why the hell *not?*" Evangeline cried, slamming her drink down and looking around, like that might somehow make Corey materialize. "When you didn't phone us I assumed it was because the two of you were too busy going at it like rabbits!"

Reyse carefully placed his glass down. If he was honest, it hadn't even *occurred* to him that he should have called his mom first.

"I haven't seen him since the day we left the house. Separately," he added. "I don't have his number and he's not online, as much as I've tried to find him. I have no idea where he lives. He knows where I live. So…"

"Oh, you poor dear," Evangeline said heavily. "You've just been sitting here, hoping." She shook her head. "You know pining is dreadfully unbecoming."

Reyse offered her a small smile and picked his drink back up again. The alcohol was already helping to decrease his fucks, even just artificially and temporarily. "I'm not sure what else to do. About anything, not just Corey."

Evangeline frowned and also picked up her glass again, swirling it and narrowing her eyes at him. "Forgive me, darling nephew, but you *are* one of the most famous people on the planet, correct?"

Reyse rolled his eyes. "Well, when you put it like that," he mumbled.

"Come on," she said cheerfully with a twirl of her wrist as she got to her feet. "Let's get this to go."

"Get this…" Reyse said faintly, then looked around. "This isn't a restaurant. And I can't *go* anywhere."

"If you're worried about Corey, leave instructions with your doormen," Evangeline insisted, knocking back the rest of her drink. "They really are *very* good. I had a dreadful fight on my hands to convince them I was family and get them to let me up here." She grinned and winked. "It was worth it for the look on your face."

Reyse chewed his lip. Actually, that wasn't a bad idea. He trusted the staff here implicitly – they were paid enough to be discreet as well as just being genuinely nice people. He *could* leave instructions with them if Corey were to turn up.

He shook his head. "This isn't just about Corey. I need to work out what the hell I'm doing with my life."

"Exactly," said Evangeline. She had already picked up the still mostly full pitcher and waltzed off into the kitchen. "Ah!" she said, finding a Thermos. "That will do. All right, stop fretting, we can discuss it on the drive there."

"Drive where?" Reyse asked apprehensively.

Evangeline's smile was maddeningly infuriating.

"You'll see," she told him.

Twenty-Six

REYSE

REYSE SHOULD HAVE KNOWN THEY WERE HEADED BACK TO Fort Ladrillo the second the private car turned toward LAX. But he hadn't been thinking straight for days now (or ever, he joked weakly with himself) so it wasn't surprising he missed it.

"Do Mom and Dad know I'm coming back with you?" Reyse asked as their car pulled up.

Evangeline just hummed and poured him some more cosmopolitan.

Reyse was resigned to his fate, though. There was no going back. He was out of the closet and everyone knew it, including his parents. As the jet took off, he tried telling himself there was nothing he could do to alter the facts now. They would react however they were going to react.

At least Evangeline still loved him. Actually, she seemed thrilled about the fact.

"So, you knew about me and Corey, too?" he asked her on the private plane. Sometimes he forgot just how rich *she* was as well, thanks to all her divorces. He was pretty sure she'd made several intelligent investments, too. But she never liked to talk about money. It was 'vulgar.'

She patted his hand as the flight attendant presented them with a very nice bottle of Champagne. The staff were doing an excellent job of pretending they couldn't hear a thing, Reyse felt.

"He's a lovely young man," Evangeline said, not directly answering his question about Corey. She was also being discreet to a certain extent in front of the crew, even if they were purposefully not listening in. Reyse appreciated that. "I'm sure it will all work out."

Reyse didn't share her confidence, but it warmed his heart all the same. Even if he never saw Corey again, he was at least glad to know Evangeline approved of him.

Luckily, the flight was very short. Reyse was feeling decidedly tipsy after mixing vodka with bubbles, and disappointed Evangeline by insisting on 'cheating' by having a bottle of water and a sandwich to line his stomach. But by the time they touched down in northern California he was no longer feeling wobbly.

He was, however, still feeling slightly sick on the drive over. But at that point it wasn't so much to do with the alcohol and more his impending doom.

He had to admit he was thrilled to hear that his dad was well enough that he'd been moved back home. If he was fit enough for that, he must be significantly improved. As apprehensive as Reyse was as to what his dad's reaction to his son's coming out would be, he was overjoyed that his health was improving.

When the front door of his parents' house opened to him, Foofy and Evangeline, however, what little good mood he'd managed to build vanished.

His uncle Dave was on the other side.

Dave didn't say anything, but his look of disappointment

and disgust spoke volumes. He turned, leaving the door open for Reyse to follow with his carry-on. Evangeline sailed straight in like she owned the place, Foofy for once calm in her arms.

"We're back," she called out, plucking her large sunhat from her head and dropping it onto the coat stand with practiced ease.

Dave had stormed off to goodness only knew where, so Reyse wasn't sure where to expect movement from. But his mom suddenly appeared at the top of the staircase, her mouth open in shock.

"Reyse!" she cried clutching her hands to her chest. Cautiously, she came down the stairs, like she was afraid she might scare Reyse off. "Evangeline – you brought him back?"

"I did," agreed Evangeline, like she was acknowledging that she was, indeed, a saint.

His mom tiptoed down the last couple of steps, looking at Reyse like she didn't believe he was really there.

"I'm so sorry, Mom," he said.

His mom surprised Reyse and Evangeline both by flinging her arms around his neck and bursting into tears. Automatically, Reyse patted her back.

"Reyse!" she scolded thickly. "Why didn't you *tell* me?"

Reyse's eyes burned, but he did his best to hold on to his composure. He was done crying. "I'm sorry," he said again.

"I love you no matter *what*," his mom wailed angrily. "You must have been so unhappy, all these years. And Corey! I should have treated him much better!"

Reyse didn't want to talk about Corey. "So, you aren't disappointed?" he asked instead.

"That my boy has been suffering all this time?" she sniffled. "Yes, I am."

"I've hardly been suffering, Mom," Reyse countered. "I've been living my dream."

His mom leaned back and hiccuped at him with big, red eyes. Evangeline huffed by her side. Two sisters, completely different, uniting under a common cause. Reyse would have been honored if he wasn't busy squirming.

"Mom, I'm a *millionaire.*"

"But where's Corey?" she asked. "I saw that interview. You were so upset about him!"

"We're working on that," Evangeline said, coming to his rescue.

Reyse blinked at the two most important women in his life, next to Bella, who he was starting to think of as an adopted sister. "You wouldn't mind if I..." he said, not able to finish the sentence for fear of rejection.

But his mom didn't need him to. "*All* I care about is that you're happy." She wiped under her eyes and managed a small smile. "I think I see now just how happy he makes you."

"Made," Reyse said glumly.

"Makes," Evangeline snapped back with a smug look on her face. "I'm telling you, it'll all work out."

Reyse didn't have the energy to argue. But he still wasn't convinced they were really accepting this as well as they seemed to be. "But, Mom, aren't you upset? I've been lying all this time. And what about grandkids?" She'd mentioned what beautiful babies he and Bella would have many a time.

"Who says you can't have kids?" she asked, apparently genuinely perplexed. "You can get a surrogate, or you can adopt, if that's what you want. Like your friend, Joey."

For a second, Reyse didn't understand what she'd said. "Like my...what?"

Evangeline sighed, loudly. "I appear not to have a drink in my hand," she announced. "This simply won't do." She squeezed Reyse's shoulder. "I'll bring us back a bottle," she told him with a wink.

Reyse nodded faintly as she strode off, Foofy trotting behind her. What was his mom talking about with Joey?

But then he realized. The reason Joey and Gabe had been forced to miss TJ and Ashby's wedding. They'd been in China.

It suddenly occurred to Reyse that maybe that hadn't been for work.

In the time it had taken for his brain to catch up, his mom had already brought up Joey's Instagram, because of course she followed the other guys' profiles, too. There were several photos uploaded already of him and Gabe with a beautiful Asian baby boy and little girl in their arms.

From looking at the dates, Reyse was able to gather that they'd only been back in the US for about a week, so he felt like slightly less of a shitty friend. But only slightly. Damn. He needed to call his friends more often.

He needed to let them *in*. What had been the very last thing he had promised Corey before he'd left? To be a better friend. He needed these guys in his life. They meant so much to him but he'd missed weddings, *fatherhood*. No more. From now on, he was going to stop this isolated crap and start *trusting* people again.

"Oh my god," he said tearfully, taking his mom's phone with a goofy grin. "Joey's a *dad*."

"And you could be too, sweetie," his mom said, wrapping an arm around his waist. "If you want to. Someday."

Reyse did think he wanted that. He'd love to be a father, as terrifying as the idea was.

It made him turn his gaze up from the screen and look up the stairs.

"He'd love to see you, honey," Reyse's mom said.

Reyse couldn't help but scoff. "Really?" he asked nervously.

His mom sighed. She was still hugging him around his

waist, so she moved her hand to rub his arm. "Yes," she said firmly. "I think you guys have some things to talk about."

"And I've brought supplies!" Evangeline announced, coming back up the basement stairs with a popped bottle of Champagne in one hand and three glasses held carefully in the other. Foofy was scampering along by her feet with the bottle's cork in her mouth, her sparkly blue bow bouncing on her head, wagging her tail and looking extremely pleased with her find. When Evangeline saw Reyse and his mom's anxious faces, she stopped and quirked an eyebrow. "Well, you two can have some later, I suppose," she said with an eye roll.

"Come on," Reyse's mom said gently to him. "I promise it will be okay."

Reyse wasn't sure if he believed her. But without any other options, he had to at least try and trust she was right.

At this point, what did he have to lose, anyway?

CHAPTER
Twenty-Seven

REYSE

REYSE LEFT HIS CARRY-ON IN THE FOYER AND FOLLOWED HIS mom up the stairs, Evangeline and Foofy bringing up the rear. The Champagne flutes clinked together, like a musical accompaniment as they made their ascent.

Reyse's parents' bedroom door was open, so Reyse saw before he entered that his uncle was standing over the bed, talking with his dad in hushed tones. Nerves immediately sprung in Reyse's belly. He didn't like the way they both turned to look at Reyse, his mom and his aunt.

"Donny," Reyse's mom said hopefully. "Look who came back."

"I'm not sure why he left," Dave grumbled as they entered the bedroom, folding his arms.

"Because I wasn't welcome here," Reyse snapped, finally sick and tired of his bullshit. He balled up his fists, planting his feet on the carpet and glaring at Dave. "You made that perfectly clear. Once I left home and it wasn't for the Army, I was never welcome back. Well, I'm here now. I know I'm not the son or nephew anyone expected or wanted, but I'm afraid it's the best I can do."

"Reyse, no," his mom cried. Evangeline huffed and plonked her bottle of fizz on the dresser, pouring a glass. Dave folded his arms and scowled at Reyse. Foofy spat her cork out by Reyse's dad's bed and wagged her tail at him.

"You need to have some respect there, son," Dave said.

"I respect people who earn it," Reyse shot back. "You're just a bully."

Evangeline whooped. When everyone in the room turned to look at her, she didn't even look sheepish. She just sipped on her Champagne, swinging her leg where she was perched on the edge of the chest of drawers, and cocked an eyebrow.

"Reyse. Is…is that how you really feel?"

Reyse was surprised to be addressed by his own father. He turned to look at him, propped up in bed wearing new-looking pajamas. He appeared a hundred times better than he had in the hospital, with color in his cheeks and an extra several pounds on his bones. His dog tags were back around his neck, where they should have been.

Reyse frowned and angled himself slightly to face the bed. It was the most direct interaction they'd had in a decade as they looked into each other's eyes. "How I really feel about what?" he asked.

"That you weren't wanted at home," his dad said without missing a beat.

Reyse's skin was clammy and his heart rate was picking up. "Well, yeah," he said. "I know I let you down. I was never…the son you wanted."

"I never said that," his dad replied. "You were never here, when did your mother or I say that?"

Reyse took a second to rein in his emotions. He didn't want to get upset or angry or start throwing accusations.

"You didn't have to," Reyse said as evenly as he could. "We never…what I mean is, whenever you were home, I knew I was a disappointment to you."

For a second his dad just stared at him. Then he shifted in his bed and looked around at everyone in the room, clearly uncomfortable. Donny Hickson had never been one to talk about his feelings. "That ain't it," he mumbled.

"It's okay, Donny," Reyse's mom fretted. She sat beside him and took his hand. "Don't exert yourself now."

"No, no," Reyse's dad said, frowning. "Getting knocked on your ass like that makes a man think. I reckon there are some things that might need saying here."

"Donny, you don't need to apologize for anything," Dave said incredulously.

But Reyse's dad shook his head. "Maybe I do," he said. He glanced at Reyse, making Reyse's skin run hot and cold all at once. His dad was going to apologize to him? "How were you a disappointment to us? I never...I couldn't provide for you and your mom enough. Never knew how to talk to you. Then *you* were looking after *us*. That ain't the way it's supposed to be. I figured...I figured you were disappointed in *me*."

"Donny?" Dave scoffed.

"Shh, let them talk," Evangeline snapped.

Reyse's throat felt like it was full of oatmeal. He tried to swallow as he flexed his fingers and attempted to make himself stop shaking. "I never, *ever* thought that," he said. "I know you wanted me to go into the Army and it killed you I didn't-"

"What nearly killed me was that damn stroke," his dad interrupted. He chewed on his lip, pausing to drink some water. He may have been on the mend, but he still looked worn out. "Yeah," he grunted. "Well, that's what a fella thinks when he has a boy, ain't it? It's what Martin's boy did, and Calvin's and Tyronne's. But you weren't like that, right from the get-go. I never knew what to say when all you wanted to talk about was music and dancing and them things."

Dave scoffed but he didn't say anything. Reyse was keenly aware of his mom and aunt watching on too. Jesus, he'd thought it was bad surviving that interview on Kimmy. This was possibly even worse.

"I wanted to come home so many times," he said in little more than a whisper. "But whenever I did, I felt like you couldn't wait for me to go. Like you were embarrassed by me."

"No, Reyse," his mom chipped in tearfully.

But his dad shrugged. "You always talked about your fancy life. Like it was so much better than all this. I figured you wanted to get back there." He chewed his lip again, not meeting Reyse's eye. "It would have been kind of nice to have you around, though. I guess."

"Absolutely," Reyse's mom cried, looking fretfully between the two men in her life. "Sweetheart-"

"I wish you'd told us," Reyse's dad blurted out. He looked embarrassed, his cheeks going pink as he averted his gaze. "About...about the gay thing. It would have explained a lot."

Reyse was aware of Dave still looming nearby with his arms crossed. Reyse hadn't planned on having this discussion with him around. But then, he hadn't planned on a lot of things.

"I didn't think you'd approve," he said quietly, amazingly keeping his voice steady and his emotions at bay.

His dad nodded, pulling at the comforter over his legs and looking like he was thinking things over. "I won't lie, it would've been a shock. But, well, I get why y'are why y'are now."

"Dad," Reyse said patiently, trying not to get riled. It was very important to acknowledge the olive branch his dad was offering him, but it wasn't right. "Gay guys can be tough and sign up to the military. Straight guys can like the arts and be effeminate."

Dave snorted.

"Be *quiet*, Dave," Evangeline said, her voice pure ice. Reyse glanced at them both, but neither looked like they were going to say anything further.

His dad sighed. "Is it bad if that helps me, though?" he asked. He seemed genuine. "If it would have helped me back then? I thought...I thought I'd been a bad dad, letting you down. Not been there enough all these months I was away. It felt like you were choosing all that singing and dancing over your family...I guess that seems pretty dumb in hindsight."

"No," Reyse said sympathetically. He took a step closer to the bed. "No, Dad. I get it. But...this is the way I was born. I always knew I would never in a million years been cut out for armed combat. I wanted to help the world in a different way. My way."

Dave scoffed again.

"I said-" Evangeline snarled.

"Oh, come *on!*" Dave exploded, flinging his arms out. Reyse's mom flinched. Foofy jumped to all fours, her hackles raised as she barked at him. "You're going to let him talk to you like that, Donny? After all this embarrassing fucking *shit?*"

"How have I embarrassed you?" Reyse demanded, balling up his fists to try and control his anger.

"By running around like a fucking fairy," Dave sneered, grimacing in horror. "Whoring yourself out for teenage girls. Bawling your eyes out on fucking TV like a goddamned sissy! Telling the whole world you suck cock!"

"Dave!"

Everyone looked at Reyse's mom, stunned. She'd leaped from the bed to her feet, doing a remarkable impersonation of Foofy. Now Reyse's mom was staring daggers at his uncle as tears ran down her face.

"You *will not* speak to my son like that!"

Reyse couldn't believe what he was seeing or hearing.

Dave didn't appear as impressed, sadly. He curled his lip and flung his hand toward Reyse. "Tina, the kid's out of control! This is what happens when you mollycoddle boys!"

"My name is Clementine," she snapped back, her voice shaky but loud. "And my son is an *international pop sensation and gay icon.*"

"Oh, bravo, yes," Evangeline cheered, saluting her sister with her glass. "Tell him, darling."

"Shut up, you *incessant* woman," Dave hissed.

"Dave, calm down," Reyse's dad said firmly.

"Yes, everyone calm down," Reyse agreed. "Shouting can't be good for Dad."

"Oh gosh, yes," his mom cried, sitting back down and taking her husband's hand. "Sorry. I'm sorry, sweetheart."

"If anyone should be apologizing it should be your son," Dave said, glaring at Reyse. "Nobody asked you to parade your perversions around in public. You're a disgrace."

"Actually, Dave," Reyse's dad said, "what was a disgrace was Don't Ask, Don't Tell." He pursed his lips together and shook his head. "I knew a fella back in Iraq that saved me from a land mine. He lost his damn leg." He looked at Reyse. "He also married his own fella a couple of years back. We ask people to offer their lives for their country, then tell them their lives ain't worth shit?" He shook his head again. "That ain't right."

Dave spluttered. Reyse felt tears pricking at his eyes. Was he actually hearing this right? Then he remembered the man with the prosthetic leg in the front room when he and Corey had first come to the house. There had been a man with his hand on his shoulder, if Reyse remembered correctly. Perhaps that was the couple his dad meant.

"So you support this?" Dave demanded. He didn't bother to look at Reyse, just jabbed a hand in his direction.

Reyse watched his dad share a look with his mom. "It don't really matter if I support it or not. It is the way it is, nothing I can do to change it. But…well, yeah. Reyse is my boy. And I'm sorry I haven't really known him all these years."

It was like something broke inside Reyse. He managed to keep a hold of himself enough that only a single tear escaped. But inside his emotions were in turmoil. Maybe his dad *did* give a damn about him.

"Unbelievable," Dave cried, raising his hands to the sky. "When Jeremy showed me those photos, I told him to leave it alone. At least before we could all pretend he was normal. Now you're all lost your damn minds."

"Jeremy?" Reyse said, swinging from one kind of utter disbelief to another. "*He* gave Dez Starr those photos?"

"He said that little dickhead friend of yours was a faggot," Dave said smugly, "so he wanted to-"

"*Get out.*"

Reyse turned back to his dad. His face was an expression of pure fury.

"Dave, I mean it. Get out. If you're going to call my son those kinds of words-"

"I didn't!" Dave protested.

"Do you disapprove of my son being gay?" Reyse's mom demanded.

"Well," Dave said, letting out a breath and rolling his eyes. "Who the hell is going to be pleased at that kind of news?"

"Me," said Evangeline, hopping to her feet. "Because it means he can stop living a heartbreaking lie. Besides, if it weeds out hideous little homophobes like you, all the better." She grinned like she was at a party. "So, off you trot. We've had quite enough of you."

Dave scoffed and turned to his brother. "Donny," he said.

But Reyse's dad shook his head, looking pained. "Dave, I

think it's best you pack your bags and head home. We can talk about this if you're willing to listen, but I need time with my son right now. I can't have you yelling at us all."

Dave opened his mouth like he was going to protest further. But Foofy shot forward and began barking nonstop at him. Every time she yapped, her whole small body jerked and her sparkly blue bow wobbled, her cloud of fluff rising and falling. *Bark! Bark! Bark!*

With every jump she made forward, Dave took a step back.

"Call her off!" he shouted at Evangeline.

Evangeline grinned and took another sip of Champagne.

Once they got to the door's threshold, Foofy stopped moving, but continued to bark. Dave looked between the dog and the four people left in the bedroom. When it was clear none of them was going to help him, he stormed off down the corridor, presumably to pack his bag.

The second he was gone, Foofy calmed down as if nothing had happened. She scampered back to Evangeline and dropped on her butt, scratching behind her ear and making her fur even more staticky.

"Urgh, that's much better," Evangeline said cheerfully. She strolled over and pushed the door shut with a little more force than was probably necessary. Then she went back to where she'd left the Champagne bottle to top herself up and fill up the remaining glasses.

Reyse pressed his fingers to his closed eyes, then blinked a couple of times. He couldn't really believe any of what had just happened. But he didn't care about his uncle or his childish tantrum.

He cared about his parents.

Evangeline pressed a glass of bubbly into his hands and also handed one to Reyse's mom. "Now, come on," she said in exasperation, looking around the room. "You all need to cheer up, lickety-split! Reyse is *home*, with wonderful news!"

"Well, I did get dropped from my record label and half my fans hate me," Reyse said heavily.

"They do not," Evangeline shot back with an eye roll. "A few hundred hysterical mommies screaming about sinners does not equate half your fans." It was a bit more than that, but Reyse didn't get a chance to protest.

"You got dropped?" Reyse's dad asked. Reyse had to say the outrage in his voice warmed his heart. Of all the ways he'd imagined this conversation going, it wasn't this.

Yes, maybe his dad was processing his being gay by using it to explain his effeminate behavior. If that helped him accept Reyse easier, it wasn't ideal, but it gave them a place to start from.

Reyse was under no delusion that they would ever be the closest father and son. But when his dad grumbled, "That ain't right," and crossed his arms, it made Reyse's heart ten times lighter than it had been in days. Weeks. Maybe even years.

"Okay," Evangeline said thoughtfully, perching on her chest of drawers again. "So, we've solved one problem of three, haven't we, Reyse?" She held up her index finger. "Spoken to Mom and Dad. And I have to say it went rather well. *Utter morons, notwithstanding,*" she muttered at the end.

"Did it?" Reyse asked, looking at his dad. "Are you really okay with this?"

Again, his dad looked uncomfortable, shifting on the bed. "Well, I can't say I get it all, son," he said shaking his head. "It seems…unnatural to me, two guys kissing and, well…" He got even redder. "Other things. But I don't reckon I need to, do I? Like when a fella's Jewish or a what-do-you-call-em? Vegan? It's not for me, but…well, that's okay, I guess?" He looked up hopefully at Reyse. "If I can be buddies with guys like that, I can get along with my own son, dontcha think?"

Reyse swallowed, but he wasn't quite able to get rid of the lump in his throat. He stepped closer to the bed, on the opposite side from where his mom was perched. He didn't feel able to reach out his hand, so he rested it on the comforter instead, his glass dangling awkwardly from his other hand.

"I can't say I understand how anyone could fire a gun at another human being," he said, afraid to voice his feelings after all these years of hiding them away. But if his dad could be honest, so could he. "But I have enormous respect for the kind of bravery that takes. The amount of training and skill, too."

He wasn't able to look his dad in the eye, so he kept his gaze on his fingers. Therefore, it was easy to spot his dad reaching out and clasping his hand tightly. Reyse bit his lip and looked up.

"I'm sorry, son," Reyse's dad said. It sounded a million times better than when Dave called him 'son.' "I think maybe we've both been a bit thickskulled over the years. But…you were a kid. Your old man should have known better."

Reyse wasn't sure if it was a laugh or a sob that escaped his throat, but he knew he was smiling. "That doesn't matter," he said. "Not if we can move forward now."

His dad nodded. "I'd like that."

"Good, good!" Evangeline cried. It was like she'd taken it upon herself to be their cheerleader for the evening, constantly bringing the mood back up. She ran around the bed and hugged her sister's shoulders, making Reyse's mom laugh. "Like I said, problem one tackled, done, fixed. Now for problems two and three!"

"What are problems two and three?" Reyse's mom asked.

Reyse sighed. "Well, I don't know where Corey's gone. It's like he'd dropped off the face of the Earth."

He watched as his parents' eyebrows raised at the same time. It would have been funny if it wasn't sad.

"Is Corey your…boyfriend?" his dad asked with some difficulty, letting Reyse's hand go. Reyse was still proud of him, though. This was a lot for him to take in.

"I hoped he would be," he said, swirling his drink around in the glass, then taking a mouthful. "We were…together. But after those photos…"

"Damn Jeremy and all these busy-bodies around here," Evangeline spat. "He was so desperate to get in your knickers, Clementine, I bet he was willing to do anything."

"What?" Reyse's dad snapped.

"Are you serious?" Reyse's mom asked. "No, no, surely not."

"Oh, yes," Evangeline said to her with a huff. "I'm sure he thought you'd be upset and come crying to him while Donny was out of the picture. I spotted the slime on him right away."

Reyse fumed. It wasn't even someone trying to make some money. This guy had ruined his life trying to make a play for his mom?

Maybe not ruined, he hoped now. But certainly drastically altered the course of it.

Reyse's mom scowled and held his dad's hand between her two smaller ones, her drink placed on the nightstand. "Well," she said, puffing out her chest. "That's the last brunch I ever invite him around for."

Reyse got the feeling that in this neck of the woods, that was the deepest insult she could offer him.

Evangeline waved her hands. "Honestly, darling," she said to Reyse. "I really believe that one will sort itself out. Besides, what did I say about moping?"

"It's unbecoming," Reyse recited with a sigh.

"Exactly," she said. "Corey's not going to come back to you if you're just sitting around feeling sorry for yourself. Which brings us back to problem number three."

"What do I do now?" Reyse agreed, taking another drink. "It's going to be a while before this court case gets up and running. I have lawyers on it, but if I can't sing…"

"All this because the label doesn't like you being gay?" Reyse's mom said, shaking her head. "It seems cruel. I'm sure there are *plenty* of gay people in the music industry. There always is in the creative arts, right?" Reyse nodded in agreement. "Well, it seems unfair that there are people out there holding them back, knocking them down. Where are the people helping them up?"

"What did you say?" Reyse asked, a thrill shooting up his spine. "What was that?"

His mom looked uncertainly at his dad. But his dad nodded in encouragement. "Well," she said carefully. "You'd think with so many gay people these days – I mean look at your old band for a start – there would be more producers or – what did you call it? A label? – out there waving the rainbow flag."

Reyse placed his glass down and gripped his hair with both hands. "Mom, you're a genius," he rasped.

"I am?" she said, not sounding convinced.

"Of course you are, darling," Evangeline said. Then she turned to Reyse. "How so?"

"*An LGBT label,*" Reyse said. "A place for queer artists and producers and writers and DJs and booking agents – whatever! They can all come together and network and support each other!"

"That sounds terrific," Reyse's dad said. "Who are they, then?"

"They don't exist yet!" Reyse said. "I'm going to start it! I already have the Below Zero guys, I bet they would jump at the chance to support something like this. And I could ask… yes…and…oh…"

His brain was running at a million miles an hour. This could work. He didn't need to find a new label. *He could start his own.*

He hadn't even noticed Evangeline come over to him, but he looked when she wrapped her arm around his shoulders. "Yes, Ricky. *Yes.*"

Ideas were flying through his mind too fast. But his train of thought went something along the lines of having ostracized himself from the community, it was now time to give something back. Big time.

"I'm going to start a new queer label," Reyse said out loud, affirming it for himself and his family. "And I know *just* how to kickstart it."

Evangeline was right. He couldn't mope around hoping Corey might find his way back to him. He was going to tell the world just how proud he was of his community. He was going to shout it from the rooftops. Not for Corey, but for *himself.*

And if him finally coming out and being proud of who he was led Corey back to him, well. That would be the greatest gift he could imagine. He would just have to hope the universe was kind to him.

In the meantime, he had work to do.

Twenty~Eight

REYSE – ONE MONTH LATER

"Oh my god!" Kimmy cried, hanging off Reyse's arm in excitement as they moved through the relatively empty Exposition Park. Soon, this place would start filling up with tens of thousands of people. But for now, in the calm early morning, there was still just the vendors setting up. "We got the rainbow cotton candy machine!" Kimmy squealed.

"We did," said Reyse happily.

He couldn't say *who* exactly had organized that. They had pulled hundreds of people together to make such a large event happen in such a short time. The past few weeks had been one giant whirlwind of activity, and although he was exhausted beyond belief, he couldn't be happier.

Well, he could. But he did his very best not to dwell on that.

There was a whole lot of work that went into setting up a new music label and signing artists to it. But in the meantime, Reyse had gone all out and organized a one-day queer music festival right in the heart of LA. Exposition was a perfect location with the cityscape in the background and the streets thrumming around all four sides of the square-shaped park. As far as he was aware, his festival was the first of its kind in California. Having sold sixty thousand tickets in less than twelve hours, it was certainly the biggest.

It had taken some time to settle on a festival name. But in the end, Reyse had gone with Iridescence. That was the name of the phenomenon when light passed through ice crystals at below zero temperatures to create rainbows within clouds. It also sounded like 'dance,' and that was what he hoped everyone did a lot of today.

There was the main stage as people came through the entrance where the headline acts would perform, then three smaller stages situated around the Coliseum stadium, which dominated the center of the park. But due to the sheer number of acts that had come tumbling forward, desperate to support Reyse and his venture, they had also erected a number of tents and marquees for DJs and unknown artists to showcase their work to smaller crowds.

Apparently, Reece wasn't the only one fed up with the homophobic nature of the music industry at large. From chart-topping pop stars to drag acts to musical theater from Broadway itself (thanks mostly to Aunt Evangeline), they had scrambled to accommodate artists from Europe and Asia as well as the Americas.

It wasn't just queer artists either, although there were a surprising number of those. They'd booked several retro acts, some of whom had been gay icons back in the eighties and nineties and had come out of retirement especially for the day. Others were just steadfast LGBT allies.

It was pretty overwhelming when Reyse considered just how many people were on his side. On his whole community's side.

He had been completely blown away at the rate which the festival had grown. It had gone from an idea of just one stage in a field to taking over an entire park. There were dozens of food trucks and pop-up bars, not to mention all kinds of queer merchandise on sale. From rainbow umbrellas to false eyelashes to leather gear to T-shirts, queer vendors had traveled cross-country for the chance to connect with the LGBT community. It was like he'd added a new date to the Pride calendar.

What was even better was that it was all for charity. Yes, he was using the event to launch his label, Clementine Creative, but the majority of the fundraising from tickets was going toward half a dozen charities that Reyse and his new team had selected from all over the state. Reyse had been serious about giving back to the community. There were organizations that worked with LGBT people who were elderly, veterans, homeless, or in need of mental health support as well as a small legal firm that specialized in taking on LGBT discrimination cases pro bono. Reyse and his team had tried to go as far across the board as they could.

A pang tugged at his heart which he did his best to squash down. But, damn. He wished he could share all this with Corey. Despite Reyse's hopes, there had still been no sign of him. It was hard not to think that he didn't want to get back in touch with Reyse, despite him finally coming out. But Reyse had promised himself he could focus his energy on that after today. First, he had a lot of work to do.

"I actually can't believe you did all this in a month," Bella said as she walked on Reyse's other side. She was hand in hand with her new official boyfriend, Tony the tennis coach, who Reyse had to say he liked very much so far. "It's incredible."

"Oh, I had a *lot* of help," Reyse insisted, grinning at Kimmy. She was still acting like a big kid, skipping around looking at all the stalls still setting up.

Kimmy's people had reached out to him immediately after the botched interview, but Reyse hadn't felt able to take the call until after he'd spoken with his family. Kimmy was distraught at what had gone down and was looking for any way to help make amends. When Reyse had suggested partnering up for the music festival, Kimmy had been beside herself with excitement. What was even better was her show had such pull at her network, her bosses had agreed to livestream the main stage performances for them online, reaching audiences all around the world.

"Ohh, look at all the little doll thingys," Kimmy cried. "Oh, oh! And balloons! Ahh, who doesn't love balloons? What's that? Do those people just stand you in a booth and spray you with glitter?"

Reyse looked to where she was pointing. "I think so," he said. "Don't worry, all the glitter here is eco-friendly."

"I *love* it!" Kimmy cried, punching the air.

By the time they made their tour around the Coliseum, it was about time to open the doors and start letting the festivalgoers inside. The sounds of several bands doing sound checks drifted through the late summer's day air. It was going to be a beautiful day.

Reyse would have loved to have experienced the festival for himself, but that wasn't possible. Still, he got to enjoy the VIP area behind the main stage where all the artists and other celebrities and patrons were invited to watch the various stages on projector screens. They also had their own bar and catering as well as trailers for changing and preparing things like hair and makeup.

Reyse was kept company by Kimmy when she wasn't doing any presenting work, as well as Bella and Tony. Reyse was deeply touched his mom and Aunt Evangeline (with Foofy, naturally) had come down to support him. Unfortunately, his dad wasn't well enough for such an excursion, but Reyse knew this wasn't his kind of deal anyway. It was sweet that he'd assured Reyse he was going to watch it on TV, though.

Cautiously, they were starting to build up a bit of a relationship together. Reyse had made an effort to read up on the LA Rams and his dad had been surprisingly insightful in Reyse's legal battle with Sun City Records. One of his ex-Army buddies had been a lawyer with the JAG corps, so hadn't been able to help directly, but had come up with the names of several good firms, one of which Reyse had gone with.

For a few hours, Reyse hung out with old friends from the music and entertainment industry, some of which he hadn't seen for years thanks to his hectic schedule. He also did multiple interviews with various reporters and presenters from blogs, TV shows, YouTube, magazines and newspapers.

He'd been very careful *not* to invite Dez Starr.

But as the evening rolled in, a fizz of slight nerves began to build in his stomach. In some ways, this wasn't any different to what he'd done literally thousands of times before.

In other ways, he had never attempted anything like this in his whole life.

He changed his mind on his outfit twice, fidgeted all the way through makeup, and had to be bullied by Bella into eating a taco. Reyse had been very careful to avoid any of the pizza trucks all day. Evangeline made him drink a Jägerbomb.

Before he knew it, he was heading to backstage and being handed a microphone. It was so weird not having Kevin around, fretting over every last damn detail. As liberating as it was, it also made Reyse feel a little anxious. Had he forgotten something?

He didn't have anything to forget, aside from himself and the mic he was tossing from hand to hand as the current band finished up their performance. Glittergasm was a fierce pop-rock five-piece who had whipped the crowd into a frenzy with their energetic songs. The lead singer, Pearl, was a petite young woman with violet hair dressed like an anime character who simply exuded charisma. Reyse was able to relax a fraction as he watched them perform their last song, the enormous crowd singing along to every word of their biggest hit.

Reyse chewed his thumb. For the millionth time over the past month he wondered if this was a bad idea. Not that there was any chance to back out now, but he still fretted. Was this going to cause more trouble than it was worth?

Making a snap decision, he vowed that was going to be the *last* time he considered jumping through hoops for other people. That was what had gotten him into so many problems in the first place. He wouldn't be fighting with Sun City for the rights to his own damn back catalog if he'd demanded to be allowed to come out in the first place.

He wouldn't have lost Corey if he hadn't been forced to pretend he was straight.

But then…he would never have *met* Corey. If Reyse's past had been so different, their paths would never have crossed. He couldn't stand there and wish for a different life. He had to take control of his future and make it what he wanted. No more jumping through hoops.

The crowd cheered their hearts out as Glittergasm wrapped up their last song and took their bows. Pearl and the girl playing bass walked off the stage hand in hand. Reyse remembered reading somewhere that they were a couple. Pearl stopped in front of Reyse as the crew raced out of the wings to clear the stage.

"We haven't met," Pearl told him.

She sounded remarkably calm considering she had just

done an hour-long, full-on set. Her glittery, shiny makeup still looked remarkably good, too. Reyse was impressed.

Pearl let go of her girlfriend and offered her hand out to Reyse to shake, which he did despite his nerves making him a little clammy. "That was amazing. You guys killed it," he said.

"Yes, thank you," Pearl said, nodding and looking out over where the crew was working as fast as they could. Glittergasm's drummer was hovering anxiously, presumably making sure they treated his kit with care.

Reyse smiled. He'd expected modesty. People liked to tell him they were terrible in comparison to him or get all shy. Pearl's confidence was refreshing.

"I'm glad you put this festival together," she told Reyse, drinking from a bottle of water her girlfriend had fetched for her. The two girls leaned naturally into each other as Pearl spoke to Reyse. It made his heart ache a little. They made a cute couple. "I'm sorry you were forced to come out, but I think it will be good for you in the end. Are you nervous about going out there?"

She jutted her chin out toward the crowd. There were no more performances scheduled for the rest of the evening on any of the other stages. So pretty much the entire festival was cramming in front of the main stage and the massive screens set up halfway down the field.

Reyse rolled his mic between his hands. "Uh," he said. This wasn't the biggest crowd he'd faced. But it was his first time performing as an openly gay man.

What if they turned on him?

"Oh, you are nervous," Pearl said, raising her eyebrows. "Don't be. You're phenomenally talented. Everyone here loves you. Here"- she thrust her water bottle into his free hand -"rehydrate. I'll get another one. Good luck."

Reyse blinked as she threw her arms around him, kissed his cheek and patted his arm.

"Bye," Pearl's girlfriend said with a wave and a sweet smile before they melted into the hustle and bustle of the backstage madness.

Reyse took a long breath in then slowly released it. He followed Pearl's advice and sipped his water. He didn't want to get bloated or have to find a bathroom before going on stage, but he didn't want to get a headache either.

The changeover didn't take all that long. The set had been the same for all the artists all day: two raised circular stages either side of the main stage, a catwalk out into the crowd in the middle, and a white backdrop behind the band. But the instruments had been cleared, leaving the stage relatively empty.

Reyse could go out there now, but he wasn't scheduled for another fifteen minutes. So he just ran over what was going to happen in his mind, visualizing it again and again, attaining that Zen-like state he preferred for performances. By the time the clock ticked around to seven, he felt like he was almost floating, like the good kind of tipsy where you're slightly out of your own body but still in control.

This was where he lived. This was the thing that Sun City couldn't take away from him. For all his doubt and regrets and anxieties, it was in this state he was finally able to admit the truth to himself.

There was only one Reyse Hickson in the world.

He could do this.

They hadn't used the hidden entrance in the floor all day. So when it was time Reyse jogged under the stage and stood on the platform that would rise up once the trapdoor had slid to the side. He gripped the safety rail with one hand and the microphone with the other. People all around him patted his shoulders and told him 'good luck,' 'you've got this,' 'break a leg.' He had sort of expected his mom and Evangeline to be there, but they must have been elsewhere. Reyse's mom had never seen him perform live at a gig of this magnitude before. It was childish, but he'd been really looking forward to her watching from the wings. Hopefully she was close by. At least Kimmy and Bella were there to see him off.

Reyse could tell when the lights changed as the crowd started going nuts before his head even rose above stage level. Background intro music thrummed dramatically, like a heartbeat in a storm.

"Good evening, Los Angeles!" he bellowed as soon as the platform became flush with the stage floor. The roar of the crowd would have been deafening if Reyse didn't have his earbuds in, feeding him the output from the speakers so he got all the levels evenly. He grinned, adrenaline pumping through his body as he stepped forward. He could see the people nearest the front of the sixty-thousand-strong crowd jumping, clapping, punching the air and crying. They were covered in glitter and rainbows and were waving flags from all corners of the LGBT spectrum. It was one of the most joyous sights Reyse had ever seen. "How are you doing tonight?"

Their collective screams and whoops made him laugh.

"I gotta say," he told them, stopping front and center, "this has probably been one of the best days of my life. This festival happened so fast, I had *no* idea we would be able to pull together so many LGBT and allied acts together. I had no idea the tickets would sell out at lightning speed. I think it shows what our community can do when we put our minds to it."

The screaming was becoming fever pitched. Reyse looked out at the crowd – *really* looked. There were people of all ages and colors, parents with kids on their shoulders, butch lesbians, sparkly twinks and leather daddies. This wasn't his regular crowd. These people weren't here for him and his music like a normal concert. They were here for each other.

"None of this would have happened without you awesome people and your support," Reyse cried, throwing his free hand out at the sea of people before him. "I wanna hear you *scream* for each other! I want you to make some noise for all our amazing artists and vendors and sponsors and the charities that work so hard for our community in this beautiful city. I want you to yell and cheer and stamp your feet for all our LGBT family across the world in spirit here with us today!"

The wall of sound was overwhelming. Reyse resisted the urge to step back as he looked over the excited, happy faces stretching out into the distance.

The sun was setting in a glorious blaze of oranges and purples and pinks and reds, reminding Reyse of the final night he and Corey had spent together. In a strange way, it was like Corey was there, right by his side. Reyse smiled, blinking back tears.

Maybe Corey would see this night on his TV and feel through the screen how much Reyse desperately missed him. Reyse didn't want to mention him by name, but he thought maybe he'd tell the world that he loved that man from those photos. Evangeline was determined that the universe would bring Corey back to Reyse, but Reyse didn't see the harm in maybe giving the universe a helping hand.

"You guys," Reyse said with a grin. He shook his head as the heartbeat music continued. "I love you." A chorus of *'we love you too, Reyse!'* boomed back at him. "Well, I guess you might have heard, I'm in a bit of trouble right now with a certain record label we won't mention by name."

The boos made him chuckle. Yeah, Sun City deserved that. He would have felt bad for any artists still stuck with them, but he'd offered to take on anyone who jumped ship for Reyse's label, no questions asked. He wouldn't make anyone come out if they didn't want to as much as he wouldn't force anyone to stay in the closest like he'd had to. But queer or straight, Reyse would take any refugees from Sun City. So he felt okay dragging them as much as his lawyers had told him he could.

"Yeah," he agreed, nodding and walking a few paces to the left of the stage. "They did a bad thing, for sure. But so did I." He continued before they could protest too much. "No, I shouldn't have let them bully me. I should have stood up for myself. Because *I know* there's nothing wrong with being gay or trans, right?" The crowd cheered again. "I also know there are people all over this country – the world – kids in particular who need people to be brave and say 'screw you, this is me!' Because I also know that LGBT values *are* family values. When it comes down to it, all of us deserve to love, to be loved, and to be free."

He gave them a second to cheer while he walked back to the center of the stage, warmth filling his heart to hear people agreeing so wholeheartedly with his words.

"But I'm here today, I'm free and I'm feeling pretty loved," he said with a smile. "And I've got *so* much love for you guys. I'm so lucky to have, like, the best people in my life, you know? A lot of them are here today. Let's give them a cheer as well."

The crowd obediently did, but he could tell it was fractionally less enthusiastic than before. Time to move things along.

"So, I bet you guys are wondering what the hell I'm going to do today if all my music is tied up in legal battles, right?" Again, the mass of people booed and Reyse grinned in appreciation. His heart rate was picking up in anticipation too. He licked his lips. "Yeah, it's a bummer," he said with a chuckle. "I'm not allowed to sing *any* of my songs." He snapped his fingers and frowned. "If only I knew some people who *could* sing them. Oh...wait..."

That was the cue.

He could tell when the lighting changed because there was a sudden, deafening *boom* that echoed across the park. It took the audience about half a second to work out what was going on before the hysterical, frenzied screaming started.

Because the white wall at the back of the stage wasn't a wall at all. It was a screen. And right now, Reyse knew without looking behind him there were silhouettes of four guys being projected against that screen.

The first notes of Hearts Bound came through the sound system and the crowd got impossibly louder. Reyse fought the tears in his eyes as he heard the screen being pulled up, the crowd losing their minds when, for the first time in almost four years, the four men stepped forward, joining Reyse in the center of the stage.

Below Zero finally stood together once again.

CHAPTER
Twenty~Nine

REYSE

Four years. And Reyse didn't just mean on stage. He hadn't even stood in the same room as all these incredible men since Sun City had dumped Below Zero. It seemed right that this should be their big reunion.

The song had a few bars of introduction, so Reyse took a second to look to his left and right, taking in his brothers. They all looked just as fucking stoked as he was.

Blake rolled his shoulders and cracked his neck. Joey grinned like a maniac and danced on his toes. Raiden opened out his arms, egging the crowd on. TJ saluted to the rest of the band, then bowed to the audience.

Reyse wasn't sure how this was going to go. They had only managed a few rehearsals over video conference calls. But there was a reason they'd been bound together all those years ago. As soon as they were all back on stage, the chemistry was undeniable.

Reyse deliberately stooped down and placed his mic in the box that had been left in front of one of the speakers for him, then waved his hands at the audience to show they were empty. Yes, he couldn't *perform* any songs still technically owned by Sun City. But hell would have to freeze over before he could stop himself singing along with the guys. He would just be doing it for himself, with no mic to capture him. The other guys had split his solos between them. But Below Zero was one hundred percent singing together today.

"Hey, girl," the first line began with some simple choreography. *"You know what's on my mind. Hey boy,"* they sang and the crowd gave them an extra loud cheer for changing 'girl' to 'boy.' All the guys had agreed that it was important to make their lyrics more inclusive if they were taking them back from Sun City anyway. *"It's just a matter of time."*

"It's the – the way that you look, and the – the way that you touch. You've got me falling. It's the – the way that you smile, and the – the way that you love. It's our calling. Ohhhhh!"

"Come on, LA!" Joey yelled at the top of his lungs. The guys all had their mics on headsets, so he held his hands up to his ears. "Let me hear you sing!"

"Heartbeat. Time's stopped," the park sang along with Reyse and the guys. *"Take heed. My love. Endless looooove, underground! In our truuuuuth, hearts bound! Oh oh oohh!"*

They'd stuck with the choreography they'd done for this song almost since its release. So it was easy for Reyse and the guys to bust it out for the crowd, despite not having blocked it for this show, or any show in the last four years.

"Oh oh oohh! Oh oh oohh! Oh oh oohh!"

The crowd sang their catchiest-ever hook along with them, deliriously happy. Before Reyse knew it, they'd flown through the next verse and chorus, taking them into the interlude where Blake took center stage for a breathtaking dance solo.

At this point, they were joined by a group of female dancers who would be performing with them throughout their set. It had taken Reyse some time to track down every single girl from that shitty misogynistic video he'd done before he'd flown home to see his family. He wasn't sure what their availability would be, but as an apology he'd wanted to offer them all a chance to come back and perform with him without being treated like meat puppets. It just so happened that the stars aligned and every one of them had made it there that evening, one of them even flying back from Mexico to make it. He'd let them have final say in the design of their own costumes, too.

That was the sense of community Reyse wanted for today and the future of his label. Everyone pulling together to make something truly magical happen.

Once Blake and the girls were done dancing, TJ and Raiden took the vocal solo that Reyse normally sang, ramping up for the final double chorus and end of the song. Pyrotechnics exploded behind them as they hit the final pose, and the stadium erupted in tumultuous applause.

But they were only just getting started.

For the next song, the girls tapped out and Below Zero was joined by five truly gorgeous guys, all of whom identified as queer and weren't wearing much at all. There was a distinctly bass-level cheer that went up at the sight of them. Reyse felt dizzy at what they were about to do and wondered briefly how many networks were about to cut their feed. But if they wanted an LGBT show, they were going to have to put up with some actual *queerness*, like it or not.

They performed 'In the Clouds,' one of their most suggestive numbers, as far as Sun City had been concerned. *"Babe, you're so sweet,"* they sang, *"Up in the clouds or between the sheets."* As they did, each band member paired off with a dancer for some pretty raunchy choreography. It was no more than they'd done with girls on stage in the past. But Reyse saw this as the litmus test as to who really supported them and who would draw the line at such a display.

The crowd ate it up, screaming and cheering and wolf-whistling their hearts out. Reyse felt giddy with daring, his partner feeding off his energy as they danced up a storm.

Seeing as they'd only had a limited amount of rehearsal time, none of which had been together, they had split the set up into various segments between the Below Zero songs. Joey sang his solo song that Raiden had written and he'd produced with Storm Sailor. Blake danced to an old disco number they'd gotten permission to use with Nessa and Karyn from his dance studio show. Reyse had worked with young Karyn in one of his own early videos, catapulting her into the limelight where she'd thrived ever since as an exceptional dancer. TJ did an acoustic version of one of Below Zero's ballads with a British singer-songwriter called Fynn Dumashie and his guitar.

While Reyse couldn't sing anything he had produced as part of Below Zero or his solo career, that didn't stop him from singing *other* people's songs. He stunned the hell out of the crowd (again) by bringing out Lolita Charisma, the pint-sized pop princess with a belter of a voice and signature long ponytail. Reyse swore he spied grown men weeping as one of the biggest gay icons of their time joined him on stage and they duetted her tracks 'Heaven' and 'Gimme What You Got.'

As evening turned into night, the band took a breather, singing a couple of their slower songs like Cherish. They sat on tall stools, and like any respectable boy band, stood up at the key change. Then they segued into Out in the Cold.

"Without your love, you left me out in the cold," Reyse sang with his brothers. *"I broke your heart, you broke my soul. Can we ever make this right?"* It had been an album track on their first release, and not a song they'd really ever performed much. But Reyse had insisted. As he poured his emotion into the words, he thought only of Corey, sitting by his side at his family's piano. *This is for you, baby,* he thought, looking out over the crowd.

If anyone noticed the single tear that ran down his check, they didn't react.

Then it was back to more of their bigger dance hits, building up to the finale where the guys would perform a medley of Reyse's biggest solo songs. It was kind of crazy, hearing his lyrics come out of their mouths as he danced along with them. But it was also immensely touching. They were here, just when he needed them.

He vowed never to shut them out again.

They ended on an epic version of 'Deny Me' with all their dancers, finally coming to the end of the show to close the whole of the first, but definitely not last, Iridescence Festival. Reyse couldn't believe it as he and the guys held hands, taking a couple of bows while the crowd cheered and cheered for them.

They'd done it. They'd really pulled this whole thing off.

Except…

The stage lights were supposed to go dark and they were all meant to file off the stage. But Reyse realized Joey and Raiden weren't letting go of his hands and the lights were still up. Panic flashed through his chest. Did they have another number that he'd forgotten about? They couldn't have. They'd pretty much sang all of Reyse and Below Zero's hits between them.

"Thank you, everyone, thank you," Blake said. He was still holding Joey's hand on Reyse's right, and TJ was on Raiden's other side to the left. Their dancers were standing in rows behind them to create a semi-circle of bodies. "It's been a long journey for all of us to reach this point, and we haven't done it alone. But for a time, Reyse *was* alone. It broke our hearts seeing him struggle. I think now he's realizing just how many people have his back. How many people love him."

Blake and Joey looked down the line at Reyse as a lump

rose in his throat. Glancing right, Reyse saw Raiden and TJ's smiles as well. "Thank you," Reyse said, his words swallowed up before the crowd could hear them by their own cheering. But he hoped Blake heard him through his earpieces.

"Did you guys know some special people from Reyse's life are here?" Blake asked. The crowd cheered.

Blake had obviously been nominated spokesperson for this little stunt of theirs. Reyse's heart swelled. He was so touched that they would do this surprise for him, but it wasn't really necessary. Agreeing to perform was enough for him by a long shot.

But Blake continued addressing the rapt crowd, who didn't look to be dispersing, despite the fact they'd finished singing. They were probably waiting for some big surprise. Reyse hoped they wouldn't be disappointed with whatever the guys had planned. If it was just a bit of chat, they could probably have done that themselves after the show.

Blake nodded to the wings on his left but Reyse couldn't see into the darkness there any more thanks to all the people standing in front of it. He didn't need to, though. He knew what Blake was going to say.

"Reyse's family came out to support him," Blake said out to the tens of thousands listening to him. "We all know what it's like to have people tell you you're not good enough for who you were born as. But Reyse's parents and his aunt are behind him, as is the lovely Bella Dalton. We all love her, right?" The audience screamed, Bella's reputation having been fully restored after Reyse's confession. "Yeah, let's give those guys a cheer. Cheer for all the awesome people in your lives who stick a finger up to homophobic assholes like Sun City."

"*Blake!*" Reyse hissed in horror.

Blake covered his mic and grinned at Reyse. "What?" he asked. Reyse could hear him through his earpieces, which meant they had been able to hear him before. Good. "My dad's a lawyer, let them come for me."

"Reyse, they have this coming," Joey said, also with his mic covered. "They screwed us then they screwed you, now it's finally time to screw them back."

"Eww," Raiden said, making Reyse look left. "I am not fucking Kevin, thank you very much."

TJ waggled his eyebrows. "I wouldn't say no to financial ruin, though," he added.

As the cheers died down, they uncovered their mics and faced the crowd again. "The trouble is," Blake said in all seriousness to them, "when people tell you you're not worthy of love, you start to believe it. Sometimes, it takes finding that special someone to make you truly understand how worthy you are."

The crowd gave him a big 'awww.' Reyse smiled. He assumed Blake was talking about his husband, Elion. In fact, he could have been talking about any of their husbands – Gabe, Levi or Ashby. His brothers were so lucky to have found their soulmates, who were all here supporting them today.

So when Blake and Joey both looked off to the left, Reyse copied them, realizing everyone on stage was currently turning their gaze toward the wings. As expected he saw there was a throng of supporters all standing there, looking eagerly back at them.

Then Reyse froze, all the blood seemingly draining from his body. Sheer habit and professionalism were all that kept him upright, because his brain ground to a halt.

Because there, in the middle of Elion, Gabe, Levi and Ashby, stood another man, their hands all resting on his shoulders as he looked out onto the stage in pure terror.

Reyse stopped breathing.

That man was Corey.

CHAPTER
Thirty

COREY – ONE MONTH PRIOR

"All right, you lot," Hamish cried as he walked into the office. One arm cradled several Speedy Pete's boxes (much to Corey's dismay), his laptop perched on top. He used the other arm to make a lasso motion. "Meeting, now, drop whatever you're doing."

"Oh, shit," Corey said, his fingers pausing above his keyboard.

But Ellie Mae shook her head. "No, it's okay. He's excited, not mad." She pointed at Hamish as he shouldered his way into the meeting room. "If he was mad, there would be no pizza."

Corey wasn't quite sure he believed her, but he followed everyone into the room regardless. He was going to have to get over this pizza issue soon. He'd told the guys in the office he was on a diet, which was no fun at all.

Being so new still, he didn't feel confident taking one of the chairs, so he stood at the back with several other staff members. Ellie Mae took a chair, then inexplicably jumped up and stood by Corey. He frowned at her but she just grinned back and twirled her green pigtail.

"Can't have you all by your lonesome, can we?" she said.

Corey blinked. Was she making sure he didn't feel left out? He swallowed. That was so nice of her.

Sure enough, when everyone piled in, Hamish grinned at them. He didn't sit at the end of the table. Instead, he stood with his fingertips resting on the table top. "So, you know how we're all in love with Reyse Hickson now?"

Corey's stomach flipped. In the week he'd been here, he still wasn't used to people continuously casually dropping his former lover's name. But he *was* Reyse Hickson. This would probably happen for the rest of his life. But right now, it was still so raw and he struggled to hold on to his poker face.

The room sighed and groaned in appreciation. "He's my hero," Jack said, clutching his heart.

Lucas scoffed. "He's been gay for a whole week now and he *still* hasn't called me." He folded his arms. "Daddy's not impressed."

"Like you're anyone's daddy," Orchid shot back with a laugh.

Hamish rapped his knuckles on the table and arched an eyebrow over his glasses. "I have dirt. Are you going to be good boys and girls and enbies, or do I have to get the naughty stick out?"

Lucas definitely opened his mouth to ask for the naughty stick. Jack slapped him upside his head. The rest of the room fell very quiet, but no more so than Corey. He felt like he stopped breathing.

"I have a reasonably long email," Hamish said, gesturing toward his laptop. "When I've dissected it some more, I'll give you the CliffsNotes. But here's the skinny. Reyse Hickson is responding to his dispute with Sun City by setting up his own LGBT Plus record label. To launch this label, he is hosting a one-day LGBT Plus music festival, right here in LA at Exposition Park. He has selected six LGBT Plus charities to benefit from this concert. Can you guess who one of those charities are?"

Ellie Mae screamed, right in Corey's ear, scaring the shit out of him. "Oh my lord, oh sweet baby Jesus. It's us! He's picked us, hasn't he?"

Hamish grinned as the fifteen or so people all packed into the room suddenly became animated with excitement.

All, that was, apart from Corey, who was too stunned to react.

His first thought was that Reyse had discovered where he worked and done some grand gesture. But that didn't make sense. Corey had been very careful that the company hadn't made his hiring public and as he'd deleted what little social media presence he had, people hadn't been tagging him in anything.

Besides, that wasn't Reyse's style. If he'd found out where Corey was, he might have done something dumb like come to find him.

The truth was, Corey kept coming back to the idea that maybe it *might* be okay for him to reach out to Reyse again. He'd even driven past his apartment building a couple of times. But he'd never had the courage to go inside. Last time, they'd happened to meet outside. But Corey couldn't exactly go in there and ask if Reyse was in. What if his security team recognized him as the random pizza delivery guy and called the cops or the press? Corey wasn't sure which might be worse.

Still, there was a part of him that had clung to life, hoping that now Reyse was out the universe might let their paths cross again. And sure enough, here they were. Corey didn't know whether to be cautiously excited or scared. He was regretting the way he'd treated Reyse, cutting him out like he had. He had thought it was for the best, but now he wasn't so sure...

"We're going to have a stall at the festival," Hamish continued, "where we'll be handing out information leaflets, selling merch, making friends, the works. I'll need people to cover it all day, but if we do it in teams-"

"I'll do it!"

Corey realized with a small amount of horror that had been his voice that had blurted out. His hand was also stretched in the air, like an overeager schoolchild answering teacher's question in class. Sheepishly, he slowly retracted it.

But Hamish wasn't mad at him for interrupting. He didn't even look at him funny for his enthusiasm. He just nodded. "Excellent. That's our first volunteer." He opened the boxes of pizza and pushed them to the center of the table. "Help yourselves. Right, who else? Let's get this schedule sorted."

People came forward and put their names down, asking about times and how much they would see of the festival. Corey didn't care about any of that. He'd stay there from dawn until dusk. The chances of him running into Reyse were minuscule. But, as much as he tried not to be superstitious, it was difficult not to take this as a sign.

He looked down at the various pizzas. For the first time in a long time, they actually smelled kind of good. Carefully, he reached down to the pepperoni jalapeño and took a slice.

He groaned as he took a bite. He was sure it had never tasted this good before.

Was it wrong to allow that little, cautious part of him that had never lost hope he and Reyse might meet again to grow?

He didn't think so.

Corey had never really been to LA Pride before. He'd been around a couple of times when the parade happened to be on, but he'd never made an effort to go specifically and he'd certainly never gotten involved. Now, looking around him at Iridescence, he was beginning to understand what he'd been missing out on all these years.

It was tricky when you were bi. You didn't always feel welcome in queer spaces. But Corey had never had any friends or dated any queer people to encourage him to participate. After spending most of the day at Reyse's festival, though, he was feeling so *connected* to everyone. People just kept hugging him and talking to him and smiling his way.

So many of them had volunteered to work at the stall from Rainbow Roofs, Corey had only been given a couple of hour-long slots to fill. The rest of the time he was free to go and enjoy the festival. But he'd not done many of those, either. The kind of festivals where you had to camp there cost a lot of money, so he'd never bothered. Besides, without any friends it wasn't like he'd felt the need to go to any local ones. So he'd been tempted to just hang around the stall with the rest of the RRT guys.

But, unsurprisingly, Ellie Mae had other ideas. She swung it so they were working the same slots. If she hadn't been very open about how much of a total lesbian she was, he might have wondered if she had a crush on him. Now, he was starting to suspect he was her new-pet project. He didn't mind. In fact, he really enjoyed her company. So he allowed himself to be dragged from the stall along with a few of the other guys to go gallivanting over the park.

Corey hadn't really bothered going to see any concerts. He always figured why bother seeing as he had all the music he liked on CDs, then streaming as he got older. But there was something invigorating about seeing songs performed live he soon discovered, even if it was only one-hit wonders from the eighties. But they saw pop acts, rock bands, drag queens and kings, comedians, Broadway stars, so called 'freak shows,' and even a magician that managed to make his show really cool and not lame. They danced their asses off in the nineties tent and bought hot dogs and drank warm beer while Ellie Mae and Lucas got their faces painted.

In all honesty, it was undeniably one of the most fun days Corey had ever experienced in his whole life. But every now and again, he would catch himself with a rush of melancholy. He was here because of Reyse. But he might never see Reyse again.

Every time he managed to pick his mood up again. He kept assuring himself that everywhere they went, there was a chance he could run into Reyse. But this wasn't a movie. There were apparently sixty thousand people in attendance at the festival. He was never going to bump into Reyse by chance.

As the afternoon drew on, he accepted that he needed to let go of that childish idea and enjoy the rest of his day, no matter how much it hurt. He and Ellie Mae were part of the crew managing the stall between five and six, so Corey had time to fortify himself with slightly stronger liquor and get a good spot to watch Reyse perform on one of the screens. There was no way he was getting close to the front. There were some people who had apparently been camped out there literally all day.

But that was okay. Corey didn't want to seem like some pathetic stalker. He just wanted to see Reyse's face again, to hear his voice for real, not through a TV. Corey still hadn't worked up the courage to watch that interview on Kimmy.

It was like he was doing his best to preserve the memories they'd shared during their short time together. How Reyse's skin felt against Corey's. The peaceful way he'd slept when they'd shared a bed. The feeling of the vibrations when Reyse had performed for Corey alone.

He was in a complete world of his own when the sensation of something tugging at the hem of his jeans snapped him back to reality. Corey blinked, remembering he was back at the stall, although traffic had slowed and Ellie Mae and Jack had it under control. Looking down, Corey realized what had pulled him from his reverie.

A small, fluffy dog had bit into the denim and was tugging at it with adorable little grunts. Corey assumed the dog was a 'she,' as she was wearing a sparkly rainbow bow in the fur on top of her head. But on a day like today, it was wrong to make gender assumptions…

His brain suddenly ground to a halt. Hang on a second…

His hands shot down, grabbing the small dog to hold in front of his face. "Foofy!" he cried in utter disbelief.

"Hello?" a voice drifted over the crowd. "Has anyone seen a small dog? Yes, you. Have you seen a dog? She's most adorable. Answers to Lady Bonniford Honeydew the Third. No? How about Foofy? Foofy! Here, girl!"

Coldness swept over Corey as Foofy wagged her tail and licked the tip of Corey's nose. Well, if he wanted a sign from the universe, he'd damn well got one. Now he just had to lay his cards on the table and see what life dealt him back.

"Evangeline?" he called out in a loud, clear voice. Ellie Mae, Jack and Lucas, the rest of his colleagues and the people hovering around the stall all turned to look at him, still holding aloft the ball of fluff that was Foofy. But he didn't pay attention to them. He just focused on the enormous sun hat that he suddenly spied bobbling through the crowd.

"Who's that? Have you found my dog?"

Evangeline emerged from the throng like the parting of the Red Seas. Beside her was Reyse's mom, looking healthier than when Corey had last seen her. Evangeline broke into a smile at seeing her dog held up. Then she slid her gaze to Corey.

"YOU!" she bellowed.

Corey cringed.

Evangeline's eyes went wide as she stormed over to the Rainbow Roofs stall with Clementine anxiously in her wake. Ignoring everyone else, Evangeline swished her long maxi dress as she rounded the corner before grabbing Foofy from Corey's grasp.

Then she threw her other arm around Corey's neck so tightly and dragged him down to her that he thought he was going to either fall over or choke.

"You *scared* us, Corey Sheppard!" she scolded him. She squeezed him once more then released him, both she and Foofy looking up at him accusingly. But she wasn't angry.

She was worried.

Corey's heart contracted as he processed that.

"Corey!" Clementine squeaked. "I can't believe it's you! You just vanished. Where did you go?"

"I – I thought it was for the best," he began.

"Well, you're an idiot," Evangeline chided with a sniff. Dear lord, was she trying not to *cry?* "It's a good job I'm very fond of you and Ricky thinks you're marvelous, otherwise I'd have to spank you."

"Who's getting spanked?" Lucas piped up.

"Shut *up*," Ellie Mae cried in disbelief, rolling her eyes at Lucas. "Corey, sweetie, is every little thing okay?"

"It is now," Clementine said. She had her hands clutched to her chest and was standing by Evangeline, smiling at Corey like he was a lost treasure.

Corey bit his lip and looked between the two women. "He…thinks I'm marvelous?" That was such an alien word for him to use, but it was what Evangeline had said and he was too afraid to paraphrase her.

Evangeline huffed. "Do you really have to ask that? Yes, he didn't leave his apartment for three days solid after that damn interview. He was so convinced you'd come back to him. Where have you been? He's *missed* you!"

"The interview?" Corey asked, his ears ringing.

"The one on Kimmy Kovac," Clementine prompted, as if there could be another interview.

Evangeline's cherry-red and glossy lips popped open as her jaw fell. "You haven't seen it, have you? Dear heavens above, what am I supposed to do with such thickskulled boys?"

"Hold on," said Ellie Mae. "You don't mean..." Her eyes darted over to Corey, as if seeing him in a new light. "Oh lordy! Do you mean the Reyse Hickson interview? Corey Sheppard! You tell me right this instant if you're the boy he was so brokenhearted over! The one he thought he'd lost!"

Corey looked defensively between his coworkers and Reyse's family. "You guys never said he said anything about the guy!" he yelped. "You said Reyse came out because he got caught out in the lie!"

"Holy fuck!" Jack exclaimed, grabbing his hair. "The guy in the photos – are you *him?*"

Corey opened and closed his mouth like a goldfish. Did he admit that he was? Was it his place to reveal that?

Evangeline huffed loudly and spun around on her heels, Foofy in her arms. "Come along, before you cause any more trouble." She did wink affectionately over her shoulder at him, though.

"Where are we going?" Corey asked as Clementine smiled and looped their arms together.

"I find it best to do what she says when she gets like this," she said sweetly, patting his arm. "She'll look after you. You do look great, honey. It's so nice to see you again."

"You, too," Corey said faintly. But he looked back at his colleagues. "I can't-" he began.

"You only have ten minutes left of your shift," Ellie Mae scoffed. "We can cover for you! Now scooch! Before I grill you to within an inch of your life!"

She was sure to still do that later. But for now, Corey was free to go with Clementine and Evangeline.

He allowed himself to be steered from the stall, waving to his bemused-looking colleagues as he left. Then they marched purposefully through the crowds until they reached a security fence.

Corey suddenly realized where they were probably going. He stopped dead in his tracks.

"Oh, no, no," he stammered.

Evangeline also stopped walking and turned to face him. But again, she wasn't angry. Her expression was actually one of complete concern.

"Sweetheart, what's wrong?" she asked.

Panic made a lump rise in Corey's chest. "I can't..." he said, trying to voice his fears. "What if he doesn't want to see me? He's going to be on stage in half an hour!"

Evangeline's face changed from concern to pure sympathy. "Oh, darling," she said, stepping closer. Her eyes flicked from side to side as she studied his face. "You actually believe he wouldn't want to see you. Okay, we won't do anything until after the show. But I promise you"- she cupped his face and rubbed his cheek with her thumb, like a mother might do -"he's going to be *so* happy to see you."

Corey wasn't completely convinced that was true. But he believed that *Evangeline* believed that. So he nodded as security gave him a lanyard pass, then walked through into the VIP area with the two women, his heart in his throat.

He was going to see Reyse again.

He just wished he knew what to expect when it happened.

Thirty-One

COREY

COREY FELT LIKE HE HAD A NEON SIGN FLASHING ABOVE HIS head blaring *'I don't belong here!'* But he stuck with Evangeline and Clementine as they passed through another security checkpoint and entered the VIP area of the festival.

Apparently, Evangeline saying "He's with me," was not only enough to get Corey a VIP pass, but also into wherever she went. They walked by a bank of trailers with handwritten signs saying 'Hair and Makeup' on them, heading to an area with a few dozen picnic tables, projector screens set far apart and a bar serving food and drink.

Evangeline must have spotted Corey looking anxiously around. "He's not here," she said as they headed toward the bar (Corey expected nothing less from her).

"He's…" Corey said.

Evangeline smiled. "I got him a shot and sent him on his way. He'll be backstage by now. But don't worry, we've got plenty to keep us entertained."

"Isn't it neat back here?" Clementine enthused, still holding protectively on to his arm.

Corey had to admit it was pretty nice. He spotted a few

celebrities, but he was more impressed with the relaxed environment. Even though the event was only for one day, someone had taken the time to wind fairy lights around all the trees, just about visible now the evening was starting to set in. The sound was well balanced, so you only heard what was going on from whichever screen you were closest to. It lost some of that live vibe, but it made up for it with comfort and easy access to amenities.

Once Evangeline had stocked up on Champagne and glasses, she carried her supplies and Foofy effortlessly over the grass to a group of three men occupying one of the picnic tables. With them was a double stroller containing a little boy sleeping inside, and one of the guys had a young girl of about four or five in his lap looking at a picture book. Corey noted that the children were Asian, even though none of the men were.

The guy with the little girl was an all-American hunk. Handsome, dark haired with big muscles and a picture-perfect smile. But the way he was cradling the girl as he talked with the other guys was immediately endearing. Corey didn't find him threatening.

Next to him was a Latino dude and a slim white guy. Although the closer Corey got, the less he was certain the last guy was actually a guy. He wore a flowery, lacy top over a flat chest with his jeans as well as cork wedges. His lip gloss sparkled in what was left of the afternoon sun.

"Look, boys," Evangeline cried as she, Clementine and Corey approached their table. "I have found us the most *wonderful* surprise."

The three guys – Evangeline had called them that so Corey felt okay using male pronouns for now – turned and looked their way as Evangeline dropped onto the bench and immediately began pouring Champagne for them.

"Hi," the guy with the young girl said, offering out his

hand to Corey as he smiled. "I'm Gabe." Apparently, Gabe didn't need to know much about someone to be nice to them. It put Corey at ease as he and Clementine also sat down.

"Nice to meet you," Corey said, shaking hands. "I'm Corey."

"Oh *shit!*" the Latino guy cried while the lip gloss guy gasped and covered his mouth. "You *are?* Evangeline, where on Earth did you find him?"

"Foofy found him, actually," she replied with a smile. "Oh, Corey. Don't look so worried. This is Elion and Ashby, Blake and TJ's husbands. Gabe sitting with Jia Li there is married to Joey. And that's little Hai in the stroller. Say hi, Hai!"

The baby yawned and continued to snooze.

Corey looked at the guys staring at him. Holy crap. These were all of Below Zero's other halves. Well, almost all. One was missing. "You know who I am, then?" he asked nervously.

"Naturally," Elion cried.

But Ashby shook his head. "No, actually," he said with an English accent, arching a blond eyebrow. "We're very confused. What *actually* happened between you and Reyse?"

"And are you here to fix it?" Elion asked, a sparkle in his eyes.

"Guys," Gabe said with a slight warning tone. He bounced Jia Li on his knee and turned the page of the picture book she was looking at with him. "Don't interrogate Corey."

"Yes, he's here to fix it," Evangeline announced to them all. "It was all just a terrible misunderstanding."

"So, does Reyse know you're here?" Ashby asked in concern.

"Um, no," Corey admitted. He felt too sick to drink, so he just toyed with the stem of his glass.

But Elion's face brightened up. "Oh, *excellent*," he said. "A surprise. He'll love it."

"Will he?" Corey asked. "I ghosted him. I walked away because I thought I'd ruined his life and left him to deal with all this crap by himself. I gave him no way to contact me and I was too scared to contact him. He probably hates me!"

He didn't realize his voice had been steadily getting louder until he shouted the last words. The rest of the table stared at him.

"Sorry," he mumbled.

It was Clementine who reached out and took his hand in her own. "We all make mistakes, honey," she said kindly. "What's important is how we deal with the consequences. Do you *want* to see Reyse?"

Corey bit his lip. He swore he wouldn't get emotional, but his eyes warmed with tears. "More than anything," he said thickly. "I...I never saw the interview. You were right, Evangeline. Did he really talk about me?"

"Not by name," said Evangeline. "But it was obvious."

"It really was," Elion said sincerely.

Ashby nodded. "He was dreadfully upset. I'm sure he'll be thrilled to see you now."

An immense cheer in the air caught all their attention. Corey joined them in looking at the main screen. His heart skipped a beat. Reyse had just appeared on stage.

"What shall we do?" Clementine asked anxiously. "Watch here or go backstage?"

"I think we'll get in the way backstage," Gabe said dubiously.

"Here's fine," Corey said, probably a little too tersely. It was crazy, having been heartbroken over the possibility of never seeing him again. But Corey couldn't face Reyse yet, not while he was midperformance. It might throw him completely. Corey had no idea what he wanted to say and he was sure Reyse didn't either.

This was a bad idea. He should go. It was never going to work. He and Reyse were from different worlds. Corey had let him down. They had no future together. He needed to get out of here before these guys put Reyse in an awkward position.

"Oh my god, you're *him!*" another British accent rang out, distracting the table from where they'd been watching Reyse speaking to the crowd. Corey barely had time to look around before he was engulfed by a pair of long arms and a squeal that sounded directly by his ear. "You made it! I so hoped you would!"

The woman let him go, and Corey realized he'd just been hugged by acclaimed actress Bella Dalton.

Bella Dalton knew who he was.

"Um," he stammered.

"Well, budge up, budge up!" Bella cried, making room on the picnic table for her and the guy she was now holding hands with. "It's Corey, right? Ahh, Reyse is going to be so thrilled to see you! Does he know you're here? No, of course not, he'd have said something."

"We're going to wait until the end of the show," Evangeline said, rising gracefully to her feet, leaving Foofy standing on the picnic table. Jia Li cautiously reached out and patted her head. Foofy wagged her tail. "I'll get some more drinks. Everyone relax, have a good time. This is going to be great fun, I'm sure."

Corey tried to chill out as Below Zero suddenly appeared from nowhere, giving the audience a surprise reunion. They heard the insane screaming from the other side of the stage. Everyone in the VIP area was enthralled watching the show, so Corey tried his best to concentrate and join them. But he couldn't really focus whenever he saw Reyse's face and his heart ached.

Had he already fucked this up beyond repair? Would Reyse forgive him for doing what he thought was best for Reyse's career?

"I've texted Blake," Elion announced after a while of general chitchat while watching the concert. "That Corey's here," Elion clarified when people looked at him expectantly.

"Oh, good," Ashby breathed out in relief. "Because I messaged Trent and I wasn't sure if I should have."

"Oh," Corey said, not sure what to think. His stomach immediately twisted with nerves.

Gabe leaned in. Jia Li had dozed off despite the noise around them, and Gabe had her sprawled across his lap. "Saying what?"

Elion shrugged. "Just that he was here. Oh!" His phone pinged and he looked up to the screen. Blake was not currently on stage. Sure enough, it was him who'd texted Elion. "He says once the medley of Reyse's songs starts to head backstage."

There was a general chorus of agreement. But Corey found he couldn't speak. "What is he going to do?"

Elion looked at him in surprise. "Oh, babe," he said, reaching out and offering his hand to Corey. Aware everyone was watching them, Corey paused, then slipped his hand into Elion's. "He won't do anything to mess with you, I promise. He knows the kind of things that can go wrong on TV. I think he'll just want to help out one of his best friends."

Corey looked at this guy he had just met, at *all* these people he'd just met.

There was kindness in their eyes. Bella freaking Dalton rubbed his back and smiled at him. Ashby and Gabe nodded in agreement with Elion's words. Foofy trotted up to him and headbutted his chest until he petted her.

Corey was so used to people not giving a damn about him, it was difficult for him to imagine complete strangers would. But Evangeline and Clementine were also looking earnestly at him. Corey thought of his colleagues who had worked so hard to make him feel welcomed, especially Ellie Mae, who seemed to have appointed herself as his personal bodyguard.

Maybe he could trust these people when they said Reyse had missed him. That he wanted Corey still.

Honestly, though, what was the alternative? Run away again? Leave the man Corey might possibly *actually* be in love with because he was too afraid to try?

Corey summoned as much of his confidence as he could.

"Okay," he said. "Let's do this."

That seemed enough to give the go-ahead to everyone. They beamed at him and began clearing the table. Gabe secured both his children (who Corey had discovered he and Joey had only just adopted all the way from China) into their stroller. By the time the mega-medley started up, they were already making their way backstage.

The music became overpowering the closer they got. Gabe had fitted the kids with mini-noise cancelling headsets, so they kept on sleeping as the group wound their way through the dark passageways of backstage. Corey's heartbeat sped up as they navigated their way in a procession up to the side of the stage.

A big blond security guy sensed their approach and looked for half a second like he was going to stop them. Then his face changed in recognition. "Elion," he shouted fondly over the music, as Elion was at the front of their line. He clapped their hands together and hugged him against his solid chest. "I thought you guys would have been here ages ago?"

Elion stood on tiptoes to speak into the guy's ear as the

group moved into a clump around them. Corey could just catch a glimpse of the stage and the couple of dozen people singing and dancing on it. The crowd was cheering along, screaming every time the song changed from one of Reyse's tracks into another.

"Hey, I'm Levi," the guy said, grabbing Corey's attention away from the stage. He automatically shook hands with the guy. "Raiden's husband. Nice to meet you." It looked like he was working security for the night, as his jacket matched a couple of other big guys' that Corey could see. But he gave Corey a warm smile and squeezed his shoulder once he'd let his hand go. "It's cool you're here."

Corey ran out of time to debate whether or not that was true. The medley ended with his favorite of Reyse's songs – Deny Me – and the crowd went wild. But it seemed the show wasn't over.

Blake Jackson began addressing the crowd, talking about Reyse and how much he was loved. Getting the audience to cheer for the people who had stood by them in their lives. Then he mentioned how finding that special someone could make all the difference.

Before he realized what was going on, Elion, Gabe, Levi and Ashby had formed a sort of protective semi-circle around Corey, with Corey right by the side of the stage. Then everyone on the stage was turning and looking at them.

Looking at Corey.

Their faces were all a blur under the powerful lights. But suddenly, Corey's vision became laser-sharp.

He'd never not be able to pick that face out in a crowd.

His heart all but stopped and tears burned the back of his eyes as for the first time in over a month, he found himself face-to-face Reyse Hickson once again.

And he had no idea what the hell to do.

CHAPTER
Thirty~Two

REYSE

It was like time stopped altogether. Reyse could feel the tension of the crowd as they watched him, trying to work out what was going on.

Reyse wasn't sure he knew what was going on himself.

How could Corey be here? Why did he look like he was going to burst into tears? Did he want to be here? Reyse's heart *ached* at the sight of him. He'd become so convinced that he would never see his beautiful lover again it came like a sucker punch to suddenly have him there now. But in the best kind of way. Well, only if Corey was happy to see him too.

He was so close. Reyse felt paralyzed. He was aware of his friends around him and all their dancers. He was aware of some sixty thousand people watching him from the crowd. He was aware of the cameras that were no doubt zoomed in on his face, waiting for a reaction.

"It's okay," Blake hissed, off mic. "Go to him!"

Reyse couldn't tear his eyes away to look at him, but TJ was nodding within his sightline. Raiden looked in confusion between Reyse and Corey, then his eyes went wide as he apparently joined the dots. "Dude, what are you waiting for?" he cried, forgetting to cover his mic as he was still holding Reyse and TJ's hands. But he didn't seem to care, nor did anyone else.

But Reyse didn't know what to do. Corey didn't look like he wanted Reyse to run to him. He looked like he might puke. He was trembling. Seeing him so distraught broke Reyse's heart all over again.

But Corey was *here*. He'd found his way back to Reyse, just like Evangeline had promised he would. Was Reyse going to let him slip out of his life for a third time?

He'd never get him back if he did. Of that, Reyse was certain.

Feeling like someone else was in charge of his body, Reyse let go of Joey's hand. Then he held his own hand out toward Corey. He could hear the murmuring of tens of thousands of people, the gasp of even more holding their breath.

Reyse looked at Corey, the other guys squeezing his shoulders and patting his back. Reyse couldn't hear what they were saying, but they were all telling him something, talking over one another.

He wasn't sure who moved first. But it was as if one second they were both looking into each other's eyes, resisting the pull. Then they both just...gave in. Reyse sprinted forward the same moment as Corey broke free of his group, charging onto the stage and straight into Reyse's arms. Reyse let out an animalistic sort of sound as they collided, screams already assaulting them from the audience. All around them, their friends bellowed in triumph and Reyse allowed himself to be crushed in the strong arms he'd been craving for weeks, inhaling Corey's unique spicy musk as he could no longer hold back his tears.

"I thought I'd never see you again," he cried into Corey's

chest. Corey held the back of his head and dug his fingers into Reyse's side.

"I'm so sorry," he replied. "I shouldn't have left you. I'm sorry, Reyse. I understand if you can't forgive me-"

Reyse leaned back, grabbed Corey by the face, and crashed their lips together to kiss him senseless. He was dimly aware that the crowd may have gone wild for the Below Zero reunion. But it paled into comparison at the hysteria they unleashed as Reyse finally declared to the world that this was the man he loved. And he was never, *ever* letting him go again.

The audience was still going beyond nuts, but Reyse vaguely heard Joey addressing the crowd for one last time. "That's all, folks!" he cried to tumultuous applause. "Thank you for joining us! I call that a happy ever after, don't you?"

Reyse was aware of the rest of the people exiting the stage around them as the white screen descended in front of them, hiding them just as it had the rest of Below Zero at the start of the set. There was confetti gently drifting from up above where a couple of cannons had gone off earlier. As Reyse and his team had planned, when the curtain fully descended again, the same projector that had illuminated the four guys came on. This time it showed a beautiful rainbow with the Iridescence logo in the middle. Reyse and Corey's silhouette appeared just below.

Reyse laughed as the crowd screamed again, but he couldn't make himself care enough to move just yet. Everyone else had left the stage, and for the first time in weeks Reyse was relatively alone with Corey again. He hugged him close and cried on his shoulder.

"You *asshole*," he said with a tearful laugh. "I thought I was never going to see you again."

"I thought that was for the best..." Corey protested weakly. Then he nodded. "Nope, you're right. I'm an asshole."

Reyse chuckled and kissed him on the lips. "No, you're not, you're gorgeous," he said between kisses. "Fuck, I can't believe you're here. I love you," he uttered as they broke to catch their breath.

He didn't even get a second to question if he'd made a mistake. Corey laughed, his face wet, and pressed their foreheads together. "I love you, too, baby," he said.

A camera flash caught Reyse's eye, making him snap his head toward the wings. He knew they were kind of exposed here, but he would have thought people would have had the decency to leave them alone for a second.

"Can we go?" he asked Corey, feeling kind of woozy. The performance and the shock had taken a lot out of him. Besides, the idea someone was snooping when that had ruined their relationship before made him uneasy.

"Definitely," Corey said, rubbing Reyse's back and kissing him again. "Shall we go find your friends?"

"Did you meet them already?" Reyse asked with a frown as they left the stage hand in hand. They had certainly seemed familiar with him before he'd come on stage.

Corey chuckled. "Well, Foofy found me, then so did your aunt and mom, then, yes, I met the Husband Club." He beamed at Reyse and raised his hand to kiss the back of it. "They were really nice to me."

Reyse stopped and kissed Corey's lips in the wings. "Good," he said, feeling embarrassingly emotional. "You're one of us now, one of the gang."

Before Corey made him elaborate on that – because Reyse was immediately aware it sounded very much like he wanted Corey to also be a husband – he tugged on his hand and led him through backstage. Nobody from the crew or any of the VIP guests bothered them as they headed out to the picnic area. Maybe he had imagined the photo flash?

Eventually, they burst out into the slightly cooler evening

air. Floodlights had been set up to illuminate the VIP area. Their group had been waiting just by the exit and instantly gathered around them. As Reyse was jostled by the crowd, he heard a big round of applause go up from the people back here. But it was too much for Reyse. His feet just sort of stopped moving and he turned into Corey, burying his face in his chest.

"All right, all right," the voice he'd come to recognize as Levi said firmly. The group fanned out over the grass. The inner circle were people Reyse knew. Friends and family. But around that were all kinds of people, hovering out of interest. Well, there was probably no hiding him and Corey now, anyway.

"Reyse, are you okay?" Raiden asked. Reyse felt him place a hand on Reyse's back before he looked back up to see his concerned face next to Levi's.

Joey was standing beside him with his new young son in his arms, Hai blinking himself awake as Joey wiped away his tears. Gabe was by him with their little girl on his hip. Blake and Elion were holding hands. TJ had his arms protectively around Ashby. Reyse's mom was with his aunt and Foofy. Bella stood slightly further back, being respectful with her new guy's hand resting on her shoulder.

These were the people he loved more than anything. He even sort of wished his dad was there to complete the picture. And Kimmy, seeing as she'd proved to be so much more than a work acquaintance lately.

That wish was fulfilled soon enough at least. "Oh my god!" her raspy, high-pitched voice rang out over the crowd. "Oh my god, Reyse! That was the most incredible thing ever! Are you okay? Reyse – where are you?"

She barged through the throng of strangers, then Raiden and Blake parted to let her through. Without pause, she flung herself against Reyse and Corey, hugging them both and dancing on her toes. She only came up to their shoulders, but she managed to rock them anyway.

"You guys!" she shrieked, pushing her glasses up her nose and staring at them. "That was – I can't – I mean – *amazing* television! Ratings are going to be through the roof! But, you know, great work in real life too." She punched Reyse's arm. Then – probably reacting to his stunned face – raised her eyebrows. "Right? We're all happy, right?"

Reyse looked at Corey. His expression was pained. "I think so?" Reyse said in a whisper.

"Nope, no," Evangeline said, letting Foofy down on the grass waving her hands. "We're not going through this again. You both tell each other what you told me, right now. I'm done with these broken hearts. They're frightfully dull and boring."

Corey bit his lip. "I never should have ghosted you," he blurted out. "It's been hell. I never saw your interview, but apparently you said some things about me and I should have just come back to your place and begged for forgiveness. I know we've not had all that much time together, but...*fuck*, Reyse, I *need* you!"

Reyse stared for a moment into his gorgeous hazel eyes. Then he laughed and hastily rubbed his wet eyes. "I need you, too," he said. "There's nothing to forgive. All that matters is you're here. And I'm *not* letting you out of my sight without taking your number this time, you jerk."

Corey barked out a laugh and buried his face against Reyse's neck. "I'm not letting you out of my sight, period," he said.

The sound of a sob made Reyse look up. His mom covered her mouth in embarrassment. "I'm sorry," she squeaked. "I'm just so happy."

"You're not the only one," Bella said, brushing tears from

her cheeks as she reached an arm around her shoulders with a smile.

In fact, Reyse realized several people were sniffing and grinning in delight.

The moment was interrupted by several explosive barks from Foofy. She had wormed her way between people's feet and was growling fiercely. The throng parted around her to reveal a guy in a Below Zero baseball cap with thick glasses and a trimmed goatee. Foofy was hopping around his sneakers, snarling and nipping at his laces. He had a VIP lanyard on, but Reyse didn't remember seeing him earlier today.

"Hey, someone call this mutt off," the guy said, waving the phone in his hand around.

"I *beg* your pardon?" Evangeline snapped.

But before Reyse, Mr. Goatee, or anyone else could respond, Ashby stepped forward. "YOU!" he cried scandalously.

"What? Who?" Reyse asked.

"Dez Starr," Ashby and TJ snarled in unison.

Reyse snapped his head back toward the guy who was doing his best to look innocent. "The guy who bought those photos of Corey and me and wrote that bullshit article? The one who drove us apart and almost ruined my career *and* relationship?"

"And ours," TJ rumbled, looking murderous.

Levi plucked the lanyard away from Dez's chest, making Dez flinch slightly. "Oh, look," he murmured with fake cheer. "A forgery."

Raiden deftly swiped the phone from Dez's grasp while he was glaring at Levi.

"Hey, that's mine!" Dez shouted.

"And you're trespassing," Levi said with a smile. He placed his fingertips on Dez's chest, as if daring him to try and push past him.

"Dude, he's got a ton of photos of y'all on here," Raiden said to Reyse in disgust. "Kissing and stuff."

"Delete them," Blake snapped.

"Damn right," Elion huffed, folding his arms.

"Wait, hang on," Reyse said. He held out his hand, so Raiden handed over the phone.

Reyse swiped through a couple of dozen very intrusive photos of him and Corey on stage and down on the grass. As furious as he was, it was kind of nice to see them together.

"No," Corey said. Reyse looked up to see him shaking his head. "We'll take more photos. Proper ones. We don't want those. They're dirty."

Relief filled Reyse's chest. Just hearing Corey say they were going to take more photos together relaxed him. Gave him faith. "Yes," he agreed.

"You can't delete those," Dez shouted, bobbing either side of Levi's large form. "Those are mine!"

"Trespassing," Levi said with a sigh, shaking his head and tutting.

"Besides," Raiden said smugly. "You've got far too many of the kids in the background of those snaps, Mr. Starr. You need their parents' permission for that."

"What?" Joey cried.

"No, no," Gabe spluttered. "No, we definitely don't give that."

"Delete them all, Reyse," Levi told him, his tone comforting.

Dez continued to fume, but Reyse just looked up at Corey. Corey nodded and kissed the side of Reyse's hair. "I *promise* we'll take more," he murmured. "I'm not going anywhere."

So one by one, Reyse deleted all the images that Dez had snapped without their permission, feeling cathartic about it by the end. "Done," he said.

Levi took the phone from Reyse and slapped it onto Dez's chest. "Now, get the fuck out of here before I call the cops. Okay? Oh, and give me that phony pass."

Levi snapped his fingers. Dez looked mutinous at all of them. But there wasn't much more he could do other than snatch the lanyard from around his neck, thrust it at Levi, then go storming off out of the VIP area. Reyse was glad to see a couple of other security guys flanking him to make sure he left once and for all.

"Oh, aren't you a clever girl," Evangeline cooed as Foofy came running back into her arms. "Did you find the bad man? Yes you did, yes you did."

Relief was making Reyse dizzy. It wasn't so much that Dez would have been exposing him and Corey this time. More spoiling this precious reunion.

"Holy crap," Reyse said shakily. "I got my band back and my boyfriend all in one night." He realized what he'd said. "I mean! Uh-"

Corey chuckled and hugged him tightly, rubbing his back. "I better be your damn boyfriend after all this," he teased.

Reyse softly kissed his lips. Not for too long, as they were in the middle of all his nearest and dearest. But enough that he hoped conveyed his love. "I'll be your boyfriend, too."

"Oh, get a room!" Joey cried, making the group laugh.

"Aww, I think it's so romantic," Reyse's mom said, coming forward to hug them both gently. Reyse rested his head against hers, sighing.

"Actually, *would* you like a room?" Ashby asked.

Reyse frowned and looked at him. Ashby had his phone out. "What do you mean?" Reyse asked.

"Oh! Oh!" Kimmy cried, looking over Ashby's shoulder. "Go for that one! That's a good one!"

"Actually, that's a smart idea," TJ said, also looking as he nodded.

"I figured with all the press attention you wouldn't want to go back to your apartment," Ashby said, waggling his phone. "So I'm booking you a penthouse suite for the night. I think you deserve it," he added fondly. "Not at *my* resort," he added hastily. "Just a nice place in LA."

"It's a really good one," Kimmy said, grinning at Reyse.

"Aww, that's so nice," Joey said fondly.

"Oh, you don't have to do that," Reyse said. Ashby was extremely independently wealthy, as well as owning a now thriving resort in Wyoming. But it didn't seem right for him to splash out like that. "I could book something-"

"Dude," TJ said, rolling his eyes. "That's the point."

"Oh, smashing idea," Evangeline agreed, also on her phone. "Let me book you a car."

"We'll escort you for the drive," Levi said, then he turned away and spoke into his team's radios.

"Oh, if everyone's getting involved," Elion scoffed, whipping out his own phone out. "How do you guys fancy room service? Champagne and steaks, don't you think, Blake?"

"Strawberries for the Champagne, too," Blake suggested.

"You'll need supplies for the evening," Bella nodded. "I can have a delivery made of pajamas and bubble bath and other lovely things."

Reyse looked from Corey, who was equally speechless, to all his friends. "You guys," he protested weakly.

"Shush," Joey said firmly. "Let us spoil you a bit. Make up for a bunch of lost time. I'm just not sure what there is left for us to give you."

Reyse looked between him and Gabe, each still holding one of their sleepy kids. "How about a hug for Uncle Reyse?" he asked tentatively.

Joey broke into the sweetest, goofiest smile. Then he stepped closer, gently handing Hai over to Reyse. Reyse cradled the chubby baby to his chest, allowing his pudgy hand to grip one of his fingers.

Reyse felt like the luckiest guy in the world as Corey hugged his side, looking down at Hai as he kissed Reyse's cheek. He really had hit the jackpot in life. But it wasn't the thousands of fans that was making his heart sing right then, although they were amazing. It was seeing so many people he loved, all standing by him. Most of all Corey.

His Corey. Reyse had found him.

And he was definitely *never* letting him go again.

CHAPTER
Thirty-Three

COREY

THE HOTEL WAS GORGEOUS. MARBLE FLOORS, SLEEK LIGHT fixtures and chrome finishes everywhere. It was even in West Hollywood, so Corey didn't feel self-conscious checking in with Reyse. Not that traveling with him anywhere was inconspicuous. But it made him relax more knowing he was in a gay-friendly neighborhood.

However, he felt he couldn't really appreciate any of the niceties as much as he should have, as he only had one thought on his mind.

Reyse was really here with him, now. They were together.

And Corey had to get his hands on him to prove it.

It was like every cell in his body was crying out to touch Reyse, to assure himself he was really there. As much as Reyse seemed to need reassuring that Corey wasn't going anywhere, Corey required the same thing.

In all the time they'd been together, he had always known the clock was ticking. He could never fully give himself over, because at some point, everything was going to fall away under their feet. And that was just with their physical relationship. He'd never been prepared to emotionally open himself up all the way, because he'd never done that with *anyone*, let alone unattainable megastar Reyse Hickson.

But for some unfathomable reason, the universe had smiled down on him. Somehow, Corey had found himself with this kindhearted, talented, crazy-sexy sweetheart of a man all to himself. Reyse was his. Just as he was Corey's. Despite everything that could have imbalanced them, they were here, as equals.

Corey didn't want there to be anything between them. Not literally or figuratively.

By the time Reyse and Corey stepped inside the penthouse room Ashby had organized them, their deliveries of food, wine, clothes and toiletries for their overnight stay had already been delivered. The damn room was even covered in rose petals. It was the kind of thing Corey had only really seen in the movies.

"Whoa," Corey breathed out as Reyse locked the door behind them.

"Do you like it?" Reyse asked, looking around their suite. The view over nighttime LA was stunning, reminding Corey of Reyse's apartment and their first time together.

Reyse had a simple satchel bag with him that he let drop onto the floor. Corey turned and slid his arms around his *boyfriend* and picked him up, laughing as Reyse squeaked and chuckled as he wrapped his legs around Corey's waist.

Corey hummed. "I could be in a field in a tent and I wouldn't care," Corey said, kissing Reyse's neck. "So long as I'm with you, it's heaven."

Reyse moaned and ran his fingers through Corey's hair. "I've missed you, Corey," he said. "To the depths of my *soul*."

Corey paused in his kisses to look into Reyse's beautiful blue eyes. He shook his head. "I'm so sorry," he said. "I left you with nothing. I didn't miss you, because you were *everywhere*. And it killed me."

"I had that one photo we took," Reyse said. "It saved me." He touched his fingertips to Corey's cheek. "I'm sorry, too, though," he whispered. "If it wasn't for me, we would never have had to split up. But that's done now. I'm going to tell the whole world you're mine. If...if that's what you want?"

Corey blinked at him. "Of *course* that's what I want," he cried. Icy coldness rushed through him at the mere thought of backing out now.

But Reyse bit his lip and caressed the back of Corey's neck. "But...the fame," he said. "You'll have to deal with assholes like Dez all the time."

"Will I have you?" Corey asked, completely serious. "Will you be faithful to me like I'm going to be faithful to you? Will you share your bed and your life and your heart with me? Will you be proud to have me hang out with your super famous friends?"

"Yes," Reyse said without pause, his eyes filling with tears. "One hundred percent, all those things. Baby, I'm in. I know it's fast, but I'm giving you – this – us – everything."

Corey pressed Reyse against the wall and hugged him so tightly he was worried he might leave bruises. "Then I don't give a crap about the bad stuff. Every relationship faces hard times. For normal people, it's paying the bills. For us, it'll be the fame stuff. But I'll take it all if I'm with you."

He heard Reyse hiccup. For a few moments, they simply clung to each other.

"I love you," Reyse mumbled. "I meant that, on the stage before."

Corey smiled, tears in his own eyes. "I love you, too, gorgeous. I can't believe how lucky I am fate brought you to me."

"I'd argue fate brought *you* to *me,*" Reyse said, wiping his tears away and smiling. "But I think we're both right. You're one in a billion, Corey Sheppard. You don't need any platinum records for me to figure that out."

"Neither do you," Corey said, turning them around and walking to the bed. "But it is kind of nice, you know?"

Reyse laughed and lightly smacked Corey on his arm. Corey retaliated by dumping him onto the bed and crawling over him. "Damn," he breathed. "I couldn't stop thinking of all the chances I'd missed to fuck you. I can't believe I've got them back."

Reyse smiled and bit his lip, looking up at Corey. "As much as I have a bucket list of *filthy* things I want you to do to me," he said. "Can we just keep it simple tonight? Make love?"

Corey's heart ached. He leaned down and captured Reyse's lips with his own. "I'll make love to you forever," he said, not caring how corny it sounded. "Filthy or sweet, it'll always be making love. But tonight, I'll take care of you as much as you want, treat you like a prince."

"I love you," Reyse said, the words thick with emotion.

Corey nuzzled their noses together and kissed him tenderly. "I love you too, Reyse," he said.

He slowly peeled both their clothes off, taking his time. There was no rush. He wanted to savor their first night together as a real couple. No more secrets. It was incredibly liberating.

Corey knew Reyse felt the same way, because he couldn't stop smiling. Every kiss was free for him to give, every touch allowed. Reyse was out and proud and it was like his true self was able to finally shine all the way through. Gone were the worried frowns and hesitations. This was the real Reyse Hickson, and Corey loved him.

Until now, Corey had always thought love was a myth

made up by Disney and Hallmark. An idea people were encouraged to chase to support the stability of society and the economy.

He didn't understand what it was like to need another person so badly it hurt your bones. To inhale their unique scent and know you were home. To feel like you were enough, just as you were, no matter what.

Now he did.

He and Reyse didn't bother untucking the bed, they just rolled around naked on top of the comforter, the rose petals sticking to their damp skin. Corey laughed as he pulled Reyse over him, running his hands down his spine and making him shudder.

"Do you want to ride me?" Corey asked. He knew before, Reyse had preferred being underneath. But Corey got a good feeling about tonight.

Sure enough, Reyse nodded and hopped from the bed to find Bella's gift basket. Corey watched him, feeling like his heart was going to burst at Reyse's easy confidence moving around the room without a stitch of clothing on, his hard cock standing proudly to attention. He wasn't shy in front of Corey. There was nothing to hide between them.

He'd worried for a second whether they'd have the supplies they really needed, but Bella had shooed him away when he'd opened his mouth to ask what she was ordering them. "I've *sorted* it, darling," she'd told him. "Don't worry about a thing." It would suck to get this far and not be able to go all the way.

However, Bella hadn't let them down. She'd actually gotten them a gift pack of different flavors of lube to try, which made them both laugh. Reyse held up a few packs of condoms. "We don't need these, do we?"

Corey grinned. They had come so far since their first night together. "Not unless you want to get tested together to make absolutely sure," he said. "But I don't think we do, no."

Reyse placed them back in the basket, bringing the box of different intimate lubes over for Corey to see.

"No pizza flavor, I see," Corey said with a sigh, making Reyse laugh. "How about strawberry? Sweet, like you."

Reyse leaned down to kiss him gently, then plucked the pink tube from the box. "Sounds good."

He straddled Corey's hips while he concentrated on squeezing out a dollop of shiny lube onto his fingers. Corey hissed as he reached back and rubbed it over Corey's hard, sensitive shaft. "Cold," he said with a grin.

"Sorry," Reyse said, not sounding all that sorry.

He added another load of lube to his fingers, then reached around to stretch himself out. Corey crooked his finger, encouraging Reyse to lean down and kiss him. It was difficult when they were smiling so much, but Corey didn't mind.

He ran his hand down Reyse's right arm, following to where it led behind his back. Reyse already had a single finger inserted into his slippery ass, so Corey covered his hand with his own, adding his middle finger next to Reyse's, helping to stretch him a little more.

Reyse moaned. "Does that feel good?" Corey asked between kisses.

"Yeah," Reyse said, nodding. "Want you inside me, Corey. Want to feel you."

They removed their fingers and Corey helped Reyse reposition himself. He held his cock steady while Reyse pulled his cheeks apart, angling his hole against Corey's tip. Then he slowly began to slide himself down.

They were making a mess everywhere, but Corey didn't care. He cradled Reyse's face with his sticky hand as they kissed and then smeared the lube in his lovely blond hair. He ran his hands down Reyse's perfect abs and gripped his hips, helping him bottom out.

Reyse panted and bit his lip as he accommodated Corey's cock inside him. His cheeks were flushed and his skin glistened with perspiration and the lubricant Corey had gotten on him. He looked so gorgeous and felt so damned good around Corey's cock. Corey wrapped his fingers possessively around his erection between them.

"Are you okay?" he asked, leaning up to kiss his neck, jaw, then the corner of his mouth.

Reyse nodded. "Good, feels so good," he uttered.

"You look perfect," Corey panted. He trailed his fingers up and down Reyse's arms, braced on either side of Corey's shoulders. "So hot, Reyse. I love you."

Reyse grinned and caught Corey's lower lip between his teeth. "Love you too, gorgeous," he said. There was a mischievous tone to his voice.

Corey liked it.

"Are you going to ride me, then?" he rasped, squeezing his fingers into Reyse's thighs. "I want to watch you come all over me, Reyse." He loved seeing how dirty talk made Reyse's eyes dilate. "You're so beautiful, baby. Come on me, don't hold back. I want to see you having fun on my big cock."

"Jesus!" Reyse spluttered with a laugh. "Shut up and let me fuck you."

Corey laughed too, looking up at his lover with marvel. "I think you promised to make love to me, sweetheart."

Reyse bit his lip and started to roll his hips. "Like that?" he asked.

Corey nodded. "Just like that."

Reyse's lithe, slim body moved on top of Corey's with the precision of a trained dancer, every muscle working together to keep his pace just right as he pleasured himself. Corey let go of his thigh to lift up Reyse's right hand, placing it on his weeping cock.

"I want to watch you jerk off," he said. He was so turned on it was unreal, but watching Reyse rub his own cock and drop his head back in ecstasy made it even better. "Holy fuck, yes, Reyse. You're gorgeous."

"I'm going to come," Reyse cried in alarm, but Corey shook his head.

"Come, baby. It's okay, I want you to."

Reyse quivered as he began to shoot his load all over Corey, just like he'd asked him to. Some even hit his chin and went into his hair. Despite still needing to orgasm himself, Corey chuckled and wiped his face as Reyse gasped for breath.

"Sorry," he said sheepishly.

Corey frowned at him, reaching up to pull him in for a hug. "Never, ever apologize for having fun during sex or for coming, okay? You looked stunning and I loved it."

"But I came first," Reyse said.

Corey brushed his knuckles against the side of Reyse's cheek. "That's allowed, you know," he teased gently. Thankfully, Reyse laughed. "Now, do you want to help me finish? Or you can lie back and just watch me jerk off, too?" He waggled his eyebrows. "I bet I can get cum in your hair as well."

Reyse snorted and kissed Corey's lips sloppily. "Can I suck you off?" he asked. "I...I want to swallow it."

Lust fizzed through Corey's belly. "I love it when you get shy about sex stuff," he said honestly. "You can ask me anything, though. I'll try anything with you, baby. A blow job would be amazing."

Reyse grinned and kissed him more slowly. "I want to do everything with you," he said. "All the stuff I've been missing out on."

"It'll be my pleasure," Corey murmured.

He watched Reyse carefully ease himself off from Corey's cock, then he kissed down Corey's chest, reaching his rock-hard, glistening member. He wiped the mess from before off with his hand, then wasted no time swallowing Corey down as far as he could.

Corey grunted and remembered when they'd done this before he'd lamented he wouldn't get time to teach Reyse how to improve his technique. Now he had all the time in the world. Not that it was going to take him long to come right now. But the realization warmed his heart.

"That's it, baby," he said. "Just relax, feels so good."

Reyse moaned and caressed his balls, massaging them in his palm. Corey bit his lip and breathed heavily. He had already been so close, and now Reyse's hot lips and tongue were unraveling his last bit of composure.

"I'm going to come," he gasped.

Reyse nodded, hardly pausing at all before increasing his speed. It was all Corey needed.

He arched his back, grabbing the bed sheets with one hand and Reyse's hair with the other. The climax ripped through him, robbing him of his breath for a second. Then he flopped back onto the mattress, gasping.

Reyse popped off his cock before it started softening, wiping his mouth and grinning. Sleepily, Corey brushed a rose petal off Reyse's shoulder he hadn't noticed had gotten attached there. "Fuck," he said, then laughed.

"Good?" Reyse asked.

Corey motioned him to come back up the bed and cuddle him. "Perfect." He sighed. "You're perfect. God, I'm so happy. You make me *so* happy, Reyse Hickson."

Reyse kissed Corey's chest, above his heart. "You make me so happy, Corey Sheppard."

Corey knew they'd sleep a little now. But the guys had

booked them the whole weekend in this suite. Corey had plans for the enormous tub sunken into the bathroom. And room service. *So* much room service.

But after that...they had everything available in front of them. At some point, Corey would have to contact his work and give them the lowdown. But he and Reyse had lives here in LA and for the first time there was no reason they shouldn't intermingle. There was no ticking clock. Corey didn't have to sneak out or worry if he should fall asleep or hide under the bed.

"What are you smiling about?" Reyse asked.

"Us," Corey said, kissing him, then reached for the box of tissues conveniently on the nightstand. He mopped Reyse's mess from his chest, then hugged him again. "It's amazing to just...be us. I'm not worrying about the future. In fact, it's kind of exciting."

Reyse smiled at him. Then his eyebrows shot up. "Oh," he said. He hopped off the bed, brushing away rose petals, and fetched his satchel. "I thought I might end up in a hotel, so I brought a couple of things. I was going to sleep in this, but, well..." he handed Corey a plain white T-shirt. "It's not mine."

Corey looked down at the T-shirt in his hands. It was pretty unremarkable, but Corey recognized the size and brand. "This is mine?" he said. Reyse nodded. Then Corey remembered the T-shirt Foofy had found that Reyse had picked up.

"I've been sleeping in it," Reyse said softly. "But I'd like it to smell like you again, please."

Corey dropped the shirt and hugged Reyse to him, burying his face in his neck. "You can borrow my shirts and my hoodies anytime you like, baby," he said thickly. "That's what boyfriends do, right?"

Reyse chuckled and rubbed Corey's back. "That's what

boyfriends do," he repeated. "I want to do everything boyfriends do."

"We will," Corey promised.

He'd never really been a proper boyfriend before. But he couldn't think of anyone else in the world he'd rather work it out with than Reyse.

Epilogue

TWO MONTHS LATER - COREY

"Do you want anything while I'm up?" Corey called from the kitchen.

Reyse looked at him from the sofa, then down at the stack of pizza boxes on the coffee table in front of him. He'd been so engrossed in the movie, he blinked and took a second to realize what Corey had asked. "Oh, no, I'm good, thanks," he said with a smile back at Corey. He turned back to the widescreen, snuggling into the cushions with Peppa in his lap, who was chewing on the hem of his pajama top.

Corey leaned against the closed fridge door, warmth filling his chest as he took in the domestic scene. As Reyse was recording his new album in LA, he'd been home at a reasonable time most nights. Their home, because it seemed ludicrous for Corey to keep renting out a room when Reyse had this enormous apartment all to himself. As scared as Corey had been to commit that quickly, he'd decided they'd wasted enough time already and to just try it. So far, it had been pretty much perfect.

His job was going well and Reyse's lawsuit had been settled out of court when Sun City realized pretty much the whole world was against them keeping Reyse's music hostage. He had also made good progress in setting up his new label and was done with his loser manager, Kevin, once and for all.

But it wasn't these things that had Corey smiling, not really. It was the two dachshund puppies – Pepperoni and Pineapple – that they'd adopted to start their little family. It was the old piano Reyse had moved out of storage that sat in the corner of the apartment, being played regularly like Reyse used to when he was a kid. It was the haphazard way their clothes were all mixed together and Reyse's Netflix suggestions now included Corey's crime dramas and cooking shows. It was the dozens of photos already mounted on several different walls, with the promise of many more to come now that Reyse didn't have to hide who he was anymore.

It had seemed so *difficult* when they had first met. Corey had felt like there was no way their lives were compatible, not when they were worlds apart. But as it turned out, it was pretty damn easy. He and Reyse just slotted together. Everything with him came naturally.

They were still working on making their communication better to avoid hurt feelings and the occasional argument. But they'd watched several self-help YouTube videos and Reyse had suggested they try a bit of therapy. They both had a lot of trust issues to work through and he thought some guidance might not be a bad idea. Corey had rejected the idea initially, but having seen how hurt that made Reyse, he agreed to give it a try. It turned out, sorting through his abandonment shit was making him less cranky about things he wouldn't have even realized bothered him before. He was glad he'd listened to Reyse on that.

Tonight was an example of just how easy things *could* be, though. It was hard to believe Reyse was known by millions around the globe when he was just…Corey's boyfriend. They were in their jammies on Halloween night, skipping any trick-or-treating this year in favor of their own stash of candy and some old favorite films. Reyse had spoiled Corey completely, bringing him candy from Japan and the UK and all the other exotic places he'd told him about.

Reyse had already booked several vacations for them and invited Corey on a couple of upcoming international engagements. Corey finally had a reason to get a passport and leave the state. But for now, Corey was just content to spend time in their own home while they were still nesting. Especially when Peppa and Pinny had only been with them a couple of weeks.

Corey was totally in love. He'd never thought he'd want a dog (or dogs, as it turned out). They always seemed like they needed so much time and effort. But Reyse's story about wanting a dog his whole life had been all it took to change Corey's mind. Now, he probably spoiled the pups more than Reyse did.

He settled himself back on the couch with his can of soda and rearranged the blanket so humans and puppies alike were comfortable. Reyse automatically leaned into Corey, resting his head on his chest and looping their hands together so he could kiss Corey's fingers.

Corey watched him rather than the movie. He'd seen The Nightmare Before Christmas a million times, but it seemed like Reyse might love it even more than he did. He'd always felt like the odd, kooky kid growing up, never knowing where he belonged, like Jack Skellington. But watching Reyse be completely enthralled by the film, quietly singing along to every single lyric, gave Corey a new appreciation of one of his old favorites.

It occurred to him that being with Reyse was going to make every experience new, and hopefully better. He had changed Corey's life so much it was almost unrecognizable from where it had been a few months ago.

And he couldn't be happier.

Reyse looked up at him with those big blue eyes Corey knew he'd never get tired of. "What?" he asked as Jack and Sally embraced on top of the hill, together at last.

Corey wasn't sure what made him say it. But it was as if the words just appeared in his mouth without him even having to think them.

"Will you marry me?"

It was no flash mob. There were no doves or grand declarations. He didn't even have a ring. It just suddenly occurred to Corey that he wanted to spend the rest of his life with this perfect man he loved so much, and he didn't see any reason to wait around.

Reyse looked at him, not moving. Then a small smile tugged at his lips.

"Yes," he said simply, snuggling back against Corey and watching the TV as the credits began to roll.

Corey grinned and kissed his hair. Apparently, he wasn't the only one who didn't want to waste any more time. Not when it felt so right.

He was sure Reyse would want to tell his boys soon enough, not to mention his family. Aunt Evangeline was going to lose her mind. Corey would be surprised if they didn't end up with Foofy as a flower girl. And of course, Corey wanted to tell his new friends at work, who had been simultaneous ecstatic and surprisingly chill about the fact Corey was dating their hero. He'd also make sure Maria and the other ladies from Speedy Pete's knew. He figured if he had anything close to his own aunts, they were them.

But just like that, he and Reyse promised their lives to one another. The earth didn't shift and Corey wasn't immediately thinking about wedding cakes. He simply hugged his fiancé and their fur babies close to him, secure in the knowledge that at some point down the line, he would stand up and tell the world that this was his man, forever.

For the longest time, the future had seemed like such a blank void for Corey. Now it was a blazing spectrum of color, like a sunset, every possibility open.

Because they would face it together.

Bonus Epilogue

SIX MONTHS LATER - REYSE

"WE'RE GOING TO BE LATE, REYSE!" COREY HISSED.

Reyse didn't care, though. He was too happy. And he was pretty sure that Corey didn't mean what he was saying, not from the way his eyes fluttered closed as Reyse slipped his lips around Corey's hot, hard cock. Reyse hummed as Corey carded his fingers through Reyse's hair.

"Just…don't make a mess of the suits," Corey said with a weak laugh before he let out a deep moan that went straight to Reyse's balls.

He knew they were cutting it close. He knew that the guests were already congregating outside and there would be someone coming to collect them any minute.

But he also knew his soon-to-be husband pretty damn well by now, in addition to being more honest with his own feelings these days.

They were both nervous.

They didn't have any reason to be, not really. Reyse was absolutely certain that marrying Corey was going to be one of the best decisions of his entire life. It was as if Reyse had been only living half a life until Corey had come flying into it like the bright light he was. He knew without a doubt that he wanted to spend the rest of their lives together.

But a year ago, Reyse had been living fearfully in the closet, a puppet of his record label, hollow and soulless. Sometimes, he still had to catch himself. His instinct was to think that he didn't deserve such happiness and that being out and proud was somehow wrong.

And Corey had been working minimum wage, carrying around a lot of anger and mistrust toward the world. He and Reyse had been forced through quite the ordeal to be together, and their new life had taken some adjusting to.

But Reyse knew that marriage was definitely what Corey wanted as much as he did. A week after his casual proposal on the couch at Halloween, Reyse had come home to find the apartment covered in rose petals and tea lights with Corey standing in the middle, dressed to the nines, with a ring box in his hand. He'd told Reyse he already knew the answer, but that Reyse was worth doing things right for. Then he'd gotten on one knee and made Reyse cry.

And now here they were, on their wedding day, about to make their commitment in front of all their friends and Reyse's family – who had already become Corey's family, much to Reyse's delight. Having thought he could never bring home a man who he loved, he was about to stand up in front of everyone who mattered and say, 'I do.'

But it was still kind of scary.

Reyse had spent more than a decade performing in front of tens of thousands of people. Yet the intimate little affair that was about to take place had him trembling ever so slightly and had Corey looking pale and withdrawn.

So the only solution for Reyse was to push his gorgeous lover against the wall, drop to his knees, and give him something else to think about.

"Reyse, baby," Corey moaned, tugging on Reyse's hair and thrusting into his mouth.

Reyse had to admit he was proud of how much more confident he was in the bedroom now. Of course, he loved it when Corey took charge. But he also loved being able to give as good as he got. Despite the fame and fortune, he never wanted Corey to feel they were unequal if he could help it.

So there he was, on his knees in his wedding suit, doing his best to relax the man he loved so they could enjoy what was hopefully going to be their perfect day.

With a cry, Corey suddenly jerked his hips, spilling down Reyse's throat. He sagged back against the wall of their suite, grinning down as Reyse finished swallowing him, kissing and licking his cock as it began to soften.

"There," said Reyse slightly hoarsely. He tucked little Corey back into his pants and zipped him up. "All better."

"Much better," Corey agreed. He tugged Reyse to his feet, then kissed his mouth sweetly. "I don't know why I'm so nervous," he mumbled against Reyse's lips.

Reyse rubbed his back and smiled at him, as lost in his hazel eyes as he had been the day they met. "It's normal," he assured his fiancé. "All the guys said they were nervous – well, except for Raiden and Levi – but that's what you get when you elope." He nipped at Corey's lip and was relieved to get a small smile out of him. "We're nervous because this is important. It matters. Not because we have doubts."

He raised his eyebrows, hoping that was how Corey was feeling as well. Thankfully, Corey sighed in relief. "That's exactly it," Corey said. "Fuck. I was starting to worry there was something wrong with me." He let out a shaky laugh and rubbed Reyse's back, kissing his neck. "I love you so much."

"I love you, too, gorgeous," Reyse said. He felt a deep contentment and sense of rightness. There were still some nerves, but they'd faded despite Corey being the only one to orgasm. Reyse felt peaceful, knowing that his man was calmer and happy again.

As if reading his mind, Corey hummed and dropped his hand to stroke over Reyse's crotch. "Would you also like some help with your nerves?" he asked, his voice warm and playful.

But Reyse shook his head. "I'm perfect, baby. I want to save it until later when I can scream my *husband's* name as loud as I like."

Corey snorted and nipped at Reyse's ear. "I like the sound of that."

As if on cue, there was a knock at the door. "Are you boys ready?" Reyse's mom called out.

Reyse met Corey's eyes, and they smiled at each other. "Are we ready?" Reyse asked.

"So ready," Corey agreed.

Reyse crossed the room with the sprawling Santa Monica beach behind him, palm trees swaying happily in the sunshine. They could have gotten married anywhere in the world, but it had been important to both of them to stick close to home and make sure all their friends and family could attend. The last ten years of Reyse's life had been about globetrotting and pleasing others.

Now he wanted to feel at home in his own backyard, comfortable in his own skin.

"Oh, my goodness," said his mom as he opened the door. She was wearing a beautiful lavender dress with the most enormous feathered hat to match. She clasped her hands in front of her chest, blinking back tears. "Don't you boys look handsome?"

Reyse beamed and embraced her warmly. "You look gorgeous, too, Mom. Is everything ready?"

She sniffed, then laughed at herself as they broke apart.

"Dear me. The ceremony hasn't even started yet, and I'm already losing it." She pulled a tissue out of her clutch and dabbed under her eyes.

"You look beautiful, Clementine," Corey said happily as he came up behind Reyse. "Sorry my husband-to-be is making you cry already."

Reyse's mom laughed and tucked her tissue away again. "Don't worry. I've got waterproof mascara on!" She sighed and looked between Reyse and Corey. "Yes. Everything and everyone are ready when you are."

Reyse turned to study Corey. It was a warm May day with a cool ocean breeze, so their gamble to wear full morning suits had paid off. They were both in black tails with white shirts. Reyse's vest and cravat were lavender, like his mom's dress, and Corey's a beautiful soft pink. Reyse brushed some invisible lint off Corey's lapel and swallowed down a lump of emotion.

"Let's do this," he said.

Corey took his hand, squeezing it, then led Reyse out the door of their suite. They'd booked out the entire beach-side resort for themselves and their guests. Reyse felt safe as they made their way through all the individual bungalows of the complex, knowing there was no one snooping around who shouldn't be. Their friend Levi had used his security firm to personally take care of everything, so Reyse had no doubts.

His heart gave a little flutter, knowing that all the guys from the band were going to be with him soon. They'd all demanded to be groomsmen, and Reyse knew the pictures of the five of them looking hella fancy in their suits were going to break the internet.

"What?" Corey asked him, and Reyse realized he'd been grinning.

He sighed, trying not to let his emotions get the best of

him. "I've been truly pleased for the guys, all getting married one-by-one. I just…I never truly believed it would ever be my turn. I'm so happy."

He was vaguely aware of his mom saying, "Awww," as Corey stopped to hug him tightly.

"Me, too, baby. I'm going to make you happy forever, I promise. Today is a celebration."

Having lost the battle with his tears, Reyse laughed and pulled away to wipe his eyes. "Yep, you're right. Okay, I think it's out of my system now. No more moping, I promise."

"It's not moping, Ricky," a voice called out. "You're *far* too fabulous to mope."

Even before he heard Foofy's barking, Reyse knew it was his aunt Evangeline. He grinned and turned to greet her, his breath catching a little as he realized that her fabulous gown was an exact match for the soft pink of Corey's vest and cravat. He hadn't known they were going to coordinate like that.

"Aunt Evangeline," he said warmly, taking in her ballgown trimmed with ostrich feathers. She looked like she was walking on a cloud as she came to embrace Reyse, then Corey on the walkway. "Well, you are *certainly* fabulous."

"This old thing?" she said with a huff and a wave. He knew she'd had it custom made, but he wasn't going to spoil her fun. "Right, chop-chop. Everything is all in order, and the only thing missing is you two handsome chaps. Shall we, Clementine?"

The sisters smiled at each other before each looping an arm through Reyse's and Corey's respectively. Evangeline (and Foofy) went ahead with Corey, while Reyse clung to his mother and took a deep breath.

This was it. The start of the rest of his life. He was committing to Corey in front of the whole world, and he couldn't be prouder. As they approached the ceremony area, he bit his lip, grinning so hard he thought he might burst.

Several dozen people were gathered beneath a mighty tree that had hundreds of twinkling fairy lights wrapped around its thick branches. The crowd all stood up from their neatly ordered chairs, a harp playing as Evangeline began to walk Corey down the aisle.

As Reyse waited his turn, he looked toward the four very excited faces of TJ, Blake, Raiden, and Joey standing by the altar. There had been a time where Reyse had worried he'd drifted too far away from them for good. He should have known there was no getting away from those crazy guys. Along with Reyse's family, their husbands were all near the front of the congregation, excitedly waving and giving thumbs-up to Corey as he neared.

Elion, Ashby, Gabe, and Levi – his best friends' loves. Now they were a family of their own, all ten of them connected by a bond that would surely last a lifetime and into their next generations. Jia Li was on Gabe's hip, and her younger brother, Hai, was being held by Elion while Joey was performing his groomsman duties. The kids were watching in awe at everything going on.

Reyse glanced at his mom, hoping that soon he'd be able to confide in her that he and Corey had already talked about adoption themselves. He knew how happy it would make her to become a grandma.

It was almost his cue to start walking down the aisle. He looked through the crowd and met his dad's eyes. Reyse almost got another lump in his throat, seeing him in his full Army dress blues. He'd already recovered so well from his stroke and looked far more like the man Reyse remembered from his childhood than the pale and fragile person he'd been in the hospital. Reyse had no words to express how happy he was that the two of them had been given the chance to start building their relationship again.

Unfortunately, things were still tense with Uncle Dave, but Reyse couldn't find it in himself to care too much. Dave wasn't at the wedding despite being invited. Reyse had wanted to allow him the opportunity to make amends, but apparently Dave wasn't interested in that.

Reyse had ultimately decided it was better not to have toxic people in his life anymore. He only deserved people who accepted him for who he really was, through and through.

Speaking of which, he was startled by an arm slipping through his free one, on the other side from his mom.

"You didn't think after all those years you'd honestly get married without me?" an English voice whispered in his ear.

"Bella," Reyse said in delight, leaning against his former pretend girlfriend to be embraced fully by her. "Holy crap, you made it."

"Yes, just not as the bride as so many people predicted," she said, her eyes sparkling with mirth. "I thought I could help your mom give you away, though? It seemed fitting."

"It's perfect," he assured her. "I'll always love you, Bells."

She winked at him. "Just not like you love that gorgeous fella waiting for you down there," she teased.

Reyse turned to see the congregation all looking at them. Corey had taken his place by the altar, and Reyse's heart leaped.

"No," he admitted softly. "Not like I love him."

With every fiber of my being.

Bella gave a little squeal, and his mom patted his arm. Then Reyse began to walk toward the man of his dreams, feeling a freedom he didn't know was possible.

It turned out that true love *was* worth going down in a blaze of glory. Because then he'd risen from the ashes stronger and more brilliant than before, with Corey by his side.

Now and forever, together.

———

To see Corey sneaking into Reyse's room from Corey's point of view, sign up to my newsletter here: hjwelch.com/subscribe

Acknowledgments

There are so many people who I have to thank in helping me complete my first series in MM romance. Heck, my first ever book series! It's been a fair old journey and whether you've been here since the start or have only just discovered Below Zero and Homecoming Hearts, I couldn't have done this without you.

Thank you to the people who have been here all the way, behind the scenes, keeping me going and bringing these books to life with me: Ed Davies, Amelia Faulkner, Conrad Rivers, Meg Cooper, Cate Ashwood, Aria Tan, Tanja Ongkiehong, Leslie Copeland and LesCourt Author Services.

Thank you to my incredible husband, whose support I simply couldn't have done without. You believed in me when I didn't believe in myself and cheered on every milestone and accomplishment. Thank you for giving me my own happy ever after.

Thank you to my friends who make *me* feel like an international pop star!

Thank you to my fur babies for keeping Mummy company in her writing cave.

And finally, thank you to every single one of *you* who has enjoyed Blake, Joey, Raiden, Trent and Reyse's stories. Thank you for all the loving reviews, for the encouragement in our Facebook Group, Helen's Jewels, the emails you've sent saying how moved you were by a book, the excitement for each new release, everything. Without you this series wouldn't have come to life. You're the best and I have so much love for each and every one of you.

Also Available

PINE COVE BOX SET BY HJ WELCH

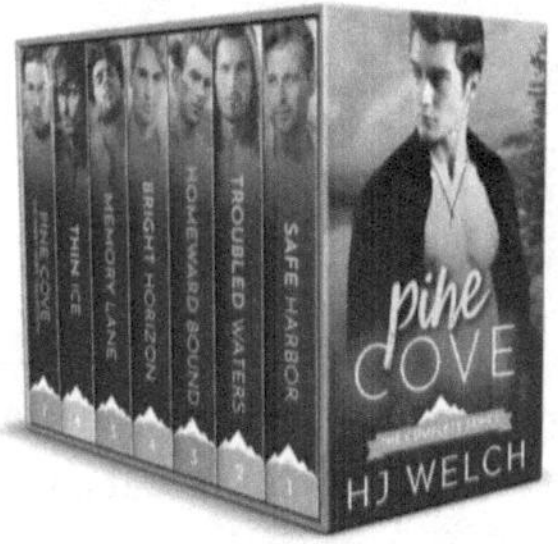

Welcome to Pine Cove, where true love lives happily ever after! **This 2000 page box set contains all six novels as well as all five companion short stories.**

Safe Harbor

Robin Coal needs a fake boyfriend for his high school reunion. He asks his housemate: a gorgeous, totally straight ex-Marine. What could go wrong? There's only one bed, and Dair might not be so straight after all... When Robin's past threatens their future, only Dair can save him.

Sweet Spot

It's Halloween and Robin has prepared a sexy little surprise for his boyfriend Dair when he gets home from work. Hold on to your horses, Marine!

Troubled Waters

Bodyguard Scout Duffy doesn't know what's worse: the fact that his scorching one-night-stand, Emery Klein, is his bratty new client, or the fact that he doesn't even remember Scout. But Emery's life is in danger thanks to his out and proud charity work, and once he finally recognizes Scout, their chemistry in undeniable.

Homeward Bound

Swift Coal just found out he's a father, and his daughter (and her cranky cat) are coming to stay. His best friend's younger brother, Micha Perkins, has nowhere to go and a wrongfully tattered reputation. He's relieved when Swift asks him to be a live-in babysitter. He just has to hide his lifelong crush. Easy, because Swift is straight—right?

Bright Horizon

With sixteen years between them, baker Ben Turner and lawyer Elias Solomon have no idea their crush is mutual. But when Ben inherits his long-lost family's estate and becomes an overnight millionaire, Elias swears to protect the innocent younger man from the vultures circling him. To unravel the mystery of the inheritance, they must go to England to confront Ben's estranged relatives…and their feelings for each other.

Crossed Paths

Raj Bhat is done living in the shadows. It's time for him to take charge of his own destiny and tell the man he's fallen for how he really feels.

———

Midnight Sky

It's the night before New Year's Eve. Taylan Demir is all alone, and he's just lost his dog. Except when his handsome customer, Hudson Perkins, comes to his rescue, Taylan doesn't just get his dog back. He's suddenly got a hot date, and maybe someone to kiss when the clock strikes midnight.

———

Memory Lane

Angel Shields saved Jay Coal's life in high school, and Jay has secretly loved his straight best friend ever since. Now Angel's back in town with amnesia after a suspicious work accident and it's Jay's turn to rescue him. He pretends to be Angel's fiancé to see him in the hospital, but with his scrambled-up memory, Angel's not sure it's fictional after all. He just knows he loves Jay more than ever.

———

Thin Ice

Kamran's ex broke his heart, tricked him into aiding a bank robbery, and now he wants him to do one last job. There's only one way to say no: seek the protective custody of the biggest, grumpiest FBI agent ever, Lee Marshall. And pretend to be his boyfriend for a week-long family reunion in their giant mansion. Wait, what?

———

Calm Shores

Gorgeous, sophisticated Dante walks into Oliver's bar and orders...a boyfriend?! Dante needs a man to keep his mother from setting him back up with his awful, cheating ex, and Oliver is up for the challenge.

———

Fresh Snow

Emery Klein is throwing the best Christmas party ever, but his fiancé, Scout Duffy, and all their friends have something more exciting in mind.

———

Each Pine Cove book can be read as a stand alone and has its own happy ever after. But if you read the whole series, you'll see a lot of familiar faces!

Available as an ebook or audiobook.

I've spent almost four years trying to get my captain Seth to notice me. He's hot as hell and knows how to boss a guy around, even one as big as me. To him, though, I'm just the team clown. But when he drags me into this graduation bet, it's no laughing matter. So why shouldn't this little cherub Gabe tutor me as well? In fact, I don't see why we can't share him in all *kinds* of ways. Seth is clearly a natural Daddy, Gabe thrives being doted on, and I'm happy to Daddy *and* be Daddied. Win-win, right?

GABE

Somehow, I've found myself standing up to the guy whose family pretty much owns Paddle Creek and put my neck on the line for two of the college's star players. Now we're spending every day together as I try and save their grades, and I don't know if I'm crazy but it's like they both *want* me. I've never had a boyfriend. I'm not even out to my overbearing parents. How could I choose between them…or do I actually have to when they *both* want to be my Daddies? After my life comes crashing down, it's their turn to come to my rescue. Maybe what me and these god-like men have isn't just a fling after all?

Heaven Sent *is a steamy, standalone MMM romance. It's the first book in the* **Paddle Creek College** *series, where it's always the quiet ones who get up to the best kind of trouble. This book features a geek tutoring two hot jocks, two hot jocks tutoring a geek in a completely different way, a trash panda with a heart of gold, a human ice cream sundae, a revenge curse, and a guaranteed HEA with absolutely no cliffhanger.*

PADDLE CREEK #2: YES, SIR BY HJ WELCH

Two men. Two secrets. Can true love set them free?

BENEDICT

Just one more year, then I can go back to my beloved Oxford University and leave this tiny town behind me. Teaching is my passion, but I have other desires that I know would get me fired if anyone found out. The only trouble is, my new TA is pushing all my buttons and I'm not sure he even realizes what calling me Sir does to me. That's nothing, however, compared to when he starts calling me Daddy.

JACKSON

Have I got hots for teacher? Oh, yes. Messing around is off the table, though, so in a way it's safe to flirt with him and see him lose that stiff upper lip. It's not like he'd be interested in me anyway if he ever discovered what I love wearing under my clothes. Tough guys like me shouldn't like satin and lace. They shouldn't want to feel pretty. But Sir makes me feel gorgeous, and I want to be *such* a good boy for him.

Yes, Sir is a steamy, standalone MM romance. It's the second book in the Paddle Creek College series, where it's always the quiet ones who get up to the best kind of trouble. This book features two people learning they don't have to be ashamed of who they are, a sassy brat who really wants to behave, a master in the bedroom who's a caring Daddy at heart, role playing so good it could win an Oscar, and a guaranteed HEA with absolutely no cliffhanger.

PADDLE CREEK #3: LITTLE PLEASURES BY HJ WELCH

One jaded Daddy. One brand new boy. A fake relationship that becomes all too real.

XANDER

It's bad enough I have to move back to Paddle Creek with my awful stepmom, but now my half-brother's best friend has decided he has to look after me—even pretending to be my new boyfriend for a family wedding to keep my stepmother off my back. What Ruben doesn't know is that I've been in love with him for as long as I can remember and spending so much time with him is torture. Until it isn't. I can't believe that he's interested in me and even wants to be my Daddy, unlocking something in me I never knew was there. But when my stepmom goes too far, can I rely on Ruben to be there for me seeing as no one else in my life ever has?

RUBEN

When my life-long best friend asks me to keep an eye on his half-brother, of course I agree. Except he's a young man now, not a kid, and he's tugging at every single one of my Daddy heartstrings. Xander has just moved back into town and between finishing his degree, part-time work, and hellish stepmother, he's stressing himself into knots. It's a long time since a boy interested me, but I just want to protect Xander from the whole world. No matter the cost.

Little Pleasures is a steamy, standalone MM romance. It's the third book in the **Paddle Creek College** series, where it's always the quiet ones who get up to the best kind of trouble. This book features a Daddy introducing a boy to his inner little, the most loyal doggy best friend, a lot of dinosaurs, a heart-stopping rescue, and a guaranteed HEA with absolutely no cliffhanger. CW: Age play but no ABDL.

PADDLE CREEK #4: FOUR PLAY BY HJ WELCH

Three hungry wolves. One pretty little lamb. The hunt for love is on.

HARPER

I'm here for a good time, not a long time. When a total cutie asks me if I'd be interested in him and his two Daddies chasing me down and having their way with me, it sounds fun. I'm only in this crappy town for the summer, after all. But what we share is *intense*. I signed on to get caught…not to catch feels. However, when I find myself being hunted for real, can I really expect my wolf pack to come to the rescue?

RICK

After my husband and I swapped military life for married life, we quickly met our sweet baby boy who we'll do anything for. When Brady says he's found a sassy little lamb for the three of us to stalk, I'm happy to indulge him. But this broken young man swiftly captures all of our hearts, even though he says he can walk away any time. There's a difference between walking and being taken, however. Now I have the scent of a fool who's about to discover what happens when he's stolen what's *mine*.

Four Play *is a super steamy, standalone MMMM romance. It's the fourth book in the **Paddle Creek College** series, where it's always the quiet ones who get up to the best kind of trouble. This book features exhilarating primal play, one hell of a paint ball match, an underwater themed motel, so many smooches, an obsessive ex-boyfriend, and a guaranteed HEA with absolutely no cliffhanger.*

reach out on Bears-4-U and go to this mixer, only to find that the new Daddy I've been talking to is just as awful. That's when Beckett swoops into my life like a hero in a story book. I know he's not looking for love, but I want to mend his broken heart so badly. When a scary snowstorm blows in and strands us, I trust he'll keep me safe and warm. I want to be in his life, in his bed, in his heart…forever.

Bears-4-U is a MM Daddy romance multi-author series, featuring a host of delicious Daddy pairings. The Bears-4-U dating app is all about putting Bears and Teddy Bears together for their honey-sweet HEAs. Psst, no real bears involved. Each book can be read as a standalone, but why not snuggle up with all the bears?

Wild Ride

When Red is chased into the woods, he seeks sanctuary at his estranged grandma's house. He doesn't expect to be rescued by his older brother's best friend, the man he was always madly in love with. Could Hunter be the Daddy of Red's wildest dreams? Especially when he unlocks a secret passion of Red's for beautiful lingerie. There's still a threat lurking in the woods, though, and Hunter realises he'll do anything to protect his beautiful boy.

Three

When three shy best friends sign up to a dating app to finally get some by the end of the year, they don't expect to all fall for the same gorgeous, slightly scary-looking Daddy. The only solution? Let him choose who he wants to bed. Except he doesn't. Daddy Wolf wants to spoil each little piggy, one after another. But when danger comes calling, will their love for each other be enough to save them all?
Includes Halloween bonus scene!

Nine Lives

When Charlie suddenly finds himself homeless and penniless, he decides to sell the only thing left he owns. Himself. For the very first time. Lucky for him he stumbles across Miller, the own of a London kink club, who saves him from those who would take advantage of him. As Miller discovers his inner Daddy, he also unlocks Charlie's kitten alter-ego. But with both their families meddling, will new love be enough to keep them together?

Available as an ebook.

About the Author

HJ Welch is an author of contemporary MM romance series, including the international bestselling Pine Cove series. She lives just outside of London with her husband and two balls of fluff that occasionally pretend to be cats. She began writing at an early age, later honing her craft online in the world of fanfiction on sites like Wattpad. Fifteen years and over half a million words later, she sought out original MM novels to read. By the end of 2016 she had written her first book of her own, and in 2017 she achieved her lifelong dream of becoming a full-time author. When she's not writing she's usually dancing, singing, filming music videos, taking long walks, working on jigsaw puzzles, drinking prosecco, or talking about Eurovision.

She also writes contemporary British MM fairy tale adaptations as Helen Juliet.

———

You can contact Helen via the following:
Newsletter: https://www.subscribepage.com/helenjuliet
Website – www.hjwelch.com
Facebook Group – Helen's Jewels
Instagram – @helenjwrites
Twitter – @helenjwrites
Book Bub – @HJWelchAuthor
Facebook Page – @HJWelchAuthor